TEMPTING
Devil

SINNERS AND SAINTS BOOK 2

USA TODAY & INTERNATIONAL BESTSELLING AUTHOR
VERONICA EDEN

TEMPTING DEVIL

Copyright © 2020 Veronica Eden

All rights reserved.

No parts of this publication may be reproduced, stored in a retrieval system, or transmitted in any form or by any means, electronic, mechanical, photocopying, recording, or otherwise, without the prior written permission of the copyright owner, except in the case of brief quotations embodied in reviews and certain other noncommercial uses permitted by copyright law. For permission requests, write to the author at this website:

WWW.VERONICAEDENAUTHOR.COM

This is a work of fiction. Names, characters, places, businesses, companies, organizations, locales, events and incidents either are the product of the author's imagination or used fictitiously. Any resemblances to actual persons, living or dead, is unintentional and co-incidental. The author does not have any control over and does not assume any responsibility for author or third-party websites or their content.

Discreet Series Edition

TEMPTING DEVIL

SINNERS AND SAINTS BOOK 2

VERONICA EDEN

CONTENTS

Author's Note	vii
About the Book	ix
Playlist	xi

1. Blair	1
2. Devlin	13
3. Devlin	23
4. Blair	33
5. Devlin	41
6. Blair	49
7. Blair	57
8. Devlin	63
9. Blair	67
10. Blair	75
11. Devlin	81
12. Devlin	87
13. Blair	97
14. Devlin	103
15. Devlin	111
16. Devlin	123
17. Blair	133
18. Blair	141
19. Devlin	153
20. Blair	157
21. Devlin	171
22. Blair	185
23. Devlin	199
24. Blair	203
25. Blair	207
26. Blair	219
27. Devlin	225

28. Blair	237
29. Devlin	247
30. Blair	259
31. Blair	267
32. Devlin	279
33. Devlin	285
34. Blair	291
35. Blair	295
36. Devlin	307
37. Devlin	311
38. Blair	323
39. Devlin	329
40. Blair	331
41. Blair	337
42. Blair	347
43. Devlin	353
44. Devlin	363
45. Blair	369
46. Devlin	379
Epilogue	387
Epilogue	395
Thank You + What's Next?	401
Acknowledgments	403
Preview the Sinners and Saints Series	405
Preview Ruthless Bishop	407
About the Author	415
Also by Veronica Eden	417

AUTHOR'S NOTE

Tempting Devil is a new adult high school romance containing dark themes intended for mature readers. The Sinners and Saints series boys are all devilish bullies brought to their knees by a spitfire heroine, so if you love intense enemies-to-lovers type stories, you're in the right place. This mature new adult romance contains crude language, bullying, dubious situations, a stalker/predator, and intense graphic sexual/violent content that some readers might find triggering or offensive. Please proceed with caution.

If you like weak pushover heroines and nice guys this one ain't for you, but if you dig strong females and smug antiheroes, then you're in the right place! Hold onto your hearts, because these guys aren't above stealing.

Each book is part of a series but can be enjoyed as a standalone in any order.

Sinners and Saints series:

AUTHOR'S NOTE

#1 Wicked Saint
#2 Tempting Devil
#3 Ruthless Bishop
#4 Savage Wilder

Sign up for Veronica's newsletter to receive exclusive content and news about upcoming releases: bit.ly/veronicaedenmail
Follow Veronica on BookBub for new release alerts: bookbub.com/authors/veronica-eden

ABOUT THE BOOK

BLAIR

I SOLD MY SOUL TO THE DEVIL.
Hard times prove who's a survivor and who's not. Me? I'm a survivor.

The plan was perfect: steal one of his cars for a payout to set us up for life. All while getting back at him for tormenting me from the moment I first stepped foot in stuck up Silver Lake High School.

But he caught me red-handed. What's worse, a jail sentence or becoming the devil's favorite toy?

My devious monster made me an offer I couldn't refuse. Now I'm selling everything to him. Even my soul.

DEVLIN

THE SECRET TO BEING CAREFREE IS LOVE NOTHING.
The puppets are fooled into believing my game of pretend. But

ABOUT THE BOOK

the way she looks at me has always pierced beneath my skin. Like she *knows*. She's a gutter rat—how could she possibly understand?

I vowed to break her. When I catch her stealing my car, it's clear she hasn't learned her lesson. She won't escape my wrath again.

Ready to play a game, little thief? The rules are simple: my way is law.

PLAYLIST

(Spotify)

Renegade—Niykee Heaton
Moshpit—Bohnes
Zombie Love—Bohnes
Bottom of the Deep Blue Sea—MISSIO
MAYDAY—coldrain, Ryo
Issues—Julia Michaels
Stomp Me Out—Bryce Fox
I'll Keep Coming—Low Roar
How Does It Feel?—Tonight Alive
The Hand That Feeds—Nine Inch Nails
Teeth—5 Seconds of Summer
Way Down We Go—KALEO
Everybody Knows—Sigrid
Lose You To Love Me—Selena Gomez
The Box—Roddy Ricch
Godzilla—Eminem, Juice WRLD
White Flag—Bishop Briggs

PLAYLIST

Blood In The Cut—K.Flay
Powerful—Major Lazer, Ellie Goulding, Tarrus Riley
Don't Leave Me Lonely—Mark Ronson, Yebba
Gone—Red
Horns—Bryce Fox
Angel On Fire—Halsey
Sitting, Waiting, Wishing—Jack Johnson
Moonlight—XXXTENTACION
Bury Me Face Down—grandson
You Don't Own Me—Lesley Gore
Dark Nights—Dorothy
I Will Follow You Into The Dark—Deathcab for Cutie
Shooting Stars—Elephante

Home isn't a place, it's the people who fill it.

To survivors, keep fighting.

ONE
BLAIR

Being here is necessary, I remind myself while crouching between the trees, scoping out my target. *It's all part of the perfect plan.*

Silver Lake Forest Estates has always made me feel out of place. Tonight's no different, even as I lurk in the shadows. My friend Gemma Turner dragged me to this community of mansions often last year for parties at her boyfriend's house on the other side of the lake. Maybe the sense of not belonging comes from being surrounded by people with so much privilege it bleeds from their ears, compared to what I have. Maybe it's that I can always feel Devlin Murphy judging my presence.

Either way, there's never been a question about it. I'm definitely not welcome here.

Now I'm staking out a place I never thought I'd willingly go: my enemy's house.

The weather has been mild for early September in Ridgeview, but I'm dressed in all black to blend in with the night. Sweat dampens the armpits of my faded long-sleeve t-shirt after hiking to my hiding place, where I have a clear view to the giant gate guarding the house. I don't know if it's from the anxious anticipation coursing through me or that I'm overheating in the outfit I scraped together for tonight from the second-hand shop. Probably both.

If Devlin catches me on his property, he'll live up to that big bad name of his. He's known as the notorious dark devil of Silver Lake High School, both for his looks and his lethal attack on the soccer field.

Douchebag devil. I hate him more than any of the jerks at my school.

One week into senior year and he's already cashing in on making my life hell once again. He cooled off a little last year after Gemma started dating his cousin and king of the school, Lucas Saint. It didn't stop him from sniping at me every chance he got, though. It just made him get more creative.

With Lucas and Gemma off at Oak Ridge College of the Arts, the high school has become Devlin Murphy and Connor Bishop's kingdom, the evil duo ruling over us with iron fists.

Today, Devlin and his soccer buddies baited me with dollar bills on fishing wire, hunting for my desperation. His vicious sneer burned my insides with acidic hatred. The most depressing part? We need money so badly that I almost gave into their cruel trap to add a few more dollars to our meager savings.

Survival always outweighs pride when it comes down to it.

A warm breeze moves the branches overhead, the creaking limbs the soundtrack to my illicit troublemaking.

The plan is to break in and take one of the things he loves most.

From what I can tell, Devlin has at least five cars—expensive ones. These aren't your typical economy class cars. It's about four more than the average person needs.

A car heist goes a little further than my usual song and dance. *More like miles further.* The corner of my mouth lifts without a trace of humor as the thought crosses my mind.

Devlin Murphy deserves it.

The bastard's had it coming since freshman year. I've endured his brand of tormenting bullshit for too long.

A twig snaps with a muffled sound beneath my shoes as I shift my weight. I tighten my ponytail to keep my hair out of my face while I work, flicking my gaze up to the stars dotting the sky above the evergreens. It's dark enough I think.

Time to get moving if I'm going to pull this off. No more stalling, dancing on the line of will I or won't I.

There is no will or won't tonight—only *have to* and *no choice.*

I blow out a breath and rub my fingertips together. My shoulders are too tense. Needing to loosen up, I give them a little shake.

The isolated house looming before me is a mix of modern contemporary style with luxe cabin touches—large windows, metal framework, white-washed concrete, and the aesthetic comforts of an oversized mountain cabin.

Cabin is being coy. This is a legit mountain mansion. The biggest in the private community of Ridgeview's own brand of royalty.

It comes off as arrogant and out of place. The house's jutting lines sprawl out like it's their right, juxtaposed against nature as the trees fight to stand their ground.

Because money gives you everything. It opens any door. Nature doesn't get to say no to money.

My mouth twists in bitter contempt as my nails dig into the bark of a tree trunk beside me. I stand and keep to the shadows.

Adrenaline tingles in my fingertips with the first step I've taken in over an hour, the sharp pricks jumping along my awareness and contorting my stomach.

No one is around. Devlin's house is spread far from the neighbors, the most remote property I've seen here. Still, I don't let my guard drop.

A flash of light makes my heart trip over itself—*headlights! Security patrol?*—and I duck behind a cluster of boulders. It moves off into the tree line, turning away from Devlin's house. I breathe out a relieved sigh and creep closer to the house.

Funny how a private community for the most elite of Ridgeview doesn't expect unwelcome intruders to walk right in, assuming guests and residents only pass through the security kiosk at the gate. Dusk settled as I hiked from the road, slipping between the homes unseen, tracing the path I mapped out to get to Devlin's house on Google Maps at the library.

A bitten-off snort leaves me. I peek around to check if the coast is clear and dart by a skinny sapling. A little farther and I'll be past the point of no return.

If the sport schedule bulletin on the school website was right, Devlin should be at soccer practice until 8pm. That gives me at least forty-five minutes to work under the cover of night. His Range Rover was in the student lot today, three spaces down from the rust bucket 2001 Corolla that gets me from point A to B.

The plan races through my head on repeat: *get in unnoticed, disable the GPS tracking system according to the YouTube tutorial, drive off like a fucking boss, watch that dick's fury from afar in school...*

I move my hand over my hips, checking the pouch hooked through my belt loops. Inside is everything I'll need for this plan.

The sense of preparedness, calculating every move, is born out of faking it until I make it. It's not like I've ever committed a crime this serious before.

My wheelhouse is petty theft—earning the stupid sticky fingers name the devil of Silver Lake High taunts me with by shoplifting what I can't afford and picking pockets when necessary.

The corners of my mouth tighten. Devlin Murphy has no idea what it's like to constantly stress about money.

Robin Hood steals from the rich, right? Well, the wealthy snobs of this town are the ones teaching me brutal lessons in survival, so I'm returning the favor.

I've long since let go of any moral guilt hanging over my head for being a survivor.

Pausing my approach to the house, I bite my lip. The undeniable consequences of what I'm here to do scroll through my head like a marquee. Devlin has more than enough money to bury me and then go after Mom. Hell, he could probably *kill* me for touching his cars and get away with it.

That crazy look that haunts his eyes when they're on me...

A shudder shakes my body. Yeah, he's messed up enough to murder someone. No doubt about it.

You're stalling. "Ugh."

I force my feet to move.

This is a big score for me, bigger than I've ever taken on. I'm not stealing cheap mascara, taking an extra carton of milk, or snagging a hundred bucks from spoiled classmates that don't notice they're short when their no-limit credit cards make up the difference.

No, this is a real crime. High risk, higher reward. The *go-to-jail-if-caught* kind.

My stomach turns over as I hesitate in the darkness.

If I get caught, Mom won't make it on her own. Maybe I should have done this at the end of junior year, before I turned eighteen in June. I tug on the end of my ponytail and chew on my lip again.

There's no other way. This is the only thing I could think of to get the money we need fast. It's a better idea than robbing a bank.

If I have to become a vigilante, repurposing some useless extra wealth to those more needy—me and my mom—then so be it. Getting back at Devlin is the cherry on top of this sour sundae.

Moving from shadow to shadow toward my goal, my resolve strengthens. It gives me the false sense of bravery I need to take this leap from my comfort zone.

I stop along the waist-high stone wall that forms a perimeter around Devlin's property line. Everything about his house screams elite, down to the cold iron gate cutting the property off from the road that turns into the circular driveway.

"A gate for the biggest house inside a gated community," I mumble to myself, shaking my head as I hop onto the stone wall and swing my legs over.

I drop off the wall into a crouch in case the community's private security patrol comes this way. My footsteps are light and quick.

The same honed focus falls over me that I feel when I'm about to pick someone's pocket or swipe something at the store. Steady breathing, exuding the confidence that nothing is wrong, and blending like I belong are the ways I get away with what I do.

This is no different. Even though my heart skips a beat at

every unfamiliar sound. I keep my cool mask in place as I reach the garage.

It's a sub-level entry from the house, the circular drive sloping down an incline to the four large black garage doors flanked by industrial style lamps. Tossing a quick glance at the main house, I dig my homemade set of lock picks from the pouch of tools on my belt and slide on a pair of driving gloves. They're not quite badass cat burglar leather gloves, but they were in the fifty cent bin in a thrift shop.

My expression melts into surprise when I grab the handle of the side entrance door, freezing as it turns. It's not locked.

Swinging my astonished gaze back and forth for another check of my surroundings, I slip inside, closing the door behind me.

Other than the foreboding entrance, Devlin's security is appalling. The keys aren't even in a lockbox. They're proudly displayed on the wall by the door, with tiny spotlights beneath the logos of each car brand.

Fucking rich people.

Their arrogance grates on my nerves. While they live with the constant expectation that they can have everything they want, Mom and I struggle to keep our heads above water. These pampered assholes are so trusting of their huge gates and private security to do the heavy lifting.

I'm offended it was so easy to get in here as I tuck my lock picks back into my zipper pouch of supplies.

The air inside the garage is cool and artificial, like there's a fancy temperature regulation system at work. Each car is parked diagonally in its own spot with an overhead light illuminating its sleek features. There are more than the five cars I've seen Devlin use—every high-end model I've ever heard of and some I don't recognize. It's like I've walked into a museum where car nuts would drool over makes and models they only dream of setting eyes on. The excessiveness of this collection turns my stomach, and a quiet scoff falls from my parted lips.

There are so many that my eyes blur and my temple throbs as I try to do the math in my head to add up the value surrounding me. I don't know what some of these retail for, but the ones I do are easily upwards of seventy grand. This entire room could wipe out the debt that hangs like a poisonous fog over Mom's head in one swoop.

It's not fucking fair.

But this is the cruelty of the world.

My hands clench into fists, the material of the gloves creaking the harder I squeeze. Dad taught me all about this harsh world at a young age before he took off.

Another collection notice from one of his gambling debts sits heavy in my pocket, the crumbled mail stuffed there after reading it made my eyes sting and a sickening panic surge on my way out of the trailer to execute this plan. The only choice was to take it with me. I couldn't leave it for Mom to find. Each one breaks her spirit a little more, no matter how strong she tries to be for the both of us. I'm the strong one and soon she won't have to worry.

I take a quick stroll down the row of cars on the left, sneering at a garish yellow Lamborghini, a gunmetal gray Audi, a shimmering pearl-colored Mercedes-Benz GLS, and a sleek black Escalade. The other side of the garage is just as bad with a vintage Mustang and vehicles that look more like futuristic flying cars.

For a moment I'm struck by indecision. I didn't realize he had this many cars. It's safer to take one of the more nondescript ones I've never seen him use. It'll be easier to move something common rather than the high profile cars. My gaze flits back and forth, considering the options.

I have to be smart about my choice.

Mom's voice still echoes in my mind when I overheard her last week, pleading on the phone for a loan she applied for. It fell through, the slimy scum of a loan officer unsympathetic to her quavering voice as she explained to him what our situation was if we didn't get that money. He didn't care, like all men. Like *Dad*. Once again reminding me why I can't trust any of them.

My throat thickens at the memory and I screw my eyes shut. I don't have time for this. I need to act now.

At the end of the row in a prominent position is a car that makes me fume as soon as I spot it.

The red Porsche.

Devlin's prized ride. Possibly the only thing he loves in this world more than himself. I've seen him practically make out with it in the school lot while his groupies watch and giggle. They probably hope he'll fuck them in the cramped back seat, but I've never seen him give any of his hookups a lift when he drives it.

The gleaming red car is a beacon, drawing me a few steps closer. I tap my fingers against my legs. The sweet satisfaction of taking something precious from Devlin sings in my blood. My indecision vanishes, obliterated by the chance of getting the ultimate revenge on him.

Stalking back to the mahogany display box on the wall, I snatch the key fob beneath the shiny Porsche logo. A smirk curls the corners of my mouth when I admire the empty space left behind.

"Karma's a bitch, Murphy."

Spinning on my heel, I hurry over to the Porsche. The door opens without hitting the button on the fob. Even the cars are barely protected, left unlocked.

I huff in angry amusement, muttering as I slide behind the

wheel. "Is that big gate supposed to keep you safe? Think again, asshole."

After adjusting the seat forward from Devlin's height, I push the keyless ignition. The engine purrs to life, sending power racing through me as I grip the wheel. A subtle rumbling vibration stirs through my thighs and I bite my lip. *Damn, this is a nice car.* My eyes crinkle with my smile. Now the driving gloves are more appropriate.

I'm searching around for a way to trigger the garage door to open from inside the car, figuring with Devlin's wealth he's probably the type to have something like that in all of his cars. My gloved fingers fumble over the visor and scan the touchscreen.

Then a shadowy figure moves in my periphery, blocking light from the window.

Within seconds my perfect plan crumbles before my eyes as my body pulses with the overpowering wrongness of someone being there. I jump when the door flies open a beat later, sucking in a strangled gasp as I fly into motion.

"No!" The shout leaves me in a garbled rush as I try to get away.

"Oh, I don't think so," Devlin snaps in a deadly voice. "Get back here!"

A strong hand with long fingers clamps over my wrist, stopping my wide-eyed scramble across the center console to escape. My heart drops into my stomach, every hair on my body standing on end. *Fuck!*

I kick with all my might, landing a solid hit against his torso. Devlin grunts angrily, but I can't break out of his hold.

He yanks on my wrist, dragging me from the car. I'm met with an angry snarl as he towers over me. "What the fuck are you doing?"

Devlin's face is etched in anger, thick brows furrowed and

his damp black hair curling across his forehead, hanging into his eyes. A muscle jumps in his chiseled jaw, sending my instincts into fight-or-flight mode.

Shit, shit, shit. My heart beats in time with my racing thoughts. He was here the whole time—but the Range Rover! It's not here. I dart my gaze around to confirm that. He's not supposed to be home yet.

Devlin shakes me, demanding my full attention as he leans into my face. His lip curls, giving me a glimpse of his perfect white teeth. With a grunt, he shoves me out of the way, pausing long enough to reach in the car to cut the engine without releasing his hold on me. I barely have time to consider if I can escape before he's in my face again.

I am so fucked.

"You are in way over your head, you thieving bitch," he seethes, tightening his grip on my wrist until it's painful. With his other hand, he digs his fingers into my upper arm. "You'll pay for this."

Every muscle in my body tenses with the need to run.

For the first time in years, I've been caught in the act. And now I'll face the consequences at the hands of someone that hates my guts as much as I hate his. Devlin Murphy, my bully.

I should've taken my chances robbing a bank instead.

TWO
DEVLIN

The house is silent as usual when I come out of the steam-filled bathroom, slipping a black t-shirt over my head. It's just as it was when I hopped in the shower twenty minutes ago. The same lifeless quiet as always.

A new book I picked up on psychology waits on my nightstand.

My phone buzzes, interrupting the Spotify station playing the haunting synth-pop rock beats of MISSIO.

The sweatpants I pulled on slouch low on my hips as I drag a hand through my damp hair. I consider ignoring the phone, but I already know who it is. I step into my bedroom and close the door, shutting myself off from the rest of the vast house.

For a second I can pretend I'm not home alone.

Bishop's name flashes on the phone screen again with a new message.

The corner of my mouth twitches and I let out a resigned sigh. This is what I get for leaving practice early. It's not like I'm invested the same way Bishop is, but that's why he's been captain of our varsity soccer team since last year. Maybe I stick with it because if I didn't I wouldn't see Bishop as much, since he lives and breathes the team.

It's something to do and keeps me out of the house. At least, until the darkness in my head spills out. That's why I had to sneak out of practice today.

I've been drifting, lost in a way I wasn't last year. It's getting worse, harder to contain, more difficult to pretend I'm carefree.

Frowning, I pass by my bed—perfectly made by the elusive housekeepers that pass through like a reset button, scrubbing even my own existence from this overpriced prison cell—to lean against the wide windowsill. Every morning I leave my bed a mess and every night before I climb in, *if* I do, it's meticulously remade. I peer out at the silhouettes of trees scattered over the mountain, glimpsing the lake between the pine needles.

Until a few weeks ago, I wouldn't be in this mood. Before it had the chance to creep in, I would have been across the lake hanging out with Lucas. It was easier to ignore that anything was wrong at my aunt and uncle's house. It calmed me down, anchored me to have somewhere to go where I didn't have to worry if I wasn't wanted. I stayed there until Lucas kicked me back home across the lake.

It didn't use to suck like this because there was always an au pair around. But when I turned sixteen two years ago, Dad decided I was old enough to be on my own with the expense account he and Mom fill up each month. Self-sufficient independence, they call it. It's just me and the invisible housekeepers I never run into, even when I try to seek them out. They're like fucking elves.

Lucas is far out of reach now that he's at college with his girl, Gemma. If I lost Bishop, there'd be no one left. I'm lucky my best friend has stuck by my side for as long as he has.

But nothing lasts forever.

I can't hold on to the same routine.

Everyone moves on.

Stop.

Rubbing my hand over my head, I struggle with the effort to push the melancholic thoughts back down in their box, locked away where they belong. Where they can't whisper their evil truths to me.

I breathe deep and slow.

It takes a minute to rein my scattered emotions, bringing them back in check from the brink of the miserable hysteria that plagues me when I let the loneliness in, where it can cut deepest.

My fingers twitch with the urge to grab the pack of smokes from the nightstand.

This is how life is supposed to be. Seniors graduate and go to college. It'll be Bishop and I doing the same after this year.

I blow out another harsh breath that burns my throat and unlock my phone to read Bishop's messages. They're sporadic nonsense until the newest one from a minute ago.

Bishop: Did you fall in the damn urinal? If you don't answer or come out in 5, I'm sending search & rescue. No bros left behind.
Bishop: Aight, I guess you ain't coming back to practice. Cool. Cool cool cool.
Bishop: [GIF of a man blinking in disbelief]

Bishop: Yo, Devil Boy, you owe me for cutting out early today.

A snort leaves me. Everyone at Silver Lake High dubbed me the dark devil, but Bishop likes to put his own spin on things.

Devlin: I had to get out of there. Leg cramp from those drills.

Bishop: Ok, your highness. [eye roll emoji] Seriously, I'm making you practice extra this week. I can't give you a break or the guys will think I give you special treatment. I ain't your whipped bitch. Besides your footwork needs it for the first match.

Devlin: [middle finger emoji] [middle finger emoji] Fuck off. I always score and you know it.
Devlin: [smirk emoji] And you know I'd treat you right, baby.

Bishop: Whatever, you dick. WYD? Wanna hang and smoke a bowl? I've got a fresh bag of Doritos with your name on it.

As great as that sounds and as much as I want to hang out with Bishop, smoking weed when my head is all twisted up always leaves me more anxious and paranoid. Like my body won't let me just chill the fuck out. It's some grade A bullshit, but I'm not rolling the dice on that tonight.

Devlin: Nah man, gotta have dinner at my aunt and uncle's.

A lie. But they'd gladly have me over for dinner if I showed up. My stomach rumbles, mocking my made up plans. If I raid the kitchen, I might get lucky and find something. Sometimes one of the housekeepers likes to leave me the extra food she makes.

Bishop: Legit. See ya tomorrow bright and early for your punishment [laughing emoji]

Devlin: [middle finger emoji] [middle finger emoji] [middle finger emoji]

Tucking my phone in my pocket, I venture down into the desolate house in search of food. My footfalls on the varnished floating stairs are the only muffled noise in the entire house. I have half a mind to connect my phone to the bluetooth speaker system and turn on some ambient sound playlist to fill the house with noise. Sometimes it helps drown out the suffocating silence.

It's eerie as fuck and I'm still not used to having the place to myself. I might never be. I don't know if it's any better on the rare occasion my parents are around, either. They keep to themselves when they're home, almost like they're not here at all.

This is exactly why I prefer to spend all my time at Lucas' house across the lake.

I wish my parents had adopted a pet instead of having me, but I wouldn't wish this treatment on any animal.

The kitchen is sterile and staged, like a real estate agent is prepared for potential buyers to swing by. Fresh flowers sit in a concrete vase at the center of the dark granite counter on the island. A stack of magazines sits beside it, one flipped to a recipe like I'm thinking about baking sugar cookies. Ridiculous.

The corners of my mouth turn down as I come to a stop before the refrigerator, staring inside once I open it.

It's fully stocked, but nothing appeals to me. My jaw moves side to side. Two containers of leftovers sit on the middle shelf. No label or note, but if I'm the only resident, it's not like the leftover food is there for anyone else.

Pinching the meat of my cheek between my teeth, I fish my phone from my sweatpants. I pull up my message with Dad and swallow at the one-sided conversation, his responses dotting the left side of the message thread far and few between. My thumb hovers over the keyboard. I don't know why I torture myself begging for his attention.

He doesn't deserve it. I don't want him to give it to me, not like I used to.

My thumbs move anyway, like I'm possessed.

Devlin: I had Frank pick up my Range Rover from school today so he can look at it in his shop. He asked if you're interested in a 1994 Ferrari F355 for our collection. I told him to hold it. We can look at it when you're home.

It seems like a million years ago when Dad introduced me to cars. The memory is distant, foggy at the back of my mind, always out of grasp when I try to examine it with clarity.

Switching over to my message thread with Mom, the words come easier.

Devlin: My AP psych teacher assigned a research topic on identity. Do you have any books on how the brain handles influences of environment at home?

A burning sensation sits heavy in the center of my chest, licking against my ribcage. I rub at it as I set my phone on the island. I brace my weight on my hands and drop my head, hanging it above my silent phone.

The granite is cold.

Give up, my mind whispers.

Pushing out a humorless puff of laughter, I shove away to make something to eat.

There's no response by the time I'm done making a protein smoothie for dinner. It's not until I'm rinsing the blender in the sink that my screen lights up, hooking a deep part of me that I keep locked up inside. The part that harbors hope.

Scolding myself with an eye roll, I flick off the water and wipe my hands on a crisp folded dish towel, tossing it on the counter before grabbing my phone.

The text is from Mom. The hope that ballooned to the surface drifts back down. Her words are clipped and sterile, even for a text. *Library shelf. Home office.*

I don't even warrant full sentences. My mouth settles into a severe line.

"Fuck this," I mutter.

It's too early to go sit on the roof and smoke cigarettes. My fingers scrub over my mouth. I could go for a run, but Bishop did work us hard in practice with dribbling drills. Pushing my legs to burn off the wild array of thoughts crowding my head will only bite me in the ass at tomorrow's practice.

For as huge as the house is, the vaulted ceilings feel like they're swallowing me up, the walls creeping in from all sides. I need to get out of here. A drive up to Peak Point sounds good.

I need to be beneath the stars as they blink into view. They always clear my mind.

After running upstairs to get my wallet, I head for the garage. Before I step through the door, a suspicious sound stops me dead in my tracks. One engine just started.

I grit my teeth against the rushing sensation of my heart pounding harder, my body on heightened alert.

Something is wrong.

My eyes narrow as I go through to the garage.

I keep close to the wall where I can peek around a partition that leads into the garage where Dad and I keep our car collection. My gaze flies back and forth, then widens when I spot the lit taillights on my Porsche.

Someone is sitting in the driver's seat.

"No you don't, you bastard," I whisper as I move like a shadow, hands balled into fists.

I'm intent on killing the fucker who thought they could come into my house and take my favorite car. I creep up to the rear bumper with measured steps, struggling to keep my breath steady. Not because I'm scared of an intruder, but because I'm shaking with rage.

Once the thief turns away, I sneak up to the window and freeze as recognition smacks me in the face.

Sticky fingers.

It's not just any thief in my car. Not some random thug looking to chop my ride. No, I've caught Blair Davis stealing Red, my prized Porsche.

Gemma's friend and the irritating, infuriating street rat that I play with for my own amusement at school.

The initial shock fades and my hands flex at my sides.

She's a thorn in my side, pulling her pickpocket tricks right in front of my boys. She doesn't fear me like she should, her stubborn brazenness like a bug I can't squash.

This little cockroach just signed her damn death warrant.

The rage comes on fast, unstoppable and all-consuming. It flares like the strike of a match, my entire body burning up with hatred for this bitch.

A rough growl tears from my throat as I rip the door open.

Blair yelps, but it doesn't satisfy me. Her sleek inky ponytail swings back and forth with her agitated movements as she scurries into motion. She flashes me a look mixed with defiance and frustration.

Not fear, though. And that just won't fucking do, will it?

"No!" Blair shouts as she tries to scramble across the center console.

I reach in after her, snatching her wrist in a blink before she can get far. Her beat up shoe scuffs against the wheel while she kicks.

"Oh, I don't think so," I snap. "Get back here!"

Her foot flies at my face, hitting my ribs when I duck back. I grunt at the burst of pain. Little bitch. The kick caught me off guard, but I don't release her wrist.

Blair Davis is going to pay for this. I'll make sure of it.

Tightening my hold on her, I yank on her arm until she yields. When I've pulled her from my ride, I cage her in and use my height to trap her against the car.

Her pale cheeks are flushed, but her whiskey-colored eyes are sharp and focused. She looks every inch a hobo, even more than usual in a faded black long-sleeve t-shirt that has a threadbare neckline. There's no trace she's sorry, only pissed she got caught.

"What the fuck are you doing?" I snarl.

Stubbornness is all I see on her face. I glare at her. She doesn't know the monster she's crossed. What I do to her at school is fucking child's play compared to what I want to do now.

Blair tests my hold and I clench her bony wrist tighter until her eyes fly around the room.

Giving her a shake, I lean into her face. She locks her gaze on me, tilting her chin up because she is the type of woman to look death in the face and fucking laugh. My lip curls back, and I hiss out a breath between my teeth.

With a grunt, I shove her aside so I can lean in the car to cut the engine. I don't see the key fob, but she could have it hidden. That's a problem for later, once I've dealt with her. I'm not letting her escape. When I slam the car door, she purses her lips.

"You are in way over your head, you thieving bitch," I seethe, tightening my grip on her wrist. To drive my point home, I grab her upper arm and squeeze. She's skin and fucking bones, but it doesn't stop me. "You'll pay for this."

Blair tenses, but still gives me a cool look that makes me grind my teeth.

"Let's go." I drag her out of the garage.

THREE
DEVLIN

Something tells me she's slippery, waiting for me to drop my guard. *Not a chance, little thief.*

Blair remains silent as we enter the kitchen. The tenacity of her fight when I first caught her in the car has bled away, but I doubt it's simply gone. She must be trying to play up that she's weak against my strength.

I don't want to bring her to my room. The kitchen's my best bet for something to restrain her.

Drawer after drawer, I come up empty. All I've done is make a load of noise as I search. Blair tests my hold, attempting to wrench away. I dig my fingers into her pale skin with a growl. Frustration sears in my chest as I search for cooking string or some shit.

Christ, how do I not know where this crap is in my own house?

"You seem unprepared for taking someone captive," Blair deadpans.

I round on her, letting my angry gaze glide over her petite frame. "If you'd rather, I've got a pair of handcuffs in my bedroom. I'd chain you up to my bed, but I don't want you to get it dirty." I pause to feign thoughtfulness. "Then again, I guess I could give you a flea dip first."

Blair's lip curls and I return to my search.

Her stare speaks volumes, pricking the back of my neck as I tug her in my wake. When I shoot a glance at her, she's taking in everything around her with a calculating interest that irks me.

Her pulse doesn't lie though. It jumps beneath my fingers when I jerk her forward another step by her wrist.

"Take it in, Davis," I spit, sweeping my arm. "It's the most money you'll ever be near."

Her brow ticks up and her pouty lips twitch, the only responses to my words. She's so practiced at containing her reactions when I attack her in school. It irritates me that she won't fight me here, either.

Fucking say something. Do something.

It becomes difficult to rummage through the drawers with one hand while I drag her in circles around the room.

Biting back an annoyed grunt, I spot the pouch attached to her belt. Maybe she's got something I can use. The poetic justice of using her own shit on her is too good.

In one fluid movement, I spin her around and hook one of the metal-backed stools by the island with my foot. The jarring scrape against the tiles makes both of us tense.

Stepping into Blair's personal space, my hands lock on her

waist. This close I can spot the tiny freckles dotting the bridge of her nose and across her cheeks.

Her breath hitches at my proximity, her eyes widening a fraction. "Get away from me!"

I smirk as I hoist her up with ease, dropping her none too gently on the stool. She shoots her hands to the seat to steady her balance. I bring a hand to her throat, grinning when her lips move together in a displeased twist.

"Don't think about going anywhere," I croon in a mocking, flirtatious tone. "You're not escaping."

I expect her to fight me. She has a fire inside to unleash against me, one I crave—if only for the chance to squash her by force. But she stills, her hands clenched on her knees. Interesting.

She could be biding her time. She'll wait all night for an opportunity that isn't coming. I'm not letting her get away with any trick.

Blair's intelligent eyes sweep the room, lingering on the doors.

I wind her soft ponytail around my hand, then dig my fingers into the elastic and undo it so her dark hair spills like a curtain around her face. It was hard to see in the struggle, but it's no longer the color of an angry storm cloud I've grown used to searching for in the halls at school. It was dyed the unnatural color when I flailed cash on a fishing wire hours ago. Now it's as black as mine.

Blair remains silent, even as I slide my hand from her hair, down her baggy shirt to her hip. It doesn't get a rise out of her. When I snatch her pouch with a quick move, she finally loses that bored expression. The corners of her eyes tense.

A brittle chuckle drops from my lips and I give her neck a slight squeeze. "What do you have in your bag of tricks?"

Blair cuts her eyes to the side, her thick lashes sweeping

over those freckles that wink at me like the stars. Her lower lip sucks between her teeth slightly instead of answering.

I set the zipper pouch on the counter and dig through it with one hand. My brows shoot up at the lock picks, pliers, a screwdriver, and a ring of keys that look similar to the set Bishop and I have for the school for our own mischief. My little thief isn't playing around.

The corners of my mouth curl in satisfaction when I pass over a thin cord. Perfect.

Snatching her wrists, I force them low behind the chair, tying each tightly to the metal backing.

"You think you're scaring me with this? You're not."

"I caught you, didn't I? You've been a bad fucking girl."

Blair twists her head far enough to glare at me from the corner of her eye, her hair cascading down her back. I bury my fingers in it and tug her silky strands, directing her head to bend backward. She meets my eyes, and a sinister grin slashes across my face.

"That's right. Struggle all you want." I lean close to touch my nose to her temple, inhaling. She smells like cheap imitation vanilla, but I like it. The sharpness of it suits her. "You're under citizen's arrest. I'm in charge and you're not going anywhere."

Blair scoffs under her breath. My fist tightens in her hair and a small sound gets stuck in her throat.

I speak against the side of her face. "Watch that attitude. Or you won't like what I do to you."

Releasing her, I check the integrity of the knots on each of her wrists, ensuring she can't wriggle free. They're snug enough to nip into her skin without cutting off circulation. Just right for discomfort. Once I've finished securing her, I come around and pat her thigh. Folding my arms, I tilt my head, considering my intruder.

"You'll stay like that until the police arrive."

"You haven't called the police." Blair cocks her head, matching my movements. She crosses her legs. "And you won't."

My arms drop and I advance on her, halting inches from her face with my hands braced on the backrest of the stool. It's tall enough that it gives her some height, but still doesn't bring us on an even level.

The bravado has to be fake. She can't think she has any leverage as the captured thief in this situation.

"Won't I? I've rained hell on people for less than what you've done." The threat hangs in the small space between us. "You were stealing my car."

"That gaudy piece of shit?" Blair taunts in a frosty tone. "What an eyesore."

I hold back a growl. This will be over too fast if I don't tread carefully. She deserves slow torture for her disrespect. I touch her hair again, twisting it between my fingers as I consider my tactics.

"Did you dye your hair black for the full criminal aesthetic? Now you really fit into the trailer park you suck dick at, don't you?"

She sets her jaw, shooting daggers at me. I flick the lock of hair away.

Blair looks like a goddess of trickery and misdeeds tied to the kitchen stool with a challenge in her eyes, a porcelain-smooth throat begging for my hand around it, and a *fuck you* tilt to her pouty mouth.

It's a tempting sight.

She'd be beautiful if she wasn't such a goddamn pain in the ass.

"Turning tricks isn't paying the bills, so you figure you upgrade from your brazen pick pocketing to this?" Another dangerous smile curves my mouth. "Or are bruised knees more your mom's area of expertise?"

"Shut up!" Blair jerks against the stool with a rough sound. Her hair hides her face as her shoulders rise with her sped up breathing.

Ah, a weak point.

I cup her face, pressing my thumb under her chin to force her face back to me. I drive the knife in harder, hitting her back where I can hurt her with words.

"So that's it. Wait until the student body at Silver Lake hears the truths I've uncovered about Raggedy Anne's home life."

She bares her teeth. The fire I've been craving bursts out. I want to fucking fight her for crossing me.

"There you are, you little demon." My thumb nudges her head back further. "I'll finally get you out of my damn school once the cops arrest you for trespassing, breaking and entering, and attempted theft."

"Asshole," she growls. "You're a pathetic shithead."

I laugh in her face, leaning closer. She rears back as much as she can in the awkward position I've put her in, her nose scrunched.

"Do you really want to dig a deeper grave for yourself?" My voice is soft, at odds with my words.

"You would've called the cops already. You haven't." She thrashes against the knots binding her wrists. "You'd rather play this sick game of pretending you have any control over me."

Everyone else at school has always seen me as a cocky playboy, the big flirt. But not Blair. No, she sees through all the stage diversions I put on. As if she *knows*. She could never know what things are like. Not a worthless gutter rat like her.

My jaw tics and I grip her face, squeezing her cheeks.

"Maybe I just want to break you first. But you're definitely ending the night in a jail cell."

"Where's that, your basement?"

A mean smirk twists my lips. "Is that what you want? You're wishing in that messed up little head of yours that this is the start to some fairytale, where I've got some tower to keep you in? I know the girls at school like to talk, but I'm no prince. I'm your worst nightmare, sticky fingers. I'm going to make you hurt for touching my car."

"I could've told them that before they degraded themselves bouncing on your diseased dick." Blair tries to grin, but my hold on her face stops it. "All I see is a pathetic asshole who surrounds himself with a kingdom of fake idiots. You can't do anything to me. You don't have the balls."

"You seem to be missing the fact I have you tied up in my kitchen. Don't wish for mercy." I snap my teeth close to her face. "You won't find any from me."

"For someone who loves that ridiculous car, you're sure taking your sweet ass time calling the authorities to take me away."

She sounds smug, like she's got me figured out. Yeah, right.

This is what drives me crazy. She acts like she knows everything about me. She knows *nothing*.

"If you're in such a hurry, then..."

I spin away from her. Once I dial, I slowly angle to face her once more, hand tucked casually in my pocket.

Blair stares me down, a crack in her brave facade. Her brows pinch together as I start to whistle. She twitches.

"Ok, wait—hang up. Seriously, I'll," she cuts off, taking a heaving breath. She uncrosses her legs, no longer playing this like I'm not a threat. Watching her pride break and hearing the desperation flooding her voice is a feast of vindication. "Devlin

—*please.*" Her eyes go wide as I open my mouth to answer, snapping my attention to the phone. "I'll do anything! Don't!"

Lifting a brow, I let the moment stretch. Her expression has lost every ounce of confidence, now that the real consequences loom. I switch the phone to speaker and slide it across the granite. It stops near her, twirling around.

"Thanks for calling Jimmy's Pizza Palace, can I take your order?"

Blair darts a shocked look from the phone to me. "You... called for delivery?"

"Hello? Pick up or delivery?"

Instead of answering her or the person on the phone, I hit the end call button. "What did you just offer?"

Blair shifts on the stool, licking her lips. Grudgingly, she repeats, "I'll do anything. Just...don't call the cops. I can't go to jail. Whatever way you want to get back at me, fine."

"Anything?" Ice crystalizes my voice, turning it jagged and sharp. "You're giving me carte blanche to take the law in my own hands." I click my tongue and shake my head, gaze raking over her. "Dangerous power to offer someone."

She shrugs.

"You know." I step closer, sliding a hand up her leg. I squeeze, my thumb pressed high on her inner thigh. "Rumor has it you'll give it up for the right price. Let's say we waive that fee for starters."

Blair visibly struggles to respond, flicking her eyes away and tucking her chin to her chest. Her breaths come fast and harsh.

"If that's what you want."

Amusement zips through me at the tortured twitch in her expression.

"On second thought..." I trail off, frowning severely. "I

don't want to catch anything from a filthy gutter rat. And I don't slum it, not when I have primo pussy on lockdown."

The fall of her face makes my mouth twist into a caustic smile.

"You're a pig."

I step back, dropping my hand from her thigh. Swiping my phone from the counter, I wave it in her face.

"Go on. Beg me nice and pretty not to call the police." I dip my chin down a fraction and raise my brows. "For real this time."

A struggle crosses her face. The way she yanks on the cord feels like a victory.

"Please," she mutters.

"You can do more than that. And you'd better."

A grunt of frustration escapes her. When it's clear she isn't going anywhere, she collapses against the backrest of the stool and looks skyward, as if she'll find an answer there.

Blair speaks to the high ceiling. "I didn't have a choice. You have so many, it made sense. You could just buy another."

"What are you talking about?"

Blair heaves a stilted breath. "I have...someone counting on me." She lifts her head to pierce me with a world-weary look. "Money isn't a commodity to you like it is to me. Plus, you're an asshole."

I stare at her for a beat. "I think I should call the police still. You don't sound sorry at all."

"I'm not," Blair snaps. "I'll do whatever it takes for the people I love."

For a brief moment, I'm thrown off by her conviction.

An idea pops into my head. I trace my lips as I turn the thought over, examining it from all sides. It's a little crazy, even for me. But it will teach Blair a lesson—one that sticks this time.

She's not sorry? By the time I'm through with her, repentance will be the least of her worries.

Touching my tongue to my lower lip, I peer at her through hooded eyes.

Destruction.

Control.

Revenge.

I'll take it all and make her wish she'd never met me.

Crossing my arms, I face her. "You can either sign your soul over to me, or the cops. Take your pick, angel."

Blair's glare returns in full force.

I tamp down on the urge to laugh. Taming her will be an entertaining experience.

"I'm no one's angel," Blair swears.

FOUR
BLAIR

"So, what's it gonna be, Davis?" Devlin leans his hip against the kitchen island.

With haunting dark eyes and a jaw sharp enough to cut yourself on his deadly edges, he's heartbreakingly handsome in the same way oleander is fatal. Pretty to look at, but its toxic poison will end you with a taste.

And he fucking knows it.

I strain against the stupid cord he tied me with. My own damn supplies hold me back. Pinning me beneath Devlin's thumb. He's such a bastard. Each time I shift a little, his gaze flicks down, watching my body.

Whatever his offer is, it can't be good. Maybe it would have been easier if I'd convinced him to fuck me for revenge. At least then he'd have to untie me, and I could make a cleaner getaway.

Though that's the one thing I've *never* put on the table to survive.

A phoenix rises from the ashes, born anew from strife. I reform and reshape the person I am, but I don't feel born again. The hardships I've faced only turn my shell harder, preparing me for the next obstacle to battle tooth and nail. I've become unrecognizable from the idealistic little girl I once was.

My lines have been drawn and redrawn in the sand each time I barreled over one, learning a new thing I was capable of losing if it meant food on the table and a tin roof over our heads.

But not my body. Never my body.

It might be one of my last lines standing, but I won't cross it.

I guess I'm glad he doesn't want that from me.

Peering at Devlin through my lashes, it's hard to decipher the mask he keeps locked in place. This differs from the one he wears in school and parties, the one that brands him Silver Lake High's dark king. That one is easy to read. Hair hangs in his eyes, but I can see the mix of calculative coldness and an uncomfortable eagerness in the sinister depths. He's probably looking forward to catching a new toy in his claws.

I scrape my teeth against my bottom lip, wishing I could reach the knots around my wrists. Gemma took me to a self defense class in Denver over the summer. If I could get loose, aim an incapacitating kick at his nuts, I think I'd make it to the woods surrounding the house before he caught me again. I'm a fast runner. But these damn knots are so tight and he tied my arms so they're separated rather than together, leaving me unable to use my opposite hand to work the restraint free.

Biding my time isn't going well. When he grabbed me in the garage, I knew right away I'd never overpower him, not while we were alone. I need to wait for the upper hand to fight him. The rules here—deep in enemy territory—are unknown. I have to figure my way out of this mess.

I've been trying to squirm free of the cord wound around my wrists. He didn't tie me with any normal knots, it seems. Every time I move they feel tighter, not looser.

The rumors spread by the bragging from girls who have been with him swim to the front of my mind, how he doesn't fuck like other guys. They call him mischievous and dangerously sexy. With the way these knots are tied...god, what kind of freaky shit gets him off?

"I really should have you locked up, but since you begged so nicely—well, not quite, but," Devlin touches his splayed hand to his chest and pretends to bow, right out of an Austen novel, "I'm willing to be a gentleman and help you out."

My eyebrows shoot up before I can hold back a reaction. *Um, what?*

It doesn't sound like a nice gesture at all, his tone and the blackness of his shadowed eyes belying the trap in his offer.

As if I'd believe he's helping me out of the goodness of his heart!

Devlin doesn't have a heart. If he ever had one, it died off long ago. In its place sits a rotten, decayed hole.

"What exactly do you mean?"

Sign your soul over to me, or the cops.

How can I pick between my nightmare and the devil that torments me?

What does he expect me to do? It's an impossible choice. But then again, so is the problem that drove me into this situation in the first place.

This feels like one of his cruel tricks, the same as his soccer buddies baiting me with dollar bills on fishing wire at school. Or last year, when he let me sit at his lunch table alongside Gemma because Lucas wanted her there, but the price was

Devlin toying with my lunch tray and dumping it on the floor in front of everyone.

Devlin waves off my question. "I'll give you what you came here for."

That gets my attention. I sit up as much as I can on the narrow stool, swallowing.

"I don't follow." My forehead wrinkles. "You're going to let me drive off with your car? Just like that?"

The corner of Devlin's mouth quirks up and a dimple appears in his cheek.

"Not at all. You're never to touch my car again." He points at me to drive that decree home. He studies me with cunning curiosity. "No, what I mean is if you play my game, I'll forget all about tonight. And if you do that, I'll give you the money you obviously need."

My lips part, lured by the temptation for a minute.

Reality catches up with me a second later. I snap my mouth shut as I seek out the part where he laughs in my face. Because what he's offering? It sounds too fucking good to be true. He'll just *give* me money? There's a catch, I know it.

Devlin? Fine with helping me?

We hate each other.

"This offer expires before you leave here." Devlin's grin is smug. "So...ready to play a game, little thief?" He slinks closer, like a beast hunting me down for sport, drowning me in the rich, earthy scent of leather and spice. He wraps a lock of my hair around his finger while the smile dances on his lips, the dimples on display. "I'll explain further. The rules are simple: my way is law."

"That's it?" I purse my lips to the side.

Things with Devlin are never simple. There are always layers, cruel pranks lurking beneath his punch line. I have a hard time believing what he's offering is as straightforward as he puts it.

"It's a one time bargain." Devlin leans in to whisper against my ear—because what's a ringmaster without the theatrics? "You might say it's a real *steal*."

Devlin's deep voice tugs at something deep inside me, his hot breath coasting over my skin.

"Ugh." I tug away from him, jerking my head. He releases me, still invading in my personal space. "Seriously, what's the fine print? No way in hell will I agree to anything you want without knowing what a deal with the devil entails."

Devlin chuckles, the sound low and raspy. "Smart. Too bad you don't have any leverage or negotiating power. Your choices are limited to what I offer, or communal soap."

"Just tell me."

"The deal is this, little bug." Devlin taps my nose. "You become mine."

My breath catches in my throat as he goes on.

"Mine to command, to do anything I say, whenever I demand it." Devlin cocks his head, hooding his eyes. "And I'll pay you for it. If you behave and do as I say."

How can I agree to that?! I'd have to be crazy! But...the money.

I have to swallow twice to dislodge the thickness clogging my throat. "Like your—your personal servant?"

"Like a well-trained," Devlin flicks his eyes to my shirt and grimaces, "...dog. Even mutts can learn to obey their masters."

Master. My stomach clenches and a cold prickle travels over my skin. Sweat beads on the back of my neck.

This is insane. I'm actually considering his offer. I have to, don't I? I'm once again left with few options.

Devlin's right, unfortunately. He threw it right in my face.

It's jail time for me if I refuse him.

I can't do that to Mom.

For whatever sick reason, he wants to give me this out. The notice letter burns in my back pocket. Debts chained to us by Dad will bury Mom and I, but this could be our way to dig out of the endless sandpit. Damn it, we need the money.

What's worse, a jail sentence or becoming the devil's toy?

My pride screams at me. Years of bullying at his hand in school flickers like a movie reel in my mind. It goes against everything in me to bow to his rule.

Last year my life was easier at school. My friend Gemma was the new girl, unafraid to stand up to people's crap. She's in college now, so things have gone back to the way they've been since I started at Silver Lake High School, the pack of vultures led by Devlin himself to pick at my pride until there's nothing left but scraps.

Agreeing to this will undermine the efforts I go to in order to rise above his petty bullshit.

For Mom... You can do it as long as it helps Mom.

"I want it in writing," I breathe, barely recognizing my strained voice.

He hums, covering his mouth. It's even harder to guess his thoughts with only half of his face visible. "Why?"

"You didn't record this conversation on your phone. Verbal agreements are paper thin. You could just turn around and decide you want to fuck me over anyway." I wet my lips and will the words out. "Put it in writing and I'll sign it. I'll—" My voice gets stuck in my burning throat. "I'll...become yours. For payment."

Devlin considers me for a long minute, tracing an absent pattern over his lips. He steps back, giving me room to breathe.

"Clever girl," he mutters as he rummages in the drawers, coming up empty. He grabs a magazine from the middle of the island and tears out a page. "Fine. Is there a pen in your thief kit?"

"Yes. You'll need to untie me so I can sign."

On the outside I'm collected, confident, and calm. Inside I'm a mess, a storm of wounded pride and hungry desperation. Survival above all else. It'll be worth it.

Devlin rifles through my pouch and bends over the torn paper to write out the terms of our agreement. After he signs it with a flourish, he frees one of my hands.

"Still tied up here," I point out, shaking my wrist out and flexing it.

"Just how I like you, troublemaker." Devlin slaps the pen down on the contract and slides it in front of me. "Sign it and I'll let you go. Of course, if you've taken to being tied up, we can leave you like that. You make an excellent addition to the kitchen decor."

The corners of my mouth turn down. Dickhead.

My hand is clammy as I hold the pen. It slips a little and I adjust my grip.

The wording is simple. The ripped magazine page states precisely what Devlin said.

Blair Davis agrees to complete any order set by Devlin Murphy in exchange for monetary payment.

There's no end date specified. I'll endure it, even if it's forever. The chance to clear the crushing debts Mom and I carry is too valuable. My life and pride are small prices to pay.

Inhaling quietly, I sign myself over to the devil.

FIVE
DEVLIN

Once she signs her name on the contract she insisted on, I dig my fingers into the knotted cord on her other wrist, freeing her.

The heat of success coils deep in my gut as I skim over our impromptu contract, her name written neatly with no frills beside mine.

Oh, sticky fingers. You have no idea what you've signed up for.

I stick my tongue into my cheek. My head is already overflowing with ideas to humiliate her. I'll teach her lesson after lesson. Not only will she regret the day she set her sights on taking what's *mine*, she'll learn to fear the monster I keep chained up inside me.

I'll be her own personal nightmare and her salvation all at once. A heady mix of power put in my hands.

The thought of making her dance to my own twisted tune fills me with so much satisfaction I go a little lightheaded from the rush.

Blair slides off the stool, rubbing her wrists. There are pink marks on her skin that will fade by morning. The cord wasn't tied tight enough to leave a lasting mark.

I should do something to mark her.

That craving gets put on hold for the time being. I need time to plan out the commands I want to give her.

Blair makes quick work of the cord, undoing it from the stool. She skirts around me to snatch up her zipper pouch. Once it's reattached to her belt, she runs her fingers through her sleek hair.

We're at an impasse. The terms of the contract are in place, but the mood of her intrusion and my efforts to thwart it hangs between us. We're not friends—quite the opposite.

Instead of reclaiming firm control once more, I let the moment stretch, curious what she'll do. Hell, she's fast enough, I wouldn't put it past her to snatch the closest thing she can and make a mad dash for the door. If it comes to that, I'm fast as fuck, too. I'll catch her again.

"So..." Blair trails off and avoids my gaze. "I'm just gonna go."

She watches me for a beat, like she expects me to go back on my word. I don't break a deal.

Tipping my head to the side, I lift my brows. "Off you scurry then, gutter rat."

She grants me a severe look, shoulders a stiff line.

Good. Keep that iron pride intact. You're gonna need it, sweetheart.

As Blair slips from the room, I trail her. I might not go back on my word, but I don't trust her at all. Desperation makes people do stupid shit, and she's got *three seconds from the next bad decision* written all over her scrawny ass.

What's some grand larceny on top of her other crimes tonight?

At the front door, an odd urge drags a question from me. "How did you get into the community, anyway?" Blair glances over her shoulder and shrugs. I circle around and prop against the door, blocking her escape. She'll answer my questions before she disappears into the darkness. "Answer me. Gemma's at college, so that option's out. You don't know anyone else here."

Blair smirks, the self-satisfaction looking irritatingly good on her. "I have my ways."

She attempts to open the door without touching me while I'm leaning on it.

If she doesn't know anyone here, I guess she hiked the mountain. It's how I'd do it in her place. If that's the truth, it doesn't sit right with me. "The woods are dangerous at night."

Her eyes dart up and she falls back a step. The movements are quick, but I watch in fascination as she assesses the other exit options, since I'm blocking her current choice.

"If you planned on walking," I clarify with a gesture of my hand. "There's a community patrol, but they don't always scare things off."

"I'll manage." She reaches for the doorknob.

"What if I make you stay." It's not a question. But it's not entirely me fucking around with control. Despite promising to let her go...I'm not ready for her to leave.

Blair freezes. I've got her there.

Her perceptive gaze finds mine. I keep my expression smooth, not giving her any hints if I'm bluffing or not. She swallows.

"I, uh, can't." She's suddenly shifty. Her fingers twist in the hem of her shirt at her side. I fold my arms. After blowing out a breath, she elaborates, "My mom will be home soon. I need to be there before that."

Blair waits me out for the span of one heartbeat to the next, then twists the doorknob.

My resolve cracks. I can't let her go out there like this. Christ, she's stubborn. I look forward to bringing that bad habit under my command.

"Seriously." I put my hand on her shoulder to stop her. "Do you need a ride to the gate? Or an Uber?"

Blair scoffs. "Still playing the gentleman act?"

Sharp laughter barks out of me. In a quick move, my arms circle her waist, twirling her around. I cage her against the door, planting my palms on either side of her head as I lean down in her space. Her body heat seeps into mine, her tits brushing against my t-shirt. If I take another step closer, I'll pin her with my body.

"Hardly," I rasp. "I'm worse than the danger that lurks outside. I don't want anything to happen to my new toy."

Her mouth twists and her dark lashes flutter. Color fills her freckled cheeks as her attention skates to my forearm flexing beside her head.

I expected big, brash reactions from her, although she never gives me a response like that when I taunt her in school. What I'm unprepared for is the way she keeps still, assessing the situation rather than trying to immediately knee my balls.

"Come on." Blair sighs and rests her head against the door. "I'll be fine. Really."

It almost works on me, but the tight tremor in her shoulders gives her away, destroying her air of casualness. I make her more uncomfortable than walking through the woods at night.

I step back and chuck her under the chin with a crooked finger. This is a discovery I can use to my advantage later.

"Don't get eaten out there." I tuck my hands in the pockets of my sweatpants. "Can't have you dying before the fun starts."

Blair stares at me in disbelief, then rolls her eyes. "You're un-fucking-believable."

The door swings open and slams shut behind her. It echoes into the exposed beams high overhead, the modern chandelier rattling with the faint tinkle of glass and metal.

Tch. I file her insolence away. She'll pay for that, too.

I wander back to the kitchen and lean on my elbows against the island. The scent of her cheap imitation vanilla shampoo clings to me. I'll have to shower again to get this shit off me.

The quiet settles over the house once again. It happens faster than expected, the oppressive weight of silence almost shocking me. For a short time, I almost forgot. Now that the excitement of the night has faded, I'm left alone in my house with only my cars and my thoughts to keep me company.

When I swallow, my throat is tight.

I rub my fingertips together and resist the nagging urge to climb to the second floor landing to see if I can watch Blair's exit. Something tells me she's already blended in with the shadows.

Taking out my phone, I skim my Instagram notifications. There's a slew of likes and comments on my picture of Red this morning and the one I shared from practice of my cleats next to a soccer ball. Bishop left a load of emojis in a comment on both posts that makes me snort. It's funny to imagine that tonight could have gone differently if I hadn't walked to the garage intent on a joyride when I did.

My thumb hovers over the screen. I've never looked before. Does Blair have social media?

A search of her name pulls up nothing. I switch to Gemma's profile and scroll until I find a recent photo of the two of them. They're on Lucas' boat in the middle of the lake, his pug dog cradled between them. Gemma grins brightly at the camera with her arm around Blair while she's more reserved, attention on Lancelot the pug.

There are two profiles tagged in the photo. One is Lucas', so the other must be Blair's. My mouth curves. *Thank you, Gem, for always being an open book.*

I click on the *@disblair* username. It's private. Her profile photo is a picture of her when she had her hair dyed blue-gray. She's wearing an oversized hoodie and holding her hand up to hide most of her face. One brown eye peeks between her fingers, taunting the camera.

"Shit."

It can wait for later. Or I could pay her for access to her account. I stroke my chin.

Swiping out of the app, I hesitate. Glaring at the message icon for a minute, I give in, pulling up my text history with Dad.

No response.

Which I knew.

A rough sound tears from my throat.

I fucking knew, and I still couldn't help checking.

"Goddamn it, you idiot."

I squeeze the phone in my hand until my knuckles turn white. My weakness pisses me off.

I briefly consider telling my parents about a break in. My breath hisses between my clenched teeth. No, I won't tell them.

I'll handle it all on my own, like everything else. They pushed me to be independent and I took it a step farther. I haven't needed the monthly guilt money they dump in my bank account for more than a year. Through investments and planning with my financial advisor, I can walk away from them whenever I want. The problem is taking that step.

My phone starts vibrating. I hate the flash of hope that bubbles in my chest.

The caller ID is my uncle.

"Hey, Uncle Ed," I greet after accepting the call. "What's up?"

"*Hey, son.*" His voice is warm.

When he calls me son, my chest aches. It's something he's always done, almost like he accepted me from birth as I grew up alongside Lucas, his biological son. Lucas and I are cousins, but my aunt and uncle have given me everything they've given him.

"*Did you eat yet?*"

"No." I scrub my hand through my hair. "Why?"

"*Come on over. Your aunt is still adjusting to cooking for two instead of three or four now that the kids are off at college.*" He chuckles on the line. "*I want to hear how the first week of your senior year has been.*"

"Yeah," I answer hoarsely, hoping he doesn't hear it. I clear my throat. "That sounds cool. I'll be over in fifteen."

It's pathetic how fast I jump at any chance to leave my empty house for a little while longer.

"*Excellent. See you in a bit.*"

When Lucas and I were kids, I spent a lot of time with his family instead of mine. My parents traveled even more often back then, and it was before they hired au pairs to raise me for them. I called Aunt Lottie my mom back then.

Secretly, I still wish she and Uncle Edward were my actual parents. But only the stars I sit under late at night hear it.

I hang up and grab my evergreen and white soccer zip up jacket from the closet in the hall before ducking into the garage, heading for Red.

Getting in, I search the cup holder and between the seats. I locate the key fob on the floor, sticking out from beneath the driver's seat.

"Christ, you're short," I mumble, adjusting the seat with a grunt until it's back where I'm comfortable.

I grip the wheel in one hand and start the engine. With a quick tap on the screen, one of the garage doors opens. I gun it, taking the curved roads and inclines at a quick clip. I know this route by heart.

It's one of the first I learned when I got my license.

One I've driven so often it's ingrained in my blood.

SIX

BLAIR

An owl hoots in the tree line at the edge of the trailer park as I trudge up to the one I share with Mom.

The streetlamp casts our faded blue trailer in flickering light and a stray cat yowls. The whole place is mostly quiet, too early for the graveyard shift residents to trickle home on weary legs bearing the weight of the world, and the elderly residents are asleep in front of their televisions. In the distance, I can hear a TV and someone having a too-loud conversation. Sound travels easily in the gravel lot between the tin-roofed homes.

I unlock the creaky front door. It reverberates as it slams shut. A sigh escapes me as I collapse back against the door, taking in our tiny single wide with a disinterested sweep.

It's strikingly different from Devlin's modern palace-sized place in the mountains.

There's a kitchenette with bland pink formica counters, the living room the length of our couch, which is the uncool kind of vintage in an ugly tan plaid, and a dim wood-paneled hall that leads to the bedrooms and the bathroom.

It isn't much, but it's home. Mom's tried to make it as cozy as possible. Over the years, she'd shoot me a cheerful look as she hung pastel curtains from the dollar store or draped a new crocheted blanket over the threadbare sofa, and say it was home as long as we were together.

We didn't always live here. Before Dad ran off, we used to have a house in Gemma's neighborhood on the other side of Ridgeview's east valley. We were a happy family when I was a little girl.

The rattle of change scrounged from between the sofa cushions echoes in my head, the memory of the last time I saw Dad floating to the surface. He didn't see me watching from the stairs after I snuck down for a cookie from the jar Mom kept on the counter. Dad muttered *need more* to himself while he dug through Mom's purse, taking dollar bills and stuffing them in his pockets. A packed duffle bag sat on the kitchen table. When I asked what he was doing, Dad had whirled to face me with a grimace.

"Blair Bear. You're not supposed to be out of bed." He patted my head. "Mommy will take care of you. Be good for her, okay?"

With that cryptic message, he was gone from our lives. After that, all I remember is Mom crying over the mail. It wasn't until I was a little older I understood her constant phone calls were with debt collectors demanding payment.

Peeling away from the door with a grumble, I pad into the kitchenette to the left, kneeling by the cabinet beneath the sink. I pull out the first aid kit and slump onto the sofa.

There's a tear in my jeans where I scraped my knee after

tripping in my rushed hike down the mountain from Devlin's house. It stings when I rub an alcohol wipe over the abrasion and I hiss through my teeth. I plaster it with an off-brand Band-Aid.

Digging the pen from my zipper pouch, I stick my tongue between my teeth in concentration as I draw a frown on the bandage. It's a personal reminder to be stronger than my mistakes.

Tonight I did nothing but mess up left and right.

My perfect plan imploded.

Uneasiness stirs in my chest as my eyes skip to the window. Devlin might change his mind, pulling the rug from under me like a sick joke. Outside the window I only find darkness instead of the flashing red and blue lights of the squad car I'm anticipating, putting me on blast to the entire trailer park of misfits as it rolls up to haul me off.

I peer out the window for a few minutes before muttering, "He better not have been joking."

With a frustrated cry, I rip the notice letter from my back pocket and smack it down on the squat coffee table I helped Mom trash pick and repaint. The notice of collections sits bent and crumpled on the table, a glaring point of why I had no choice in accepting Devlin's twisted offer.

I scrub my hands over my face and get up to put away the first aid kit. Scooping up the notice, I slip it into the stack that lives next to our toaster. The pile never shrinks, only seems to grow and grow and grow. I rifle through opened and unopened bills, other collection notices and debts past due—everything Dad shackled to us before he high-tailed it.

A sick dread upsets my stomach when I look at this pile of despair. I rub my belly to abate the feeling of my insides turning into solidified bricks.

"Fuck you, Dad," I growl to the bills.

My temple throbs and I swallow. I need to take my mind off everything that went wrong tonight.

Spinning on my heel, I retreat to my room. It's a tiny square with a futon bed, library printouts of my favorite art pieces tacked to the wall alongside photos where I'm posed with Gemma and Mom, and stacks of paperbacks under the window.

They're my collection from the twenty-five cent bin at the thrift store. Most of them are beat up, with cracked spines and yellowed pages, but I love digging through the bin once a month to find a new treasure to add to my collection.

Wriggling out of my dirty clothes, I toss them in the corner to be dealt with later. I pull my hair up into a twisted bun and put on my old track pants and SLHS girls track team t-shirt to relax in. My hand smooths over the green shirt and a wistful smile tugs at my lips. I don't need the track team to run regularly, but I do miss the way it occupied my time. It was something I had for myself, and those are far and few between.

Yet another disappointment to credit Devlin for...

Sighing, I shake my head and cross to my paperback stacks. I sit on the floor and trace my finger over the spines to pick out something suited to lose myself in until Mom gets home.

I don't have as many as I'd like. If I could, I'd fill my room with floor-to-ceiling bookshelves. But we don't have the space, so I limit myself to only titles I want to hold on to the most. The books I don't love, I donate to the free book exchange shelf at the Ridgeview library.

My finger pauses on a biography of Frida Kahlo. The corner of my mouth lifts. *Perfect.*

I'll read anything, but books on art and artists are among my favorites.

Picking out my book, I flop on my futon, dragging a pillow over to prop myself on.

* * *

The racket of the front door snaps me out of reading Frida's biography.

"I'm home, Blair!" Mom calls from the main room.

I roll off the futon and flip my book over to save my place before heading out of my room.

Mom is at the sink washing her hands. She finishes, then turns and holds her arms out to me.

The light blue waitress uniform hangs from her thin frame more than usual, and it makes a pang of worry spear through me. Her brown hair is tied into a low bun, but a few gray fly aways fall around her face. Her skin has a waxy quality that I don't like one bit, and her blue eyes are sunken with bags beneath.

She's been working way too hard lately.

"Hey, how was work?" I step into her arms and give her a tight squeeze, tucking my head under her chin.

This is our ritual when she comes home from work. When I hit puberty, the hormonal imbalance made me an asshole and I told her it was stupid. She always insisted, and now I live for her hugs. For a few seconds, I don't have to be the strong one between us.

"Work was good." Mom smooths a hand over my bun and drops a kiss on top of my head. "I brought you home a slice of apple pie. It's in the fridge."

"Thanks. Want me to make some tea? We'll split it."

I rummage through the cabinet where we keep tea, instant coffee, and some ancient lemonade mix that I'm pretty sure has crystallized into a singular mass. I hold on to it because that shit would hurt if I chucked it at the drunkard two trailers over who tries to enter our trailer every few days. I like to be prepared because I don't trust him if he ever makes it in here.

"You can have it, sweetie."

Mom works her fingers into her shoulder, a grimace twisting her features. I abandon the tea bags on the counter and guide her into a seat at our tiny bistro table in the corner. Her protest doesn't last long once I rub her shoulders to massage out the aches and pains of standing on her feet at the diner.

"We're splitting it." I bend to kiss her on the cheek and continue taking care of her discomfort. "Do you have a shift Saturday morning? I was thinking we could make pancakes."

Weekend pancakes are one of the few treats we have kept alive since I was a kid. No matter how little we have, we treat ourselves to a homemade pancake breakfast.

Mom sighs, tipping her head back into my stomach. "Yes, hun. Sorry. What about on Sunday?"

"Sure, don't worry," I assure her gently. "There's no rush on pancakes."

Mom taps her nails on the tabletop. Her red polish is chipped. "But after, it might be my last shift for a bit. They're changing the waitress shifts around."

"What?" My insides go icy and I bounce my eyes from Mom to the messy stack of bills by the toaster. "Why? You've been there for long enough that you should have seniority over shift choices, they can't just—"

"Blair." She pats my hand and I loosen my tense grip on her shoulders. "I'm going to go lay down, I think. It's late and I'm tired."

The words hit me like a slap, though she spoke quietly. "Of course. Sorry, Mom."

"It's okay." She releases a soft groan as she stands. Her hand cups my cheek. I've never seen her face so pale and colorless. The weariness around the corners of her eyes makes my heart hurt. I'm worried her health is declining faster than we're prepared to handle. I've already had to take her to the doctor before school. "Have the pie, okay?"

Working as hard as she does is destroying her, tearing away little pieces bit by bit. Despite our shitty lot in life, she still manages to find a warm smile for me.

"Yeah," I rasp. "Get some rest, Mom."

She hums and tucks a stray piece of limp brown hair behind her ear. I flick my nails together, a terrible nervous habit that I know she hates. I stop and lace my fingers together before I upset her.

My stomach tenses as I watch her slow retreat into the shadows of the hall. A moment later, her bedroom door clicks shut.

When my shaking knees give out, I collapse into the chair at the bistro table, cradling my head in my hands.

She's getting worse.

Dad did this to her. First it was stress, but now I'm not so sure. Can stress slowly kill someone, sucking away their life force like a parasite over the span of years? I chew my lip, wishing I could see Dad right now. I'd scream my head off at him for being so irresponsible and selfish. Then I'd punch the bastard.

Men are such untrustworthy worms, the whole rotten lot of them.

I don't know what to do. The bills are already so much to handle. If she collapses like she did last year, the medical bill from the emergency room is going to destroy us.

I'd quit school and get a job myself, but I'm on scholarship at Silver Lake High School. Attending the school alone is enough to open doors for me I previously believed were jammed shut for life. Graduating from Silver Lake High will be the difference between Mom and I struggling to eke by the rest of our lives and the chance at a full ride to any college I want.

Devlin better not screw me over.

My eyes burn as I flick my watery gaze over to the window, searching for flashing red and blue.

I wait for so long, my body grows stiff. The cops never come.

SEVEN
BLAIR

Nothing has happened yet.

I held out through the weekend, classes on Monday, and all of today—nothing.

Waiting for the shoe to drop is giving me an early ulcer. Not even the fresh mountain air can settle my nerves.

Devlin and I share Mr. Coleman's English class together, but he ignored me while I ended up shooting glances his way two days in a row.

Part of me wishes he would make his move, because Mom and I need money as soon as possible, but another part of me has been walking around the sprawling campus of Silver Lake High School like an attack will come from any corner.

After the last period of the day let out, I went to the athletic fields behind the bleachers and beyond where the soccer team trains. It's the outer field where the track and field teams like to hold practice.

The track coach blows her whistle and the girls take off for meter dashes. I tug a fistful of grass from the spot where I'm watching from, a far enough distance that they won't be weirded out.

After all, I'm not on their track team anymore.

The mid-afternoon sun keeps me warm. I lean back on my hands and cross my stretched legs in front of me. The baggy sleeves of my secondhand button-down shirt droops down my arms.

People are always breaking the school's uniform requirements. They'll go around in beanies and whatever shoes they want, but while they are expressing themselves, I'm going against regulation because the blazer for the uniform is too damn expensive. I can't find a used one. I gave up sophomore year and have worn only the white shirt and the skirt ever since. The administrative board thinks the uniforms blur the lines of class differences between the student body, but all it does is set us apart even more in my mind.

With the next shrill of the whistle, another group of girls sprint from their starting position. I lick my lips and release a sigh.

My phone lights up beside me in the grass with a text from Gemma. It's a used iPhone I bought from a guy with a shopping cart full of devices on the shadier side of Ridgeview's downtown. The phone isn't the latest and greatest model, like the spoiled rich kids who get a new phone every time an upgrade releases. This one is at least four generations old. It works, despite the spiderweb of cracks in the screen. Mom and I can barely afford the cheap monthly plan, but it's for emergencies since we don't have a landline.

The text is a selfie of Gemma on her college campus with

her boyfriend, Lucas, partially visible. She looks so happy compared to this time last year, when we first met. A smile tugs at the corner of my mouth. The phone buzzes with another message.

Gemma: Just found this new location and omg I'm dying to do a shoot there with you. I want to show you so much here. Come visit me soon!

A visit with Gemma sounds incredible.

But it's also impossible. Money, my mom, money, my junk box car, *money*. There's too much keeping me from living the life a normal teen would.

A pang hits me in the chest. I miss Gemma. Before she befriended me last year as the badass new girl, I was a nobody in this school. Other than crossing paths with Devlin, I kept my head down and focused as much as I could on my studies while the vultures at this school called me names and taunted me for being poor. Gemma made so much of that go away.

Her boyfriend—the previous king of the school—wasn't even so bad once Gemma got his head screwed on straight.

Why did Gemma have to be a grade ahead of me?

The heaviness of being left behind weighs down on my shoulders. I dig my fingers into the grass.

"Keep it up, ladies," the track coach calls, her encouragement floating my way.

I pretend that she's still offering me a boost.

A light breeze shifts my skirt, the evergreen and white plaid material riding up my legs. The blades of grass tickle the back of my knees.

I want to run. Maybe I should change into my gym clothes and jog the track around the football field.

"That's it, girls! Go, go!"

Even though I was kicked off the track team last year, at the end of the cross country season, I still come to watch them. It was a shock when the coach told me she had no choice but to take me off the team. The rules were clear, she'd explained, and I had too many demerits on my school record.

Ridiculous.

My teeth scrape across my lip as I dig harder into the grass, tearing at it. I release my fist and watch the blades flutter to the ground.

I know exactly who to thank for getting thrown off the team.

Devlin.

Evil fucking bastard.

He retaliated against me picking his friend's pocket last year by fabricating more detentions on my school file. With a best friend who is the son of our principal and his elective as an office aid, it was probably easy for him. And because I don't have a rich family to donate to the school, no one noticed anything amiss with my file.

When it all went down with my coach at one of our last practices of the season, Devlin made sure he was close by to watch the showdown, of course. He smirked as he wiped his mouth with the neck of his soccer jersey. When the burn of his smug stare became too much to ignore, I swung my gaze to him. *Told you*, he mouthed.

Because he'd warned me not to try him.

I muffle an irritated sound in my throat and slam my fist on the ground.

The cruel king can take away my spot on the team, but he can't take running from me. I still run anyway.

"Nice, Katrina!" My old coach praises a girl as she reaches the group.

Sitting up, I tuck my legs into a pretzel, leaning my elbows on my knees as I hunch over.

I don't think many of the team liked me, but running with those girls filled a gaping hole in my chest, just a little so the loneliness didn't bend in on itself like an aching empty stomach wracked with hunger pangs. The team was sort of like a family. It's not the running I miss, but running with other people who have my back.

Another text interrupts my moping. It must be Gemma, since I didn't respond.

It's from a number I don't have in my phone. My brows pinch together. *What the hell?*

Unknown: Do the first english essay for me. $250.

Realization dawns on me. My entire body goes hot and cold with emotion all at once. It's from Devlin.

"Motherfu—" I cut my annoyed curse off and tap my fingers against the side of the phone. "How did you get my number, you tricky devil?"

I wrack my brain, trying to think of the few people who have my number and where my cell is listed. There's no way he weaseled it out of Gemma.

Knowing him, he probably invaded my privacy and nabbed it off the emergency contact form in my student file. Or he had his best friend, Connor Bishop, do the digging. I've heard that guy knows everything about everyone at school, trading secrets for favors and payment.

A huff of disbelief escapes me.

I should've known Devlin would be the kind of morally gray prick at ease with pilfering personal files for his own gain.

The question is, can I trust he'll keep his word if I do this?

EIGHT
DEVLIN

Blair doesn't answer my text right away. I hover at the edge of the soccer field with my water bottle in one hand and my phone in the other. Behind me, Bishop's shouts to the guys become background noise as my attention zeroes in on Blair.

My head jerks with a snort.

Does she think she's being subtle, sitting near the girls track team? She's pathetic.

Her head is bent over, her hair creating a curtain of black as it falls around her face.

My eyes flick down to the screen, anticipating three dots popping up any second with her response.

After I bribed Bishop with a little mischief and the number of a Coyote Girl he wanted to steal from the football player she was dating, he gave me the password to unlock the current student files stored on the computer system. This morning during my office aid elective period, I found her cell number on a form for a field trip in sophomore year. With a smirk, I programmed her into my phone as *Little Thief*.

"Dev, quit slacking off," one of my teammates calls.

I lift a brow in his direction and slowly bring my water bottle to my mouth, taking a long gulp.

He flips me off.

The phone buzzes, but it's a message from my aunt letting me know dinner is at seven tonight.

What is taking so long? I squint at my phone and bounce my gaze between the screen and Blair. The task I set is hardly difficult. After the shit she pulled with my car, I could've plunged her into the deep end and paid her to run around school in her underwear. She should be thanking me.

As Blair begins to pack up her things and swipe grass from her skirt, I glare from the sidelines of the soccer field. I send another text.

Devlin: Or I could give my uncle a call. He's pretty friendly with the Ridgeview police department. I'm sure they'd love to hear all about the security footage I have from the other night. Don't forget the rules of this game.

It's a bluff. I don't actually have a security feed set up, though after Blair's stunt I've been considering telling Dad we should take measures to protect the house as a precaution. The security patrol is clearly losing its touch if they can't catch a mangy stray wandering in.

Devlin: I'm letting you off easy and paying you triple what I pay for homework from my usual guy.

I drift a few steps in Blair's direction. The texts stopped her in her tracks. I can't see her expression from here, but she glances around, body rigid. Blair rubs her forehead and drags her fingers through her hair.

My phone vibrates and the corners of my mouth curl up in victory.

Little Thief: Kk.

An amused sound huffs out of me. It's essentially a *fuck you*. But she agreed.

Game on.

"Dev," Bishop calls. He jogs over and claps my shoulder. "Man, let's go. I don't want to get up early again this week to make you practice a double. Friday morning was bad enough."

Bishop leans his weight on me and moans dramatically. I shake my head, fighting back a smile. Bishop can always get me to smile with his antics.

He leans in, whispering, "I've got the lowdown on the location of a secret fight ring. Tonight. Landry is taking bets until seven. We get thirty percent of the cut."

My smirk breaks free, wicked and devious. "His parents wouldn't be pleased if they found out. What did you have on him that he needed to pay you so steeply?"

"A positive drug test that would ruin his football scholarship. Oh, and footage of him getting blasted at that boat party in July."

To the rest of the school Bishop is this angelic face and the principal's son, but to me he's my partner in crime with a mischievous streak a mile wide. We're best friends because we fit together like a matched set—charming and handsome on the outside, but underneath our irresistible veneers lies a darkness sure to consume anyone that gets too close.

"Cool? Cool." Bishop smacks my back. "Now get your ass back in the game."

I cover his face with my hand and give him a shove. "Yeah, yeah. Get your own ass in gear, captain."

NINE
BLAIR

The essay doesn't take long to complete. I type it up in the library before school starts.

I didn't put my full effort in, but it's enough to get Devlin a fair passing grade. He never specified that it had to be a good essay. He's not as clever as he thinks he is. If he wanted full marks, he wouldn't get them from me.

Devils don't deserve an A+.

I'm jittery through the first two classes of the day, eager to get my hands on my $250. I cycle through nervous habits, chewing my lip practically raw, twirling my pen, bouncing my knee, and flicking my nails until students glare at me for being disruptive.

The anxiousness grows to a flurry of butterflies in my stomach as I slam my locker between periods.

A sea of students mills around me as I make my way to English class, the girls in green plaid skirts and black blazers with the school's golden crest, and the guys in slacks, green and white ties, and the same blazers. Little rebellions crop up everywhere, students with their shirts in various states of disarray, wearing jackets and hats that aren't part of the required uniform, and every kind of shoe imaginable. Few wear the regulation shiny black loafers.

I wrap my arms tighter around my books, Devlin's assignment tucked inside my textbook. My incomplete uniform and beat up black Chucks aren't a show of self-expression. I pieced together what I could find and afford.

Freshman year I didn't even have the right uniform. I wore a cream shirt instead of white because it was what I found at the thrift shop for a few bucks, and a brown plaid midi skirt.

I reach class as the bell rings. Devlin is in his seat in the row next to mine, talking to Connor Bishop. A few of their usual cohort hang around nearby, pretending like they're not listening to every word from their kings.

It's hardly noticeable to the brainless masses at this school, but there's something off about Devlin when he's surrounded by his sycophants. People can't see past the end of the silver spoons stuck in their mouth. But now that I've been in his house alone with him, the fake cockiness in his actions is even more obvious.

Despite the carefree, flirty demeanor, when no one's looking I see a flicker of brooding edginess beneath his dimpled smirks.

Whatever Devlin mutters under his breath makes Bishop laugh and ruffle his light brown hair.

These two are a fearsome duo, and my insides clench at the thought of what they could be plotting with their heads bent together. With the arrogant, attractive tilt to his mouth, even I can reluctantly admit the devil is handsome. All tempting things are perfectly wrapped to lure you down the path of depravity. Devlin props his elbow on his desk and traces his mouth with his fingertips. His eyes land on me when I start down the aisle to my seat.

The spark in his eyes can't mean good things.

As I reach Devlin's desk, I slip his essay to him, placing it on top of the psychology book he has out. His hand covers mine before I can take my seat.

"Proclamations of love are not being accepted at this time," Devlin drawls.

Bishop snorts and jabs Devlin in the shoulder.

Devlin's mouth tugs up at the side as they exchange a cruel glance. He finds my gaze again.

"But if you're especially desperate," he takes me in head to toe, then makes a face, "eh, on second thought. I still don't slum it, gutter rat. Move along. Your desperation is stinking up the place."

My hand curls into a fist beneath his hand, crinkling the essay assignment underneath. I speak through my teeth in a low mutter. "You know what this is for."

"Oh, is yours an extra special confession? Did you write me some emo girl poetry?" Devlin swats my hand away and lifts the essay. He pretends to examine it closely. "Hmm, this is sweet. Who knew the impoverished could be so eloquent."

Bishop steals the essay away from him. He skims the page, his eyes flicking to Devlin for a beat.

"Oh, wow, you guys," Bishop says as he waves the page around. He chuckles and shakes his head, pulling words out of his ass, "I can't stop thinking about you, my sweet, handsome prince. My heart beats for you alone. Ever since I first saw your midnight eyes and your silken locks. I hope you'll return my feelings, and make my dreams come true. Take me to prom?"

The others crack up, leaning on each other for support and cooing at me meanly.

Humiliation burns under my skin.

Bishop dumps the essay back on Devlin's desk and shoots me a wink.

My teeth grind as I lock my jaw. "Listen—"

Devlin clicks his tongue, wagging his finger at me. "I don't like the way you look at my dick. It's not sexy to think you might bite it off because you mistook it for a hotdog."

"Oh, damn," Bishop chokes into his fist to muffle his laughter. "Bro. That mental image. My eyes!"

A low growl rips from my lungs. I take a step toward Devlin, but the look he flashes me halts my attack. My stomach clenches.

What if he ends our deal right now and calls the cops?

This is bullshit! I just want my money. It was stupid of me, not realizing that Devlin's games are only fun for him. When you think you're winning? You're actually losing.

Gritting my teeth, I remain their punching bag to toy with, enduring their taunting laughter.

"Whatever. You're disgusting."

Resisting the urge to kick the hell out of his chair, I take my seat.

"Oh, come on, sticky fingers," Devlin croons with his chin propped in his hand. The vicious curve of his mouth is so punchable. "I've heard you get up to way worse for anyone willing to pay. But not me. I don't pay for it, and I sure as fuck am not touching you with a ten-foot pole. There aren't enough condoms in the world to double up before I let your mouth or your cunt near me."

I glare at him, seething. The titters of our other classmates grate on my ears.

"Devlin, you're so bad." A giggling blonde girl named Nina

drapes herself over Devlin's back, looping her arms around his neck.

He hums and preens under her attention. She leans her breasts into his back and nuzzles against his neck. He plays with her hair and draws her close enough to kiss. He speaks against her lips, but his words are for me.

"It's better for trash to know where it belongs. Can't have it thinking it has a chance of climbing out of the dumpster." His eyes cut to me as his lips graze across the mouth of the sighing girl he's turning to putty. "She needs to understand I'm not her Prince Charming. I'm not here to save her."

Devlin leans away from Nina. It's subtle, but I catch the flash of hardness in his eyes and the way he nudges her away. He pushes his black fringe back from his forehead and sighs at me like I'm causing him a huge inconvenience.

"I don't want this. It's pathetic."

Devlin picks up the essay and shreds it right in front of me. He tosses the torn pieces across the aisle. I stare at him as they flutter to the floor between us. People all around us cheer and clap and howl like coyotes because these animals consider themselves one with our school mascot.

My gaze falls to the ruined essay. He just...ripped it up and threw it away. Am I still getting paid?

Devlin covers an evil grin with his splayed hand when my eyes fly back to him. Another sheet of paper sits on his desk, the essay topic in bold print at the top of the page. He didn't need my essay. I came to school early for no reason, except to sate the whims of a total dick.

My nostrils flare. If this is how he wants to play, I can take it. His words mean nothing to me as long as he fucking pays me.

I knew I was a fool to trust this asshole.

"Are you still going to—"

"You shouldn't treat people like that."

Both of us turn to Thea Kennedy, twisted around in her seat in front of Bishop's. Her cheeks are pink, and she looks a little surprised she intervened, but she holds her ground, gripping the back of her seat with white knuckles.

"It's not right." Thea licks her lips, taking a breath. Her eyes dart to Bishop before swinging back to us. "So please stop."

Thea is a quiet, nerdy girl in our grade with kind eyes and wild auburn hair. Today it's tamed into a braid with several fly away curls escaping. Her uniform is on the frumpier side, even more than my oversized shirt, and she's usually wrapped in some kind of shapeless knitwear.

Devlin's brows shoot up in surprise.

This is the most I've ever heard Thea speak in four years of school together. We usually have at least one class together and she has a reputation for keeping quiet.

Bishop breathes out a harsh laugh and leans close to Thea. Whatever he whispers to her, it makes her blush beet red. Thea ducks her head and tugs on the cuffs over her blazer that's at least two sizes too big. Bishop reclines in his chair with a mean twist to his smile that makes him lose that charming jokester vibe. He kicks his feet up to rest on the back of Thea's seat while he pulls out his phone.

I narrow my eyes, but don't voice what's in my head. If Thea can speak her mind, then she is capable of handling her own shit. I didn't ask for her help and I have my own monster to deal with in Devlin.

"Let's get started," Mr. Coleman announces at the front of the room.

My shoulders slump. I debate hiding my phone under my desk so I can demand Devlin pay me. I'll corner him later.

For the whole class period, Devlin ignores my attempts to catch his eye, appearing vaguely bored with the lesson. Bishop's attention is glued to his phone and I can make out a pinch between his brows, his smarmy attitude falling away. In front of him, Thea squeaks. Like, actually squeaks. Bishop shifts in his seat, unaware of Devlin's suspicious glances.

As Mr. Coleman talks with his hands at the front of the room, my attention drops to the shredded essay on the floor.

I can handle his game, can't I? How much worse can it get?

TEN
BLAIR

On my way to lunch, I stop by my locker to drop off my morning books and grab my notebook for my next class. I pause when I open it.

An envelope is inside, sitting askew on top of my stuff. It must have been shoved through the slot in the locker door. Glancing at the other students at their lockers, I grab it.

Thumbing the flap open, my breath catches. *Money.* Crisp bills fill the envelope.

A small sound escapes me as I lean my shoulder into the cool metal.

There's no note or anything written on the envelope. It's plain and nondescript.

Devlin wasn't kidding after all. My lips twitch as I turn that over in my head. I wanted the payment, but now that I have it, alarm bells are going off like sirens in my head.

Sure, he's loaded, but it doesn't make sense. Why is he actually giving me money after I was stealing his beloved car? I rub my chin and ignore the echo of slamming lockers in the hall.

This was all his idea, but I wasn't sure he would follow through. I didn't trust doing what he wanted would result in money in my pocket. After English earlier, I thought he might dangle the carrot and laugh when I tried to jump for it.

An uneasy wariness buzzes through me. I tap the envelope against my hand. For now, I tuck it deep in my locker, hidden between a thick book on the art history of Japan from the school library and a math textbook. I squeeze the hard metal door, then shut it.

My thoughts swim as I bleed into the flow of milling students on my way to the cafeteria for lunch.

I don't trust the hand feeding me. I'm prepared to bite it at a moment's notice.

When I get to the cafeteria, the lunch period is in full swing. I join the line and pick up a tray. The lunch lady nods to me and slides my meal across. While the others buy pizza and the stuff offered that's not on the main lunch menu, I get the food assistance program meal. Today's is a scoop of mashed potatoes, steamed broccoli, an apple, and a cut of roast chicken breast. It's almost the exact meal Devlin took off me last year and dumped on the floor to be a douchebag.

Without Gemma, I've returned to sitting alone by the window at the table I get to have to myself. No one else wants to sit with the notorious sticky fingers. Not after Devlin put my tricks on blast on TikTok in retaliation for stealing from his soccer buddies. Those idiots challenged me to my face when they heard I could pick pockets. Before people avoided me because I'm the poor girl, but now everyone keeps their distance because Devlin branded me as a thief.

If only they knew where that landed me.

I pick at the food on my plate and consider what my back-up plan is if the deal with Devlin goes south. There's no way Devlin has a hidden heart of gold behind his cold eyes. There's not a helpful bone in his demonic, athletic body. He's not giving me money because he wants to, he's doing it to show me he has the power here.

Things that are too good to be true often are. Men are all the same—they take what they want and leave you to pick up the shattered pieces.

Either I follow along with his rules, or he turns me in. Both give him full control over me.

With a sigh, I drag my fingers through my hair. What have I gotten myself into?

* * *

After the last period, the afternoon sun beats down on the student parking lot. I tip my face into the rays with my eyes closed and lean against my car before I put my stuff in the backseat.

I need to get home to cook dinner so Mom has something to eat when she gets in. She's on the dinner rush shift today, and she always seems so haggard when she comes home. There's never time for her to eat when the diner gets customers from the interstate and the lower-class families on the outskirts of town.

All around me, flashy luxury rides surround my crappy Corolla. Two rows over I see Devlin's Porsche sandwiched by a BMW and a Hummer. An indignant breath rushes past my lips. These damn students are so spoiled.

A buzz from my phone pulls me out of my thoughts. I reach behind me to grab it from the top of my books I set on the hood of my car while I enjoyed the sun.

My gaze narrows when I look at it. Instead of the Instagram DM I'm expecting from Gemma in response to the video I sent her of a pug I found on the explore page, *D-bag Devil* taunts me with a new text notification.

The message is short enough to read the whole thing on the lock screen: *Walk to school tomorrow. No car. No Uber. No public transport.*

Another simple enough, if annoying as hell, task.

Chewing the inside of my cheek, my gaze moves around the parking lot, passing over Devlin's sports car. He's not there. I peer up the steps that lead up the hill to the main campus, where the school sign sits in front of the stone columns of the north building. Bingo. Devlin leans against one of the coyote statues that flank the sign.

From this angle, the pointy pine trees that stretch into the sky on either side of the school look like devil horns poking from his head.

Devlin is watching me. He waves his phone in the air.

I fold my arms and refuse to drop my gaze first. Devlin holds my stubborn stare.

The command from Devlin echoes in my thoughts, his voice a smoky sound that churns my insides.

As much as I can feel in my bones that I've signed my name in blood in a contract with the dark devil of Silver Lake High...I need the money.

Nothing else matters. I have to play his game by his rules until I find a way around them.

If this cocky, rich asshole gets off on me pretending to be under his control while he hands me the money I'm desperate for, I'll endure.

I've suffered through far worse—the clawing cramps of hunger pangs, the panicky weight on my chest as I urgently scrape together enough money to make rent so Mom and I aren't out on the streets, the anguished sobs from Mom late at night when she thinks I'm asleep, the leers of sleaze bags who assume I'm down to suck dick for cash, and the ugly, naïve hope in those early years that if I wished really hard on shooting stars, my dad would want Mom and I as his family again.

The rush of memories burns my eyes. A flash of drawing stars and a dark-haired boy with sad eyes, wishing with all my might, not knowing when my daddy would be back to see the star drawing I made for him flickers in my mind. I tighten my arms around myself. Fuck, I haven't thought about some of that in years. It's hard to breathe for a minute, air rattling in my throat, scraping it the length of my esophagus like a sharpened blade.

Devlin Murphy? He doesn't even rank in my top ten. I've handled his bullying for three years. What's one more? After this year, I'll be heading to college on a full ride because I'm going to work my ass off to earn it. By playing his game, Mom and I get to finally have some breathing room in our finances.

Glancing at the text again, I release a sigh, resigning myself to doing what Devlin wants.

ELEVEN
DEVLIN

The chessboard is set.

I watch with an eagle-sharp focus from my position at the top of the steps until Blair's shoulders slump in defeat. Satisfaction unfurls in my chest, blooming like a moonflower. It's something beautiful that only comes out in the shadows.

That's right, little thief. This is how the game works. You understand now.

Her shocked look when I tore up the essay before class was like speeding down the road in my pride and joy with the windows down and the wind in my hair. It was thrilling and I crave more. I'm already itching to chase the high.

Blair agreed to our deal to stay out of jail, but what she doesn't know is the true extent of this arrangement. I'll make her do anything I want in front of the whole school, pulling her strings like a puppeteer. It's all part of my revenge plan. I'll break her pride and her spirit so she knows beyond a shadow of a doubt she never should have dared to steal from me.

The door of her piece of shit Corolla slams hard once she gets in, the echo traveling up from the parking lot to where I'm standing watch. As she drives off, the car makes a horrible high-pitched screeching sound.

Turning away, I wet my lips and nod to Bishop as he ambles in my direction from the shaded terrace in front of the north building with Sean and Trent from the team, along with a few hot chicks from the cheer and dance squads. I'm not in the mood to hang out with the plastic puppets that surround us, but it's easy enough to fool these idiots into thinking I give a shit about them.

Other than Bishop, I don't.

But they'll never guess my secret. The reason I always appear so carefree. The trick is loving nothing.

The only love I have is reserved for myself and the select few I grant my real attention to—Bishop, my aunt and uncle, Lucas, and Gemma. That's all my black, twisted heart has the capacity to care about. Everyone else? Useless pawns to use up and toss aside when they've served their purpose.

Blair Davis is going to serve a very specific purpose by playing on my court.

"Hey, bro." Bishop knocks his shoulder into mine.

We're off from practice today. Bishop has his *up to no good* look on. My mouth curves.

The girls laugh with Trent and Sean, hanging off their arms. Nina, the peroxide-blonde with big tits that hung all over me in English as I shredded Blair's essay, flashes me a hooded leer. It's her secret code for begging for a ride on my dick. A pleading look I haven't answered this year. I'm not interested in her fake moans and her obsession with the notoriety of my parents' national medical research firm.

"Where are we going today? Peak Point?" Trent asks as he untucks his shirt and loosens his school tie. His blazer is off, tossed over his shoulder.

He's one of those idiots that thinks he has the entire market on swagger, but he's really just like any other wannabe at this school—covered in Axe spray, always searching for willing pussy, and waving his mom's black card around. Sean's a little more bearable, but he's a follower with no original thoughts. It's like someone stuck a hand up his ass, shut off his brain, and controlled his mouth.

Nina clicks her tongue. "Please, what are you, a freshman? No senior girl wants to go to Peak Point to make out with you." She shoves her manicured hand in Trent's face, the gold bangles on her wrist clinking. "Do better, darling."

Irritation simmers beneath my skin. Everything feels tighter, but maybe that's the way my fists are balled in the pockets of my slacks.

"We should drive to Denver and raise hell." They want something devilish to excite them? I'll give it to them. My gaze finds Bishop's. "In the principal's Escalade."

Bishop's brows hike up and a whoop leaves him. He slaps me on the back. "*Hell* yes. Now you're talking. My old man will flip his shit when he tries to leave campus today."

Nina and her friend, Bailey, giggle into their hands.

"Where will we go?" Bailey asks.

Idle boredom leads to temptation. We're all craving something that makes us feel alive.

"We'll head for the university." I make sure Nina is paying attention before stepping into Bailey's space. She's not as short as Blair, but still much shorter than me. I slip my fingers into her soft wavy hair as she gazes up at me, star-struck. "Then we'll find a party to crash."

When I peek at Nina from the corner of my eye, hers are narrowed and her arms are folded tight beneath her breasts. *You don't own me, sweetheart.* I wink at Nina, selling it like the playboy flirt they all know me as. It feels like more of a mask this year than ever before. She pouts and threads her fingers with Sean's.

I almost laugh. She can't make me jealous. I'd need to want her for that to work.

"Oh," Bailey breathes, leaning closer to me without subtlety.

I drop my hand and turn to Bishop. "Stash all the cars at the lake and we'll ride over in one of my dad's cars."

"Yeah, perfect," Bishop agrees with a knowing look.

We'll get at both of our fathers with one stone.

Bishop turns to address the group, hands up. "All right, people. You heard our Devil Boy. Hop to it, chop chop."

He claps his hands. As everyone spurs into action to follow our lead, I hang back. Bishop waits with me. Once the puppets are far enough down the steps, we begin our descent without anyone to eavesdrop.

"What else do you know about Davis?" I mutter, glancing in the direction she drove off in.

Ahead of us, the girls have run to their cars and Trent honks his horn while he peels out of the lot, Sean not far behind him. The girls howl like coyotes as other students watch their antics.

Bishop shrugs, raking a hand through his hair. He's distracted by whatever he's looking at on his phone. I smack his arm with my knuckles.

"Not much, dude." It seems to take him a lot of effort to put his phone away. My eyes narrow. He's as addicted to the damn thing as anyone I know, but something's off. Bishop ticks off on his fingers. "Outside of the school records and the backlog of forms I gave you the code for, she's like a ghost. I asked around, but your little lady is only known around here as a charity case for the school district's economic diversity quota."

My mouth pulls to the side as we reach the parking lot. I was worried he would say that.

We all immediately hated Blair on sight for not belonging.

She stands out in every way, from her incomplete uniform to her food program lunches. She's inescapable. I hate that I find her impossible to ignore for the nobody she is.

Ignoring Blair has never been an option for me. Whatever it is about her, it demands my attention like a goddamn moth to flame.

Blair looks at me like we're on the same level. *Dead wrong, little bug.* I want to crush her beneath my shoe for her insolence.

If I'm going to put her back in her place, make her understand that she's never clawing her way out of her position on the lower rungs beneath me, then I need to know what her weaknesses are to press her buttons harder. The more I push her, the closer I get to total control over her.

"If you hear anything, let me know." We pause beside my car. I unlock it, lean in, and swipe my pack of smokes. I tap one out, sliding the cigarette between my lips. Bishop declines when I offer him one. "Let's get fucked up tonight."

Bishop smirks. "You better have your hangover cure ready for me before school then."

"Fuck that, I'm cutting tomorrow." My mouth tips up at the corners in a cocky grin. "And my captain better not fault me for it."

"Fair, fair." Bishop laughs. The amusement falls away when he checks his phone and gets sucked in again with laser focus. What is up with that? "I'll, uh...probably cut tomorrow, too."

Bishop walks off to his ride and I get in my car, dangling my cigarette out the window.

Using my connections and access in the office to orchestrate Blair's dismissal from the track team wasn't enough. I'll crush her, *break* her beyond repair. She signed a deal with the devil, and when I'm finished with her, she'll be nothing but the shards of the girl who crossed me.

Blair's fatal mistake was believing this game could end happily for her. She has my hatred and I'm going to bury her alive with it.

TWELVE
DEVLIN

The lunch period has been one long exercise in precise self control this year.

I lean back against the table on my elbows, turned to face the room. My legs are stretched out, crossed at the ankle. Blair's across the room, seated at the table by the window.

Just like last year.

With the semester barely underway, I've had to hold myself back from snapping several times. Today I'm coming dangerously close to my limit. I need something to burn off this angry energy before it swallows me whole and unleashes my inner monster.

Maybe it's the lingering hangover from yesterday.

Should've stayed home, but giving that sneaky bitch a respite isn't on the agenda.

I need to punch something. Or smoke. Preferably both.

Aunt Lottie and Uncle Ed will see right through me if I show up to dinner tonight in this mood. They always know when something's off with me.

I tip my head side to side to crack my neck, but it does nothing to dispel the itch crawling under my skin.

Bishop is here, at least. The rest of the people that flock to us like we're gods drive me crazy.

Last year it was easier to fake interest in Lucas' lunch period, but he was like a shining star drawing in admirers, golden and perfect. It was obvious to see why people loved the star quarterback. It's a shame I'm not like my cousin—too flirtatious, too vulgar, too dirty, too this, too that, *too much*.

Now I have to work to hide the fact that I care about very few people in this world. If I don't care about them, then no one can stop caring for me, either.

Our table at the center of the room is packed with people—all plastic and fake. Bailey sits close. I can tell she's working up the courage to stake her claim on me by the slight twitches of her mouth. Maybe she's talking herself into it, reasoning that even though I flirt with every girl in school, somehow it was special when I was charming to her.

It wasn't special. Simply a well-crafted mask to keep people in their place.

My attention focuses on Blair once more. Her dark hair hangs down, forming a curtain around her bent head. Her shoulders are in a straight line, prideful even when she's got the scorn of everyone in school, including me. She couldn't put up more of a *leave me alone* vibe if she hung a banner in bold letters overhead.

Bishop's holding court on my other side, his deep voice the only one that reaches me above the din of background chatter.

Everyone's eating out of the palm of his hand, their shrieks of laughter grating.

"So, Dev's got this frat boy's girl in his lap, right." Bishop snickers into his fist. "The guy is jacked as fuck, but Dev's like 'No, you're right. If your name's on her ass, we should check. Fair's fair.' and the poor girl thinks he's messing around. Legit, he stands up, and the frat boy is shitting bricks when he gets a load of how tall our boy is."

"You're so fucked up, bro," Sean laughs, pushing my head from behind.

It catches me off guard. My shoulders go rigid. I was too busy watching Blair instead of keeping an eye on my surroundings.

"Hah, yeah, well." My voice is brittle and chilly. Sean's hand disappears. "I wasn't going to pull her skirt up in front of everyone without her consent." I shrug. "She was into it. She wanted a Daddy, if you know what I mean."

I wink at Bailey.

In truth, that girl wanted something dangerous to excite her. I was mysterious and available when she found me smoking outside, and she liked the thrill when my hand slipped beneath her skirt under the flashing neon lights in the frat house. I didn't touch her, but she acted like I was finger fucking her for anyone to see.

Bailey makes a small sound beside me. She's blushing and wide-eyed. I can see the internal struggle in her expression, debating whether to move away from me or stay close, because being near me comes with a higher status on the chain of social hierarchy.

My lip nearly curls at her pathetic willpower when she moves closer instead of running away, even after hearing the story. It makes me want to stand up on the table and scream at all of them that I'm not good or nice or some tall, dark, and handsome knight.

If anything, I'm the fucking villain, the thing that lurks in the shadows of nightmares.

I take a second to focus on my breathing before anyone else notices the way I'm dragging air into my lungs. My fingers twitch. It's a miracle I keep my knee from bouncing at this point.

I'm nothing without the vigorous control over my devious trickster mask. Everyone focuses on what I want to show them. While they see my distraction, I hide my real face inside, distorted and ugly and an unlovable terror.

Thorns encase my heart in a mess of brambles. My own parents don't love me, so there must be something wrong with me. I belong in darkness.

Across the room, Blair pushes her empty lunch tray to the side and has her nose in a book. It rankles the burning itch making my skin too tight. She doesn't get to relax and enjoy herself while I'm ready to crawl out of my body from everything locked up inside me.

Fuck that.

If I suffer, she's going to feel my wrath tenfold.

"Hey."

With one word, the table snaps to attention. All eyes are on me. Bishop and I might rule this school together as top dogs, but when I speak, they all fucking listen. I smirk at my unsuspecting target.

Bad move, my little toy. Rule number one: always be prepared. If you're not, I'm going to wreak more havoc.

"Who wants to see a neat trick I've perfected?" I tip my head back to survey them, forcing my body to relax into a sprawl against the table.

The devil king is in session on his throne.

Bailey lights up first, as if I've personally offered to kneel between her legs. "Oh, yes, yes! What sort of trick? Magic?"

My mouth quirks up. "Sort of like magic. You'll see."

I slide my phone from my pocket and find my message thread with *Little Thief*.

Devlin: Come here.

Blair's head pops up across the room. She frowns. I crook my finger and she stands with an eye roll.

The tasks have been far too easy.

It's time for that to end and the real game to begin.

As Blair nears the table, someone behind me scoffs. "What do you want?"

Blair stops in front of me, arms crossed. There's attitude in every inch of her posture as she cants her hip to the side. I let her hold on to that bit of headstrong independence, prepared to rip it from her with this command.

"It's part of the trick," I murmur. Angling my head to peer at everyone, I allow a sinister smile to break free. "Watch this. I've got Raggedy Anne trained good. She'll do anything I tell her to, like my little doll."

Blair makes a choked sound and I give her a gloating look. I reach for a big canteen of water Sean carries around and hand it to Blair. It's full to the brim. Her fingers are cold when they brush mine, accepting the bottle. Discreetly, I mouth how much she'll earn—three hundred bucks.

"Dump it on yourself."

My order is cold, hard, void of emotion. Bailey gasps beside me. Some of the packed tables around us are looking over, watching the scene unfold.

Blair remains still, jaw locked as she stares me down with fire burning in her eyes.

My hostile grin stretches wider. "Do it."

Everyone around waits with bated breath, collectively leaning in. The tension and anticipation presses in from all sides. No one eggs Blair on, possibly aware of the same thing I am. The struggle is clear as day in the rigid line of her body and death grip on the bottle. I can guess what's going through her head—pride versus how much money she needs.

To earn it, she'll submit to my whims. She's fucking crazy to do it, to willingly humiliate herself. But when she releases a small breath and inverts the water bottle over her head, the thrill that zips through me is undeniably satisfying.

In seconds Blair is soaked, her bra visible through the white shirt sticking to her skin. Her chest heaves and she tilts her head to let her hair hang in a dark clump covering her eyes.

A rough chuckle huffs out of me. "What a good girl you are, sticky fingers."

Cheers and laughter erupt around the room. Jeers fly.

Blair stands there, dripping wet, shoulders trembling.

"You trained the bitch!" Trent crows.

"Good girl, good girl!" People taunt and shout amidst their raucous amusement. "Wet dog alert!"

"Something stinks!"

Several people at the next table over make kissing sounds to call to Blair like they would call a dog.

Blair endures it all in silence. She gave up on comebacks and reactions freshman year once she figured out people would go after her no matter what.

Her silent obedience is my reward to reap, the cruel laughter music to my ears.

"Dude," Bishop mutters, plopping next to me on the bench. "What gives?"

I offer Bishop a secretive smirk.

My gaze sweeps over Blair, meeting the glare she gives me

from behind her hair. The searing fury in those deep brown eyes tugs at my chest and lower, my stomach tightening. The room narrows to the intensity Blair directs at me.

In an odd sense of wonder, I look at her like this is the first time I've ever seen her.

With her attitude stripped back to this simple strength in her vulnerable state, I see beauty.

Blair is hot, if you can get past the fact she's a criminal.

My fingers twitch for a different reason than the agitation I battled ten minutes ago, fingertips rubbing together to keep them from the sheer temptation of her perky, petite tits. Shit, if she moves a step, I might grab her.

"We have an arrangement," I explain, snapping out of the weird bolt of heat that passed between us. Must be the see-through shirt. "This is part of it."

Blair takes a breath and hands me the empty canteen. "Lunch is almost over."

"I'm not done looking at you yet," I counter, leaning back on my elbows, taking my time studying her.

Bishop snorts. "You're an evil dick, bro."

"Don't worry." I waggle my brows and stick my tongue into my cheek. "She'll get her reward."

The guys at the table take my meaning to be sexual, reacting like a bunch of animals.

Blair sends another glare at the ground. The angry pinch between her brows is something I have the urge to trace and learn the shape of with my tongue.

What is this...

My head is more messed up today than I thought.

"Um." Thea Kennedy comes up behind Blair with napkins. She offers them. "I brought you these."

Bishop tenses, sucking in a sharp breath. I toss a questioning glance at him. His focus is completely locked on Thea, his expression like a hungry lion opening its maw to chomp on a rabbit.

"Thanks," Blair mumbles, accepting them.

Thea hovers while Blair pats herself. She shoots Bishop and I a disapproving look. This goody-goody is a little buzzkill who probably thinks the world is sunshine and rainbows.

Bishop explodes from his seat and gets in Thea's face. It's laughable because he's a giant next to her, almost needing to lean over to reach her. Thea is shorter than Blair, even.

Thea freezes, clutching the napkins to her chest. "U-um, Connor."

"Were you invited over here?" Bishop demands.

Thea blinks. "No. That doesn't matter, though." She tips her chin up. "Blair needed help."

"*Blair* needed help?" Bishop mimics, circling behind her. He clamps his hands on her shoulders. "You hear that, Dev?"

"Sure did." With a grunt, I rise to my feet and amble into Blair's personal space. "Did you need help, Davis?"

I communicate what her answer better be with my hard gaze. Blair works her jaw, then sighs.

"No," she mutters in a monotone.

The caged rebellious energy flows from her almost as if it's a living entity, brushing against me like a lure. I want her disobedience and mutiny so I can take extra enjoyment from making her bend to my will. I smother the urge to brush wet hair away from her cheeks.

Thea's big eyes dance between Blair and I with her lower lip tucked between her teeth. "Well—"

"You know," Bishop drawls next to Thea's ear, grinning at her flinch. He traces her shoulders, plucking at the chunky sleeves of the sweater she's wearing instead of the school blazer. "The only thing a girl next door is good for is warming my dick." He leans closer enough that her auburn curls touch his lips as he speaks in a sinister hush. "You offering, neighbor? You can leave your granny sweater on."

I catch his words because they're standing beside us.

Thea trips over her own foot as she stumbles out of Bishop's grasp. "You...You—"

"Me," Bishop declares with a proud sweep of his arms. "All me, baby."

The way he says it hints at something more to the meaning.

Thea seems to understand perfectly. She shakes her head like she can't believe her eyes. Her expression crumbles and she rushes off, dashing tears away.

Bishop watches her retreat with his jaw clenched. Darkness clouds his eyes. I glance from Thea to Bishop. I'm worried about what's been on his mind lately.

When I turn back to the table, everyone's watching the two-for-one show play out. There's a thirst for blood in every face, the drama unfolding too good to ignore.

"Make the dog do another trick," Trent suggests.

Sean and the others bust out in cackling laughter.

THIRTEEN
BLAIR

It's fucking cold. And wet. Uncomfortable.

My clothes stick to my skin. The laughter isn't so bad, but that douche Trent called me a *dog*.

Fuck. This.

"Ugh," I snarl under my breath.

My shoulder crashes into Devlin's chest as I leave the cackling assholes behind. The door bangs when I barrel into it, howls following in my wake.

This school is nothing but a rabid pack of hyenas.

Further down the hall, I catch the disappearing blur of Thea Kennedy as she rounds the corner in a rush. I could go after her and thank her for standing up for me, but I'm pissed off and stuck in wet clothes.

The heavy wooden door clanks open behind me. I whirl to find Devlin. Great. My savage *master* followed me into the hall.

Can't a furious girl catch five minutes alone?

We stand there for a moment. My fists flex at my side while he props against the wall, considering me. He's too focused on my breasts.

"Give me my money," I demand, flinging my hand out expectantly. "I did it, so pay me."

Everything about Devlin is sharp, cut and chiseled like marble. Cold. Hard. Unmoving.

Devlin strokes his chin, cocking his head

"The question isn't whether you followed orders, but how quickly you obeyed."

"What?" I breathe, stalking toward him. "Are you kidding me? You didn't say I had to do it with a time limit. You called me over and told me to—" I lose my words, burned away by my anger. I fling my hands around to fill the space. "—in front of *everyone*."

"Don't fret." Devlin hitches one shoulder, careless, unfeeling. "You don't have a reputation to ruin in the first place. You're only your labels to them. Gutter rat, trash, unwanted charity."

My chest heaves as I drag in stinging gasps. My emotions are running away from me, slipping through my fingers. I work so hard not to let anything that happens in this hellhole get to me. Something inside is cracking in warning. The dam is splintering, threatening to unleash the torrent of everything I hold back.

With a frustrated sound, I shove Devlin. "Pay me, damn you!"

"No." Devlin grins, arrogant and mean. "Earn it next time. Those are the rules."

"You haven't told me all the rules! You keep changing them!"

He grabs my wrist when I go to shove him again. "Yes, I did. My rules are what I say goes."

Devlin releases me with an unimpressed scoff.

The crumbling barrier inside of me fractures in another spot.

I hate him! Why did I think I could trust he wouldn't go back on his word? He's a man, of course he's going to trick me.

Getting in Devlin's face, I hiss, "I knew I couldn't trust you. I should've known your word was fucking worthless!"

Something malevolent crosses Devlin's eyes, a flash of truthfulness behind his pristine veneer. The hatred I spew in his face is a distraction. While he's focused elsewhere, I slip my fingers into his pocket with practiced deftness and dexterity, plucking his wallet. I'll pay my damn self what I'm owed.

"Your mother must be so proud to have such a lying snake charmer for a son."

Devlin growls and moves so fast I don't have time to process. One minute my hand is seconds from liberating his wallet, the next he has my wrist in his hand, wrenching it above my head.

I gasp. "Wh—"

"Still want to keep running that mouth? This is the most you've ever spoken to me, I think."

There's a dangerous undertone in his voice, a jagged sharpness that pricks at my nerve endings and makes my heart race. The scent of leather and ginger surrounds me, intoxicating my senses. My skin feels hot as he leers at the outline of my breasts, the wet shirt plastered to my chest thanks to a full canteen of water.

Devlin looks to my trapped wrist with a predator's precision. "You want to get in my pants?"

Heat throbs between my thighs and embarrassment spears through me.

What the hell?

I shift slightly and Devlin's grip tightens on my wrist.

"If you wanted in my pants so badly, all you had to do was ask."

He crowds me, shoving my body back against the chilly tiled wall. It bites through my shirt, seeping into my skin, juxtaposed by the heat that rolls off him when he steps into me. My heart pounds in time with the throb in my clit.

I bring my other hand up to push him off me, but as soon as my palm lands on him I freeze.

Devlin's chest is hard, muscled, and...*warm*.

He slaps a palm next to my head, making me stifle a startled jump. His eyes slit, keeping me pinned in place with his body and his piercing gaze.

"I'll make you earn your nickname for real, sticky fingers," Devlin murmurs in a rough undertone. He releases my trapped wrist in favor of touching my waist, teasing his thumb up my rib cage until he grazes the underside of my breast. His nose touches my clammy temple. "I'll come all over them and leave you a mess."

My insides start a riot, melting and exploding left and right. I press further into the solid wall and Devlin follows, not allowing any relief from his body heat or the feel of his abs. He inhales, tracing his nose down the side of my face.

"What are you doing?" My voice is edged with a tremor. I clench his crisp shirt in my grip. "We hate each other."

I should hate him for this. I have to find it before this gets out of hand. But searching inside for any scrap of logic, I turn up none, only the insane spark of attraction.

How can I be turned on by the wicked look in Devlin's eyes

as he holds my waist and breathes against my skin? This is crazy.

I need to stop this. Need to retaliate. I want to slap him across the face, but I'm afraid of breaking one of his arbitrary unspoken rules. What if he ends our arrangement with some bullshit breach of contract? Losing the only cash flow I have isn't an option.

"Haven't you ever heard of hate sex?" Devlin chuckles into my neck, and, oh, *fuck*, that shouldn't feel as good as it does. I'm mortified by the way I claw at his shirt with both hands. "If you try that shit again, I'll have you on your back with your hand or mouth around my dick so fast you won't be able to catch your breath."

His lips skim against my neck when he speaks. It sends a rush of tingles across my skin, the burst of hot and cold rippling. I shiver, unable to muffle a small sound as I clench my thighs together in an attempt to relieve the pressure coiling tighter.

"Devlin," I whisper, intent on finishing that disgustingly breathy sentence by telling him to get the fuck off me.

He gives me an answering rumble, the deep primal sound making me squirm. Unfair and un-fucking-cool. How the hell is he capable of making a sexy sound like that?

Devlin chuckles into my overheated neck. It's quick, but I jolt at the hint of his teeth scraping over my sensitive skin.

"What—"

The bell rings, interrupting whatever is going on right now.

Devlin tenses. I feel the clench of his abs against me. Right before students spill into the hallway, Devlin leaves me cold, wet, and alone, plastered against the wall with my face flaming. His face is an unreadable shield, like he's unaffected by the cruel new way he devised to toy with me.

Taking my limp hand, Devlin slaps a wad of cash in it and

pushes me through the nearby bathroom door, muttering, "Clean yourself up, you fucking pest."

The door slams behind me before I have the chance to whirl around and tell him off. I poke my head into the hall, but he's gone.

Pursing my lips, I retreat into the bathroom, claiming the stall farthest from the door, and barricade myself inside. I lean against the wall, scrubbing my face.

"What the actual fuck," I mumble against my palms.

I pound the bottom of my fist against the stall, savoring the satisfying thump it makes.

My whole body is shivering and uncomfortable from my clothes, but underneath it all a buzzing has awakened from deep within me.

This battle of wills is far more dangerous than I thought. I need to be careful so I can figure out how to skirt Devlin's arbitrary rules that give him full control.

He's got another thing coming if he believes I'll hand him power over my body, too.

FOURTEEN
DEVLIN

As impossible to ignore as ever, Blair remains stuck in my head for days like the stubborn thorns of a rose.

She invades my school, my house, and my thoughts.

In the boy's locker room, surrounded by the other guys on the team, I slouch on the wooden bench. My soccer uniform is half on, my jersey slung over one shoulder and my cleats beside me.

It's a game night, but my head couldn't be further from focused. My aunt and uncle are out by the field to watch before we go out for dinner.

Across from me, Bishop seems to be in the same boat for once. He shoves his backpack in his locker and sits on the bench with his blazer off, shirt unbuttoned, and tie half undone and forgotten.

My brow furrows for a second before I smooth it. Bishop is usually the first one ready before a match so he can prowl the aisles of the locker room as we change, bombarding us with reminders about our opponents. He rarely misses an opportunity to give a pep talk, but tonight his head isn't in the game.

Bishop never shuts up about soccer, the one thing he lives and breathes, so something is definitely up with him.

Instead of preparing for our match, he's absorbed in his phone again.

Glancing around to make sure Trent and Sean have left to grab the ball bag, I brace my elbows on my knees.

"What's up, man? Is it more stuff with your parents?"

Bishop's eyes dart up to meet mine. "What?" He blinks. "No, no. It's—Don't worry about it. It's nothing."

Before he hides his phone, I catch a glimpse of the girl on the screen, a little hottie from the looks of it, with her chunky sweater pulled up to expose her stomach and hint at full tits peeking from beneath. I snort, shaking my head. Bishop's this twisted up over some chick?

I was worried for nothing.

"I see." Chuckling, I hit Bishop's knee with a playful tap. He smirks, tucking his phone away. When he meets my gaze again, he's my soccer-obsessed best friend. "There he is."

"Let's crush these guys. They won't see us coming."

I bump my fist against his when he holds it up.

The varsity soccer team might be less flashy than our football team, but between Bishop and I, we're a force to be reckoned with. We're both calculative players. Our unyielding two-man attack razes our opponents every time when Bishop picks up the ball from the defensive line and moves into attack plays alongside my offense position.

I pull the jersey over my head, running a hand down the #6 on my chest. The soccer field is where I cultivated my nickname as the devil. Bishop always jokes that as a striker, my assigned number should be #9, but I insisted on playing as #6 once my reputation as the dark devil spawned and grew.

Bishop puts on his #10 jersey and stands before me. "You coming?"

"Right behind you."

"Two minutes." Bishop taps his wrist.

I wave him off as he jogs around the locker room to round up our teammates.

The echo of slamming lockers and the chatter of the other guys travels through the room.

Closing my eyes, I picture the girl on Bishop's phone, but her luscious curves automatically change to pale skin, petite tits, and a cascade of shiny black hair. My dick twitches with interest.

It bothers me that I felt nothing looking at that photo Bishop had. Sure, it was quick, but long enough to make out the gist of the sexy photo. No rush of heat to my groin.

I sit back against the locker.

The only girl on my mind is Blair, my thoughts filled once more with the replay of what went down between us in the hall during lunch.

The heat I expected before coils low in my stomach. I breathe through it, balling my hands in my shorts.

Blair didn't shove me off, like I suspected she might when I touched her. For a survivor, she has terrible self preservation skills. Knowing I can press her buttons with my best asset, I plan to use it to my advantage.

The chessboard shifts, reforming and adapting to something that I'll take supreme pleasure with.

* * *

In the morning, I wait by Blair's locker. I want to be here when she opens it to find the special package I stashed inside with the help of the janitor before school started. A few people stop to say hi and ask about my weekend plans. I can see the curious suspicion in their eyes, wondering why I'm over here instead of out in the parking lot with Bishop.

Blair pauses several feet away when she arrives. I didn't warn her with a text this time. I won't give her room to breathe between commands, applying pressure harder.

She closes the distance between us and ignores me as she twists the dial on her locker. I prop against the one beside hers, watching. Her hair is partially damp from a morning shower and I catch a whiff of that cheap imitation vanilla wafting off her.

Blair cuts a look at me before she opens her locker. "Why are you here?"

I shrug carelessly. "In school? The state mandates a minimum number of days for students to grad—"

"Oh my god, shut up," Blair groans. "Why are you at my locker?"

"Why did you have to come to my school?" I counter, leaning over her.

She stands her ground, squinting up at me. Stubborn little thing. Once she opens that locker, she'll know better.

I make a show of checking the time on an invisible watch. "Better hurry. You'll be late for homeroom."

"Doesn't that mean you should move your ass along, too?"

"I have office aid for homeroom this morning. Taking attendance."

When she rolls her eyes, I grin.

The locker swings open and I relish the exact moment Blair pauses.

"What the hell," she mutters, reaching for the gift bag. She freezes when she peeks inside. "What. The. *Hell.*"

She swings a confused gaze to me. I give her a challenging smirk in response.

"What is this?" Blair gestures sharply at the locker.

I peer into the bag and withhold a sadistic grin at the brand new Silver Lake High School uniform, complete with a blazer and new shoes.

On top sits an extra special item: a leather collar.

It has a silver nameplate that reads *Sticky Fingers*. My note peeks out from under the collar, where I wrote directions to wear everything in the bag to school or else there will be dire consequences—like no payment.

Below that I wrote $750.

"I think you'll find all the answers you need inside this bag." I wave a hand lazily and prop my shoulder against the edge of the locker. "Looks like you won't stand out for having an incomplete uniform anymore. How generous."

Blair sneers and jabs a finger at the collar. "And *that?* Are you fucking kidding me?"

My mouth stretches wider as amusement blooms in my chest. "Not in the slightest. Are you saying you'd rather take the other option from our agreement?"

I pull my phone halfway out of my pocket.

Blair clamps her hand on my wrist, squeezing hard. "No!" When I hum, she blows out a breath. "Jesus."

She releases me and rubs her forehead. Her gaze bounces around the hall. One of her locker neighbors a few spots down makes her gulp.

I pretend to check my non-existent watch again. "Tick tock, Davis. Don't want to be late for homeroom, remember? Should I mark you absent when I go to the office?" I *tsk* disapprovingly.

"Too many absent days will increase your demerits, you know. Could put your scholarship status at risk."

"Shut up," Blair snaps.

I shift to block her between me and the locker, bracing my hands on either side of her head. A cold expression settles on my face. "Watch it, little bug. With that attitude, you're making me want to squash you under my heel."

Blair's jaw clenches as she makes herself as small as possible, keeping a few inches of space between us. She doesn't want a repeat of what happened the other day.

"Do as the note says, or it's game over."

I trace her neck with a delicate touch, then press into the soft spot under her chin, driving her face to angle up to mine. Blair's throat works as she swallows. Her glare is mutinous, shooting acidic poison at me with her rich whiskey-colored eyes.

Blair is an uncontrollable flame that I want to touch whether it burns me or not as I tame it under my control.

I stare into her eyes, pinching her chin between my thumb and forefinger. My attention drops to those full, pouty lips. They're chapped today, like she licks them too often. Shifting my thumb, I brush the edge of her lower lip with my thumb.

Blair pushes out a harsh breath, breaking my concentration on her mouth. She wraps her fingers around my wrist and digs her short nails in, almost hard enough to break the skin. The sting spurs on the urge to pin her against the locker and take her mouth as mine.

I shove the desire down and lock it away with the rest of my real emotions. Everything is compartmentalized, buried deep under layers of fake smiles and flirting. By pushing it all down, I don't have to care. I can remain numb, my heart protected in my ironclad fortress.

"Get the hell off." Blair bares her teeth and shakes damp,

partly dry tendrils of hair from her face. "I'll wear it. You better pay up."

Plastering my signature cocky mask on my face, I grin at my feisty little toy. "You don't get to tell me what to do."

Blair makes an angry, muffled sound and shoves away from me. She snatches the bag from her locker, slamming the door shut with a loud bang that draws the attention of the students lingering in the hall before school begins. They all look between Blair and I with interest.

The devious school king and the school pariah? It's a juicy show.

The chatter dies down as Blair stomps away in the direction of the bathroom, flipping me off the entire way.

A slow, genuine smile unfurls on my mouth.

I hide the secret expression behind my hand until I get myself under control. With my social armor in place, I amble down the hall in the opposite direction with a lazy swagger in my step.

Anticipation sings in my veins for our English class.

FIFTEEN
DEVLIN

The uniform is a perfect fit compared to the oversized shirt and ill-fitting skirt Blair had before.

I follow behind her on the way to English, keeping far enough back that people don't mistake us for arriving together. The skirt fits like a glove over her small waist, flaring over her hips. Without meaning to, my eyes fall to her ass as she glides down the hall toward the classroom.

Blair's hand keeps flying to her neck. The self-consciousness has me fighting back amused enjoyment.

People give her double-takes as she passes by. No one is used to seeing her in the full uniform. She looks hot.

A guy on the basketball team eyes Blair up and down with his tongue poking out of the side of his mouth. He catcalls her. "Damn, girl! You can come right on over here, baby."

Blair ignores him, and the other wolf whistles that assault her as she enters the class ahead.

Something dark slithers through me. Gritting my teeth, it's a struggle not to stop and punch the guy. Blair belongs to me.

"Yo, Dev! Sick match last night. That goal in the last half was amazing." He nods to me as I walk by, but I ice him out.

I don't show my annoyance or make any effort at all. Everything I do is a performance to maintain. The guy isn't worth my time.

In the corner of my eye, I see his expression fall. I make a mental note to ply Bishop for whatever he has on the dude later, so I can get revenge when it suits me.

Giving into a baser urge to punch this dick for looking at what's *mine* doesn't serve me at the moment. I don't work in the light, I only operate in nightmares.

Mr. Coleman isn't in the classroom when I stalk through the door. Neither is Bishop. Blair sits at her desk across from mine with her chin tucked to her chest and a hand splayed over the collar of her shirt. It's buttoned tight, but she's not chancing anyone finding out what she's wearing for me. Twin spots of color tinge her cheeks as her eyes dart to people that come too close.

I move down the aisle between the desks like an ominous shadow, tapping on each desk as I pass. Stopping by Blair, I drop my bag and perch on top of her desk. She sits back, a tetchy sound escaping her as she leans away from me. Her lips form a line as she avoids my gaze. Those dark lashes sweep over her freckled cheeks.

For a moment I'm lost in exploring the constellations I see in the freckles across her nose.

Blair folds her arms beneath her breasts, hugging herself. She turns her head away.

The buttons on her shirt pucker. I smirk when I see that

peek of the collar beneath her top, locked around her porcelain throat.

Leaning over her, I murmur low enough for only her to hear, "Meet me later."

"What?" Blair turns her head sharply, her sleek black hair swishing like silk around her shoulders. "Why?"

I lift my brows, silently saying *because I said so*.

Her chin juts and she purses her lips. With that rebellious tilt, they're an undeniable enticement. I sink my teeth into the inside of my lip to keep myself focused before I swoop down and steal a taste of those lips for myself.

Mr. Coleman strides into the room, clipped words calling the class to attention. "We have a lot to cover today. Take your seats."

Sliding from Blair's desk, I open my mouth to set a meeting place, but I'm interrupted.

"Devlin, sit down." Mr. Coleman snaps his fingers at me. He starts writing on the chalkboard. "Today we'll be talking about the reading from this week."

I shoot his turned back a narrow-eyed look of annoyance. Taking my seat, I prop my chin in my hand, bored with the beginning of Mr. Coleman's lesson.

Mr. Coleman is one of those young teachers that puts on airs like he's great with his students because he's hip or whatever. He calls on the girls in class more than anything and they hang on his words.

Except Blair. She doesn't go out of her way to participate the way the other girls in class do.

With neatly coiffed brown hair, a straight nose, identical dimples, and a strong chin, he's the all-American dream of wholesomeness. He appears like someone you can trust, which is exactly why I don't. No one is trustworthy.

He pisses me off.

Glancing at Blair, she's equally disillusioned with the lesson. Her notebook is open, but her focus is elsewhere. There's a worried tilt to her brows. Does she ever stop worrying for a second? I suppose I'm to blame for some of her trouble, but she brought it on herself.

I stare at her neck and picture how the collar looks. I want to see it. Touch it.

Mr. Coleman pauses going over the reading when the door opens ten minutes into class. Bishop comes in.

"You're late, Mr. Bishop." Mr. Coleman props his hands on his hips like a mockery of an authority figure. No student here takes a teacher under thirty seriously. "Care to explain yourself?"

"No," Bishop says with attitude, raising an eyebrow.

"Excuse me?"

I choke back a snort. A small identical sound to my right tells me Blair finds this as funny as I do. A warmth bleeds through my veins at the bright mirth dancing in her eyes when they meet mine for a beat.

Bishop passes Mr. Coleman like he's not late. As he comes down the aisle, his surly expression morphs into a betrayed glare that he directs at Thea. She tucks her shoulders and slouches. He finds his seat, sighing agitatedly.

Dead air fills the room. Bishop glances up at the teacher and waves his hand.

"Well?" Bishop snaps his fingers in a perfect mimic of the way Mr. Coleman tends to. "I'm here to get an education."

Titters move through the room. I nudge Bishop's back in a show of camaraderie.

Mr. Coleman works his jaw, but lets Bishop slide. "Let's get back to the lesson. Can anyone tell me your thoughts on the protagonist's passage on page forty-three?"

Thea's hand shoots in the air, along with several other

students. The girls he has eating out of his palm flail their arms with their eagerness to answer.

"Yes?"

"I think the passage means that it's important to be true to yourself," Thea says in a soft voice, her arm still partially raised.

"Yes, Thea," Mr. Coleman praises in a warm tone, pointing at her energetically. "Excellent."

His teeth are too white, the gleam blinding and disconcerting. *Fake.* It's easy to spot his false mask because I'm so good at hiding that mine isn't real, either.

Going off what I've read in my psychology books on disorders, I cycle through possibilities for what lurks beneath Mr. Coleman's shiny disguise.

Thea laughs, flustered by the encouragement. I can picture the shy smile she always gives him and the stars in her big doe eyes.

In front of me, Bishop clenches his pencil in a tight grip. The tip breaks against his notes when he presses it to the page on purpose. An angry red flush sneaks up the back of his neck. Bishop's knee bounces for a few seconds, then he explodes from his seat.

"Mr. Bishop, you're disrupting—"

"Fuck off," Bishop barks. "I'm out of here."

"If you leave class, you'll earn detention."

Bishop tosses his hands in the air and slams the door behind him. The window pane in the door rattles.

Thea squeaks and darts her hand up. "Mr. Coleman, may I be excused to use the restroom?"

Mr. Coleman stares at Thea, the defeated slump of his shoulders completely manufactured. He waves in permission and she's off like a shot.

My curious gaze flicks from the door to Mr. Coleman. Something is going on.

Unbidden, that saucy photo from Bishop's phone the other night pops into my head. Thea wore the same type of sweater today. There's no way she's the girl in the photo, is there?

I put it from my mind.

Mr. Coleman asks another question to get the class back on track, but I tune it out. Instead, I write a time and a place at the bottom of my blank page. *Beginning of lunch, in the courtyard.* I tear it off and fold it a few times into a small square.

When the teacher has his back turned, I discreetly slip the note onto Blair's desk.

Blair covers the note with her hand and for a second I think she's going to swipe it off the desk without reading it. Her cool gaze snaps to me. Unfolding it with deft fingers, she skims the note. Blair's lip curls.

Tucking the note under her notebook, Blair returns her attention to the board.

It's hard to focus on the class. For the first time, I can't even follow the general gist, when normally school comes easily to me.

I keep studying Blair in my periphery.

It's not until near the end of the period she acknowledges me again. A sharp point pokes my arm while Mr. Coleman rifles through a stack of handouts. I grunt in surprise, rubbing the tender spot where my bicep was jabbed. Blair holds a folded note between her fingers. It's folded so many times the corners of the paper have become prickly weapons.

I snatch it before she pokes my arm again. Opening it up, I find it's the same note I gave her twenty minutes ago. Her only response is a checkmark beneath my writing. Simple, succinct.

The corners of my mouth twitch up. The bell rings, interrupting Mr. Coleman mid-sentence.

"See you later, sticky fingers."

Blair stiffens, plastering her hand against her buttoned up shirt as I lift my bag to my shoulder and stroll from the room.

* * *

Stepping out into the courtyard, my grin flashes before I can tame it. She's there, waiting for me by the stone bench. The leaves on the aspen tree stretching above the bench haven't turned gold yet, though a few on the spindly branches have faded to a yellow-green.

It makes Blair stand out starkly, next to the thin white bark of the trunk with her inky black hair.

Blair turns around. "What do you want?"

I tuck my hands in my pockets. "Eager to get to your steamed broccoli and mystery meat? I hear it's very nutritional."

"Please, you don't even get the regular menu." Blair rolls her eyes. "Why did you call me out here?"

She's not as careful now, though her sharp gaze flicks to the exits every few seconds. I cock my head and enter her personal space. Blair matches me step for step until the back of her knees hit the bench. My mouth curves.

"Now you're trapped."

Blair huffs indignantly. "Hardly."

She goes to sidestep me, but I catch her around the waist.

"We're not finished yet."

Blair's eyes narrow. "So get on with it. You're wasting my time."

"Is that any way to talk to the person who pays you?"

"Pays me to humiliate myself," she mutters.

The collar peeks between the buttons done all the way up to the stiff top of her shirt. In a nimble move, I undo the top two buttons before Blair's eyes go wide. She smacks at my hands and covers her neck, scrambling to move out of reach with stone pressed into the back of her bare legs.

"What are you doing, you psycho? We're in the middle of the school!"

Her gaze flies around, checking the windows. With a lazy glance, I check with her.

"No, you're alone with me in the courtyard. Only I get to see this." I cover her hand with mine and tug. "Now show me."

Blair's throat bobs. She resists my pull, pressing her hand harder to cover the collar.

I hood my eyes. "Show me. I want to see the proof you're my little pet."

Blair struggles for another beat, flustered. With a rough scoff, her hand drops to her side. She cuts her gaze away, dark lashes outlining her brown eyes.

Smirking, my attention falls to the leather collar on her neck. The silver nameplate looks perfect. I hook my finger in the collar and pull her closer, near enough that my lips could brush hers if I leaned in. Blair avoids looking at me, color bleeding into her cheeks. This close, I can inhale imitation vanilla and count the galaxy of freckles speckling her cheeks.

Those pouty, full lips slide together. My heart thuds and an excited tingle spreads over my skin.

"Good girl," I rumble. "Look at you. No one would know you're a mangy stray."

Blair squirms against me, making a strangled sound. I chuckle and graze the back of my knuckle over her cheek. It's warm and soft beneath my touch. Blair blinks quickly.

A giddiness bubbles up inside me, fizzing like top shelf champagne along my nerve endings. This feels fucking good. I want more of the expression on Blair's face, this crack in her insolent confidence and years of silent indifference. I'm finally getting under her skin as much as she digs under mine. The thrill of it sings in my veins.

Whenever I'm around her, I feel alive. For a short while, I can forget about my demons.

My finger curls tighter, tugging her a fraction closer. Her breath fans across my neck with her tense exhale. I'm fascinated by the micro-expressions twitching in her features, filled with wonder as I watch her struggle to control herself to keep me from knowing exactly what this is doing to her. But I can see it all.

A chant repeats in my mind: *all mine, all mine, all mine, mine, mine.*

If she'll obey me in this, what else can I tell her to do? I picture laying back in my special spot beneath the stars, staring up at the vastness as she rides my cock.

I've never shown anyone my spot. I don't bring girls back to my house, but I can picture her there on the roof with me.

The scene shifts and I imagine waking up in a warm bed with her lips wrapped around me and that pretty rosy tinge to her cheeks. The images in my head coalesce together, idea after idea racing faster than the quick beat of my heart.

My hard cock strains against my fly.

I could make her mine and only mine.

The siren song of her lips is as hypnotic as the drug of controlling her like this. They're plump and pink. When her tongue darts out to lick them, I touch my nose to hers, intent on kissing her this time. Blair freezes.

The air goes still and the courtyard blurs.

Blair finally meets my hungry gaze with a shocked look. She tips her head up. I think she's going to let me kiss her. I inch closer.

"When are you going to pay me for this?"

Her hushed question snuffs the heat flaring in my stomach. I narrow my eyes to slits.

"What?" I rasp.

For a minute, Blair made me forget my own rules. Made me set aside years of hatred and the thirst for revenge. Made me want her, and nothing else.

We're not some sweet love story. We'd be a hate fuck at best. Raw, angry, and dead set on hurting each other as much as possible. Blair and I are oil and fucking water doused in kerosine and lit in hellfire.

Blair blinks slowly, pretending she is unaffected by my proximity and unaware of my internal war.

This must be how she does it. If she makes the sorry fucks who pay for her body feel something more than an itch to scratch, she must make more money. How else could trailer trash like her survive in a place like this? How many guys in this school has she kneeled for? That rumor about her rings true as a goddamn bell.

How could I not see it before? She's as fake as the rest of them.

I repeat my mantra, my sacred rule in my head. *Love nothing, let no one in close enough to hurt.* With those thoughts on replay, I squash the inkling we could be anything more than a means to an end.

It's the cool trickle of ice I need to get my head on straight. To stop thinking with my cock. Those fucking lips still entice me. Goddamn it, I will have them. I'm going to *take* that kiss, and I don't give a fuck if she doesn't like it.

Once I have a taste, things will go back to how they were before.

"You said $750. Give it to me."

I'm nowhere near finished with her yet. She still has a lesson to learn.

My grip on the collar flexes and I can feel the way my knuckle digs into Blair's throat. She clenches her teeth.

Rubbing my nose against hers in a mockery of a romantic nuzzle, I grin humorlessly. Blair shivers.

Money. That's the only reason she's here. I had the chance to send her away, but I was selfish. I wanted to make her pay by my hand.

When I speak, my voice is wrapped in shadows and shards of glass. "You really need this money, don't you?"

She jerks against me. "What part of that wasn't obvious?" Her hands come up to claw at my wrist until my choices are let go or get my arm shredded. I release her with a grunt. She hisses, "I didn't steal your car for the fucking thrill of it. You're such an ass."

I step back, running a hand through my hair, feigning indifference while she rants.

As soon as I give her room, Blair stomps a few feet away, breathing hard. She whirls on me, cheeks still pink.

"You think I'd put this on if I didn't have to?" She gestures to the collar. "This is all to take care of the person I love. I can't do that if I go to jail."

A muscle in my jaw jumps. I don't like the sound of that. It makes my chest tight and uncomfortable. I don't know why. Stuffing my hands into my pockets, I ball them into fists out of sight.

I take a breath and master the raging emotions battling inside, crushing the broken, hopeful boy, and remind myself I'm only a monster now.

Thumbing my wallet, I take it out with practiced disinterest. I count out the bills and fling them at her feet. They fly everywhere like the splash of a wave. Blair yelps.

Before she can bend down to collect the money, I get back in her face, wrapping a hand around her throat over the leather collar. The nameplate presses into my palm when I squeeze.

"If I'm your salvation…" I pause to smirk, flicking a vicious glare over her. With my other hand, I capture a lock of her hair between my fingers, twirling it around. "Welcome to hell."

I memorize the look on Blair's face. Hatred. That's all. Not desire, not love.

Because that's not something we'll ever share. No one feels that way about me. I won't make that mistake again, lured in by those kissable lips and the thrill I get telling her what to do. Maybe in another life, one where our circumstances were different, we could've been something that worked.

Blair and I aren't a maybe or an almost, we're just two people that fucking hate each other, trading hits back and forth to destroy the enemy in an effort to distract ourselves from our pain, trying to survive the bitter ass lemons life dealt us.

This is an arrangement designed to torture her. I can't forget that goal by allowing her to yank on the parts I keep tucked away, buried under brambles and chains to protect myself from hoping. Those parts are weak and useless.

She's doing this because I'm paying her, not because she wants to be. I can't forget it, or allow myself to lose sight of crushing her beneath my heel.

Tonight I need to sit under the stars to settle the anger searing in my blood.

"I'll give you everything you deserve. Punishment, humiliation, repentance." My grip on her throat flexes with each word. "I'm in control of your sins now, my demonic angel." Releasing her, I walk away, tossing over my shoulder, "Better button up if you don't want anyone to know who you belong to."

SIXTEEN
DEVLIN

The blare of the fire alarm grates on my ears. I skirted out of sight from the secretaries as soon as it went off while they shuffled out of the office. They think I've bled into the mass of people flowing through the halls to follow protocol, but really I'm waiting for the hive of offices to empty from my hiding spot in the coat closet.

"Third one this month, isn't it?" Denise's muffled comment makes me grind my teeth.

Hurry up, I think, wedged between a musty peacoat that's been in the closet for two years and a forgotten raincoat. She's taking the longest to leave.

I only have so long once the room clears out to find what I need, and it's costing me.

Blair's payment sits in my pocket, rolled up and wrapped in

rubber bands. If I find what I need, I'll pay her for pulling the alarm to provide the distraction for my snooping. It's twice what I offered for this task, but the greedy little demon negotiated a better deal for herself because of the potential trouble she'll get in if she's caught. The idea that she cares about consequences is laughable.

I bite down on a smirk. What Blair doesn't know is the alarm I told her to pull is in the same hall Principal Bishop always walks to take his secret morning smoke break.

She still did what I ordered, and I get an electric thrill from having so much power over her. I underestimated how addictive it is. Having her bend to my whims touches a long-hidden part of me I've smothered and suffocated for years.

For now, she's not going anywhere. That thought keeps running through my head at night when I sit on the roof watching for shooting stars.

My obsession with her willing compliance is growing, feeding the beast. It's voracious, starved for more of her obedience now that I've had a taste. I want to know exactly how far I can push her.

When no sound comes from the office other than the shrill ring of the fire alarm, I slip from the closet.

Vice Principal Sanford's door swings open and I duck behind the circular desk before I'm busted. I hold my breath as he lopes across the room. I give it a few more seconds, then poke my head over the edge of the desk where my half-eaten donut sits.

The coast is clear.

I wonder if this is how Blair feels when she's knocking over convenience stores or whatever delinquent trouble she gets up to as I go to the room at the back of the administrative hub. The doors are unlocked during the day, saving me the trouble of breaking in after hours with the set of keys Bishop and I copied sophomore year.

Thankfully, the room muffles the angry trill of the alarm once I'm inside. The permanent records of every student are kept here. It looks like something out of a stuffy old gentleman's club rather than a high school, with a muted style stuck in time. There's a leather chair in the corner, like someone enjoys leisure time with the student files, and polished wooden file cabinets line the walls. The only staples missing are a fireplace and cigar smoke.

Finding the drawers for the *D-E* names, I get to work. There are only minutes to swipe her file.

This mission is necessary. I need to find out more about Blair. Knowledge is ammunition to my arsenal against her.

I rifle through the first drawer and come up empty. Dragging out the next, I flick through the thick and thin files. *Dabrowski...Dacosta...Daniels...Davis!*

Smirking, I pull out the manila folder and lean against the file cabinet. The more recent stuff is obvious—dismissal from the track team, student lunch program paperwork from the state, suspension and detention slips.

There are a few late excuses from the first week of school, dated before she broke into my garage to steal my Porsche. One explains Blair took her mom to the hospital as her reason for arriving during third period.

My eyes narrow. Is this why she needed money? To take care of her mom's hospital bills?

It tugs at my core. Jealousy runs down my spine in an icy-hot slide. Blair has to have a strong connection with her mom to be the only person around by her side each time she has to go to the doctor.

I trace over Blair's handwriting. It must be nice.

When I picture myself doing the same, it's difficult to

imagine what it should feel like to take a parent to the doctor. Would I be anxious? Would they reassure me everything would be fine?

In my pocket, my phone's silence screams at me. It's been days since I've heard anything from my parents.

They could've died and I wouldn't know about it.

I could've died and *they* wouldn't care.

Agitated, I drag my fingers through my hair, wincing when I pull too hard and rip a few strands from my scalp. A rough sigh makes my shoulders sag. This is about Blair, not me.

Digging through the file, I discover more late slips from last year that mention additional hospital related incidents. It's far more hospitalizations than normal. My gut tightens as I consider the first thing that comes to mind in situations like this —an abusive father or maybe the mom has a fucked up boyfriend putting her in the hospital repeatedly.

It sends an unwarranted pang of worry spearing through me.

I freeze, shocked at the unfamiliar feeling. My brows furrow as I shove the unnecessary protectiveness aside.

Unbelievable. I'm searching for ammo against her, but here I am fucking worrying that she has a dangerous home life. What is wrong with me?

I already told her I'm not her white knight.

There isn't room for sympathy, only the ways I can use information to control the pieces on the board. Blair's mom could be a drug addict, using up city resources for free care. I shouldn't give a fuck about their home life.

I scoff and flip earlier, reading over comments from her teachers at middle and elementary school. They all say roughly the same thing about her.

Blair shows great aptitude for the material and appreciates the challenges presented. She has a strong interest in art and history subjects. Individual work is excellent, but in class she is quiet and slow to participate.

Miss Davis is polite and reserved, but often isolates herself from her peers.

Blair shows great intelligence in her school work given the recent changes in her family situation. However, she has gone from a bright, smiling, happy young girl to withdrawn. When other classmates engage her, she shies away.

A frown tugs at my lips.

The alarm finally shuts off. Glancing at the clock, I realize I need to hurry up. There isn't time to run to the copy machine in the other room, and I don't want to leave behind evidence. My phone will have to do.

I lay out the folder on the chair, flipping quickly through the pages and snapping photos of Blair's pitiful history.

Smart but sad, how cliche.

A jagged rock lodges in my stomach, sitting heavy.

My grip tightens on the phone. She's not like me. It's not the same.

I work backwards through everything, caring more about the relevant information than what a delight she was to her preschool teacher. A creased note on an earlier page near the beginning of the file makes me pause. I missed it in my first skim. Flipping it open, I find it's from a guidance counselor at Little Boulder Academy.

"Huh." The curious sound puffs out of me before I can contain it.

I went to Little Boulder Academy, too. So did Lucas and Bishop. Most of the people in our circle attended the prestigious private elementary school. I try thinking back, searching distant memories for any of a dark-haired little pest. How could a girl as poor as her afford the tuition of the private school?

I always thought the trash spawned her into existence, low class through and through. Blair has always been the girl from the dirt who somehow managed to earn a scholarship to Silver Lake High. I never considered our paths might have crossed before high school.

Plucking the memo from the file, I read it with pinched brows.

Macy Davis called to inform the school that Blair will withdraw from Little Boulder Academy due to a change in financial circumstances. The transfer will go through next month. Macy expressed concern for Blair's reaction to her father's desertion and disappearance from his family. Please inform all of Blair's teachers of this change and keep an eye on her while she remains a student at Little Boulder Academy.

My heart pounds harder as my eyes fly over the words. I don't realize I've wrinkled the note from my clenched grip until the paper crinkles. Inhaling, I smooth the creases while I try to calm my pulse.

The unwelcome sympathy seeps back into my bones. I want to dig into the marrow and cut it out. I don't like feeling this way about Blair Davis. The heavy ache inside me expands in my chest like a balloon.

I rub my eyes and push my hand into my hair. Grudging understanding sparks to life. Her dad left her and I know what that feels like.

I blow out a breath, shaking my head.

As I put the memo back in the file, an exit interview from

the counselor catches my attention. A little girl's handwriting fills the page in big, blocky print. Stars dot the I's.

Squinting, I draw it closer, crouching to kneel rigidly over the open file. I recognize this handwriting. Blair's name is at the bottom with the same star punctuating the letter in her name.

You look sad. Don't be sad. Here, wish on my star.

The soft, high-pitched voice echoes in my head along with a flash of long dark hair and brown eyes. My throat is thick when I swallow. The memory of my third grade art class assaults me in snippets, skipping like a broken movie reel.

There was a girl my age, both of us older than the other kids but too young to join the grade ahead of us. She came up to me during arts and crafts to show me her drawing of stars. They filled the page, lopsided and quirky, just like her smile.

I had been shirking the teacher's directions to draw because I was sulking. Everything sucked and I wasn't getting my way. Mom and Dad kept leaving me alone. I didn't like the lady staying at my house. She didn't know the book I liked to read with Mom.

The little girl didn't mind or notice the way everyone kept their distance from me, taking the chair next to me without asking. I glared at her, but she ignored that, too.

You can have my stars, they'll make you happy again. Make a wish! The wishes you make on shooting stars always come true.

I couldn't yell at her to leave me alone. Instead, I remained quiet and surly, pinching the edges of her drawing while she started on a new page. At the bottom of the page she wrote her name, Blair with a small star over one letter. A look of concentration settled on her face, tongue poking out between her teeth as she drew. Two pages filled with crooked stars and her random bouts of humming later, the anger making me shout at everyone bled away, leaving me calmer.

Suspicious, I asked her, "How do you know the wishes work? Have you tried it?"

Blair had blown out a gusty breath that moved her hair. "No," she said with a pout, pausing from drawing. "Mom says they come out after my bedtime, but she swears it's like magic! Magic is *awesome!*"

Her eyes had grown so big and were full of such sincerity, I had to believe she was right.

I clung to her words like a lifeline after all the anger, pain, and frustration I felt from my parents noticing me less and less as they stayed away from home for longer stretches. I don't know what I did to make them not want to be around me, but the hurt was suffocating. Blair's promise about wishing on shooting stars helped. I looked for one every night before bed, staying up until my eyes were dry and itchy. When I saw one, I was going to tell her about it, eager to boast that I had wished on a real one before she did.

Blair sat beside me in every art class, talkative enough for the both of us. Her enthusiasm was contagious. She made me laugh, struck with a spark of life again after I'd felt numb to the world.

Then she was gone.

Like my parents.

No one wanted to stay with me.

Her chair remained empty and the tingling numbness crept back in without her smiles to fight it back. The teacher told me she had to go away when I asked where my friend went.

It wasn't until after Blair was gone that I finally saw my first real shooting star.

For my first wish, I wished for her to come back. I was mad that she could leave me behind so easily.

Well, I wished for Blair once, and she did return to me. Only it was far too late. I was already broken beyond the repair of her magic shooting stars by the time I found her again.

The quirky friend from my childhood is my little thief. I can't believe it.

My breath comes in harsh pants and I cover my eyes, dragging air into my lungs. The world feels like it's tipped sideways and tumbled me around. I haven't thought about the girl from my art class in years. I kept her buried deep under layers of everything else, locked in her own box with the rest of my emotions and memories.

Does she even remember me? I can't blame her if she doesn't. The irrational anger I've always felt when I looked at her makes more sense now. I might have shoved the memory of our brief, strange bond down, but the grief of losing that connection so easily seeped out between the cracks.

This discovery doesn't change my plans. Blair still needs to pay.

The crooked smile that used to light up her face pops up in my head. With it comes other memories from that time in my life, ones that leave me raw and humming like a live wire. I clench my teeth together hard enough to feel the pulse in my ears. My hand covers my mouth as I wrestle the memories back into place, where I can forget about them.

This is all her fault. I'll make her squirm for breaking past the sturdy barriers I erected. My next move begins to form in my head.

You won't escape me so easily this time.

The slam of a door and muffled voices makes me jump.

"Fuck," I whisper gruffly.

My time is up and I haven't made my getaway.

Shooting into action, I scramble from my crouch, gathering the manila folder of Blair's educational life. Footsteps pass the door of the student records room. I freeze, holding my breath.

"Devlin's not back yet?" Debbie asks someone. "Let me know when he's here. I need him to make copies of this right away."

Damn it, Debbie, calm your tits. Being quiet, I carefully open the drawer of the wooden cabinet and slip Blair's file back in place. I need help to escape the records room unnoticed. The office sounds full again.

I send a text to Bishop.

Devlin: How close are you to the office?

Bishop: [GIF of a man sprinting away in the distance.]

The corner of my mouth lifts. He hates coming down to the office when his dad is around.

Devlin: Come flirt with Debbie. Need her distracted so I don't have your dad riding my ass for being in the student records room.

Bishop: Oh shit!! You devil. [smirking devil emoji]
Bishop: On my way.
Bishop: [GIF of Superman flying through the air]

I lean heavily against the doorframe as I wait for Bishop's help. I can't get Blair's voice out of my head.

The wishes you make on shooting stars always come true.

A humorless smile twists my mouth. Out of all the countless wishes I've made on stars, this one comes true. I skim a hand over the side of my ribs, where the magic Blair once told me about is inked into my skin.

Guess I got what I fucking wished for.

SEVENTEEN
BLAIR

Hell is humiliating.

It's filled with Devlin Murphy's impish smirk, his friends' comments about my desperation stinking up the school, nasty taunts from the student body in the form of dog barks, and whatever that weird feeling was last week when he made me wear a collar.

I thought he might kiss me, so I panicked. The ridiculous flutter in my stomach had been confusing and I hated myself a little for it. I hated him more for causing it.

That embarrassing collar went straight into the dumpster behind the trailer park when school was over.

It's all hell, but at least the cash I need is coming in with each completed trial of willpower versus my battered pride.

Devlin always delivers, even when he toys with me first. He

pays me in stacks of crisp bills, the unmarked envelopes stuck in my locker, or in my beat up junker. I won't even fathom how he manages to get in without the key. His world is automatic electric systems on luxury cars, so how would he know to use something to jimmy the door on the Corolla beneath the window seal? It's a small mercy that he locks it when he's done.

The bastard is like a twisted Batman, a dark knight that will turn on me the second I stop playing by his rules.

After I pull into a parking space in the student lot, a fresh envelope tucked between my seat catches my eye when I go to unbuckle the seatbelt. I must have missed it.

"Damn him," I mumble, plucking it from the hiding spot.

Flipping it open, I count out four hundred bucks for pulling the fire alarm yesterday. I'm lucky I've mastered the art of being light on my feet. Principal Bishop almost caught me, but I was able to scurry far enough down the hall before he found me standing next to the pulled alarm.

I'm thinking of buying Mom a new mattress with the money to help her get more rest. She's been incredibly pale and worn lately, it's really making me worry about her. I don't want to see her get so bad we have to go to the hospital for another bout of exhaustion. Mom has never had the best health, but the transition in seasons doesn't usually hit her so hard. This year it's taking a brutal toll on her.

I have to do whatever I can to make her life easier.

There's a note tucked between the twenties. My gut clenches.

Your "car" is an insult to real cars everywhere.

His cynical voice fills my head as I read the note. My brows lower.

"Asshole."

It irritates me that he thinks he can insult the car I put blood, sweat, and tears into saving for. The day I bought it was one of the happiest of my life, and I can count those days on one hand.

So what if it's not a flashy luxury brand? The only people that can afford that are the stuck up rich kids. The rest of us work damn hard to get what we can.

It's called surviving.

I jump when I get out of the car. Devlin is parked in the spot opposite mine, waiting for me with sunglasses that probably cost more than a month's rent at the trailer park. He's propped against the back of his car, palms resting on either side of his Range Rover's bumper, long legs crossed at the ankle. I must have been really daydreaming to miss him when I pulled in. Damn it.

I was too busy making a mental tally of the money I've saved so far from being Devlin's bitch.

"What, not feeling your ugly red compensation for your dick size today?"

Devlin's lips twitch up. "Thinking about my cock again, sticky fingers? The Range Rover is more spacious." He nods to the SUV. "Climb in the back and I'll show you what you can't stop thinking about."

A few students passing by on their way to the steps snicker. One guy high fives Devlin, which he accepts with a wide, self-assured smile.

I can only guess Devlin changes up his rides to flex his absurd wealth, shoving it in the faces of people like me that he is dripping with privilege while I wonder if I can afford gas for my car this week.

"You're disgusting." I cross my arms. He's alone, not even his horrible other half in sight. "No cohorts to kiss the king's rings today? What a shame. Probably for the best, though. Reality hits like a sonuvabitch and once you graduate, you'll figure out this is your peak."

Devlin's shoulders shake with his snort. He touches the corner of his lower lip with his tongue. "Wanna bet?"

I grit my teeth. No one makes my blood boil like he does, with that unbearable arrogant attitude.

"You think you're untouchable."

Devlin leans forward. "I don't think. I know I am."

I'm done with this. Rolling my eyes, I shoulder my backpack and head for the stairs up to the school.

Devlin falls in beside me, an annoying pep in his step.

"Did I invite you to walk with me?" I give him a shove when he doesn't answer. "Fuck off."

"No." A smug smile dances in the corners of his mouth, fighting to break free.

I stop, gripping the straps of my bag. "What do you want now?"

Devlin pauses a step in front of me, half-turning to glance over his shoulder. "I have another task for you."

The morning light gleams off the black hair hanging in his face. With his chiseled jaw and high cheekbones, he looks like every beautiful temptation. If he wasn't a total dick. An untrustworthy snake in the grass. A *man*.

He tips the sunglasses down his nose, peering at me over the edge. My stomach bottoms out unfairly.

I shove down the stupid fluttering sensation, telling my heart to shut up. It's confused. The misguided little traitor doesn't understand that nothing good would come from liking Devlin Murphy.

Swallowing to soothe my dry throat, I shoulder past him. "What do you want me to do now? Take over the office? Quack like a duck in class? Hotwire the principal's car?"

"That last one has some merit."

The hair on my arm tingles under the uniform blazer and shirt, aware of Devlin's presence beside me. His body heat seeps into my personal bubble. I sidestep to gain some distance. A second later, he closes it, his arm brushing mine.

Leather and spice drifts on the air, seductive and hypnotic.

"You better pay big if you seriously want me to commit a criminal offen—"

"What, you have morals now?" Devlin chuckles and pats the top of my head. "Good little angel, so wholesome and pure."

His mocking tone makes me grumble under my breath. We reach the steps and begin to climb. It's weird to be walking into school with Devlin.

"I'm bored of our game. Time to change it up."

"What? You don't get to change the rules now!"

Devlin laughs. "It's my game. I can do what I want."

I purse my lips. Damn Devlin Murphy back to the demonic pit he crawled out of.

He gives me a leering once over. "I want to show everyone how much school spirit you have locked away behind your thrift shop emo girl aesthetic." His tongue peeks out to swipe his lower lip and heavy innuendo laces his voice. "How much you support the athletes." He bounces his eyebrows suggestively. "You'll know it when you find it."

With that mysterious hint, Devlin jogs ahead of me, leaving me in the dust on the steps.

Ugh, bastard. School spirit... Whatever he has planned, it's bound to be even more humiliating than being labeled Devlin's *dog*. Unease spreads through me for the new hell Devlin cooked up.

By the time I reach the top step, he's long gone. Sighing, I head for my locker.

Once I reach it, I'm distracted by the safety pin bursting off my busted zipper. Groaning quietly, I fiddle with it as I open my locker. Swinging the door open, I go to hang the backpack from the hook to fix it, but my gaze locks on the telltale green and white heap of fabric waiting for me inside. My frustration melts to horror faster than an ice pop on fire.

Oh, hell no. *Hell* no.

Screw you, Devlin!

Nina happens to be nearby. She peers into my locker and scoffs. "Thinking of joining the squad, Raggedy Anne? I don't think so."

My spine snaps straight at her sneering voice.

"Speak for yourself, Nina." Trent from the soccer team slings his arm over her shoulders. She sticks her huge boobs out more, like a proud peacock. Trent takes me in with a sweep of his eyes that makes my skin crawl. "I'd like to see her in the cheer uniform. And then I'd like to see it on my floor."

Gag. To guys like Trent, the women around him are nothing but objects for him to ogle.

"Can you do a split, Davis?" Trent leans into my space. "How flexible are you?"

Ignoring them becomes impossible. "Get lost, Trent," I bite out. "Or I'll show you exactly how high I can kick."

When he doesn't move, calling my bluff, I raise my brows to drive home my threat. Holding up his hands, he backs up a step.

Nina surveys me with a narrowed gaze, tipping her chin up. She seems to have found some begrudging respect for me standing up to Trent's shit.

"There's no way you're good enough for the squad," Nina drawls. "Pick another pathetic way to get Devlin's attention."

I roll my eyes. "I have no plans to become a cheerleader."

Scrunching her face in annoyance, Nina flips her hair over her shoulder and struts down the hall with her big rack stuck out.

I snatch the Silver Lake High cheer uniform from my

locker before anyone else sees it, balling the material up in front of me. A crisp note on thick, fancy paper sticks out of the neckline. Hunching over the bundle, I read the message.

Change into this for the rest of the day for $1000 plus a $2500 bonus to cheer from the sidelines of today's soccer practice. Give me a big kiss on the field when we're done, and really sell it, or you earn nothing.

My heart stumbles over a beat and I suck in a breath so fast my throat burns. Is he insane? Yes, I remind myself. He's an unhinged psychopath. My pain is his pleasure.

Somehow this is way worse than dumping water on myself or being known to the school as his trained dog. This is an actual nightmare. I can't blend in wearing this. It paints a target on my back, turning me into a big green beacon of false school spirit that will draw the attention of every single gnat in this school.

Bending to his cruel pranks was awful, but this is an all new low. This is the last thing I would ever do. *Probably the precise reason he picked it.*

I roll my lips between my teeth, blinking in time with my rapidly beating pulse. The blood rushes in my ears, muffling the sound in the hall. All I hear is the steady *throb, throb, throb* in my eardrums.

These tasks are escalating. Devlin is offering more money, but the things he demands are becoming increasingly difficult to complete.

I'm selling everything to Devlin, even my soul.

I work through his possible motive like a puzzle to solve. What will he gain from making me put myself on display? Why does he want me to kiss him?

It has to be another one of his ruthless mind games.

My pride screams at me. *Is this worth it?*

I close my eyes and draw in a fortifying breath. It has to be. For Mom.

With my hands shaking from how much I want to punch him, I shut my locker and go to put on the cheerleading uniform.

EIGHTEEN
BLAIR

The worst part about spending an entire day in a skimpy cheer skirt and sleeveless vest that exposes a strip of my stomach isn't that I wouldn't be caught dead in it otherwise. It's the way it changes how everyone looks at me. There's nowhere to hide from it, either.

None of my teachers care that I'm breaking dress code, not for the sake of school spirit. Mr. Coleman even squeezed my shoulder and told me he was glad to see me getting involved.

Girls are annoyed, and I don't think it's simply because the uniform doesn't look bad on me—I checked for a whole fifteen minutes in the bathroom this morning before I worked up the courage to brave homeroom. I'm guessing it has to do with the way every guy in school can't take their eyes off me. Including Devlin.

His dark gaze is an inescapable curse against my skin.

The leers of the guys follow me all day.

Lunch was excruciating, sitting at my table by the window in plain view of Devlin's smug expression as he ruled over his court at the center table.

My skin felt too tight, suffocating me as I smothered the urge to squirm under his gaze. He drank in the sight of me in a way that made my heart pound.

The day only went downhill from there. Someone taped a sign to my locker that said *Give me a D! I! C! K!* with a crudely drawn penis next to a sad stick figure cheerleader. In my history class, the girl that sits behind me was watching some stupid TikTok video that turned out to feature me being rated fuckable now that I stopped being "all goth and shit" by some sleazy underclassmen twerps.

It's a nightmare, but I'll weather anything for the amount of money Devlin promised.

At the end of the day, the walk to the soccer field for the practice match is both a relief and its own drawn out torture.

I tug on the hem of the skirt. It's shorter than the school uniform and I am so not wearing the right underwear. I clamp my palms against my thighs, trapping the skirt when a breeze threatens to expose me.

There are other people hanging out on the sidelines as the soccer team stretches for warm up. I pause a few feet away. Sometimes a few girls watch practice, I used to see them during track, but not this many. They all turn to me, eyeing me up and down.

Their judgement is obvious as they whisper to each other.

The urge to sprint to the tree line and pick up the trail that winds through the pines grips me. I'm seconds from springing into action when strong arms wrap around my waist from behind, enveloping me in a familiar masculine scent. Devlin.

"There you are," Devlin murmurs into my hair. I stiffen as he tickles the bare strip of skin where the uniform doesn't cover my stomach. "Hmm, having you dressed this way certainly improves my motivation. Cheer me on so we win our practice match. Nice and loud—and remember it's spelled d-e-v-i-l."

I can hear the smile in his voice.

"You're twisted," I breathe.

His chuckle is dark and smoky, traveling down my neck and drawing a shudder from me. That sound should be illegal. I struggle not to clap a hand over my tingling neck.

"You have no idea, little thief."

The girls along the sideline glare in our direction. I'm treading all over their territory simply by being here. Devlin's teammates on the field smirk.

"You all owe me fifty bucks," Bishop calls from the center, his arms stretched overhead as he bends.

A round of groans sound from the other players. Great, now they're betting on something they know nothing about. They probably think Devlin and I are some weird *thing*.

I have a few steamy books in my paperback collection. I'm familiar with the idea of hate turning into love. Bullshit. Not in our case.

"Why are you making me do this?" I hiss. "What messed up satisfaction is this giving you? And—the other thing you want?"

Devlin's arms tighten around my waist. He nudges me forward and I walk awkwardly with him wrapped around me.

"Because." His voice is hard next to my ear. "I want to make you squirm for me."

My stomach twists into a tight knot. A hot pulse of heat throbs between my legs. Does he need to talk right next to my ear and breathe all over my neck like that?

We reach the sideline and he releases me, only to circle around. He draws me close, his hands settling on my hips.

I peer up into his eyes, trying to read the mystery clouding the blackness. I don't believe the interest in his expression is for me. It's for show. For whatever reason, he wants them all to believe he wants me.

"Did you bring pom-poms to cheer with?"

The question startles me out of trying to figure him out.

I snort. "Yeah, I can totally hide pom-poms in this crap."

Flashing a quick smirk, Devlin toys with the edge of the skirt. I open my mouth, only to clamp it shut when he drags his fingers up my thigh. He moves higher, skimming beneath the vest, stroking my stomach. His touch heats my skin and makes me fight off a tremble.

I hate that he can make my insides coil. What is wrong with me?

Devlin hums thoughtfully. "I see what you mean. No practical storage space."

My jaw drops. Devlin's shoulders shake with a silent laugh. He's...having fun. While he torments me with an audience.

"Stop enjoying this," I snap in an undertone, glancing at the group of girls nearby.

If they didn't hate me before, they definitely do now. I have their favorite hottie all over me. I don't want to watch my back for mean girl attacks on top of Devlin's games. He's making me more visible, painting a bigger bullseye on my back in blood.

"But it's oh so fun." Devlin tips his head to give me a smile.

This one startles me because it's not like his fake ones. I think it might be genuine. It makes him appear...less evil. My heart thuds and my eyes drop to the dimple winking at me.

"Cut it out." Flustered, I press my palms to his chest and push. "Go play soccer."

Devlin covers my hands with his, squeezing them against his jersey. "Wish me luck. You're my personal pep squad."

"You don't need it." I need him out of my space. I have to clear my head, find my happy place to do what he ordered.

The threat of the kiss clause hangs over my head.

"Blair."

I dart my gaze up to meet his. Hair hangs across his forehead. One side of his mouth tugs up as wicked amusement dances in his gaze.

Oh, god. I haven't really thought about it all day, too busy enduring the humiliation of wearing the cheer uniform. If I don't kiss him at the end of the practice match, I don't get paid.

Devlin squeezes my trapped hands again. "You suck at this. Say 'good luck, Devlin' or something."

I lick my lips. Devlin zeroes in on my mouth.

"Good luck, asshole."

"Dev, let's go!" Bishop calls.

"In a minute," he shouts back, staring intently at my lips. His thumb brushes over them. "You're here to cheer for me. When I win, I'm coming to claim these."

My stomach bottoms out.

Devlin grins at whatever he finds in my deer-in-headlights expression, then pinches my cheek before jogging onto the field. The girls gathered squeal for him, forming their own squad. I stand there, dumbfounded.

I touch my lips, where his soft caress lingers. His words repeat in my head.

When I win, I'm coming to claim these.

My entire body is wracked by a shiver from the hot and cold sensation traveling over my skin.

How can I be turned on right now? Doesn't that make me some kind of fucked up, to want a kiss from the guy who has bullied me for three long years?

Scrubbing my face, I think I finally understand the dilemma Gemma faced last year.

I never thought I'd grapple with the same problem.

"You know," says one girl that breaks off from the group and crosses over the invisible line in the sand between us. "Devlin doesn't do girlfriends. He does hookups. So whatever you think you've got with him, it's not gonna last."

Normally, I'd ignore her. Hell, I agree with her. But it's getting hard to take people's crap around here while I hold my tongue. The fiery need to fight back stirs beneath my skin.

Tipping my head, I click my tongue in sympathy. "Aw, are you jealous? That's cute. Did you know jealousy derives from feeling threatened?"

The girl squints, curling her lip. "You're trash. He won't want you for long." Her eyes rake over the cheer uniform. "Why don't you go try out for the dog show instead? That's where you belong, bitch."

I choke back an incredulous laugh. Devlin doesn't want me, period. This whole thing is an exercise in making me jump as high as fucking possible for his game.

"If Devlin only does hookups, I guess that means you don't have a chance to be his girlfriend, either. Better go gold digging somewhere else."

The girl's eyes go wide with outrage, and she stomps off to lick the wound caused by the truth amongst her friends. They all shoot me nasty looks.

Whatever. They're the ones fighting over a guy that doesn't even notice they exist.

The other team arrives for the practice match against Silver Lake High. A few of them spot me on the sidelines. They smirk and smack each other. One brave one heads for my end of the field to warm up, flexing his biceps to stretch the yellow jersey. There's a dark blue #11 on his chest.

He waves to me.

I lift my eyebrows, unaffected.

Devlin appears behind the guy, a whole head taller. The expression on his face isn't any different from his mask, but I see a deadly fury in the tense set of his chiseled jaw and the tight corners of his eyes.

He mutters something to Eleven. Whatever he says, it makes the guy stalk off to his team's end of the field to finish his warm up. Devlin remains where Eleven set up, dribbling the ball with some fancy footwork.

Devlin glances my way, sticking his tongue between his teeth in a smug grin when he finds my attention on him.

Showoff.

Once the practice match begins, it's time for me to cheer. I've never gone to a game and I make a point of avoiding the cheerleaders in school.

When Devlin runs by with the ball, I clap and give a sad, "Woo!"

Devlin catches my eye a few minutes later. His unimpressed expression says it all: *do better*.

Sighing, I raise my efforts.

When Bishop faces off against two offensive players from the other team and steals the ball from them, I cup my hands around my mouth to cheer him on. Bishop points to me, grinning as he weaves the ball between his feet to keep his possession.

The game moves fast. One minute the ball is down near our goal keeper, then in the next Bishop and Devlin are moving in formation with the rest of the team. It's kind of fascinating to watch. They're quick, strategic, and damn good at moving the ball.

Bishop and Devlin are a force to be reckoned with, both on their own and when they attack together.

The ball passes in a blur from player to player on our team. I find myself cheering with more heart.

"Come on guys!"

I shuffle down the sidelines, closer to the group of girls who haven't shut up since the first whistle. They're better at this than I am. I listen to what they're saying for ideas, but all they've got is endless girlish squealing when Devlin has the ball.

"You've got this, ten!" I cup my hands around my mouth and jump when Bishop pulls off a cool twist that cages the ball between his feet. "Get the ball!"

Bishop must hear me, because his wide smile is energetic as he drives down the field, passing to Devlin. Together they sprint as a coordinated force. Their opponents don't know how to counter their attack. Devlin has the ball and he lines up a shot, kicking it hard. It flies in a beautiful arc and misses the diving goalie's outstretched hands, landing in the back of the net.

The whistle sounds, confirming Devlin's goal.

"Woo! Go Coyotes!"

I have no idea what's come over me, but I'm getting sucked into the game. It's becoming easier to cheer them on. I don't have to fake my enthusiasm. Most of the team smiles at me when they run by, like I'm their personal one-woman cheer squad.

Halfway through the match, I remember what's coming at the end. I freeze mid-clap.

Crap.

The game has swept me up so much, I forgot that cheering isn't enough. If I want to get paid, I have to kiss Devlin.

It's the last thing I'd ever do, but...

As my eyes track him moving around the field like a bullet,

my stomach flips. I'm not dreading a kiss. The energy of the game is feeding my adrenaline.

Heaven—or maybe hell—help me, I'm anticipating his lips on mine.

The resounding truth in that thought makes me sink my teeth into my cheek.

I want to kiss Devlin Murphy. Even if it's fake.

Devlin catches my eye. His expression is hungry. My heart pounds faster and my breath hitches.

God, I'm messed up.

Devlin winks before stealing the ball lightning-quick from #11, a vicious grin stretching his face as he directs the ball around. Eleven seems pissed off. Devlin heads for the net, unstoppable as he closes in on the target. I hold my breath, my palms tingling. If Devlin scores now, the game is over.

"Go!" I yell, breathless.

Devlin lines up the perfect shot between the two defenders. His foot connects with the ball and my heart stops as it soars into the net.

I clap so hard my hands hurt. This is only a practice match, but something about the win has my excitement exploding free.

Bishop and the other Silver Lake High players yell like banshees. Defeat hangs over the opposing team. Devlin circles the field with his fist in the air, ending his jog a few feet in front of me. The rest of his team's celebration fades into background noise as Devlin's arm slowly drops.

This is it.

His intense look pulls me in, making my feet move like I'm possessed. I'm still clapping as I reach him. My cheeks hurt from beaming.

"Nice goal." I swallow thickly.

Devlin makes a rumbling sound in response, stepping closer. His hands find my hips. He smells musky as he hovers his lips over mine, hair hanging in his face. Devlin breathes out and it coasts over my mouth. I swallow again.

An ache twists low in my stomach and between my legs.

Devlin cups my jaw. His warm touch lights me up. It feels like damnation, luring me in and dragging me under into the sweetest hell.

He brushes his thumb over my cheek and pins me under his heavy-lidded gaze. "You want to earn that bonus?"

His words sting with the truth of why we're doing this, but I don't care. I'll face that later. I tilt my head up to accept the kiss.

With a quiet growl, Devlin covers my mouth with his, immediately pushing his tongue past my lips.

When we come together, we're volatile. Rough. A violent storm hellbent on battering each other.

He claims my lips with power, control, the same unstoppable force from the field putting me under his spell. My fingers fist in his white and green jersey.

The kiss heats like a five alarm fire, blazing and engulfing us in desire. I didn't expect him to kiss me like this, like I'm his favorite meal. I don't know if he is equally taken aback, but judging by the muffled groan that vibrates against my chest, I have an idea.

A sound hitches in the back of my throat as his tongue slides with mine.

Devlin's fingers press into my cheek and jaw. He wraps his arm around my waist, holding me close like he wants to be the only one to possess every part of me.

The ache between my legs intensifies. This is too much.

I push away from him, gasping. I press my hand over my swollen lips.

Devlin's eyes are hooded, his pupils bottomless pits that

swallow his dark eyes. He drags his fingers over the sides of his mouth.

His attention falls to my tingling lips. He tightens his hold on my waist, like he wants to pull me into another kiss. I plant a hand on his chest to stop him from sweeping me up again.

Before either of us can say anything about the kiss, Devlin's teammates crash into us, celebrating the win.

"Yeah! Man, that was such a good shot!"

"Did you see that play?"

"The devil is back!"

They absorb me into their huddle, patting me on the back. Even Trent and Sean seem happy to have me there.

"Good job cheering, Davis." Bishop ruffles Devlin's hair. "You should come to our official matches, too. You're a good luck charm."

I give him a strained laugh, feeling weird about being crushed in the middle of a huddle of tall soccer players. They all stink. It's not nice and earthy like Devlin's scent.

"I think you guys are fine without me. Don't you win all the time?"

"Yeah, but not like *that*." Bishop nods to Devlin. "I haven't seen you play that way since JV. Like you gave a damn about winning."

Devlin brushes him off. He breaks free of the huddle and walks away, leaving me in the middle of the herd of sweaty soccer players.

"Wait!" I push through the tangle of limbs and struggle to get out. I jog after Devlin to catch up. "Where are you going?"

"Shower."

"Okay," I drag out on a long syllable. "And—what you owe me?"

Devlin stops, cutting a heated look my way. "You want more?" He huffs out a sensual laugh, the curve of his mouth obscene when he sweeps his eyes over me. He grabs my wrist. "Fine, come to the showers. I'll pin you against the tiles and have your screams echoing through the whole locker room."

My entire face flames and my insides rearrange. What's his problem? I did what he wanted.

"Stop being such a dick!" I yank my hand out of his tight grasp. Lowering my voice, I ask, "What about my money?"

The shift in Devlin's expression is subtle, but I can see the way he shuts me out. I don't get what his deal is, but somehow I've pissed him off.

"You'll get paid," he snarls, stalking away from me.

I watch his back retreat into the building, no longer caring that the short hem of the cheer skirt moves in the breeze.

NINETEEN
DEVLIN

Hot water runs over my head, sluicing down my arms. They're braced against the shower tile in the locker room, flexing with each harsh breath I drag into my lungs. The water doesn't drown out the pounding rush of blood in my ears or distract from how hard my cock is.

I won't touch myself while thinking about her.

My hands ball into fists. I beat one against the slick tile with a grunt.

"Fucking pest," I mutter.

My cock throbs as soon as the words leave me. The kiss replays nonstop, bombarding me with Blair's breathy sounds, the way she clung to me, and the rush of desire to devour her right there on the field in front of everyone.

I can still taste her on my lips.

I swipe the back of one hand across my mouth, ignoring the throb in my groin.

Once again, Blair made me forget about the game. While kissing her, I lost sight of the fact she only wants my money. It's the damn lure she has all over again.

She's skilled at invading my senses, undermining my plans, and intoxicating me with her clever whiskey-colored eyes.

I thought humiliating her with a kiss from her worst enemy would burn this little obsession from my system, but no. Instead, it thrived to life. This new curiosity is growing out of control now that I've had a taste of those plush fucking lips.

My cock jerks, the twisted little fucker too stupid to realize I have no intention of sinking to Blair's level. I'll never let her beat me. Not at the game I'm best known for.

"Yo, you dirty devil, I'm heading out if you're not done jerking off," Bishop calls.

"Fuck you," I grouse, raising my voice above the shower.

Bishop's snicker echoes off the tiles. "You got your little lady in there after putting on that show?"

"No."

Bishop laughs again and slaps the wall outside of my stall. "But you wish she was."

My body certainly agrees with Bishop's knowing tone. Sighing, I shut off the water. "Leave it."

"Whatever, man. I'll see you later."

"Yeah."

Bishop leaves and I'm left in an empty locker room with my head a mess.

* * *

I hoped after a day or two, I would come to my senses. I hate being wrong.

Blair is more inescapable than ever. My attention seems glued to her whenever she's near at school. I've kept my distance, but it's impossible not to watch her, even when I don't intend to. Inevitably, my gaze seeks her out.

She's in my dreams, too. Plaguing me whether I'm awake or asleep.

I've never felt so drawn to someone before.

This campus suffocates me. I might cut out early for a drive through the mountains. Fuck coming back here until I can rein myself in.

As I sit through another boring as hell English class, all I can focus on is Blair at the desk next to mine. My peripheral gaze is magnetized to her presence. I can't stop thinking about the kiss on the soccer field—can't stop thinking about *Blair*.

Thoughts run through my head, intertwining with the stuttering thrum of my heart when I catch a hint of sweet vanilla shampoo. I toy with the idea of paying her to take a ride with me, driving her home, and keeping her to myself. Trap her away until I've had my fill. She's slippery, though. It wouldn't last long enough to stamp out this addiction to her.

I can't let my impulsive side run loose, no matter how strong the urge to wrap her in my arms is.

It's insane how much she's invaded my thoughts. When I'm close to her, my stomach clenches. It's a challenge not to draw her into a secluded corner. The desire to flirt with her just to see her freckled cheeks blush fills me to the brim.

Giving into this means giving her power over me.

What I need to do is step back.

It's time to cut my losses. If I can't control myself, then the next viable option is to remove the temptation. I've given her the payment for the kiss, and that'll be the last she gets from me.

Blair's eyes flick over, catching me watching. *Fuck—when did I stop looking at her from my periphery?* Her gaze jumps down to my lips and heat sears my insides.

I want her.

And that's exactly why I have to stop.

TWENTY
BLAIR

The tasks from Devlin have dried up. It's been almost a week.

After the last payment for making a spectacle of myself in a cheer uniform and the kiss, Devlin has gone radio silent on me.

Plagued by anxiety that I've somehow fucked up the deal, I've bitten my nails down to the beds. They haven't been this bad since last year. It feels weird to have no nails again. I can't stop prodding my fingertips.

I tear my attention from my sad nails and refocus on my homework spread across the coffee table. It's hard to concentrate with the itchy tweed of the ugly plaid couch irritating my thighs and leaving indents in my skin. I shift around, adjusting my cotton shorts.

Five more minutes of trying to work on my history essay—a subject I normally love—and I close my eyes, falling back against the couch with a defeated groan. I cover my eyes with the sweater paws of my oversized hoodie.

The damn kiss with Devlin won't leave my head. The sweep of his tongue, his grip on my waist, and the muffled groan he made are all seared into my memory. I had no idea kissing could be like that. The few kisses I've experienced have been sweet, awkward, or void of feeling.

Kissing Devlin was overwhelming. Uncontrolled. Unforgettable.

Ruinous.

A coil of heat twines my stomach into a delicious tangle. "This is ridiculous. And pathetic. Get it together."

I'm confused. That's all. There's no way I'll let him convince me to kiss him again. Even if he pays me one million dollars.

Well...

Okay, it wouldn't be a hardship for that much. I fall sideways on the couch, stretching my arms above my head. A lopsided smile lifts the edge of my mouth as I daydream. With one million bucks I could buy Mom a nice house, a reliable car, wipe out the debts and bills, and still have some left over to pay for college.

In the middle of imagining picking out the perfect art history classes for my college schedule, the rattle of the door startles me into sitting upright.

Mom walks through the door hours before she's due home from her evening shift at the diner. Her shoulders droop and her face is too pale, making the bruised bags beneath her eyes stand out starkly.

"Mom!" I pop up from the couch and rush over. "What are you doing home?"

She releases a shuddering breath and takes my hand. Her fingers are ice cold.

"Oh, baby girl," she whispers raggedly.

I don't like the broken sound of her voice. Worry weighs down my stomach like bricks covered in sludge, sticking together and creating an enormous mass of discomfort.

"Come sit down." Lacing my fingers with hers, I guide her to the small table in the kitchenette.

Once she's seated, she puts her head in her hands, bony elbows on the table. Her waitress uniform hangs from her small frame. If I'm skinny, Mom is almost deathly thin. She could never keep weight on. And it has always been hard when our meals are rationed throughout the month.

It would be better if we qualified for food stamps, but Mom makes too much. The system is a joke to everyone like us, slipping through the cracks because we have too much income to qualify for government assistance programs that would be a huge help, and have too little income to sustain ourselves without worrying. Ridgeview is still an expensive place to live, even on the rough side of town. Most of Mom's paycheck from the diner goes toward rent on the trailer, then the bills in order of priority and consequences. It's a horrible existence to constantly dread if we can afford our bills or if we'll get to eat from week to week.

An anguished sob escapes Mom and she scrunches her hair in her clawed hands. My heart shatters as I wrap her in my arms.

"Don't cry," I whisper, as broken as she is. I hate seeing her cry. It wrecks me, stabbing my heart like lethal daggers. "It's okay. Just breathe, Mom. Whatever it is, we'll figure it out. We always do."

The words feel hollow, but they won't stop coming. I have to do *something* to stop her tears.

Mom turns with a strained whimper, banding her arms around my waist and burying her head in my chest. Tears sting my eyes and clump my lashes as I stroke her hair, soothing her with gentle shushes. We stay like that until she calms down.

"I'm sorry, sweetheart," she says repeatedly in a tight voice. "I'm so sorry."

"It's okay."

Helplessness shackles me, clamping me in iron. How can I fix this?

Mom pats my back and pushes me off gently. I lean back to give her room and she peers up at me. She immediately bursts out laughing.

"Oh my god," she breathes through weak laughter. Her shoulders shake under my hands. "You look like a raccoon."

I blink, swiping away tear tracks from under my eyes. My thumb comes back smeared with mascara. I huff out a laugh and shake my head.

Giving her a wry smile, I hug her. "Let me go wash my face, then I'll make some tea."

When I return, Mom has her name tag in her hand, tracing the plastic letters that spell *Macy*. I plug in our electric kettle that I found at the thrift shop downtown and pull out cups and tea bags. As I make the tea, Mom remains quiet.

It scares me when she breaks down. She doesn't usually cry in front of me, so for her to lose her composure instead of going to cry in her room, I know it's bad.

"Here," I say as I set down a steaming mug of tea in front of her.

Mom sets aside the dinged up plastic name tag and curls her hands around the mug. There's something about a warm drink that has magical calming powers. No matter how bad things get, it helps ground us.

I take the seat across from her and chew on my lip as I work out how to broach the subject. "So..."

Mom sighs, weary and beat down by the world. It makes

my heart twinge, the fractures like the prick of a thousand needles. I swallow, my throat thick and tight.

"I was let go from the diner."

A lump lodges in my throat. I wheeze when I try to breathe around it.

Mom rubs her temple, scrunching her face up. "I don't know how we'll make rent by the end of the month. I'll have to start looking for another job right away."

"I could get a jo—"

"No." Mom cuts me off with a fierce look. "I've told you a hundred times, Blair. Focus on school. I'll take care of us. I just want you to worry about your studies. You worked so hard to get your scholarship. I won't see you waste that opportunity because of money worries."

"But it's not even your fault! It's all because Dad left like a goddamn—"

Mom slams her hand on the table. I jolt. I'm glad she has some fight in her still, even if it's to scold me.

"That's enough. It doesn't matter anymore. We just have to keep moving forward. Dwelling doesn't do us any favors."

I lean back in my chair, sighing. I tap my nail-bitten fingers against the side of the mug. There is another option. I was going to save it up, but since Devlin hasn't talked to me all week, I might as well give it to her now.

"I'll be right back."

"Blair?"

I hold up a finger as I go to my room. I wait for a second, hands planted on my hips. Sighing, I go to the mattress of my futon and lift the corner. In the closet, I dig money out of two different pairs of boots. From my sock box, I retrieve the last of my saved stash of cash. The stack is thick, all twenties and fifties earned from playing Devlin's game.

It's everything I've saved up so far.

Going back to the main room of the trailer, I put the stack in front of Mom. "Here. We can use this for rent. I think there's enough for two months at least."

Mom gapes, whipping her shocked gaze from the money to me. "Wh—Blair, where did you get this?"

I shrug, picking at an angry red cuticle on my pinkie. The stinging bite of pain keeps me anchored.

Mom thumbs through the money, mouthing the count. The higher she goes, the more her eyebrows creep up on her forehead. "Blair," Mom rasps. "This is almost five thousand dollars."

"I know."

"Where did you get this much money?"

I skirt the question. "I've been tutoring some people at school. They're all rich, so they pay great. Just take it. Will it help?"

Mom shakes her head in disbelief. "Yes, but..."

Covering her hand with mine, I implore her. "Please, Mom. Let me help. I'm not a kid anymore and I don't want you to stress over this. This way you don't have to kill yourself searching for a new job. You can get some rest first."

I take in her sunken eyes, the exhausted creases at the corner of her eyelids, the limpness to her low ponytail, and the alarmingly pale pallor of her skin. Mom is only 37. She married my dirtbag dad at 18, young and so in love. He gave her the world, and she gave him me at 19. She works so hard and looks like she's ten years older than her age.

Mom has been through too much.

Her lip quivers and her eyes turn glassy, filled with fresh tears.

"Oh, baby girl."

I squeeze her hand. "We'll be okay, Mom. I love you."

"I love you, too." Mom gets up and drops a kiss on top of my head. "Have you eaten yet? How about we splurge on a pizza?"

"Sounds perfect."

As Mom calls for delivery, I gather my homework from the coffee table and set it with plates. While she's ordering, I grab my phone and tap out another text to Devlin to find out what's up with our deal. If Mom can't get a job, then I need him now more than ever. As much as needing him makes my blood boil, he's the easiest way I can make money right now.

Blair: Don't know why you're ignoring me. Are we done?

I can't believe I'm actually upset about Devlin's cold shoulder. Not that long ago, it would've been a dream come true to stop existing on his radar. Now I want to jump up and down in front of him in the SLHS cheerleader outfit again to get his attention.

My cheeks heat.

I absolutely do not picture what else I might get from him by wearing it.

Definitely not.

Not at all.

Nope.

My phone buzzes, sending my heart free falling into my gut. It's not Devlin. He's still ignoring me.

Switching to Instagram, I open the direct message from Gemma. I haven't told her about getting tangled up with her boyfriend's evil cousin.

@brightgem: Dyyyying!
@brightgem: [sent @pugsly_daily's story]

The Instagram story is hilarious and lifts the weight from

my shoulders for a few moments of pure pug-induced happiness. The pug in the video is our favorite pudgy Instafamous dog account sinking into a beanbag, barely visible until he explodes from the beanbag with an amusing flail.

@disblair: omg [heart eyes emoji] sweet lumpy prince!

I close out of the app and prod the side of my phone to feel the squish of my fingertips. Willing a message from Devlin to come doesn't work.

Maybe I should hope for a shooting star instead, like Mom used to tell me.

But that won't work either.

I should know, after all the wishes I wasted hoping Dad would come back and take care of us.

* * *

Mom and I are only on our second slices of pizza when there's a knock on the door. We pause our chewing, glancing at each other.

"I hope that's not Alexei wanting to collect the rent." Mom wipes pizza sauce from her mouth and goes to get up.

"I'll get it."

I spring up before she can. She deserves to rest.

As I swing open the aluminum door, I've got what I'll say to Alexei the landlord ready to go. But instead of Alexei's thinning bleach-tipped hair, gray whiskers, and beer gut, someone I never thought I'd see here waits at the bottom of the steps.

Devlin.

He stands at the edge of the pool of light spilling out onto the weeds and gravel in front of our trailer, hands tucked in his pockets. It's a mild night, the heat of the day not yet dipping into the cooler temperatures.

After barely seeing or speaking to him this week, he's here on my doorstep in a henley and jeans.

"Hi." I brace my hands on the doorframe. "What are you doing here?"

Devlin takes a step forward, into the light. He peers up at me, eyes hooded. There are bags underneath them, a sign he's not rested. I've never seen him like this.

Glancing over my shoulder, I find Mom nibbling on her crust, trying to look like she's not listening. I close the door behind me and sit on the top step. An uncomfortable tightness sits in my chest. It chafes to face Devlin while sitting in front of my sad house. The trailer could easily fit in his garage. Twice, probably.

When he still doesn't answer me, I pry further. "You've avoided me all week."

We haven't spoken since the kiss at his practice match. Even in English, Devlin arrives right when the bell rings and leaves as soon as class ends.

Devlin takes out a cigarette and lights it, the amber glow of the flame flickering over the sharp planes of his face. He takes a deep drag, then tips his head back slightly to exhale. The plume of acrid smoke curls in the air, tickling my nostrils.

I cover my nose with the sleeve of my oversized hoodie to filter out the smoke. "So we're just going to have some one-sided conversation here?"

His gaze snaps to mine. A muscle in his jaw jumps. His cheeks hollow as he inhales another puff.

"Talk to me," I demand, getting annoyed. I jolt to my feet and rush down the steps to get in his face. At the first hint of leather and ginger, my heart skips. I actually missed it. I'll make him answer me. "Why did you come here if you're still ignoring me?"

Devlin plucks the cigarette from between his lips, ashing it with an absent flick. He's infuriating.

Throwing my hands up, I ask, "How do you even know where I live?"

Devlin grows agitated, the sharp line of his jaw tense as he tosses his half-finished cigarette to the gravel and crunches his shoe on it. He sweeps his gaze away, only to cut back to me like he needs to keep me in his sight.

I'm worried something happened to his family or something to put that haunted shadow in his dark eyes.

"I followed you home once. So I'd know how to get to you if you got away."

A chill zips down my spine. "You...*what?*"

Devlin purses his lips and shrugs. "I needed to know, so I followed you. I've known where you live this whole time."

"Okay, stalker. That's wrong on so many levels."

He plucks at the long sleeves of my hoodie. It's then that I realize I'm in cotton shorts with yellow ducks printed on them. He lifts a brow and grazes my thigh right under the hem.

My pulse thunders. When I stumble away, I wince, stubbing my bare toe on a big piece of gravel.

Devlin drags me back by my hips, skimming his fingers under the hem of the hoodie. I swallow, fighting back the flutter. Our kiss wasn't real, and neither is this. He's playing with me.

Struggling to mask the true hurt in my words, I mutter, "I thought you threw me away."

"I don't throw people away," Devlin says, cold and precise. His grip on my hips flexes. "I use them when they're useful to me."

My head jerks back. "That's the same thing."

He slides his hand higher to the side of my stomach. His touch is hot, sending sparks over my skin.

"It's not."

Devlin presses his face into my neck and exhales. The hot gust of air makes me shiver. His tongue darts out and tastes my skin.

This is crazy. He's the one who stayed away all week, and now he's holding me like a man possessed, unwilling to let me go. After hesitating with my hands hanging in midair, I rest them on his sides, playing with the soft material of the henley shirt clinging to his abs.

"What kind of wicked siren are you?"

"I don't know what you mean."

He leans back to give me a brooding look. "You make me want impossible things. Ever since you kissed me, I want—"

His attention drops to my lips. He leans in, hovering his mouth over mine.

"The kiss was one of your orders for the deal," I whisper, wide-eyed. "It wasn't real."

Devlin stills. He buries his face back in my neck, remaining quiet for another beat. He murmurs something I can't understand, words muffled against my neck.

This is a different devil than the one I know.

Concern wins out over everything else—my annoyance at him for avoiding me and the stress. "What's wrong?"

Devlin turns to marble beneath my hands, rigid and impenetrable. He leans back to face me, his hands locking together at the small of my back.

"Move in with me. Live at my house."

Disbelief crashes over me. For a long moment, I can't speak, only gape at him. When I find my voice, it's shrill.

"Excuse me?" A nervous giggle bubbles out of me. "You opened your mouth and fucking *crazy* came out."

Devlin's expression is a blank mask.

No.

No, no, *fuck* no.

I shove at his chest, but he keeps me in place, tightening his embrace.

Glaring up at him, I list all the ways that's never fucking happening. "You're out of your mind! What makes you think I would agree to that? What would you even get out of that? No. No way! People at school would talk and get the wrong idea and, more importantly, my mom would never let me!"

"Ten thousand." It's Devlin's only response, passive and bored.

What the fuck?

I smack his chest. He doesn't budge.

"*Why?*"

"I don't have to explain it to you."

"You do if you expect me to agree!"

"Are you backing out of our deal?" Devlin crushes me in his arms. "Whatever I say goes. If you can't comply, I'll shred our contract and drop you off at the police station."

"No!"

It's difficult to control the train wreck of emotions.

On one hand, ten grand is a lot of money. All I have to do to get it is live with Devlin. That's way less of a public humiliation, unless he brings people home while I'm there or lets me ride to school with him.

On the other, I'd have to live with Devlin. Enemy territory, unfamiliar and uncharted. It would put me in a vulnerable position, dependent on him in every way.

Jesus, what would he do with access to me night and day? He's a twisted and ruthless demon. I'm afraid to imagine what he might come up with in his fucked up head.

The water from the sink turns on inside the trailer. I can

hear the muted sounds of Mom shuffling around. Shit, I can't let her find out about my deal with Devlin.

"You're psychotic and entitled! I won't do it. You can't just throw money at me to make it happen. The world doesn't work like that, Devlin."

This has gone so much further than navigating Devlin's playing field to keep myself out of jail.

A muscle jumps in Devlin's jaw as it clenches. "In my world, it does. The money doesn't matter. Anything I want, I get it."

He slides his hand into my hair and tugs a fistful, drawing my head back. A strangled cry catches in my throat. He puts his teeth on the stretched column of my neck, scraping against the skin. I jerk in his hold, heat spearing through me and throbbing between my legs. I hate the way he can manipulate my body.

"Haven't you learned the rules by now, little thief?" His tongue chases the same path as his teeth. I grit my molars stubbornly to hold in a moan. It's not fair, it feels so good. "You don't get to say no."

I buck against him to throw him off. "Let me go!"

Devlin releases me with a grunt and I stumble over the gravel. It digs into the bare soles of my feet. Clenching my teeth doesn't help stave off the pain.

"You're coming with me tonight."

"I don't fucking think so."

Fed up with Devlin, I push up my hoodie sleeve and slap him. The crack of my hand on his cheek echoes in the air.

"I'm *not*."

Devlin touches his cheek gingerly, staring at me in surprise. Good.

Yanking back some control from this entitled asshole feels awesome.

There's a gleam of respect in Devlin's eyes for a second before it vanishes. He makes no move to retaliate. I don't trust him, so I square off against him with my guard up, prepared for whatever he wants to throw at me next.

My chest heaves on a frustrated breath. "You might pay me to do whatever you say, but that doesn't mean you control me."

Devlin considers me, cocking his head like I've made a play he wasn't expecting. The corners of his mouth twitch up.

Before our argument can continue, a loud crash sounds from inside, drawing our attention. I spin on my heel, icy dread freezing my veins.

"Mom!"

Devlin is right behind me as we rush inside the trailer.

TWENTY-ONE
DEVLIN

Macy Davis lies in a slump across the cheap linoleum floor where she collapsed, white as a sheet. Sharp pieces of a broken plate are scattered around her. The faucet in the sink is on.

This is not how I expected things to go when I drove over here to get Blair, no longer able to stand avoiding her.

"Oh my god," Blair croaks.

Something stirs to life inside my long-frozen heart as Blair crashes to her knees beside her mother, barely missing cutting her knee open on a piece of shattered glass.

Blair's devotion to her mom is obvious. It's undeniable she loves her.

Dazed, I step around them to turn off the faucet. An uneasiness prods at me from the inside as I watch Blair tend to her mom. The pieces of the chessboard scatter in my head, strategy knocked askew by an urge to help.

"Mom? Mom!" Blair gently rolls Macy over and touches her cheek. "Mom, wake up."

It simultaneously calls on the mangled shard inside of me that longs to fit into my family again and makes me burn with jealousy that these two women have a strong connection. A bond I'll never get to have.

"Can we get her into the car?" Blair asks. "We have to get her to the hospital."

"Why the hell would we drive her ourselves? We don't know what happened to her and neither of us have emergency medical training. We can't transport her safely."

Blair covers her face with one hand. "We don't have insurance."

The concept is foreign to me. With parents renowned in the medical field who pressure me to follow in their footsteps, I feel as though I've been spoon fed the importance of medical care. My family has never faced being uninsured. I can't wrap my head around being sick and not being able to see a doctor.

"We'll worry about that later." I whip out my phone and dial. I have to do something. "The sooner we call for professional help, the better."

Blair flashes me a frazzled look. She hesitates, pursing her lips. "Fine. Call an ambulance, then! We need help."

I lift my brows, phone pressed to my ear. "Already on it. Don't move her too much, you don't know what caused her to collapse."

Blair's eyes widen, probably panicking that she rolled her mom over. She takes Macy's hand and presses her forehead to it.

"Her hands are cold and clammy."

"Okay. Check for a pulse."

Color drains from Blair's face. As her fingers fumble over Macy's wrist, she whispers, "Oh my god."

A woman's calm voice answers the phone. *"911, what's your emergency?"*

"I need an ambulance at 502 Spruce Lane, in Pine Hills Park. A woman collapsed."

"Okay, sir, I have help on the way. Is she conscious?"

I lean in for a better look. "No. She's passed out."

"Is she breathing?"

"Yes."

Blair murmurs to her mom, carefully stroking her hair, arranging it out of her face. Tears cling to Blair's inky lashes and she bites her lip. I've never seen her like this. For some reason, I want to take her tears away, make her feel better.

I want to protect her, because only I get to make her cry.

These tears aren't for me.

"It'll be okay." Blair flinches and swings her gaze to me. My chest cinches tight around my heart. "Your mom will be okay."

Blair's big whiskey-colored eyes shine under the fluorescent lighting. She nods. It's strange to find her beautiful right now, with her nose pink and runny, her eyes puffy, and tears streaming down her face.

Beautiful and mine.

Mine to protect. Mine to care for. *Mine.*

I don't know why I gave into the urge to comfort her. I owe her nothing. In fact, she owes me and her debt is yet to be paid.

Watching her gently hold her mom's hand as tears drop from her chin, I forget about the lingering sting in my cheek where she slapped me. An invisible band around my chest renders it hard to draw breath. I fight against the instinct to crouch beside Blair, gather her into my arms, and inhale the scent of her vanilla shampoo.

She's belonged to me since she signed that contract. Before that, even.

Possessiveness rears up and takes over. I set everything between us aside. The only thing that matters right now is control.

Minutes later, flashing red lights flicker through the windows, illuminating the walls. I open the front door. Once the paramedics bustle in, I scoop Blair into my arms, and lift her away from Macy.

The emergency responders kneel on either side of Macy in the kitchenette across the narrow room. One is a woman with her braids twisted into a bun on top of her head and the other is a stocky man in an EMT uniform.

"Wait!" Blair cries, flailing her legs as I step out of the way.

Even as she struggles, she weighs nothing in my arms. Her tiny shorts with the duck pattern ride up the more she flails, driving me crazy. I wish I could see her like this under different circumstances.

When all of this is done, I'm making her wear the shorts again.

"Calm down." I set Blair down by the couch, resisting the twitch in my hands to pick her up again. I jerk my chin. "There's broken glass all over the floor and you're barefoot."

Blair peers down. "Oh."

"Go find shoes. You'll probably need them if they have to take her."

Blair's features crumble. She rolls her lips between her teeth and nods. Turning away, she scurries down a dim hall.

"Patient is female, mid-thirties, unconscious," the woman announces to her partner. "Breathing is shallow. Patient presents with symptoms of hypotension. Any known conditions?"

I peer down the hall Blair disappeared. "Not sure."

The EMT makes a note on his tablet.

When Blair comes back out with a pair of black Chucks on, I tuck her against my side as the emergency responders check Macy's vitals and flurry around her prone body, avoiding the glass. We hover on the other side of the room, next to the world's ugliest couch and a beat up coffee table. Blair trembles, digging her fingers into the material of my shirt. Holding her close feels right, soothing the weird possessiveness. I stroke her back, feeling both awkward because I've never comforted anyone, and like the action is the most natural thing to do.

The whole time I ignore how good it feels to have her leaning on me. I shouldn't enjoy having Blair in my arms. I came here to drag her back to my tower in the mountains because I'm a selfish monster.

She's only taking comfort in my embrace because she's distraught, and I took charge of the situation.

"Okay, let's get her loaded." The paramedic turns to us in the cramped space while her partner sets up a stretcher. "We'll be taking her to Ridgeview Memorial. I can only let one of you ride in the ambulance."

"Me," Blair pipes up. She swipes under her eyes and pulls away from my side, leaving it cold and empty. "I'm her daughter."

"Okay, come on." The paramedic gestures to the door.

Outside, Blair freezes, looking down at her hoodie and those cute little shorts. When she came out of the trailer in them I wanted to bury my hands under the hem and palm her ass.

"Just go," I murmur in her ear, squeezing her shoulders from behind. "People show up in all kinds of wild shit when there's an emergency. Where's the house key? I'll clean up the glass, then lock up and follow behind you."

Blair hangs her head, scrubbing her face. "Hook by the door. Thanks."

"I'll be right behind you."

"Okay." Blair's voice is so small.

It's bizarre to see her like this, worn down and razed to the ground. I'm used to her quiet strength, the stubbornness to rise above the taunts at school. I want to freeze the moment so I can examine this fascinating new facet from every angle, but there's no time.

"I promise." I don't know what pushes me to offer her reassurance. Rubbing her shoulders, I explain, "Ridgeview Memorial is good. My godfather is the chief of medicine there."

A flicker of hope sparks to life in Blair's eyes. "Thanks." She glances at the ambulance as her mother is loaded in the back. "I know you came here for a different reason. But, um, I'm glad you were here."

Blair touches my arm briefly. My poor little pest is shaken, unsure. For all that she takes care of things, in this case she let panic rule her.

I lick my lips. "You can pay me back later."

The deliberate cruelty of my words is used to regain the higher ground. She doesn't get a pass. It doesn't drive away the lack of control I'm grappling with.

Blair tenses.

Taking a breath, she jogs away. I watch from the front step of her trailer as she takes the paramedic's hand and climbs into the back of the ambulance. I swallow the urge to rip her away from the EMS guy. He's doing his job, not coming onto her.

As the ambulance pulls out, crunching over the gravel, I chain up the monster inside and go back into the trailer.

Inside, I pause. I could unearth all of Blair's secrets. She shouldn't have trusted me to be in her trailer alone.

Locating the broom, I take care of the remnants of the

broken plate. Every second I spend in the trailer, inhaling hints of vanilla, is another second a tether pulls taught in my stomach.

A week without talking to her was torture. I was going to let everything go—the agreement, the break in, even forget her existence. My goal was to go back to the way things were before she broke into my garage, before this game started between us.

It messed me up after she kissed me like a siren, then asked for payment.

And it's my own fault. My own game has destroyed me.

The idea of making her wear the cheer uniform and make a fool of herself in front of everyone, then kiss me to top it all off, was supposed to be a way to toy with her. Instead, I'm the one plagued by that fucking kiss.

It wasn't supposed to spark this desire in me.

The taste isn't enough. I'm an addict, desperate for my drug of choice.

After kissing Blair, I want to fucking devour her.

The time I spent restricting myself, ignoring her in class and avoiding her in school has only heightened that need. It did the opposite of what I wanted. Instead of getting her out of my system, she dug her claws deeper. I couldn't stay away any longer.

She's in my bloodstream and she's not going anywhere unless I do something about it.

I don't want to go to my depressing empty house in the mountains, and I'm not leaving her alone right now.

Forget snooping for Blair's secrets.

I'm going to get my girl.

* * *

Blair's voice reaches me as I search through the emergency room.

"I don't care about your procedures! That's my mom and I want to go back with her!"

Turning the next corner, I find Blair fighting with a nurse.

"Miss, I can't let you beyond this point." The nurse seems completely done, like she's repeated herself multiple times. "You can wait in the lounge over there."

I close the distance between us in four long strides, sliding between Blair and the nurse.

"Stop. You're just making a scene and getting nowhere. That's not how you get what you want."

Blair glares. "So what? I want to go back there."

The nurse disappears behind the *No Entry Beyond This Point* door while Blair is distracted.

"Quick, she's gone. We can sneak in."

I almost smile. Pesky little troublemaker.

"Come on." Steering Blair away from the restricted door, I take her to a lounge area. I kiss her temple. "Wait for me."

There's a vending machine for coffee nearby. It's probably bitter and shitty, but she needs something warm to drink. I punch the buttons and watch the cardboard cup fill.

This area of the hospital isn't busy right now. I passed a few people in the emergency room reception when I came in, but this section is deserted. The lighting is too bright, everything smells of stale air and astringent antiseptic. It creates a sense of liminal space.

I don't like hospitals.

One of the few memories I have before my parents began dumping me on others was when I was young, maybe four or five. I was playing with Lucas, who could climb better since he was a year older. I wanted to do anything Lucas did. He was my idol. My only friend.

When I tried to climb as high as Lucas, I fumbled my footing and landed badly on a rock. They made me stay overnight in the hospital, alone, with too many beeping machines.

Grabbing the piping hot coffee, I return to find Blair biting on her abused thumb nail. Her brows are furrowed and she stares into space. I pass her the coffee.

"In the ambulance she started seizing or something, I don't know," Blair mumbles, looking rattled. "Once we pulled up to the hospital, they took her away."

I tip her chin up. Her eyes are bloodshot and swollen. "I'm going to find my godfather. Just wait here."

Blair blows out a ragged breath and shrugs. Taking a sip of coffee, she grimaces.

"This tastes like shit."

The corner of my mouth curls up. "Tough."

"Seriously, this is the worst cup of coffee I've ever had."

I leave her with her crappy hospital coffee and head for the elevator in the next hallway. I ride it up to the third floor, questioning what I'm doing the whole way to my godfather's office.

Whatever it is, I'll see it through. There's no point in stopping at this point. If it gets me to my endgame, then it's worth it.

Uncle Craig is inside the office, seated at a glass top desk with a pair of reading glasses drooping low on the bridge of his nose as he goes over medical records. A white lab coat is draped across a black leather sofa.

Craig is a barrel-chested man with a broad, gleaming white smile, light brown skin, and warm eyes that make you feel his love. He's not my uncle by blood, but I've known him my entire life. He always insists I treat him like family, which I'm glad to. As far as I'm concerned, we are family.

I knock on the open door. "Hey."

Uncle Craig looks up and beams at me, waving his hand to

gesture me in. "Devlin! What a surprise. I was just talking to your dad a couple of days ago. Have a seat."

Of course. Dad can talk to his colleagues, but not to his own son. I haven't had a conversation with Dad in over a week. He ignores most of my texts.

I should take the hint and stop dragging myself over hot coals because there's nothing to gain from him.

I stand on the other side of Craig's desk. "Actually, I can't stay long. My—" I falter. What is Blair to me? We're still not friends. What do you call the girl who drives you crazy that you pay to control? The thought rattles through my head unpleasantly. Craig's graying brows hike up at my verbal fumble. I'm not usually tongue-tied. "—friend, her mom was brought in. I want to make sure she gets the best care possible."

"Hmm, I see." Craig scrubs a big palm over his shiny bald head. He drags his open laptop closer. "What's the name?"

"Macy Davis."

The keyboard keys clack as Craig types. Craig pushes his glasses up his nose. His eyes bounce back and forth as he reads the information on the screen.

"Okay. She was given a bed in the emergency department for evaluation of the symptoms she presented with upon arrival. I can't tell you exact details."

"Can you have her transferred into a private room?"

I picture Blair biting on her nails and sitting in her duck shorts downstairs. A sigh drags out of me. I can't provide her with my own health insurance, but I can throw money at the problem.

A niggling instinct has been picking at me since I saw Blair on her knees next to her mom. It's something fighting against the darker shades of my mind intent on getting what I want out of this.

"If they admit her to the floor, then yes."

"I want to take care of all of it."

Craig plucks off his reading glasses and strokes his chin. "Some friend. Are you sure? I can see this patient doesn't have insurance on file."

I wave my hand. "Whatever gets her the best testing and care. Make it happen. Will you keep an eye on her case?"

"That's part of my job." Craig studies me. "Is everything okay? You look like hell."

My mouth pulls to the side. "Studying hard, you know? Dad expects me to ace this year to look good for pre-med programs."

Craig shakes his head. "Get some rest, Devlin."

I release a relieved breath. "Thanks, Uncle Craig."

As Craig types on his laptop, I leave the office.

Blair hasn't moved from where I left her, and that sends a satisfied hum into the pit of my stomach. She listened. Obeyed.

Before I can tell her the good news, the same nurse Blair argued with comes through the double doors.

"Miss Davis? We're admitting your mom upstairs. Come with me, I'll take you to see her."

Blair jumps to her feet and abandons her cardboard coffee cup on a stack of magazines. "Is she okay?"

"She's stable. The doctor taking over her case will likely run some tests to find out what caused her low blood pressure."

The nurse walks briskly as she talks. Blair scurries to keep up on shorter legs. I tuck my arm around her waist as we follow the nurse to another bank of elevators.

It's ridiculous, but I struggle against a bout of irritation. I wanted to tell Blair.

As the nurse directs us through the pristine hallway, Blair stiffens beside me.

"What's wrong?"

"These are all private rooms. I thought hospitals had some where you share."

"Your mom's getting the best care possible. Isn't that what you want?"

Blair shoots me a conflicted look. "Yes, but...aren't private rooms expensive?"

Her brow pinches. The math is adding up in her mind. She's probably factoring in the cost of the ambulance ride, and whatever the charges will be for the emergency room doctor.

"Here we are," the nurse announces as we arrive at a room at the end of the hall.

Corner room. It'll have a nice view of the mountain range that stretches across Ridgeview in the morning. I suppress a sigh. I did tell Uncle Craig to take the best care of Macy.

I shouldn't worry. It won't even put a dent in the account my parents dump money into each month. Their guilt money.

As if their money could substitute for real parenting.

Besides, if it drained the account, I have my personal accounts I've grown with my financial advisor through investments.

"Visiting hours are until 8pm, so you have about twenty minutes to see her."

"Thanks," Blair says.

The nurse nods and heads down the hall to the nurse's station.

"Do you want me to stay?"

"Uh, I'm not sure." Blair glances anxiously at the hospital room. "I don't have a ride home."

"Yes or no?"

"No...?"

Sighing, I pull out my wallet. "Here." I hand her a twenty. "Take a cab home."

"Thanks."

Leaving is the last thing I want to do.

I want to drag her to an empty room and tear those tempting cotton shorts off her. It's torture to have her so close all night after a week of resisting and not be able to kiss her or touch her the way I want.

Blair peers up at me, hesitating. "You've been...not what I expected. I really appreciate your help."

I stare back at her. She's the only thing I've wanted all week. She's right in front of me, thanking me.

And I'm not done taking from her.

Her debt isn't repaid.

Not even close.

I've jacked the price she owes me higher. I'll have whatever I want from her. All of it.

Blair is mine. Nothing will change that now.

"You can thank me later." I cup her shoulders. "Because I got your mother this room and better care."

Blair's features go slack. "You what?"

I lean down to murmur in her ear. "You can consider what I did payment. I'll be there this weekend to pick you up. You'd better be packed and ready."

A minute ago she was thanking me. Now she stumbles back a step, glaring at me.

The demand destroys any bridge I've built with Blair by helping her through the situation tonight. Instead of crossing it, I choose my selfishness over everything else. It's the only way I know to keep the pieces on the board under my control.

"I hate you." Blair's glare is fierce, but she doesn't argue.

I smirk. "I know."

The problem isn't that Blair hates me. It's that I no longer fully hate her. It's seeped away, overcome by the growing obsession with the way she makes me feel alive when I'm around her.

The only thing I care about is having her.

And I always get what I want.

"Go be with your mom." I begin to back away, keeping her locked in my sight. Pure fury rolls off Blair in waves. "See you this weekend."

TWENTY-TWO
BLAIR

This month has felt far too long with everything that's happened.

It's the last weekend in September and the weather has spiked into the mid-80s all week with a late in the season heatwave. I'm craving the cooler temperatures of fall, when the aspen trees turn golden and the scent of woodsmoke fills the air.

The ancient window unit died in August, leaving me to suffer in an oppressively hot trailer as I haul my small box of books out to the car.

Devlin isn't helping, the bastard.

I want to slap the smarmy, triumphant smirk from his face.

He leans against the Porsche with sunglasses on, arms crossed, showing off the defined curve of his biceps. In his basketball shorts and a white and green SLHS varsity soccer t-shirt, he looks damn good. I'm annoyed at myself for giving into baser instincts. How can I be attracted to this jerk with tousled black hair and a cut jaw?

Devlin shifts, sliding a hand beneath his t-shirt to scratch an itch, showing off his abs as the shirt lifts.

God. Damn. It.

Fuck my lizard brain. Fuck it right to hell.

I hike the heavy box of books higher as my attention falls to his exposed tan skin. Heat pools low in my stomach. When I dart my eyes back up, his smirk stretches. What an ass. He knows exactly what he's doing.

Well, it won't work on me. I won't let it. Our fake kiss is all he'll get out of me.

"Would it kill you to lift a finger?" I gasp.

Sweat trickles down the back of my neck. The box is hard to hold in my slippery grip.

Devlin shrugs. "It might."

Rolling my eyes, I get the burden into the trunk without his help. It's filled with my favorite books. I'm not bringing much else with me. A patched up duffel stuffed with some clothes sits next to the box. Other than that I have my backpack full of school supplies and my two uniforms.

Devlin insisted on picking me up to make sure I wasn't backing out. His mechanic is supposed to pick up my Corolla later and drop it off.

We have Monday off from school. I'll be trapped for three days straight in Devlin's giant house.

This is insane.

I'm moving in with Devlin.

All because the arrogant asshole considers footing Mom's medical bills payment for his demand.

Grateful relief brawls with the part of me outraged that he's using his financial assistance to manipulate me. Now he believes he owns me even more than before. This no longer feels like a game to humiliate me as payback.

It's darker, more twisted and sinister.

I have to adapt again to his mind games. If I don't, he'll swallow me whole in damnation and hellfire, consuming me until my last breath.

The problem isn't dancing with the devil.

It's that I'm willing to keep selling my soul to him if it means Mom gets better treatment and top of the line medical care.

We would never be able to afford that private hospital room, let alone the ambulance ride with our lack of insurance and limited income.

"Is that everything?" Devlin surveys my measly collection of belongings. "You don't have more?"

He probably sees junk, but to me I have my most treasured possessions—my book collection and a few of my favorite print-outs of folk art I got at the library. The carefully pieced together set of books is one of the few things I've saved for myself.

I shrug. "That's it. The rest can stay here."

"Then lock up your rat-sized shoebox and let's get the hell out of here. This place is depressing, and your neighbors keep staring at Red."

"They're mentally pricing what they could get for your rims alone."

Devlin slides his sunglasses down and peers over the frames. "I won't offer them the same deal I have with you if they touch my ride."

The look he sends me tangles my insides in knots. A hot and cold sensation travels across my skin, leaving me shivering.

Shaking it off, I jog back to the trailer and hesitate at the open door, peering inside. There isn't an ounce of attachment for the place. Without Mom, it doesn't feel like home. Just an empty space with mismatched furniture making an attempt at creating a comfortable space.

People are your home, not the places you live.

Nodding to myself, I lock up.

Rent is paid on the trailer for the next two months. With Devlin covering the medical bills, I was able to use the cash I've saved so far to keep our trailer. Just in case Mom's condition improves. I want her to come home from the hospital without worrying.

It's been four days. Every day after school I've gone to sit with her, doing my homework at the foot of her bed. She looks better. Her color has returned, but the doctors won't clear her release without more testing first.

At the very least, she's getting a nice break with a cushy private hospital room to rest.

All on Devlin's dime.

I cast a glance at him as we climb into the red Porsche. He adjusts his sunglasses and flicks on a playlist once his phone connects to the Bluetooth. A haunting lo-fi beat fills the car.

The gravel grinds beneath the tires as Devlin revs the engine and peels out of the community of misfits I've called home for the last several years.

Watching the trailer park shrink in the rear window as we drive off is weirdly bittersweet.

I've been looking forward to escaping this place for years. To go to college and land an opportunity to improve our lives. Is this what that freedom will feel like?

"You'll get a neck cramp if you plan to sit like that the whole time."

Huffing, I shift in the seat, plucking at the frayed edges of my cutoff shorts. We quickly leave the rougher parts of

Ridgeview. Nicer houses fly by the window as we approach the Rockies.

Devlin seems relaxed. He slouches back in the driver's seat, shifting gears like it's second nature. One hand rests over the wheel, air drumming to the beat of the song playing. This one has more of a rock style mixed with some synth beats. I wouldn't have pegged him for listening to stuff like this.

I twine a piece of denim around my finger to keep busy. I'm trying not to pick at my nails so much. The further the car climbs into the mountains, the more my stomach flutters with nerves.

"Since we have off on Monday, I'm going to see my mom."

Devlin hums.

"Gemma texted me last night. Her and Lucas are driving down from Oak Ridge College for the weekend."

I'm hoping to get some time to see Gemma, since Lucas lives across the lake from Devlin.

"Don't tell Gemma about our deal." Devlin shoots me a sidelong glance. "Or Lucas."

I snort. "I don't really talk to Lucas. And your rules are bullshit."

"I'm serious. Don't tell anyone. This isn't the same as making you quack like a duck because it's funny."

"Whatever."

I lean an arm against the window as we pull into the huge entrance of Silver Lake Forest Estates. My stomach turns inside out like the drop in a roller coaster. Devlin remains quiet as we wind through the community, passing tennis courts and a pool. I sneer at the sign for the rock climbing gym. These stuck up rich people have it all.

Devlin pulls through the iron gate at the front of his property a few minutes later, parking out front on the circular drive.

The huge modern contemporary meets cabin style mansion looms into the trees guarding it. In the daylight, it's beautiful.

"Grab your shit." Devlin saunters up the front steps, leaving me to haul my things by myself.

Narrowing my eyes, I hoist my duffel onto my shoulder, following Devlin into the house.

It may be beautiful and dripping in expensive taste, but it's empty. The air inside the entrance is still and oppressive.

I peer up at the high ceiling with exposed beams and a modern chandelier made of glass and metal. It's hard to believe it was only a few weeks ago Devlin pinned me to this door after catching me stealing his precious car.

Devlin doesn't wait for me to take in the wonder of his wealth, continuing into the belly of the house without me. As I follow, I'm baffled. The house is so much bigger than the parties Gemma took me to last year at Lucas Saint's, and *his* house is huge.

The kitchen is where I find Devlin. It's just as luxurious as the first time I saw it, though I was a little distracted then. My attention cuts to the metal-backed stools he tied me to. The room looks like something out of an upscale interior design magazine with frosted glass-front cabinets and dark granite counters.

Devlin leans in the open fridge, sighing even though it's full to the brim with food.

An eerie silence blankets the house.

I allow my duffel bag to drop at my feet on the cool tile. "Where are your parents?"

Devlin shuts the refrigerator and shrugs in a stilted way, like I've driven a spike into a nerve. He avoids me as he sidesteps around me to grab a beer from a smaller fridge at the wet bar on the other side of the room.

"Traveling for work, as usual. New York, last I heard."

A flash of pain crosses his face before he smooths his stony veneer.

He lives here by himself? All alone?

There's a tug in my chest that feels alarmingly like sympathy.

I scrape my fingers through my hair to fight it off. "I'll get my other stuff from the car."

Devlin takes a long sip of beer, lips wrapped around the mouth of the bottle as he watches me with hooded eyes.

On my way out I rub at my chest, but the pang of sadness doesn't leave. I might have next to nothing in this world, fighting tooth and nail to survive day to day, but I'm not alone. I have my mom.

Doesn't he have that?

"Don't be ridiculous," I mutter to myself, hitching the box of books on my hip.

Devlin has everything he wants under the sun. I can't feel bad because the sad little rich boy sits in his lonely mountain tower alone. He's an over privileged asshole, too accustomed to getting his way.

I can't let myself feel bad.

Devlin can choke on his silver spoon for all I care.

I strengthen my resolve and make two trips to bring in the rest of my belongings, leaving them by the front door. Voices echo from the kitchen as I drop my backpack next to the box of books.

"*It's supposed to be hot as shit tomorrow.*" It's Bishop's voice.

I find Devlin leaning over his phone at the island in the kitchen, peeling at the label on his half-finished beer bottle. He hums in response.

"*I already talked to Lucas. Beach party tomorrow, dude. It's gonna be lit.*".

Devlin meets my gaze as I linger in the doorway. "Beach party, huh?" His eyes skate down my body in a slow drag that makes my skin prickle with heat. "Yeah, sounds good. We'll be there."

"*We?*" I can hear Bishop's eyebrows flying up through the phone by his intrigued tone. "*Do you have a girl over? Like, you actually let a girl into your house instead of driving out to Peak Point to fuck?*"

Bishop's laughter fills the kitchen through the phone speaker.

"Bye," Devlin says, jabbing the end call button. Sliding his amused gaze back to me, Devlin's cocksure attitude rears its head. "Let me show you to your bedroom."

* * *

The house isn't only huge, it's also a maze. Devlin showed me up the main staircase and pointed out a random guest room I can use. A shelf of artfully placed knickknacks drew my attention. Devlin said it was my room and I could do whatever with it. Pure elation spiraled through me as I moved the decor from the shelf, intent on giving my books a real bookcase.

After getting my things up a stupid amount of steps and slumping on a soft bed, I groan.

Damn, I'm getting slack. I need to pick up on my runs. The prospect of trail runs in this gated community is exciting. I bet there's a nice trail that wraps around the huge lake behind Devlin's house.

Devlin leans against my doorframe with mischief dancing in his dark eyes. He took great pleasure in watching me cart my stuff to my room. I'm glad I only brought the essentials.

"What?"

"Well, for one, those shorts make it look like you have an ass, so I'm enjoying the view."

"Ugh!" I roll over to deprive him of staring at my butt. "Dick."

"Mm." Devlin licks his lips. With a fluid strength, he pushes off the doorframe and stalks closer to the bed. He leans over, planting his hands on either side of my hips. "Two...I bought you that."

I look over at the closet. A maid costume hangs from the door.

"Wh—Are you fucking kidding?" I screech, scrambling up the bed. "No way in hell."

Devlin follows me like a beast on the prowl, the muscles in his arms flexing as he crawls up the bed to cage me in again. He's enjoying this. My trickster devil has me at his mercy with no escape.

Narrowing my eyes, I push up on my hands to get in his face. Devlin's eyes flash and he grins. A bolt of heat zips down my spine. I fight the screaming need to let my legs drop open, where he could fit his hips between my thighs.

I take a breath and snark at him. "I'll make you regret it. I'll find your room in this insane pampered maze and smother you in your sleep."

A flirtatious smirk pulls Devlin's mouth into an attractive curve. He dips his head down to drag his nose over my cheek, breathing on my neck. My body seizes up, my core throbbing steadily, hot and insistent.

"If you come into my room after dark, you better be prepared." Devlin's voice is deep and full of forbidden promise.

I bite my lip. "For what?"

"Anything I want, little thief," he whispers roughly.

He nibbles on my neck, making me squirm at the delicious sensation of his teeth on my skin. My nipples tighten to hard buds and my body demands more. I want to wrap my legs around him, grind with him until I scratch the needy itch for release.

Devlin growls, the sound tugging at the heat building in my stomach. His tongue swipes over my pulse point, ripping a gasp from me.

Cool air prickles in a wave across my body as Devlin pulls back. His lids are heavy. I blink, coming to my senses.

"You—Get out."

"You don't tell me what to do, Blair." Devlin's gaze goes from heated to cool in seconds. He traces my collarbone and holds my neck without pressure. "You're mine and I decide when I'm done."

My pulse rushes in my ears. His hand around my neck is my shackle, a collar to control me. And I don't hate the feel of it.

The thing growing between us since the fake kiss is becoming a slippery slope. If I'm not careful, I'll lose my footing and find myself enjoying this.

"Get out," I repeat, voice steadier than my liquid insides feel.

Devlin stares me down for a long stretch. I hold his gaze, pushing all of my resolve into it. My heart pounds. He can probably feel my rapid pulse beneath his fingertips. I don't look away, refusing to back down.

After another minute, Devlin sits back. "There's plenty of food in the kitchen. The housekeeper makes sure it's stocked." Dragging a hand through his tousled hair, he nods to the maid costume. "That was a joke. I wanted to see your face. But I won't say no to you wearing these or your duck shorts around the house."

A heated flushed engulfs my face at the sultry lilt of his

voice. "Perv. Don't think about whatever it is that's putting that look on your face."

He leers at me, dragging his teeth over his lower lip.

It's only the first day, not even twenty-four hours in his house, and I'm already grappling with maintaining the balance between us.

The line in the sand is blurry at best.

I push against Devlin's chest, and he cups my hands, trapping them. "If this is my room, whatever I say goes in here."

He squints. "Fine."

"Good. So get out."

Devlin leaves me to my own devices. For the first time all afternoon, I face the fact that I'm living with my monster. I fall back on the bed. It's so comfortable, I can't contain another grateful groan.

This may be the craziest thing I could agree to, but right now I'm planning to enjoy this bed.

I stay in my new room for a while, marveling that my futon could fit in here, like, five times. It's big, but plain, with a large closet, a window with a deep ledge perfect for a book bench, and the biggest bed I've ever been in.

After dozing until it's dark, my stomach starts to growl. I venture out into the house to explore on my way back to the kitchen.

The house has so many rooms. I pass a nice study with a real fireplace and cedar shelves built into the wall, filled to the brim with so many books. The staircase has floating risers, giving the illusion I'm levitating on air as I descend to the lower level.

Throughout the house there's modern art. I pause in front of an abstract painting to study its muted tones and the shapes used. I love art, but not a single piece in this house makes me feel anything.

There's no connection. It's all lifeless. Cold.

Wrinkling my nose at the painting, I navigate my way to the kitchen.

There's no sign of Devlin. It's kind of creepy. How did he feel when it was only him in this house? I frown, considering how lonely a big place like this would be by myself.

Maybe it's why he grew into such an unbearable jerk.

I wonder if he ate as I raid the fridge. I go for a handful of baby carrots so I don't have to find anything in the cabinets or work the microwave that looks like something designed by NASA.

On my way back to my room with my snack, I halt in the hallway.

Devlin emerges in a cloud of steam from the bathroom. He's freshly showered and wearing nothing but a low-slung towel. There's a tattoo on his ribs, beneath his heart.

It's the first time I've seen it.

The tattoo is a cluster of shooting stars, delicately inked. Awareness tingles in my back, where my own star tattoo marks my body.

We're the same—black hair, tarnished hearts, and star tattoos.

Devlin runs his fingers through his wet hair. His muscles ripple with the movement.

Holy hell.

I swallow, clutching my carrots.

Devlin prowls over, following me when I stumble back a step, my back hitting the wall. He presses his body into mine, his strong torso rubbing against my breasts through my thin t-shirt. My breath snags in my throat.

"What do we have here?" Devlin teases in a playful tone. He tucks some of my hair behind my ear. "Lost?"

The heat of his skin bleeds through my shirt.

"No."

"Oh, I see." Devlin chuckles and drops his hand to the towel. "Were you sneaking around out here hoping to get a good look?" He acts like he's going to rip off the towel. "Want me to drop it?"

My throat is thick when I swallow. "No."

"No?"

I shake my head.

"You sure?"

His voice is a sinful caress against my skin, the low rumble stealing my breath away. I bet he can feel my hardened nipples against his chest.

"Devlin." My gaze zeroes in on his lips.

His mouth curves into a slow, smug smile, dimples on display. "Your room is that way, roomie."

Devlin peels away and goes into his room. It's the door on the other side of the bathroom.

The room two doors down from mine.

I gulp and zip into my bedroom, leaning against the closed door.

"What have you gotten yourself into now?" I mumble.

Be careful, troublemaker. The voice in my head sounds like Devlin's.

Time to adapt once more. But are the rules the same?

Are we even playing the same game?

TWENTY-THREE
DEVLIN

After discarding the towel and changing into briefs, I sit on my bed with the crinkled magazine page we wrote our contract on.

Having Blair here is more intense than I imagined. She smelled so enticingly sweet as I caged her against the wall. Walking away from her in the hall when I had her right where I wanted her was a challenge. But after forcing her to come here, I couldn't ignore the voice in my head telling me to leave her be. I think it might be my conscience.

Who knew the rusty old thing was alive and kicking?

It's forcing an awareness of what a dick I've been to the front of my mind, messing with my plans.

Releasing a sigh, I trace Blair's signature. It doesn't have an ounce of the quirky way Blair used to write her name with a star. Now it's neat, straightforward, and to the point. Has she changed as much as I have since we were kids?

The question lingers as I map the letters in her name. Even with my penchant for stargazing, I'm nothing like the boy I was then.

The sadness I carried grew with me, festered, and pushed me into the shadows.

We might be too different from the kids we were and the people we've become to ever regain the brief bond we shared. Are we even the same now as we were when we made this contract?

I picture Blair's feisty expression as I proposed this arrangement, her arms tied to the stool.

My tongue swipes over my lip as I search for the same hate I harbored for her that night. There's even less than before. It's bleeding out of me by the day, replaced by the urge to chase her for another taste of her lips.

The creased page makes a faint sound as I shift to my feet.

If I put it away, I won't have to face why she's here. I can just enjoy it while it lasts.

Crossing to the closet panels along the wall, I tuck the contract out of sight beneath a stack of shirts on a low shelf. Rubbing the back of my neck, I return to the bed.

So much of my energy is focused on fighting for control, but I don't have it. I never did. Not just over Blair, but over myself, too. Everything I've done is a futile attempt to gain control.

It's always been easier to strive for it than face the reasons I want control so badly.

Blair is here, but now what? If I keep on the same path, she'll only meet a monster at the end. Blair deserves more than that.

If she sees my demons head on, there's no question about it —she'll walk away, just like the others.

Maybe I can change that.

TWENTY-FOUR
BLAIR

Waking up in an unfamiliar room makes me jolt out of bed in the morning. It takes a few seconds to catch up with my reality: living with Devlin.

Climbing out of bed, I tug on a pair of leggings and a gray wide neck t-shirt that drapes off my shoulder.

Turns out, Devlin is easy enough to avoid in such a big house. I give him the slip as I explore it more in the light of day. I learn where the exits are and commit them to memory, mapping out the giant property until his commanding voice fills the house over an intercom system.

"Get your ass to the kitchen for breakfast, troublemaker," Devlin demands. His wicked chuckle fills the room. "Don't make me come find you. I'll hunt you down and take whatever I want as a finder's fee."

I scramble to the kitchen, wary of what he might do.

Devlin stands at the stove with a fresh pan of eggs. The shock of him making food stalls me in the doorway. The savory scent of bacon makes my mouth water, and I inch closer. A strange warmth blooms in my chest at the sight of him dishing out the food he made.

"Do you want to eat or not?" He sounds amused.

"It smells really good. Thanks for cooking."

Devlin hums, setting a plate of toast down. Circling the island, he clasps my wrist and pulls me over, where he has two plates set side by side.

It's so...domestic. Normal. Like a family used to eating together. I've only ever had that with Mom.

The blooming warmth expands.

"Wow, you really cut up fresh fruit, too? I don't think I ever pictured someone like you cutting up your own fruit."

"I like cooking. My aunt taught me." Devlin takes the seat next to me, the one he tied me to the first time I was here. "You're not going to starve while you're here. Eat."

"You didn't poison it, did you?"

Rolling his eyes, Devlin crunches into a piece of bacon.

It smells divine. Who knew the devil could cook?

I take a bite and clap my hand over my mouth, groaning involuntarily.

A small satisfied smirk curls Devlin's mouth.

We eat in silence for a few minutes. I'm having a full on experience. It's a surprise that he would lift a finger, but finding out he actually is a good cook is blowing my mind.

"I'm going to go for a run before the party later," Devlin says, breaking the quiet.

"You are?" I perk up.

Devlin quirks a thick brow. "I assume you'll follow me on

the trail anyway, so you might as well join me. Did you bring shoes?"

"Yeah." I don't mean to sound so breathless, but I haven't gone for a real run in so long. "I want to come, too."

We finish eating and the world doesn't grind to a halt. It's a miracle. Maybe we stopped being bitter enemies when I wasn't looking, but it's hard to keep hating the guy who fed you gloriously fluffy eggs and paid for your mom's medical expenses.

We're not friends, but maybe we could be. If he can apologize for being the world's biggest jerk for the last few years. I'll even say I'm sorry for attempting to steal his car.

When we're on the trail an hour later, the fresh air fills my lungs.

Stretching my legs and pumping my muscles as we jog through the mountain trail is amazing. It's the most I've felt like myself in months.

My legs burn in a way I love as we push on.

Devlin keeps pace with me as I learn the unfamiliar path. His perfect running form is as precise as the rest of his cultivated habits, only giving the impression he's loose and effortless while he cuts through the trail with amazing speed.

I find myself watching him more than the trail at some points. He's a beautiful runner, his tousled black fringe pinned back from his face by an elastic band.

When we near the end and his house comes into view, he darts ahead.

"Hey!"

"Race you!" Devlin throws over his shoulder.

I follow, thriving on the burst of competition. I pull on my reserves to close the distance. Once I pass him, he lets out a grunt as he chases me. I look back, finding him in hot pursuit with a wicked gleam in his eye.

Our race ends with me beating him to the front step by a hair.

"Yes!" I gasp.

"You cheated," Devlin snarks.

"You cheated! You started without saying anything. I won fair and square because I'm fast."

An easy laugh puffs out of Devlin. "Yeah, you are."

As we pant, I can't hold back a wide smile while I catch my breath.

Maybe living with Devlin won't be such a hardship.

TWENTY-FIVE
BLAIR

By early afternoon, the sun is baking the world alive as Lucas pulls the Jeep into the parking lot at the beach. Party music drifts through the air, along with boisterous laughter from people already here. The sun sits high in the sky and a slight breeze makes small waves lap across the surface of the lake.

"Oh my god, I can't wait to dive into that water," Gemma groans, fanning herself on the bench seat beside me. "I hope it's frigid as fuck."

"Mood," I agree quietly, tying my hair into a sloppy bun on top of my head to keep it off my neck. "Where is fall?"

"That pumpkin spice bitch better show up soon," Gemma says. "I just want to wear flannel and my leather jacket."

I smile. I really missed Gemma and her sharp humor.

Devlin and Lucas hop out of the front of Lucas' Jeep to grab the cooler they stocked before we left.

When we arrived at Lucas' place earlier, Gemma had blinked in surprise that Devlin showed up with me in tow, then gave me a goofy grin, hooking her arm with mine. "What the hell is going on?"

I shoved her as we got into the Jeep to ride around the lake to get to the beach. "*Nothing.*"

"Uh huh. Sure." Gemma and Lucas had exchanged a look of silent communication in the mirror. They certainly have come far from when they first met and were at each other's throats constantly. "So much changes when you leave for college, huh, babe?"

Lucas cut a sly glance at Devlin, who flipped off his cousin. Lucas chuckled. "So much."

Devlin wouldn't let me skip this beach party. I tried hiding in the closet, but he found me and dragged me out, hoisting me over his shoulder while I protested.

A few high-pitched squeals pierce the air, followed by splashing.

As we hover by the back of the Jeep, I twist my hands on the strap of Gemma's beach bag. She takes one of my hands and tugs me toward the beach.

"We're grabbing a spot!" Gemma calls over her shoulder.

"Right behind you, Gem," Lucas says.

I never told Devlin I hadn't packed a bathing suit, but somehow a bikini in my size was waiting for me on my door handle when I woke up this morning.

It's fucking red.

At least I have Gemma with me for moral support. Her pretty blonde hair falls to her shoulders in french braids. She picks out a semi-shaded spot on the soft sand—totally shipped in, a high altitude lake like this should have a rocky beach—and gestures for her striped bag.

"I packed a ton of sunscreen. I'm not dealing with a sunburnt Lucas. He got so sulky on our vacation to Jamaica over the summer. The first day, too! Pitiful beefcake."

Gemma shakes her head, but she sports a fond smile, and her eyes are faraway. She's in love.

I hand over the bag, losing my reason to stand around and keep my oversized t-shirt on to cover up.

"Take that off." Gemma gestures to the shirt that hits above my knees. "I'll do your back."

Chewing on the inside of my cheek, I cast a glance around the crowded beach. Bishop chases Bailey, Nina, and a third girl through the shallows, splashing around. Half the soccer team is here, plus most of the popular crowd that bow down at Bishop and Devlin's shared throne.

They don't matter. It's fine.

Crossing my arms and grabbing the hem of the big shirt, I peel it overhead, tossing it down on the blanket Gemma spread in the sand.

"Damn, girl," Gemma says admirably. "Will you pose on the rocks later? You know I have my camera with me. This look is killer and I need to capture it."

"Stop, it's not even mine." I cover my face. I peek between my fingers. "It's okay?"

"Dude." Gemma gives me a once over. "You look hot."

A relieved exhale leaves me. I peer down at the red bikini. It's bold, something I'd never have gone for. The sun kisses my pale skin. I'll probably have fresh freckles dotting my cheeks by sunset.

Gemma shucks off her white shorts and strips out of her Oak Ridge College tank top, revealing a military green bikini that crosses over her boobs. I feel less out of place with Gemma beside me. She's used to the party scene, but it's never been for me. I kind of wish Lucas brought his sweet pug dog, because he's my best friend at these things.

"So," Gemma drawls, squinting at me. "What's the deal with you and Dev? Are you, like, a thing now?"

"I, uh." There isn't a straight answer I can offer. "It's...complicated."

"Hah, I know what that's like," Gemma says with a burst of laughter. "But seriously. Is he being chill? Do I need to kick his balls into his teeth?"

"No. He's a smart ass dick, but I handled it." I'm not about to have Gemma fight my battles for me.

"Good. You'd tell me if you needed help, right? Because I have your back, even if I'm not in Ridgeview."

"Yeah." I grant her a thankful smile.

"Cool. Now come here, pasty."

"I'm coming for you, sweetheart!" Lucas interrupts before Gemma has the chance to apply the sunscreen.

He grabs Gemma in his big, muscular embrace. With a deep whoop, he scoops her up and runs for the lake.

"Lucas, no!" Gemma shouts, breaking off into laughter. "You freakin' caveman!"

"Ayyy!" Bishop cheers further down the beach, following up with a coyote howl. "Get her, Saint! Watch out, a king and his queen coming through!"

Once they hit the water, she screams, wrapping her arms and legs around his waist as he free-falls backwards into the lake. The splash they make as they breach the surface is huge, spraying high. They look like the perfect couple, the handsome ex-football-star-turned-architect-student and the sassy photographer he fell hard for. No one would know their start was rocky and fraught with tension.

Bending down, I grab the abandoned tube of sunscreen.

Strong arms wind around my waist, and a solid, warm bare chest plasters to my back. My heart skips a beat as Devlin's decadent, spicy musk envelopes me.

"Fuck," Devlin rasps in my ear, his lips pressed to my lobe. "I've changed my mind. No one else gets to see you like this. I have a dock. We can swim at the house. How much would it cost me to drag you home right now?"

The way he says *home* makes my stomach flip over.

"Too rich, even for your blood," I sass, turning my head to view him in my periphery. "You did everything to make sure I was here, so I'm staying. Plus, Gemma wants to take photos of me later."

Devlin splays a hand low over my stomach, skimming the bikini bottoms with his pinkie.

He groans in my ear. "You're in my color."

"You put me in this color."

He hums and nuzzles his nose into the crook of my neck.

His color.

Red, like the Porsche I attempted to steal.

I shouldn't like the sound of that, but it sends a thrill through me.

The pull of attraction is undeniable. He's hard to resist when he's being sexy like this. The thing between us has been steadily growing since that fake kiss. It's close to the breaking point. I can't ignore the way I feel when he's like this with me.

"Now I'm picturing you wearing my number." He sucks in a breath and I can feel a hardness pressing into my ass. "Shit. Add that to the list of what you should wear around the house. The cutoffs, those duck shorts, my soccer jersey."

He squeezes me and presses his dick into my ass.

"Devlin!" I swat his arm and put an inch of space between us. My heart thunders in my chest. This is the first time I've *felt* his attraction. We've been dancing around it. The elastic band that draws us together is pulling tighter. "That better not be what I think it is."

"No one can see." His exhale coasts over my neck, eliciting a shudder. I squeeze my thighs together. "If we were home, we could skinny dip."

I don't know where this is coming from. He's flirted a little with me, but this is the first time he's taken it farther than flirtation. The first time he sounded serious about taking a step over the line. Is he joking?

"Don't tease me."

"I'm not," he swears. "I'm not playing around at all. Christ, if I had you to myself right now...fuck." The muttered curse seems directed more to himself than to me. He drags his finger over the edge of the bikini bottoms. "Am I making your heart pound? Are you getting wet knowing I'm hard for you? What would I find if I slid my fingers into your bathing suit right now, little thief? Would you make my fingers as sticky as yours if I filled your pussy with them?"

My breath leaves me in an uneven gust, face flaming hot. Anyone could look over and see this going down. Devlin chuckles, the sinful sound vibrating against my neck, plucking at every string inside me, threatening to leave me a puddle of goo.

Licking my lips, I wriggle out of his hold. "I have to put sunscreen on. I don't want to burn."

"Hold up." Devlin plants his hand on my stomach and tugs me back against his body, keeping me in a possessive hold. "What's this?"

I shiver as his fingertips trace between my shoulder blades, mapping the outline of my star tattoo. I got it somewhere it wouldn't be seen often, since it was for me, not to look cool. Kind of like Devlin's, hidden on our bodies. A private piece we keep tucked away.

"You have a star," Devlin murmurs, wonder filling his tone.

"So do you."

Devlin traces the tattoo twice more. His touch ignites a thousand tiny sparks. They erupt across my skin in a rush. My breathing becomes shallow.

Across the beach, Bishop entertains the in-crowd. Nina and Trent sneak off to a secluded spot in the tree line. Gemma and Lucas share a kiss in the water, wrapped around each other in their own little world.

The whole time my body trembles as Devlin lavishes my tattoo with his rapt attention. It's not an erogenous zone I was aware of, but it's sending electric heat straight to my core. I slide my legs together, enduring the sensual torment for as long as I can.

"Devlin, what are you doing?" My voice is unsteady.

"Learning something new about you. Why a star?"

"I like them. I don't know, they were my thing when I was little."

Devlin pauses. "Is that all?"

I don't know what else to tell him. The truth is I was obsessed with stars to the point I would use them in my handwriting the same way other young girls put hearts on their *I*'s.

"It was just a thing. My mom promised me they were magic. It reminds me of her."

I still like the stars, even though I know the magic Mom filled my head with as a kid isn't real.

If it was, I would've gotten Mom and I out of our troubles countless times over with all the wishing I wasted on stars.

"That's it?" Devlin presses.

I shrug and it breaks the moment enveloping us in a bubble.

"Whatever. Forget it." Devlin sighs and takes the sunscreen from me, slathering it on my back where I can't reach.

I return the favor for him. Keeping my breathing even is a struggle as my palms glide over the muscles and sharp planes of his back. He keeps still for me, angling his head so I have a view of his chiseled jaw and a hint of his profile.

"Going to cop a feel while you're back there?" Devlin taunts.

"No," I mutter, pinching his side.

His deep laughter rolls over me like the blanket of the night sky, speckled in starlight. I like the sound of his laugh. Curling my fingers in hesitation for a beat, I let myself be as bold as my red bikini, soothing the spot I pinched and skating my touch up to his shoulders.

Devlin goes still, reaching back to brush his fingers against my hips.

Bishop interrupts, plopping onto Gemma's blanket with his attention glued to his phone.

"Thought you were chasing Bailey around," Devlin says mildly.

Bishop hitches a shoulder seconds later in a delayed reaction, humming. "Sean's into her. I've got something better, anyway."

As Bishop sprawls on his back, I catch a glimpse of his screen. My brows fly up.

"Holy shit. Is that—?"

Devlin steers us away before I finish my question. I'm pretty sure Bishop had a risqué photo of Thea Kennedy filling his screen. But that couldn't be right, Thea isn't the type to send a photo like *that*.

Especially to someone like Bishop, who is awful to her with his constant taunting.

"Pick your chin off the ground," Devlin murmurs, arm slung over my shoulder possessively as we approach Sean and Bailey near the smoking grill.

Bailey lights up. "Dev! You have to try Sean's kebabs, they're, like, so awesome."

Sean fist bumps Devlin as he flips the skewers. He winks at me, taking in my suit. "Looking good, Davis. You should hang with us more often. My parents have a boat we take out in the summer. You're definitely invited if you wear that."

Devlin grunts, snaking his arm tighter around me so I'm pressed against his side. I place a hand on his abdomen to keep my balance.

"Are you going to do the race with the guys?" Bailey asks Devlin.

He grants her a smile that's totally fake, the construction a precise facet of his mask. The shift is subtle from how he was when we were by the blanket alone. It's odd, but I can tell the difference.

"I don't know why they bother. They all know I'll win. I'm the fastest swimmer."

Devlin's muscles ripple beneath my hand as he puts on a show of flexing, falling into his usual arrogant persona. I'm tempted to pinch him again to bring back the real Devlin, the one that cooked me breakfast and accused me of cheating because I'm a faster runner.

"What about you, Blair?" Sean asks. It's the first time someone from his crowd has ever used my name. I blink at his perfect gleaming smile. His eyes drop to my chest. "Will you join the girls in cheering us on? You're so good at boosting the team morale." Sean drags his teeth over his lip. "I'd so want you to get me to the finish line."

Heavy innuendo laces his tone. Is he...flirting with me right now? What bizarre world have I woken up in where the popular guys want me around for more than someone to laugh at?

Narrowing my eyes, I smirk. "Hell no. I'd join the race and show you all up." I bump my hip against Devlin's. "Tell them how I beat you this morning in our race through the wooded trail."

This bikini is like a magic charm, instilling confidence I haven't used before. I've never cared to engage with these people, but something about Sean implying I'm only worth his time in a cheer uniform or a bikini lights a stubborn fire in me.

Glancing at Devlin, I find a proud, matching smirk on his face.

"You're a speedy little demon," he confirms. "You owe me a rematch before we go to bed tonight."

My lips part. Devlin might as well have told them I'm living with him. Even Bishop pointed out Devlin doesn't do girls in his bed, let alone allow them into his house.

Not that I've seen his bedroom. Yet.

Sean's eyes widen more as Devlin's hand glides down to rest scant inches above my ass. Devlin's smallest finger tucks into the band of my bikini bottoms. He claims me in front of his teammate with that single gesture. Other nearby guys from the soccer team and people from Nina's friend group glance our way with surprise etched in their expressions.

Devlin might flirt openly with girls at school, but he never makes a public gesture that screams *this is my girl, back off*.

Warmth floods my chest and pours through my body.

"Come on, let's take a walk." Devlin threads his fingers with mine.

He leads me away from the others, taking us to the wet sand where a passing speedboat creates a ripple of waves that rush over our feet. Devlin keeps holding my hand.

Ahead of us, Gemma has her camera out, taking photos of the party and the landscape. Lucas stalks up and she snaps the shutter. His predatory grin spreads right before he scoops her into his arms. Gemma's shoulders shake with amusement as

Lucas' hands roam her body. They kiss, their lips connecting lazily.

"I should buy you an engagement ring," Devlin says. "It'll beat back the other guys who think they can touch what's mine."

I sputter. "Sorry—*what?*"

Things just went from zero to sixty.

"What?" Devlin smirks. "They already suspect I must be fucking you if you're here."

My eyes narrow. That escalated quickly. He was so sweet all morning, but this taste of the viper lurking beneath Devlin's mask reminds me I shouldn't trust him.

"First of all, fuck you. I'm not wearing a fake engagement ring. We're eighteen. That's insane." I pull my hand from his. The corners of his mouth tighten, but it serves him right. "If you buy a ring, I'll hock it at a pawn show for the cash the first chance I get."

Leaving Devlin with my snarky retort, I find a secluded spot far down the beach, away from the bustle of the party. I sit on the sand, sticking my feet in the water. From this distance, I can watch whatever goes on.

Trent and Sean attack each other with neon water guns, then turn on the girls, squirting Nina's big boobs. She pouts, then gets all the guys howling like coyotes for her as she piles her long wet hair on her head, showing off her curves.

Someone turns the music on and a dance party starts up. Devlin hovers around the edge of it for a while, a plastic red cup dangling in his grip. Bailey and Nina both approach him. I hold my breath, digging my toes into the sand.

He's not yours, I remind myself. He might want to claim me as his territory so none of the other boys come onto me, but Devlin isn't my boyfriend.

I expect him to hook up with Nina. She flashes her bedroom eyes at every guy here.

But Devlin walks off to stand with his feet in the water, surprising me.

Still. He's not mine.

I stamp out the happy bubble that has no right to exist.

TWENTY-SIX
BLAIR

For a while I watch the clouds drift by. The sun warms my skin and the sand. I could fall asleep like this.

Gemma's yelp draws my attention. She's running toward me, splashing through the water's edge. Lucas chases her and Devlin follows close behind.

"Come on, B!" Gemma calls as she approaches.

Gemma and Lucas cut through the water. Devlin reaches me, grabbing my hand. He hauls me to my feet with a secret smile playing on his lips, bringing out his dimples.

"What's happening?" I gasp.

"War," Devlin says, mouth pressed to my ear from behind. His arms lock around my waist and he carts me deeper into the water, heading for Lucas and Gemma. The lake is chilly and refreshing as it licks at my hips. "We're playing chicken. I need you for this. You're on my team against Lucas and Gem."

Before I can answer, Devlin dives under the water, hoisting me onto his shoulders. I shriek, nearly losing my balance as he stands. He secures his hands around my legs, wading deeper into the water.

"Wait—Devlin!" My only choice is to hold on tight while his splayed palms burn into my skin like iron brands. "I don't know how to play chicken."

Instead of pool parties in the summer, I rode a bike around Ridgeview looking for cans to take to the recycling center. I'd do anything when I first noticed how much Mom watched our funds.

While other kids had a regular childhood playing games, I spent most of mine forgetting about idealistic dreams and learning harsh realities.

"It's easy. You wrestle Gemma. Lucas and I are the support. You win when you knock Gemma off her cocky steed."

"I heard that," Lucas snarks.

Devlin laughs.

I have no idea where to put my hands, so I hold on to his hair. The wet strands glide through my fingers. "She's stronger than me. What if she knocks me down first?"

Devlin squeezes my thighs. "You're scrappy. You can do it."

The resolute confidence in his tone pierces into my heart, putting a crack in the stone wall I keep around it. Devlin believes in me.

"Okay."

"Bring it on!" Gemma crows.

"We're taking you down," Lucas promises.

Devlin slides his fingers higher up my legs, tickling the inside of my thighs. "Ready to fight for it?"

My breath shudders out of me at his distracting touch. "Yeah. Let's do it."

The four of us circle each other. Water laps at Lucas and Devlin's stomachs, though we're pretty far out from the shore. Gemma comes at me once we're in range. We clasp hands, pushing and pulling to win the battle.

A laugh breaks free as I try different tactics to throw her off her game.

"Come on," Devlin heckles, throwing his own distractions. He moves us forward and back, creating an unwavering base of support so I don't feel like I'm falling. "You stop playing football and all of your footwork goes to shit."

"Shut up, you little dick." Lucas grins, swiping at Devlin. "Damn it! You can do it, babe."

Gemma squirms for better leverage. I lock my shins against Devlin's back, giving a good push. Lucas wobbles, but finds his balance again. We back up a few paces, luring our opponents into deeper water.

Devlin's fingers creep higher, tearing a gasp from my throat.

"What are you doing?" I hiss. He keeps going, teasing the sensitive skin of my inner thighs. "Devlin!"

Heat pools between my legs. I shift to relieve the building pressure, but it only gives Devlin room to graze his fingertips against the edge of my pussy. I bite down on the sound threatening to escape.

"You're crazy."

"You make me this way," Devlin murmurs, his touch teasing in a way that makes me want more. "Is your pussy soaking wet again?"

"Focus on the game, you heathen." I yank on his hair. My eyes flutter in surprise when he groans quietly. I squeeze my thighs to trap his hand. "Let's win this."

"Fuck, yes, angel. Once we win, you're all mine."

I gulp at the filthy hint underneath his promise. My cheeks are on fire, embarrassed and turned on. The thrill of the stolen moment climbs my spine like the flash of lightning.

"Quit flirting over there and fight us!" Lucas calls, closing in on our position.

My stomach swoops. Are we that obvious?

"Show everyone what a fighter you are, Blair." Devlin tilts his head, squinting at me with one eye closed against the sunshine. "They're all watching you."

Glancing to the shoreline, I see we've drawn a crowd.

Gemma lets out a wild yell as she and Lucas rush us. I throw my hands up as we crash together. We both grunt and giggle as we fight for victory. Gemma's smile is infectious. The happy bubble I crushed earlier expands and pops inside.

This is fun. It feels nice to sit on Devlin's shoulders, to feel his steady grip on my legs as my best friend laughs with me.

"Ah!"

Gemma gives me a look of surprise when I twist her hands to the side. She tips over Lucas's shoulders, taking him down with her because her legs are twined around his chest.

"Winners!" Devlin pumps his fists in the air, spinning in place.

He leans back and we crash into the water. I splutter as he pulls me to the surface with a sure grip. Water clings to my lashes and clumps his inky black ones, creating tiny spikes around his eyes. Droplets of water dot his lips. He can touch the bottom of the lake, but it's too deep for me to reach without treading water.

"We won." Pinning me with his gaze, Devlin grips under my thighs and wraps my legs around his waist.

Under the water, I feel his abs between my thighs, pressed against my pussy. Devlin drops his rapt attention to my lips.

I'm trapped by the tether tugging between us.

There's nowhere to go. Nowhere I *want* to go. I'm right where I should be.

Devlin takes my chin between his thumb and forefinger. My breath catches as he meets my gaze. There's a silent question in his eyes. One I need to answer.

This time there's no promise of payment.

It's different. And I want it.

I lean forward a fraction, pleading without words. Devlin releases a rough sound and swoops in, sealing his lips over mine. I close my eyes as we come together in a rush of lips and tongues.

Devlin's kiss is like a black hole. It swallows me up, and I'm diving in head first, desperate for more.

If Devlin staked his claim over me in front of everyone earlier with one small gesture, he devours me with his kiss, branding me from the inside out. His tongue puts me under a spell as his strong arm keeps me in place against his hard body.

We're so absorbed in kissing, we don't hear the others until someone drives us apart with a loud coyote howl—the universal Silver Lake High call. It's Bishop.

Gemma and Lucas are on the other side of us with matching expressions, seeming pleasantly surprised by this development between Devlin and I.

I touch my lips. I can't believe I kissed Devlin, and the world didn't end in fury and hellfire.

Devlin squeezes me and grumbles under his breath. "Goddamn cockblockers."

"You can make out later," Bishop says slyly.

He splashes us and I gasp, clinging to Devlin.

"Oh, it's on, Bishop," Lucas says, joining in with his own splash attack.

"Hold on." Devlin maneuvers me around to hang from his back, piggybacking me to free his hands for retaliation. I snort at his flailing attacks. "Are you just going to sit back there like a damn barnacle?"

"I don't know." I lean up, affecting a regal tone. "I think I like this throne."

Devlin reaches back to hike me higher, taking the opening to squeeze my ass. "Fight back with me, angel."

A wide grin stretches my mouth.

Fight *with* Devlin. Not against him.

Gemma joins the fray with an unbridled laugh, ducking behind Lucas when I direct a wave of water her way. The five of us horse around, flinging water in every direction.

It has me laughing so hard my sides hurt. I lean heavily on Devlin to catch my breath. He shoots me a charming smile over his shoulder, whipping us around without warning so I have to hang onto his shoulders while he sends water flying.

A yell builds in my chest and I release it, tipping my head back to the sky.

My heart is happy and full for the first time in a really long while.

TWENTY-SEVEN
DEVLIN

A few weeks pass and Blair settles into living at my house. Such a simple thing shouldn't make me as happy as it does. The house isn't so still with her there.

Blair's vanilla scent lingers in the rooms, in the hallway between our bedrooms, in the bathroom. I don't care that much for sweets, but I would gorge on her. I've become an unhinged madman, hunting it down when she disappears with a paperback.

Whenever she isn't visiting her mom, I've found her sitting with her feet in the natural rock-edged hot tub on the lower level of the teak deck out back with her nose in a beat up paperback and her toes splashing in the heated water. She's also claimed the low cushioned ledge in the open layout lounge area, sprawling on her stomach beneath the large window.

It's become a new game, prowling the house to find the spots she hides in.

Our joint runs quickly becoming a routine on the weekends. Soccer practice isn't enough to tire out my thoughts, so I train with additional runs to keep out of my head. Blair likes running, too. I think it's the same for her. There's something about the burn in your legs and the rhythm of your breathing while you push yourself that is an addictive form of therapy.

Our runs are filled with bursts of sprints where we race each other. The competition flirts on tipping into something else. Blair makes me want to chase her until I catch her.

I've ducked a couple of invitations from Aunt Lottie and Uncle Ed to come across the lake to their house for dinner. I think they're picking up on the change in my habits, since I've had dinner with them at least once a week since the start of senior year.

At school, I keep Blair close. The idiotic puppets accept the change easily enough, because they defer to my rules. If I turned on Blair again, they'd spin a tale about how it was my plan all along. But no matter how much I remind myself of the original objective, Blair turns my goals inside out. I search for an ounce of hate for her, but it's a dried up well.

The only thing left is the need to kiss those pouty lips.

It's an urge that bleeds into all of my actions.

In our English class, I partner with her instead of Bishop for paired reading work. He's too busy giving into his new obsession with Thea anyway. Blair takes this in stride with minimal sass.

The stubborn fight in her rears its head when I pull her to my center table in the cafeteria. I buy her lunch, but she still tries to use her food account, stirring my annoyance. This is one way of apologizing for being a dick up to this point, but she remains suspicious when I pay for the nicer lunch options available to the students that can afford to eat off the standard menu—something almost no one at this school eats from except for Blair.

Macy's condition has stabilized. Uncle Craig couldn't tell me much, but I overheard his phone call with Blair. She visits her mom every other day after school.

When she goes to visit, I follow her and watch from the car —one from Dad's collection that doesn't get much use so she doesn't notice me tailing her junker. Macy's corner room window provides the perfect view to see Blair's tender smile as she spends time with her mom.

I grip the wheel whenever I watch. The jealousy of her relationship with her mom is still there, but when it swirls through my chest on these stakeouts there's something new. An emotion I don't understand, but whenever I look at Blair it's present. Unavoidable.

The feeling entwines with the whisper in my head to stop being an ass.

Nothing has happened since the kiss at the beach party the weekend she moved in. Not for lack of trying on my part. I want more. All the time. I'm like one of Pavlov's dogs, attuned to her quick and subtle movements, turned on by every little move she makes.

Blair isn't like the other girls I've fucked, though. I need to work out a better way to seduce my little thief so I have her falling apart in my arms. My cock grows hard simply picturing it.

If I can't have her yet, I'll have her in my fantasies when I jerk off.

* * *

An instinct has been bubbling in me for a few days. It nearly jumps out of my mouth when I come across Blair putting together a snack, one of her paperbacks open and turned over on the kitchen counter to save her place.

She's wearing my SLHS varsity soccer zip up jacket, the cuffs giving her sweater paws. My heart lurches in a tailspin at the sight.

I've given her actions to make up for my behavior, but I need to do more. Maybe I should give her my words, too.

"Oh, hey." Blair's lips purse in excitement as she sprinkles seasoning over the bowl of popcorn. "I was going to read on the deck."

Say something.

I flounder, searching for a way to not blurt out what I have floating around in my head. I've never apologized before. Every ounce of strategy flees now that I need to craft my words carefully.

"Want me to light the fire pit?"

Blair hums in consideration as she fills up a glass of water. "Thanks, that would be cool."

"I see you've commandeered my hoodie." I circle the island and pluck at the sleeve.

"It totally looks better on me."

"It does." I swallow.

The material almost covers her athletic shorts, giving the illusion that she's wearing my jacket and nothing else, driving me wild with the runaway thought.

"Listen, there's been something I've wanted to say." I tug on my ear as Blair tosses popcorn in the air, aiming to catch it in her open mouth. Heat shoots into my groin. "Blair."

"Yeah?"

"I want to—I've been—" This is ridiculous. My tongue

refuses to cooperate with my brain. Why is this so hard? "The way I've treated you..."

Blair's eyebrows hike up. "Dude. Get it together. This is weird to witness. It's ruining my image of Mr. Control Freak."

I huff out a laugh. *Tell me about it.*

"I shouldn't have," I wave my hand, "been such a shit to you. The things I've said about you, I mean."

Blair stares at me as she gathers her inky hair into a ponytail. "Are you having a stroke?"

I scrub a hand over my face, peeking at her through my splayed fingers. "Maybe. This is harder than I thought."

"What is?"

My stomach flips over. "Apologizing."

"Is *that* what you're trying to do?" Blair laughs. "Damn, you suck at this."

"I mean it, though. It wasn't right."

Blair shrugs and eyes me warily. "Are you saying you want to end the, um..." She gestures between us. "The deal."

"What? No."

I muffle a groan behind my hand as I cover my mouth. This is a disaster. She's not getting it at all. I'm just trying to say I'm sorry for treating her like a bug and playing stupid pranks on her. Is there some way to make her believe me? How can I make up for what I've done?

"Should I leave the popcorn stuff out?"

The water glass catches my eye and spurs an impulsive thought. I always strive for control, but right now this feels right. If she doesn't understand, maybe I can show her. We're not in the cafeteria, but this will have to do for now.

I swipe Blair's water while she rummages in the fridge. "Blair."

She turns to me and I dump the glass over my head, blinking through the rush of cold water soaking my head.

Blair's jaw drops. "Wh—"

She busts out laughing, hugging her stomach.

Water drips from my hair into my eye. "I mean it."

"Okay, you mean it." There's a light in Blair's eyes as she reaches up to push the wet clumps of hair back from my forehead. "You're so weird."

A weight lifts from my shoulders and a soft smile curves my mouth. "I'll grab some logs to put in the firepit."

Blair gathers her popcorn, book, and a new glass of water to take out on the deck. My chest feels warm as I watch her go.

* * *

Later, a rare conversation with Dad drove me outside. Like an idiot, I answered the call. Any morsel of attention Dad offers makes me forget logic and the patterns he follows.

All he wanted to talk about was his expectations for me. He has my whole life planned out. Pre-med. Medical school. Continuing the renowned reputation the Murphy name carries in the medical field.

Fuck anything I might want. Fuck the fact I don't really want to do whatever he expects. Fuck that I'm his son.

Dad only cares about his goals and plans.

I sit in my spot on the roof outside of my bedroom window with a lit cigarette dangling from my fingers. I take a drag and tip my head back to blow out a plume of smoke. The nicotine takes off the edge.

Agitation grips me, making me jittery and belligerent. I'm filled with an angry energy, prepared to whip the jagged lash at anything.

It's always like this whenever I talk to Dad. Mom, too, to a lesser extent. At least she pretends she has a maternal bone in her body, but it's never been enough.

They both leave me hollow, opening the chasm of my insides to brim with the lonely rage engulfing me, drowning me beneath choppy waters. I can't keep my head above the current.

Squinting at the sky, I spot a shooting star. *Make a wish.*

It's stupid, but I started doing it as a kid and can't stop.

A heavy sigh leaves me. *But I didn't just start it, did I?* It's because of Blair. Weeks later and I'm still reeling from remembering our brief connection, and realizing she's the reason my private ritual began thanks to what Blair told me when we were kids.

Her encouragement to wish on stars was my single saving grace that kept me from being swallowed all these years.

I massage my temple with my thumb knuckle and let the cigarette burn down to the butt, mesmerized by the ash.

I've told the stars so much in my life.

They wait for me as I peer at the sky. Blair's freckles pop into my head. They remind me of the stars.

I lick my lips and rub my fingertips together.

Blair was my first wish, but I always thought it didn't come true.

I also wished for a brother and sister. Lucas was always there, but I wanted more family to play with. I even wished to be a part of Lucas' family instead of my own.

I begged the shooting stars to send my parents home for longer than a few days. To make them talk to me. To take an interest in me past how much money they've sent, how my grades are, and if I'll go pre-med.

I'm their son, not one of their petri dish research experiments.

The work they do as doctors might be important to help so many people, but can't a kid just want the attention of his parents?

None of the wishes ever work, but something about

sending my deepest, secret desires to distant balls of burning gas and fragments of rock falling into the atmosphere makes me feel better. It's a ritual that calms the ocean of bitter pain for a brief moment.

Tossing the cigarette into the ashtray I brought out, I think about calling Bishop or Lucas to see what either of them are up to. I've calmed down somewhat from talking to Dad, but speaking to them would help.

"Here you are. I was looking for you."

I whip my head to the side. Blair climbs through the window nimbly and navigates the narrow ledge that leads over to my spot on the roof. The wind disturbs her ponytail as she stands over me, taking in the view.

The vulnerability burns. No one's ever found my spot. I swallow.

"Are you going to sit?"

Blair settles next to me. "It's cool up here."

"Yeah." I try to picture it with fresh eyes, forgetting everything I've confessed up here. "I come up here to think."

"There's a spot in the woods between the trailer park and the convenience store where I used to hide out when I didn't want to be found."

Blair tucks her knees to her chest and wraps her arms around them. She's wearing the same oversized hoodie from the night her mom collapsed, her fingertips poking out of the big sleeves. I pinch the pant leg of my sweatpants to keep from reaching out to take her hand.

We're quiet for a few minutes. My pulse turns erratic. I'm plagued by an awareness of her presence and every movement.

"I know your secret," Blair murmurs in a conspiratorial tone.

I dig my grip into my sweatpants, out of view. She can't.

"Doubt it," I scoff. I tap my chest, near my heart and the shooting star tattoo. "I keep them all under lock and key."

Blair rests her chin on her knees. Her gaze holds mine. "You want everyone to think you're this carefree playboy. But you're not. Your secret is that you care. More than anyone."

My stomach drops at the truth in her assessment. In my pocket, my phone sits heavy like lead. Three texts sent to Dad after our phone call go unanswered.

The puppets at school believe my mask is the real me, but it's not. They see what I want them to. Blair's right. The truth is I try hard as hell not to care about anything. I compartmentalize it all, burying the hurts deep where they can't get to me.

How does she do that? How does she always see through the armor I've constructed to protect myself from disappointment?

Maybe Blair hides a chained up monster, too, because her little claws scrape at the box I've tucked all of the weakness into. Sometimes it seeps out, like Pandora's chaos escaping a cage not strong enough to trap the torrent of horror desperate to get out and spread.

Blair's voice is soft when she continues. "I think it's why you try so hard to control everything around you. Down to the exact curve of your smiles."

I laugh jaggedly to play off how she blindsides me when I least expect it. Dragging a hand through my hair, I turn my attention up to the sky. "I didn't let you sit up in my secret spot with me so you could psychoanalyze me. Quit it, or you're getting the boot."

"Sorry."

More surprised that she apologized to me than the fact she figured me out, I cut a quick look at her. She fiddles with the cuffs of her hoodie.

"Me too," I offer.

The rest gets stuck in my throat. I mean all of it—sorry for internalizing so much anger because she left, sorry for making her my favorite target, sorry for trying to drive her to leave all these years.

"I'm sorry," I repeat, trying to push all of my meaning into the apology. "I know I muddled it before and you didn't believe me, but I am. Do I need to find another glass of water to dump on myself?"

Blair laughs, the bright sound drifting in the night. "No need, though I think I do prefer you wet." She sends me a sly look from the corner of her eye. After a beat, she flaps her hand. "I guess I'm sorry for making a move on your car, too."

"I'm not." Blair's brows lift in surprise. I shrug. "If you didn't break in, I wouldn't have you here right now."

It's fucked up that my revenge plan led to this, but I can't say I'm mad at the turn in the tide.

She smiles, the corner of her mouth tugging up. "I like it up here."

The stars blink down at us, faintly twinkling.

I haven't asked the stars for the thing I want most of all lately. The secret I thought Blair figured out.

It's impossible, too much for even the magic of a wish.

Blair studies at me with an unreadable look, the moon painting the side of her face in pale light.

My stupid, messed up heart thumps, aching at her beauty. Her full lips slide together to contain whatever she's holding back from saying.

"What?"

She blinks like she's coming out of a daze. "You reminded me of someone I used to know. A long time ago."

"Who?" I swallow past the shards stabbing my throat.

Does she remember, too?

"A sad boy I knew once. I told him about shooting stars."

Her brow wrinkles. "You have the same kind of look in your eyes."

Tell her, my mind screams. *Tell her you are that boy. That you knew her, too, but she left.*

Like the others. All of them leave. No one stays.

Part of me doesn't want to tell her. If I do, she'll see my weaknesses. She could leave again. She *will* leave eventually. Because she's not here for me. Blair is only here for other reasons.

Not because I'm worthy of her company.

Not because I've earned her trust or her affection.

Not because I deserve any second I steal with her.

My wretched heart lurches as I stare at her.

Maybe it was always coming, wanting her as much as my next breath. I've just smothered it. Learned to survive around it.

Now it's a force I can't contain, the need for her living in my veins and my bones like vines wrapping around every part of me.

I rub my fingers together and turn my attention to the sky. When I spot a shooting star, I point it out. "There's one. See it?"

Blair hums in acknowledgement. "There's another. Mom used to read me this book about a falling star." Her expression turns fond and tender, like it does when she visits her mom in the hospital. "It was one of my favorites."

I study her profile in the moonlight.

The urge swirling inside becomes too much. I've fucked around with plenty of girls, but I need something else right now.

The words leave me before I've fully formed the thought. "I'll pay you five grand to sleep in my bed tonight. Just sleep."

Blair's head snaps around. "W-what?"

"Five thousand," I repeat, clenching my jaw.

If Blair's stubborn, I'm a stone wall. I'm selfish and I can't help myself.

It's the first order I've officially given her since she moved in, because I want a guarantee.

If this is my only chance, I want it. This time I'm not waiting on the stars to grant my wishes, I'll take it for myself.

"What's your answer?"

Blair slides her pouty lips together, sucking the bottom one into her mouth. "Yes."

TWENTY-EIGHT
BLAIR

We climb through the window into his bedroom. He goes first. I take his hand to balance as I hop down from the wide windowsill.

It's a surprise he doesn't have much in here. It barely looks like a teenager's bedroom.

The first few years after Dad left, I would pick catalogues out of the trash, imagining the house Mom and I would get if we won the lottery. I went through a period where all I wanted was fairy lights to hang over my bed and a sheer purple curtain to drape around it.

All that money, and Devlin's room has a big bed that's meticulously made, a wall of modern dark wooden panels that I think are closet doors, and a stack of books on the nightstand next to a pack of cigarettes.

It looks more like a hotel room than someone's bedroom. Clean, but impersonal. Like he can't express himself in his own private space.

Even I have some photos, my book collection, and some print outs from the library of my favorite art pieces from around the world in my room.

I take off my hoodie, draping it on a lacquered live-edge wood bench by the closet. If I sleep in it, I'll overheat. I'm left in leggings and my SLHS girls track team t-shirt.

Padding over to the nightstand, I tilt my head to read the spines of the books. The Social Animal, Influence: Science and Practice, and The Lucifer Effect: Understanding How Good People Turn Evil are the top three in the stack.

"You really like psychology, huh?"

Devlin hovers at the bottom of the bed. "I like knowing how things work. Human behavior is..." He circles the mattress and stops in front of me. Cupping my shoulders, he pushes me to sit down. "Fascinating."

I watch as he strips out of his gray henley with languid movements, leaving his chest bare. The sweatpants hang low on his hips.

My mouth goes dry. The cut V in his hips leads down into the waistband of his sweats. His body is chiselled like a work of art, lithe with athletic strength.

I tuck my hands under my thighs to keep from reaching out to trace his abs.

Devlin has claimed me with a kiss, but that's as far as it's gone between us. Kissing me in the lake doesn't mean he wants me.

"Scoot back," Devlin rumbles. "That's my side."

A flutter tickles my stomach as I move across the mattress. "You have a *side*? What are you, eighty-five?"

Devlin peels back the covers and climbs into bed. "I like my side."

Once we lay down, Devlin turns out the lights, plunging us in darkness. The only sound in the room is our out of sync breathing. Devlin breathes, then me. Inhale, exhale.

The distance between us is palpable, like a wall I could press against. It's only several inches, but it might as well be a cavern.

I'm about to open my mouth and say something to break the awkward air, but Devlin's hand lands on my hip. His touch is hot, seeping through my leggings.

"Okay?" Devlin's normally authoritative voice is hushed and hoarse.

"Yeah. It's okay."

Devlin doesn't just take an inch, he takes a mile. His arm snakes around my waist, dragging my back against his bare chest. He's like an octopus, wrapping himself around me. For someone I once believed was cold like marble, his body heat envelopes me.

A rough sound chokes out of Devlin. His breathing turns tense and edgy. He slides his big hand beneath my t-shirt, caressing my belly and up between my breasts. I don't have a bra on. His thumb traces the edge of one breast, drawing a gasp from me. My nipples pucker, the friction of my t-shirt making me squirm in a burst of oversensitivity.

"Devlin," I breathe.

He said he only wanted to sleep. Does he want more? Does he want *me*?

Devlin's nose buries against the back of my neck. His stiffness relaxes and he hugs me tighter. He nudges his knee between my legs and I can feel his half-hard cock against my ass.

I shift my hips, rolling them against his length.

Devlin growls, his arm locking tighter around me. He presses his hips against mine in response, his dick growing harder.

"Sleep, troublemaker."

I bite my lip. The spark of fire he ignited in my stomach leaves my skin tight and my clit throbbing. We're really going to sleep like this?

"What about—"

Devlin cuts off my question about his cock with another grumbling sound, nipping at my neck. His tongue follows, making me arch against him.

"Christ," he groans into my neck. "Go the fuck to sleep."

My body protests. I want him to stop teasing the curve of my breasts with absent touches because it's driving me crazy.

"You wanted me in here."

His teeth and tongue graze my neck, torturing the same spot. Is he giving me a hickey? How can he touch me like this and ask me to go to sleep?

"I want you to sleep." Devlin settles, tucking my body into his.

When he exhales, it sounds content. Almost happy.

I lick my lips and try to slow the rapid beat of my heart as I curl up to sleep. I'm surrounded by his scent, the hint of ginger wrapped in leather tickling my senses. It's in the sheets and all around me with Devlin holding me close.

As drowsiness quells the rush of lust, sleep eludes me. Devlin drops off into unconsciousness with his lips pressed to the crook of my neck.

I've never sold my body. It's the one line I have left. But somehow this feels different, sleeping in his bed. Maybe it's the thing growing between us that changes everything.

It's what I tell myself to finally drift.

Devlin's lips move against my neck in his sleep, like he hasn't had enough.

I think I understand the way he was tense, then able to relax once we were tangled in each other. It soothes me, too. It's…nice.

Cuddling with Devlin, I'm able to fall asleep, no longer feeling so alone without Mom.

* * *

When I arrive at Mom's hospital room with an armful of books, she's alone. Mom is propped up in bed, looking better than I've seen her in years. There's healthy color in her cheeks and her eyes are bright.

Nothing was more terrifying than running into our trailer to find her passed out on the floor.

"Hey," I greet brightly as I enter.

"Hi, baby girl." Mom's smile is full of radiance. She pats the bed. "Come sit."

"I brought you some entertainment." I perch on the side of her bed, setting the books from my collection on the tray table. "I figured you might be getting bored and need something to occupy the time. Will the doctor discharge you yet?"

"Not yet. We're waiting on the latest results from the blood test."

I hold back a sigh. Things at Devlin's house have been better than I expected, but I miss Mom. I pick up the brush from the side table and get to work with our routine. I visit, brush her hair, and do my homework as we talk.

When she holds her arms open, I lean in for a hug. She pets my hair and for a minute everything is okay in the world.

After we part, Mom checks out the books. "Some of these are new additions to your library."

"Yeah, I picked up some new ones." I was able to buy a whole box the library was planning to get rid of. I point out the one she has in her hand. "Look, same author as Stardust."

"Ah, one of your favorites." Mom laughs. "You used to beg me to read it again every time we finished it."

I wrap my arms around her shoulders and hug her. "You did the voices better than me. I loved it."

A wistful look lingers in her eyes, crinkling the lines around them as I finish brushing her hair and pull over the armchair.

"What is it? Are you tired?"

Mom waves a hand. "No, no. I'm just glad you were happy. That's what's important."

My heart clenches. "Of course I was." I take her hand, stroking her knuckles. "As long as I have you, I'm happy."

A wrinkle appears on her forehead. "I'm sorry, sweetie. Being in here for so long, I've just been thinking a lot."

"Mom," I breathe, squeezing her hand.

"I'm sorry for your father, you shouldn't have had to worry—"

"Mom, no. It wasn't your fault." My strong expression nearly crumbles. I want to take away all of her pain and swallow it. The burden can try to burn me from the inside out, I'll survive it. "Everything will be okay now."

She dashes away a tear before it falls. "Why don't you tell me about how school is? The doctor mentioned your friend told him about a college fair coming up."

"Right."

Devlin left college brochures on the island in the kitchen. Gemma sent me the link for Oak Ridge College, too. But I can't go to art school to study art history. I should go for something practical. Nursing, maybe. I haven't decided yet. I'm more worried about picking schools that have scholarships and grants I can apply for.

Neither of them have to worry about their futures. Gemma had her heart set on one goal and Devlin can select any school he wants.

"I know we haven't talked about it much, but whatever you choose, we'll make it work. I want you to follow your dreams, Blair."

I look up from picking at my nails. "I haven't decided on a major."

Mom leans back against her pillows, smiling. "I'm so proud of you."

"Thanks, Mom."

The nurse bustles in a few minutes later, checking on Mom and dropping off her dinner. We split the jello and laugh at TikTok animal videos I pull up on the hospital's WiFi.

One video features a boy that looks like Devlin. Just like that, I can't get last night out of my head. It keeps popping up. Concentrating in English earlier was hell.

"What put that look on your face?" Mom gives a teasing gasp. "Are you blushing?"

"I—*no*."

I cover my flaming cheeks. Oh god, I am blushing. I can't help it, not when my mind shoots to the faint red mark I found on my neck this morning. I tied a bandana around it to hide it. My cheeks heat more, replaying the feeling of Devlin's mouth on my skin, leaving his mark.

A vibration in my pocket provides a perfectly timed distraction. Hopefully Gemma has a good Instagram story to share of a dog to get Devlin out of my head.

Except...the text is from Devlin.

The cycle starts all over.

I roll my lips between my teeth as I shift in my seat.

Devil: Will you be home soon? Want to go for a night run?

[moon emoji] It's supposed to be a clear night. I want to take you to the lookout point where there's a good view of the sky.

After the lake party, I dropped the *D-bag* part off of his contact name, but left the *Devil*. He's still my dark devil, though now he makes my body tingle with something other than loathing and resentment.

Does a joint run at night count as a date when we're living in the same house?

With my heartbeat skittering all over the place, I type out a quick reply.

Blair: Visiting my mom, but be back soon. You owe me a race, so I'm in. Loser makes dinner?

Devil: You drive a hard bargain, little thief. That's called a rigged bet.

Blair: [GIF of a cute young girl shrugging unapologetically]

Devil: Deal. See you at home. [smirking devil emoji]

"Wow, you've turned red." Mom laughs, delighted. "Is it a boy?"

"Uh, yes. But it's, um." I don't know what to say. Devlin isn't my boyfriend. The butterflies that come to life in my chest as I read his text again can fuck off. "A friend from school."

It's the best I've got to explain the complicated thing Devlin and I have. Enemies to frenemies? I don't know what's going on.

Nothing seems to have anything to do with revenge between us anymore.

"It's nice to see you happy with a crush," Mom says.

Crush.

Oh god.

My lips part. Is that what it is? The feeling that makes it hard to breathe around Devlin?

It's not just that he's hot or that his kisses reach in and batter my heart.

I think I actually like Devlin.

Mom cracks up at whatever expression my face is locked in.

TWENTY-NINE
DEVLIN

When I'm around Blair, something brings me to life. Makes me feel in ways I've kept numb. I thought it was the thrill of the game, of controlling her. But I think it's more than that, it's just *her*.

She's in my head, my dreams, my fucking veins. And she won't get out.

Every breath I take is tinged with the hint of vanilla.

This might have started as a way to torment her for revenge, but she's dug her way so deep into me, I don't want it to end. I want her stubborn spirit and her moans. The desire to break her from pleasure, then put her back together to do it all over again has surpassed the savage part of me hellbent on destroying her.

The game has changed forever, because now I'm playing for keeps.

But Blair is only here for the money, right?

Take that away, and she's gone again. Back to spitting fire and fury at me.

I rub a hand over my mouth as I stalk from my bedroom to hers. Halfway there, I pause. The shower is running.

A faint, cut off cry of pleasure reaches my ears, muffled by the rush of water. I remain stiff in the hallway, staring at the bathroom door. Another moan follows, high and fucking divine.

My mouth curves in a sedate, predatory smile.

It's time I tested my theory. I have to be strategic and pick at her piece by piece, just as I have when I used to hate her. I'll make her see her place is by my side.

When I grab the handle, my smile stretches. The door isn't locked.

Oh, you naughty little hellcat. You want to get caught? The monster is coming for you.

Turning the handle with stealthy care, I crack the door and peer inside. The glass-walled shower is partially fogged from the steam and speckled in water droplets. My mouth goes dry at the sight of Blair.

Her head is arched back, putting that tempting neck on display. I lick my lips, wanting to clamp my teeth over her pulse point. Mark her fucking *mine*.

"Ah..." Blair's breath catches as she tweaks a pert nipple with one hand and slides the other between her legs. Her hips rock in slow rolls, moving against her hand as she takes her pleasure.

My cock goes rock hard and a lust-drenched growl threatens to tear from my throat. I keep quiet, pressing the heel of my hand against my throbbing dick.

The monster inside roars, clawing to be unleashed. To dominate. To *devour*.

Blair's lips part on a breathy moan. Fuck, I want her. I don't care if I'm a creep, watching her in secret. She's mine to watch.

I've fought the pull to own every inch of her for too long. The obsession is no longer something poisoning my actions. No, it's taken over.

The only thing I want is Blair. Her pouty lips made to wrap around my cock and kiss until they're swollen. Her tight little ass. Her stubborn attitude. Every inch.

All of her.

Blair is mine and I'll have her. No one else will ever get these sounds, see her perfect body, have the thrill of her fighting until she submits.

I throw the door open and stalk up to the shower. Blair gasps when I yank on the glass door. Warm water splatters the front of my clothes.

"What the fuck, dude?" Blair's voice is husky and hoarse. She covers her body, cupping between her legs and wrapping an arm over her tits. "I'm showering, here."

"Too late, angel. I've already seen. Drop those arms." My gaze drags down her body and my dick twitches. "Now."

Blair's freckled cheeks are pink from the hot shower, but they flush more, color flooding her face. She puckers her lips and tightens her arms.

"Fuck off."

Blair's fight is false. It's clear in the way her pupils expand, black desire taking over her eyes. She was already turned on from touching herself. This is heightening the arousal.

This is as much of a rush for her as it is for me. Maybe it's why I'm so obsessed with her. This dance between us is a tango from beginning to end, a seduction from fight to fucking.

At the thought of fucking her, a hot pulse tugs at my cock.

Yes.

I keep her pinned in a hard, dominant gaze, silently demanding she do as I say. It's our rule. That's how this works.

"Do it. Show me those tits you were teasing and that pussy you were touching."

A small, strangled cry escapes Blair.

After another minute of chewing on her lip, she lowers her arms to her sides. Her fists ball and she trembles, the tight peaked nipples begging for my teeth and tongue. She's a gorgeous, enticing siren.

I take my time gazing at every naked inch of her, enjoying the subtle shifts as she tries to stay still. The muscles in her thighs flex as Blair rubs them together.

I smirk. "Good girl."

Blair darts her eyes down, smoky lashes fluttering.

"No. Look at me." My command is deep and firm.

Making another bitten-off sound, she brings her gaze up to meet mine. Her eyes are wide, tits rising and falling with each breath.

My tongue moves over my bottom lip slowly. "Good."

Blair trembles as I admire my prize. The strained energy rolls off her in waves. She needs the release I stole from her.

So many possibilities run through my head, rushing by all at once until they bleed together. My dick strains against my pants.

"I'm joining you."

"What? You're—" Blair gulps. "And if I say you can't?"

A chuckle rolls through me. "What rule did I give you about saying no?"

Her lids fall to half-mast, drowsy with how much my rough, demanding tone turns her on.

That's right, hellcat. The monster has you in his sights. You can't escape this.

"I'll give you twenty-five hundred."

Before the words have left my mouth, I'm stripping my t-shirt overhead and flinging it aside. My sweatpants follow and my cock springs free, bobbing heavy between my legs.

Blair's eyes stretch wider as she takes it in. I flex the muscles that make it bob again, just to see her squirm. Amusement spirals through me at Blair's expression.

"So..." She takes a breath, gesturing at my cock. "You're paying to shower with me now."

I hum as I step under the spray with her. She inches into the back corner, plastering herself against the glass wall. I keep hold of her gaze as I drag my fingers through my hair to wet it. Water cascades down my chest and I follow its path with my fingertips, reaching around my cock at the base and squeezing. A satisfied groan leaves me, echoing off the tiled wall.

As I stroke my erection, I place my hand next to her head, leaning in. "How much to know what you were thinking about while you touched yourself? Was it me?"

Blair's lip pops from between her teeth. It's pink and plump. I want to bite it.

"Can't a girl masturbate? Goddamn..." Embarrassment tinges her tone. She brushes my abs with a tentative touch that grows bold. She explores, moving up to my pecs, then over my tattoo. "Guys do it like you're breathing and it's normal."

"Of course. I think it's sexy as hell that you were getting yourself off." My attention slides down her body. "Taking your pleasure. Were you so horny you couldn't take it anymore? Was your pussy begging to get fucked after the other night?"

Blair gasps. The sound is incredible. I need another one, preferably with my hand around her throat while I pound into her body.

I release my dick and graze the skin of her belly, dragging my hand up to circle her tits. I tweak one nipple, enjoying the way Blair's head bangs against the glass, then close my fingers around her throat. Defiance mixed with lust flashes in her eyes when I squeeze enough to show her I'm in control.

"Is that what you want me to admit? That I was thinking about you?"

"I know you were." I lean in to lick the side of her face, lapping the water droplets from jaw to earlobe. "Are you as twisted up about me as I am about you?"

Her nails dig into my chest as she curls her fingers. "You're just saying that because your dick is hard."

I shake my head, panting against her ear. "I'm not. I can't get you out of my head."

I don't want to hold back anymore.

In a swooping move, I claim her lips, kissing her like it's the only air I'll get. The kiss is hot and addictive. She kisses me back, making tiny sounds as her arms twine around my shoulders.

It's not enough just to kiss her.

Parting on a rough sound, I hold her hips in a punishing grip. My thumbprints will be there on her skin when I let go. Blair makes a sound of protest and goes on her toes to kiss me again. Rumbling, I give her a peck.

I drop to my knees and look up at the demonic dark angel who has her sharp claws in my soul. She's a perfect match to the monster inside me.

Gripping Blair's thigh, I maneuver her leg over my shoulder and hover my lips over her pussy. She's spread for me, a needy sound tearing from her.

"How much?" My breath ghosts over her sensitive folds.

"Dev," Blair breathes, threading her fingers in my hair. "I don't..."

Fuck, when she says my name like that.

Blair struggles to find more words.

"How..." I swipe my tongue over her pussy, groaning at the first taste. "...much?"

"Please. Please, just—"

As soon as she breaks, begging for my mouth, I devour her. I suck her clit as I grip her ass cheeks. Blair's piercing cry sounds over the rush of the shower. I feast on her pussy until she's shaking apart for me.

She begs and gasps and grinds on my face as I tongue-fuck her.

"Oh, god, I—Devlin, I'm—"

"Yes, fuck," I groan against her sensitive skin when she comes with a fierce scream. "Louder. Let me hear you."

Her sounds of ecstasy echo on the tiles.

I keep going, sliding two fingers into her as I tease her clit with my tongue. Her pussy is so wet for me. I growl against her, curling my fingers and fucking her with them.

"Oh my god! F-fuck!" Blair moans, tugging on my hair.

I pull back to wet my thumb between my lips and Blair cries out.

"No!"

I grin around my thumb as I fuck her with my other hand, pumping my fingers. "Patience, angel. I'll make you feel good."

My mouth is back on her pussy, teasing her folds and clit. As she's climbing higher and higher to oblivion, I pull her ass and massage my thumb over her hole. She stills for a beat. When I follow suit, stopping everything, she squirms.

"Damn it, Dev."

I hum, giving her a tiny hit of divine pleasure vibrating over her swollen labia.

"Okay. Okay, fine. Please, I need—"

"I know."

My mouth and fingers move in symphony. I let her relax, rewarding her with more pressure from my tongue. When my thumb presses into her ass, she shudders, arching away from the glass. At first I let her get used to it, slowing down to a torturous pace, playing with her just to feel her ass squeezing my thumb. The sounds she makes are sublime, spurring me on.

I suck on her clit relentlessly as I fuck her pussy and ass with my fingers.

"Shit! Oh god—*Ahh!*"

She comes again, her entire body quivering in pleasure.

Blair fighting back is a beautiful, addictive drug.

But Blair coming undone?

Fucking stunning.

She leans against the glass for a long stretch, gasping and whimpering from aftershocks of her orgasm. My cock aches. I want nothing more than to drive into her right now, but not yet.

I get to my feet, licking her taste from my lips. She catches me in her net with neediness flooding her gaze. With a rumble, I cage her against the wall and kiss her, slow and dirty. I can feel her heartbeat thundering in time with my own, the heat of her skin bleeding into mine. Steam surrounds us and the rush of water drowns out our ragged breaths.

Pulling back, I rasp against her lips. "Do you taste yourself on my tongue?"

"Yes."

"Good."

The hypnotic mood lingers, blanketing us as we rinse off and leave the shower. Blair follows me into my room.

My erection hasn't faded and if she's in here, she's accepting that we're not done.

Letting the towel drop, I sit on the edge of the bed. Blair hovers near the door, clutching her towel.

"Come over here."

She shuffles over, unlike her usual light-footed grace.

"Drop the towel."

It falls to the floor in a rustle of fabric.

I spread my knees to give her room. "Kneel."

Blair's throat moves with her gulp. The order takes her longer, but after a minute she gets on her knees between my legs. She tilts her head up, looking at me with big eyes, star-speckled cheeks, and full lips begging to fit around my cock. Fuck, that's a gorgeous sight.

I run a thumb along her lips, pulling on them. "Open."

Blair inhales and opens for me.

A growl leaves me as heat spears into my gut. I press into her mouth, gripping her jaw. Blair tentatively touches her tongue to my thumb, then sucks.

"Fuck, angel." I can only imagine the fire filling my eyes as our gazes lock. "Yes. Keep that up."

I stroke my cock, watching her mouth intently as she takes my thumb deeper, growing more confident.

"You look so good on your knees with that pretty little mouth on me."

My impending orgasm is rushing up like a surging tide, sweeping me away the closer I get to the edge. Blair's tongue curls around my thumb, exploring, tasting. *Fuck.* My grip tightens on my dick.

"Is that how you'd suck my cock?"

The heat builds when Blair looks up. She releases my thumb with a pop. I grunt as my fist flies over my shaft.

Blair grows bold. Tucking her wet hair back, she opens that fucking mouth again and closes it over the tip of my cock. A feral groan tears from me as her tongue swirls on the crown. I cup the back of her head and thrust deeper. She makes a startled sound, but adjusts to accommodate my cock filling her mouth.

"Oh, fuck, baby. Like that, god, suck my cock."

She peeks up at me through those inky lashes. A hint of

power fills her eyes. Heaven and hell, it's a sexy look. My little thief is getting off on having my pleasure under her control while I've got her on her knees with her mouth on my cock.

I don't last much longer. The sight of those damn lips on my dick is too much. White-hot pleasure takes over.

With a groan, I come, hand tangling in her hair.

I hunch over her, leaning an elbow on my thigh so I don't topple over from lightheadedness. She sucked my soul out through my dick and left me on cloud fucking nine.

"Jesus," I murmur.

Blair sits back on her heels, grimacing.

A breathless chuckle shakes my shoulders at the way her jaw works, a drop of come left on her swollen lips.

"What do I do?" Blair cries, unintelligible with her mouth full of come.

My groin tightens and I suck in a breath. Even after coming, I still want to pin her to the bed and fuck her until she passes out. Christ, she'll be the death of me.

Snorting, I stroke her hair. My limbs are loose and unwound. It feels like the first time I've relaxed the tight control over myself in years.

"Up to you whether you spit or swallow. That's where you hold all the power. It's one of the few liberties I'll let you have, so enjoy it."

Blair's nose scrunches. Her mouth is full of come after she sucked me off like a little temptress and yet I find her adorable right now. I graze the back of my knuckles over her cheek.

Casting a searching look around the room, Blair crawls over to the trashcan near the bed and spits. A grin spreads across my face and I lean forward to smack her ass.

Blair yelps. "Dude!"

"Don't shake your ass in front of me and not expect me to

slap it. Now bring that ass back over here, I'm not finished with you yet."

"You're not?"

"Not even close."

When Blair's back in reach, I tug her into bed and kiss her deeply. She's not leaving my bed tonight, or ever again if I have my way.

THIRTY
BLAIR

It's past midnight, I think. After a short nap in Devlin's bed, we raided the kitchen for a late dinner of peanut butter on toast and spicy chili Doritos, then ended up in the in-ground hot tub under the back deck.

Naked.

I can't explain the incandescent feeling settled in my bones, but it's been expanding all night, refusing to extinguish. It's keeping me light, like I could float up to the sky.

The warm, bubbling water envelopes us in humid steam as our breath clouds the chilly night air. It's getting colder out. Devlin stretches his legs, leaning back against the natural rocks lining the edge of the tub. He swipes his damp fringe back from his forehead. The curve of his bicep and the veins in his forearm distract me.

There's something about him that's changed. The curve of his mouth is softer, more relaxed. I like this side of him. It's as if I'm getting a look on the other side, behind the curtain of the puppet master.

I scoot down on the seat, letting the soothing water cover my shoulders. It laps at the flyaway hairs falling from my topknot, curling the wet strands against the back of my neck.

Moonlight shines down on the lake, illuminating the calm body of water and the ridge line.

One thing has been bothering me since I started living at Devlin's. It's been almost a month and I haven't seen anyone come by. Devlin wasn't kidding about his housekeepers being silent, I've never met them. But more importantly, his parents haven't been home once.

How long do their work trips last?

Thinking of spending that long away from Mom makes my shoulders sag under the water.

Living like this, so isolated, can't be good for him. It's no wonder he turned into such a bitter asshole. My heart twists and I swirl my hands through the water, watching the rising steam.

I thought it would be torture to live with him, but all I feel now is a twinge in my chest. Am I the only person keeping Devlin company at home?

Swallowing, I gather my courage. "Where are you parents? Really?"

Devlin cracks his eyes open. He sits up with a frown, and a knot of worry tightens in my stomach. He was relaxed and... happy, I think. Now he's putting his mask back on, shutting me out.

I tuck my hands under my thighs, biting my lip. "It's just. You're alone up here. You don't even go to your aunt and uncle's. The Saints, right? I know Lucas is your cousin and I know they live here."

"I do usually go to their place for dinner once or twice a week." Devlin shifts, slinging an arm behind me on the rock wall. His fingertips graze my shoulder. "I've been declining their invitations to make sure you get something to eat."

I freeze. It's true, he's made dinner most nights. Even when it's just reheating some leftovers the housekeeper left. The corners of my mouth tug down.

"Have I kept you from seeing your family? That's not right. You should—"

"It's fine." He guides me closer and I lean into his side. Devlin looks to the stars. "I'm not alone. You're here."

My throat thickens with emotion. I haven't always been here. Jesus, my trailer with Mom is more of a home than the way Devlin's been living.

"How long?"

Devlin hums inquisitively.

"How long have you pretty much lived on your own?" My voice is small.

His arm tightens around me. "Worried about what kind of monster it bred, angel?" He drops his voice lower to a gravelly tone as he kisses the top of my head. "It's fine now."

My heart fights to leap out of my chest. I think it wants to burst free to burrow into Devlin's.

We're quiet for a few minutes. It's a comfortable sort of silence.

An idea begins to form in my head. One that makes the corners of my mouth twitch up and warmth spread. I'm going to surprise Devlin with something I always wanted. I'll spruce up his sparse room in the way it deserves. Those string lights I've always coveted will be perfect.

I curl into Devlin's side, picturing the kind shaped like stars. They'll look great hanging over his bed.

Maybe Devlin will want to keep me. This. Us.

Devlin caresses my side as his lips feather over my cheek.

I haven't quite acknowledged that we've crossed into the unknown, past the point of return. When this deal ends...I don't know how I'll go back to the way things were before I knew the devious way Devlin kisses. Heat pours through my limbs just thinking about Devlin kneeling on the shower floor, mouth hot and insistent, driving me crazy until I came.

My cheeks prickle and a bead of perspiration runs down my temple. Devlin's tongue is there to catch it. He nibbles on my earlobe, calling on the pit of fire he's set ablaze inside me. The bubbling water ripples as I gasp.

For now, I'm going to see where things go. Maybe I don't have to lose this when the deal ends.

We match. Black hair. Blacker hearts, dark and frayed by circumstance.

But maybe we can heal our bruises together. Two broken souls finding solace and salvation in the depths of each other's darkness.

"Come here." Devlin pulls me into his lap and kisses the back of my neck. "I need you again."

"Again?" My laugh turns into a moan as he finds a sensitive spot.

"Over and over. I can't get enough of you."

His hands wander over my body from behind, massaging my breasts and dipping lower, between my legs. My thighs part for him, spreading wide on either side of his legs as he wastes no time with teasing. With clever fingers, he rubs my clit.

"Why are you so good at..." A groan steals my words as I roll my hips against his hand.

Devlin plays me like his personal harp, masterfully

plucking and creating harmonies with my body to bring me over the edge. I tip into a sea of pleasure that erupts inside my core.

"Ah!"

Devlin bites my neck with a pleased sound. He palms my thighs as he grinds his erection against my ass.

"Do you have a sexy cat burglar outfit in your closet or do I need to buy you one?" He pinches my nipples, twisting them until my back bows. His voice is a hot murmur in my ear. "I want to role play as the cop who catches you red handed."

The sensations dancing across my skin leave me breathless. I arch into each teasing touch, seeking more.

"You've already caught me."

"Fuck yes, I did. Caught you and I can do whatever I want with you."

"Yes." I'll agree to anything if he lets me come right now.

Devlin groans, lifting me out of the water as he stands up. It's freezing. Shivers tingle over my body. He spins me around, sets me on the seat so our height is better matched, and squeezes my ass so tight I cry out.

"Gonna mark you so everyone knows who you belong to."

"*Yes*," I moan, lost to the dirtiness of his promises.

I wrap my arms around his neck as he hikes my leg on his hip, grinding against my clit. His hard length sends delicious friction straight to my core.

"Look at you. This is where you belong. Right here, rubbing that pussy against my cock."

Devlin squeezes my ass and grinds his dick up and down. With his hold on my backside, he controls the pressure, making me shake with need.

"Please." I'm delirious, unsure what I'm begging for other than the sweet bliss of orgasm. My body throbs, pulsing as I reach the precipice. "Devlin, please."

"Come for me, baby."

The explosion of release ripples through me with so much force, I nearly slip and lose my footing. Devlin's there to catch me, pressing open-mouthed kisses down the length of my neck to my chest. He guides me back down to the seat in the hot tub and takes his cock in hand, standing over me.

"Open."

The command in his voice makes my lips part automatically.

"Yes, fuck." Devlin's cheeks hollow as he pants, jerking off. "I'm going to fuck that perfect mouth again soon. Come down your throat."

I open my mouth wider, inching forward to flick my tongue over the tip of his dick.

He hunches as he comes, grasping the rock wall behind my head. His release splashes over my tongue, my lips, my chin, and the tops of my breasts. The sound that rips from him shoots straight to my core.

Devlin leans his forehead against mine. He smears his come over my lips, dipping into my mouth. I can taste it as I suck on his fingers.

"My filthy angel."

He makes a splash as he drops into the water, pulling me back to his lap so I straddle it. His arms loop around and link behind me.

"How will I survive in school without touching you?" He splashes water over my breasts to wash off the come, then cleans my chin. "I'll want you even more when I shouldn't."

"Don't expect me to meet you under the bleachers, perv."

Devlin grins, salacious and full of mischief. I pinch his nipple and laugh at the way he bucks beneath me. My fingertips trail down his chest, following the path of the shooting stars inked into his ribs.

"Seriously, though, I'm not cutting class. I need to keep my grades up." I move up to trace his shoulders, mapping out the muscles. Devlin watches me, eyes hooded. "I don't have the luxury of a safety net. I'm aiming for a scholarship for college."

Devlin considers me for a moment. My heart gives a faint flutter at opening up to him.

"In that case, prepare yourself. I'll wear you out every night to get my fill."

I snort, but my insides coil. My body is pleasantly loose with overstimulation and we haven't even gone all the way.

Devlin smirks. "You laugh all you want. I'm serious."

"I believe you."

"Stay in my bed tonight."

My breath hitches. "Okay."

Devlin's lips quirk up. He grasps my chin and flicks his gaze between my eyes. There's a question behind the unbridled way he looks at me like he wants me.

"Do you have a date for winter formal?"

I wasn't expecting that. "No."

"Will you go with me?"

I wasn't planning on going. My cheeks prickle from more than the hot tub.

Is this real?

I have to know if this is part of his game or something he genuinely wants.

"How much do I get for it?"

Devlin tenses. A hard look crosses his face. He pushes out a harsh breath and cuts his gaze over my shoulder to the lake behind me.

"The pleasure of my company."

"So, no payment then." My pulse speeds up. "You actually want me as your date?"

Devlin relaxes a fraction. Some tension lingers in his posture. "I do."

I squeeze his shoulders at the admission. Then—?

Maybe the kisses at the lake and in the shower tonight weren't flukes. I thought we'd gone back to the deal when he began offering payments along with his orders again. And because I was weak to my desire, I let it all happen. I let him pay to use my body.

With each kiss, each touch, my resolve crumbled, and I erased the last line I've held tight to because Devlin was too hard to resist.

But was it really destroying my line, selling my body to the devil?

There's nothing on the table this time. No demand. Devlin is asking me out.

I've never gone to any school dance with a date.

"Yeah. Let's do it."

Devlin pulls me in for another toe-curling kiss.

THIRTY-ONE
BLAIR

In the span of a week, we've tipped into a new territory. Devlin makes good on his dirty promise. If we ride to school together, he can hardly make it home without pulling over to bury his head between my legs.

I know his body almost as well as I know my own, but we haven't had sex.

Any more orgasms and my legs might turn to jelly permanently. Devlin is insatiable—touching, tasting, and never stopping.

I'm still coming down from this morning, where Devlin woke me with his fingers buried inside my body as he sucked on my neck. Waking up on the verge of coming is amazing. I'm planning to test it out on him, curious if waking him up with my mouth on his dick will give me an even bigger sense of power over him.

Anytime I'm not visiting Mom at the hospital, he's hunted me down and devoured me.

Her condition remains stable, and she insisted I have time to myself instead of worrying about her so much. It was a tough sell, but she promised she's feeling fine.

It's the weekend and I intend to spend my Saturday afternoon curled up in a blanket on the cushioned window seat in the lounge while I listen to the steady patter of rain outside. If I can just find my book first...

I come out of my room, which I've only used to store my clothes and my book collection. I haven't slept there all week.

Pausing in the hallway, I tap my chin. I know I didn't leave it downstairs. Maybe I took it to Devlin's room, in my growing stack of paperbacks on the nightstand.

When I check the pile, it's not there. I go to Devlin's side of the bed and shuffle through the psychology books he reads.

"Aha!"

I snag my paperback on the Japanese art of Kintsugi, a poetic craft of repairing broken pottery with gold to symbolize accepting flaws, transforming what's broken into an even more beautiful piece of art. It's a favorite practice of art I love reading about because I feel a connection to the beauty in embracing scars and fractured pieces.

I flip the book over and find a new bookmark sticking out of the top. It's a real bookmark, unlike the scraps of paper and receipts I usually use. "What were you doing over here?"

"I pilfered it. Along with a few others."

Devlin leans against the open door, hands tucked in the pockets of his jeans.

"Now who's the thief?"

Smirking, I check the stack of books on his nightstand and

sure enough more of my books are between the psychology titles. Even Stardust, the book I mentioned Mom reading to me the first time I sat on the roof with him. When did he take these?

I hold up the book. "Did you read all of it?"

"I did." Devlin peels off the doorframe and comes over. He circles my waist from behind. "It reminded me of when my mom would read to me. I was pretty young." His voice drops lower, tinged with melancholy. "I can barely remember it clearly. Just murky slips of memories with a nightlight that cast stars on the wall."

I put Stardust down and spin in his embrace, looping my arms around his neck, threading my fingers into his thick hair. "Sounds like she spent a lot of time with you. Hold on to those memories."

Devlin hums and pulls me into a kiss. It quickly sweeps both of us away, stoking a fire in my stomach. We fall onto the bed, where Devlin puts me in his lap as he kisses down my chest before stripping my shirt off.

"I want you," he murmurs into my skin. "All of you. I want to keep you for myself and let no one else in our bubble."

Our bubble.

Gasping, I hold on to Devlin as his lips drag over my skin, whispering the things I've been too jaded to wish for. Because I'm no longer the little girl that believes in wishing on stars.

But for Devlin? I might be able to find a way to believe again, to hope. To trust he isn't lying.

Things grow hot and heavy, his hands following the same path as his mouth. He pauses, leaning back to look at me.

"What is it?"

"Let's go out tonight." Devlin brings his mouth to mine. "We'll go out of town. We could even get a hotel room."

"Like a date?"

"Yes."

I blink twice, searching for the punchline. "What's wrong with hanging out in town? The pizza place on main is popular for dates. Or, uh, so I hear."

"I want to do this right." He clears his throat, dropping his eyes. He goes on, mumbling, "It's what you deserve. You're worth it." He inhales, meeting my eyes once more. Some of his confidence seems restored. "I figure go big or go home."

A laugh bubbles out of me. "Okay. Sure."

Devlin grins, recapturing my mouth in a searing kiss.

* * *

When I come out of the shower later, there's a gorgeous black dress laid out on my bed. Spotting the tag, my jaw drops. It's designer. High-end and *new*.

There's no way in the short hours since asking me out Devlin managed to get this. Has he been planning tonight for a while?

The dress isn't all, there's also jewelry and shoes.

My eyes bulge as I tally the worth of the design labels. It's enough that I consider selling it all on eBay. I could cover another three or four months of rent, or pay for Mom's medicine for the autoimmune disease she's been diagnosed with. It would be the practical thing to do.

Touching the luxurious material of the sexy dress, I sink my teeth into the inside of my cheek. It's the nicest gift I've ever received, and it's beautiful. Perfectly suited to my style, if I had one other than thrift store chic.

When Devlin asked for the date out of town, I didn't think he meant like *this*.

I'm about to go question him, when I find him watching me from the door as he buttons his suit jacket. It's tailored and his hair is combed back with some product, but still appears touchable. My stomach bottoms out at how sexy and dapper he is in the suit.

"Damn," I drawl appreciatively, eyeing his ensemble.

Devlin gives me a crooked smile that rearranges my insides. "It's all for you. I want to give you something nice."

"It's beautiful." I gesture to the dress. "Help me figure out this zipper. I'm not used to this fancy shit."

Devlin's answering laugh is deep and untethered, free in a way he rarely indulges in.

* * *

In the limo ride on the way back, Devlin is absorbed in tracing my hand, palm to fingertips, driving tingling sensations up my arm. "You make me greedy, Blair."

The way he says my name is a spell coiling around me. It doesn't just pluck on my heartstrings, it fuses with my entire being and touches a place deep inside of me, one I've ignored for so long.

Our date was so utterly right. When I had been apprehensive about going out to dinner somewhere upscale in the city, Devlin had chuckled and admitted he was in the mood for pizza. We spent over two hours working our way through a huge pie, enjoying making up stories about what other patrons thought we were doing there so dressed up. My favorite was the story where we were mafia royalty and a secret spy, star-crossed but defiantly in love. I wanted to bottle the brightness lighting up Devlin's eyes and the happy curl of his smile.

As we approach Silver Lake Forest Estates, the streetlights create intermittent pools of amber light spilling across the back of the limo.

This isn't my life. It's so far from my reality, where Mom

and I split frozen meals for dinner and sleep in a trailer with thin walls. A life I was forced into, where it was adapt or die.

But I want it to be.

I always live with the single goal to help Mom get out of Dad's gambling debts, to assist with the monumental financial burden, to pick a sensible college major instead of something I'm truly interested in. With Devlin, I get to be selfish. I get permission to love Mom as her daughter, have a normal teenage life. I no longer have to push aside every frivolous thing.

With Devlin, I get to be the idealistic version of myself I thought I crushed years ago. The survivor in me doesn't have to fight so hard every day.

I turn into Devlin's touch, kissing him, pushing all of my racing thoughts into the glide of our tongues, the scrape of teeth on skin, telling him with my mouth how much I want this. Want him.

There's a tangible energy when we return to the house. It follows as Devlin helps me out of the limo, when he sends the driver away, and inside the house. Devlin stops me in the entrance, grasping my wrist.

Our eyes meet and an answering pulse of heat echoes in my core.

I can feel it before he kisses me, the steady build of arousal growing, licking higher and higher like flames as it takes over both of us. With a low growl, Devlin scoops me into his arms and carries me upstairs to the bedroom.

I bounce on the mattress when Devlin tosses me there. He's on me immediately, attacking my mouth, biting my neck, sliding my dress up with hot hands. He grips my thighs in a bruising touch, slapping them apart. I spread my legs to give him room to fit between them.

The roughness is exciting.

Our clothes come off with the telltale sound of tearing

fabric—his, I hope, because I like the dress he bought me—until we're completely bare.

Devlin's teeth sink into my lip, tugging it with a possessive brutality. His hard cock ruts against my slick folds.

"You wet for me?"

"Yes." I suck in a breath when he enters me with two fingers, curling them in a way that has me throwing my head back. My pulse pounds in time with our ragged breaths. "Oh my god."

Devlin's laugh is downright corrupt. "We're just getting started." He thrusts his fingers in deeper, drawing a sharp cry from me. "I'm fucking you until you break."

His teeth clamp around my nipple. I arch up, clawing at his back from the mix of pleasure and pain. A rumbling sound vibrates in his chest.

Devlin lifts my calf to his shoulder and positions himself, gliding the head of his dick over my entrance. He leers at me, looking like a vengeful god with his sinfully attractive features. "I don't care about the others. I'll fuck each and every one of them out of you." His grip flexes on my thigh. "I'm going to fuck you until you only feel my cock inside you."

It's hard to catch my breath from the rush of overwhelm crashing over me. I liked the roughness until I realized that might make this hurt more.

I part my lips, searching for some way to slow down. My heart beats erratically. "Devlin."

His dark eyes meet mine. Some of the lust clears, making way for shock as he studies me.

Devlin lets my leg fall to the bed and grasps my chin. "Are you...have you ever...?"

Emotion clogs my throat. It's stupid, but I'm helpless to fight the sting of tears. None of the rumors about me are true. I shake my head.

Devlin is still for a long moment, breathing hard. The way he kisses me feels like he's holding back a tide of possessive force, but he keeps it in check. His kiss is searing and slow. I moan, locking my arms around his neck.

The emotion threatens to spill over. Without me saying anything, he understood what I need.

Devlin takes me apart with steady focus, kissing my entire body with feather light brushes of his lips until he settles between my legs. He strokes my hips, glancing at me through his lashes.

"Okay?"

I nod.

The corner of his mouth lifts. "You won't be, when I've finished. You'll be crying and begging for me. I'm going to own every inch of you."

I shudder as his mouth descends on me. "Ah!"

My hands fly to the back of his head to hold him where I need him. His tongue and fingers are devious and so damn good. He murmurs against my sensitive folds, whispering filthy encouragement as he eats my pussy.

"There! Right there, please!"

My hips roll, desperate for release, riding his tongue until the explosion of pleasure ripples through my body.

"That's it, angel." Devlin lifts his head. His breath coasts over my throbbing clit. "Come for me, come on my tongue."

He goes back for more, wrenching another two orgasms from me until I can't take it anymore. I try to wriggle away, but he pins my hips in a dominant grip, shooting me a filthy grin.

"Please," I beg, tangling my hands in his hair. "I need more."

"You think you're ready? Are you loose and wet for me?"

I nod frantically, trembling. "Yes!"

"I don't think you've come enough times yet." Devlin

nibbles on the tender skin of my inner thigh, filling me with his fingers once more. "One more. I want this pussy to soak my cock when I fuck you."

"Ah!" I wail as he tortures me with his mouth.

Impossibly, another burst of pleasure spirals in an explosion from my core. How can he make me come so much? Delirium floods my senses. A deep-seated urge for more connection grips me. I know I want to feel his cock filling me, feel our bodies joined.

"Devlin, please! I need you! Please, please, please!"

As he shifts up the bed, grinding his erection against me, I moan with abandon.

"You beg so pretty, my dirty little thief." He strokes my cheek with his knuckles. "Is this what you want?"

I make a needy sound and try to push him inside by digging my heels into his ass. "Give it to me. I want you inside me."

Devlin gives me a monstrous, feral look that turns me on. He may be a devil, but he's *my* devil. I want him to consume me in his hellfire.

He leans over to dig for a condom in the nightstand. Once it's on, he cages me in his arms.

"Just remember...this is what you begged for."

"Yes," I breathe, cupping the back of his neck to draw him down for a kiss. "Do it. I want it. Fuck me."

"You're so perfect," he says against my lips. Devlin lines up and pushes in. "Fuck." He drops his forehead to mine. "You're mine, angel. Be mine."

He goes slow at first, achingly slow, giving me time to adjust. The tight sensation of fullness builds the further his cock sinks into my body. A different kind of overwhelm crashes down on me as the tightness eases. He pets my hair as a small sound escapes me.

Devlin pulls back and thrusts with sharper force. My back

arches and my nails drag down his back. There's pressure, but it doesn't hurt.

"More," I demand.

"*Yes*," Devlin growls, face buried in my neck. "Tell me. Tell me how much you need my cock fucking you good."

Devlin wraps me in his arms and lifts me from the bed, plunging into my pussy. We pant as one, clinging to each other as we chase our release. He fists my hair and kisses me, his hips snapping faster.

I tremble as he hits me deep enough that a galaxy bursts behind my eyes. I almost tip backwards, but Devlin holds me close, groaning.

"Yes, baby. You're so tight, I can feel you coming. Your pussy is gripping my cock."

His thrusts turn more frenzied. Then he tenses, letting out a sound of pure ecstasy. His cock throbs deep inside me as he comes.

Devlin's voice is hoarse as he repeats, "Mine."

"Yours," I whisper.

I feel like I'm floating as Devlin gently lays me down. He disappears from the room, returning a few minutes later with a damp towel. Devlin watches me with one of the few unguarded looks he's granted me as he carefully wipes me clean.

All of my limbs are useless. "I can't move."

"Good. Just how I like you."

Keeping my eyes open is hard. I'm flooded with drowsiness.

Devlin's chuckle makes me smile. His soft lips press against my forehead. "You're all fucked out. It's cute. I'll have to keep this in mind for when I need a way to tame that stubborn streak."

I hum, too far gone to formulate a sassy response.

With an impressive reserve of energy, he picks me up under my knees and around my waist. Holding me close, he treks through the house, and sinks into the welcome warm water of the hot tub.

A contented moan leaves me.

I feel safe, loved, and at peace laying my head on Devlin's shoulder while he combs his fingers through my hair.

I feel...home.

THIRTY-TWO
DEVLIN

Blair dozes for a while, coming in and out of consciousness. I really wore her out.

It's a challenge to restrain myself from playing with her tits and slipping my fingers into her pussy right now. I want to do everything I did to her tonight all over again. The need I feel for her is too big to contain, spilling over with an endless amount of desire.

"What are you doing to me, my little thief?"

When she shifts shortly after, waking up, I hold her closer.

"Look."

"Hmm?"

I point up. "See Polaris?"

"The North Star?"

Tracing the shape in the sky while I outline the star tattoo on Blair's back, I point out, "You can see the Little and Big Dipper constellations."

"Cool." Blair sits up, leaning toward the sky. "They're part of bigger constellations. I have a book on mythology upstairs that tells the story."

"Actually, I stole that book. It's on my side." I point out a different pair of constellations. "I've always enjoyed the story of the king and queen, Cepheus and Cassiopeia."

My heart bangs hard against my ribs because I like this, having Blair within the walls I've erected. She cut through the brambles and rusted chains locked around my heart to get in. Our lives might look different, but our insides match, calling to each other.

Blair shoots me a sly look and splashes me. "Now who's cultivating a criminal habit?"

"What can I say, your corrupt nature really rubs off on me." To illustrate my point, I grope her tits, playing with her nipples.

She leans back against my chest with a delicious little moan. I circle my arms around her.

"I think you'll find *you're* the corrupt force of nature at work here, you dirty devil."

I press against her ass, letting her feel the evidence of her statement.

"Oh my god!" She exclaims in exasperation, reaching back to pinch my side. "You're freaking insatiable. Is that normal?"

"It's all your doing." My lips find her neck, my favorite part of her to nibble and leave my marks. I like seeing peeks of them when she can't hide them at school. "You've stirred a hungry beast. I want to be buried in your body all the time. When you walk around school in that fucking skirt I want to flip it up, rip your underwear aside, and slide into your pussy while I've got you bent over begging for it."

Blair shivers as I attack her neck with tongue and teeth. "Very stereotypical dude-lizard-brain of you."

I snort, nipping at her neck. "In my fantasies you talk back, but not this much."

"Obviously the real deal is better," Blair says airily in the sassy tone that makes my dick hard.

"Watch that mouth, or I'll fill it up."

"That's not really a threatening punishment if I like doing it so much."

"Fuck, you kill me."

Blair laughs. I want to bottle the relaxed sound. "In all seriousness, though, I'm pretty sore."

I direct her face around for a kiss. "That's why I brought you down here."

She bites her lip, a beautiful, affectionate expression lighting up her eyes. It cracks into my heart, wrapping it in a soothing balm.

We enter a comfortable silence after Blair snuggles back against my chest. I point out more stars and tell her the mythology behind the visible and non-visible constellations.

The question I've been wanting to ask makes my heart thud. I can't contain it any longer.

"Do you still draw stars?"

Blair jolts. "What? How did you know I used to like drawing stars?"

"You went to the same school as me. Little Boulder Academy."

"Wait, seriously?" Blair turns in my arms to face me.

"We had an art class together in third grade. You showed me your stars." I tug her closer, playing with her hair while I murmur my secrets. "You knew I was sad, even though I didn't say anything. Despite my efforts to be the grumpy little shit I was, you came right up to me and sat down."

Blair gasps, recognition morphing her expression.

"You told me to make a wish on your star and I did." I wet my lips. "Whenever I felt alone, I wished on stars."

Blair cups my face. She's surprised, awe-struck. "You really were the same boy."

I turn my cheek into her palm. "I was. I didn't remember until recently. After you left, I wasn't happy." I lock my arms around her small waist. "I wanted you to come back."

"I wish I could've." Blair's expression falls, then hardens with bitterness. "That was because my dad left. He ran out on us. Dumped all of his gambling debt on my mom."

The explanation clears up what little information I pieced together from what I found out about her. With the filled in gaps, I can guess how it shaped Blair to go through that as a kid, and why she fights so hard to protect her mom.

Blair shakes her head, an angry wrinkle marring her brow. "He destroyed everything we had because he was selfish. He left Mom to clean up the mess."

I press our foreheads together. "I'm sorry. Not just that you went through that, but for being a dick, too. I'm sorry I hurt you."

Not entirely sorry for what my actions put in motion, though. My morals run gray. If I hadn't started the war between us, we might not be here right now.

She chuckles. "Damn right. But, I mean, I'm not totally innocent here. I did try to steal your car for revenge against your supreme assholery."

I hum, massaging her ass. "That's what I like best about you, angel."

Blair ducks her head, biting my shoulder. We wrestle playfully for a few minutes.

Leaning back against the rocks lining the hot tub, I rake a hand through my hair.

"All this time..." I trail off, leaving the rest left unsaid.

"Yeah," Blair echoes, picking up on what I didn't voice.

All this time I wasted on hating her, and here she's the one who gave me one of my only salvations.

The little girl with the stars and the stubborn thief who steals all of my attention, one and the same.

The way my heart thunders around her is new and unfamiliar, but I think I'm beginning to understand what it means.

THIRTY-THREE
DEVLIN

A week of bliss passes where Blair and I are wrapped around each other every minute she's home.

I've been working up to asking if she wants me to go with her when she visits her mom in the hospital every other day after school. It's a silly idea, maybe. But I want to be with Blair all the time.

Then we're in the middle of dinner when my parents come home out of nowhere. No notice. They intrude on my bubble with Blair.

The fork pauses halfway to my open mouth when Mom and Dad stand in the entrance to the kitchen, dumping their things without acknowledging us.

Blair darts an unsure look from my parents to me. I'm as surprised as she is. This hasn't happened before, either.

"Mom." I clear my throat, setting down my fork. "You're home."

Dad tosses a dismissive look at the kitchen island where Blair and I sit side by side on our usual stools. He leaves the room without a word, his footfalls sounding on the varnished floating risers that lead upstairs.

Mom frowns after him, her expression pinched. "Hello, son."

With perfunctory efficiency, she gives me a drive by kiss on her way to wash her hands in the sink. When she's done, she grabs a water bottle from the fridge and leaves the room.

They didn't greet Blair at all.

"Um," Blair says after a door upstairs shuts. "So, those are your parents?"

"Yeah." I rub my jaw, stabbing my fork into the chicken on my plate. "Congratulations, you've witnessed happy reunion number thirty-eight."

Blair's head jerks back at my caustic tone. I can't help it. My parents always put me in this dour mood.

"Sorry. Finish up, then we'll go study for midterms."

She seems like she wants to talk more, but nods and returns to eating dinner. Her worried peeks in my direction wind my spine tighter with tension as I sit in silence.

After dinner, the plates clink when we set them in the sink. We go up to my room and spend an hour on the floor going through spread out flashcards Blair made for the English exam. When it's late, she casts a longing look at the bed.

"I'll, uh, go back to the other room tonight."

She hasn't called it her bedroom in weeks, much less slept there. We've been living in a perfect cocoon until my parents showed up. I don't want to sleep without her in my bed. I sleep better when I'm wrapped around her.

"They don't care. You can stay in here if you want."

"Still. I don't really know how to do the whole awkward 'hi, I'm Blair, and I've been sleeping in your son's bed for weeks' conversation. Amongst...other things."

Blair turns a pretty shade of pink. I drag her to me, kissing her deeply. Her eyes are darker when we part, pupils dilated and lashes fluttering.

A growl tears through me. "Fuck."

Blair gives me a soft, shy laugh. "Deal with it. You'll survive."

"But at what cost?" I drape myself against her side.

She pushes at me with a wry grin. "Goodnight."

Blair gathers her flashcards and grabs a paperback she's been reading from her nightstand before leaving the room. I stare at the closed door after she leaves, willing my twisting heart to calm down.

"Stupid," I mutter to myself as I climb to my feet.

Going to one of the panels of my closet, I open it and take out the magazine page with our contract agreement written on it. My fingers brush over it, tracing where Blair signed her name.

Now that I've caught her, do I get to hold on to her?

Or is the contract the only thing keeping Blair by my side? I wonder if she would go if I tore it up.

* * *

For two days, I'm braced for my parents to say something —*anything*. It's what parents should do, but they don't. There's barely any acknowledgement of Blair's presence at the house, and she's been jittery anytime we're all in the same room.

It leaves me angrily floundering.

"Midterms this week?" Dad asks, nursing a cup of coffee when I come downstairs.

I grunt in response, pouring a mug for myself.

"Are you prepared?"

My grip on the mug turns white-knuckled as I grit out, "Yes."

Dad hums, appeased. All he cares about is that I make the grades for pre-med. We don't have a father-son relationship. We don't have any kind of relationship that's salvageable as far as I'm concerned at this point.

I'll have to be the one to cut the mangled thread holding the last shred of hope we could be a real family, but I'm not strong enough.

Blair enters the kitchen, slipping in with silent stealth. Maybe if she made more noise, my parents might speak to her.

"Want some coffee?"

Flashing a look at my dad, she nods. I want to sigh wearily. That's not the fighting spirit I love. I pour her coffee and hand over the mug.

The atmosphere in the kitchen is brittle and hostile, my perpetual baseline of anger impossible to control when my parents are home.

"Um, Mr. Murphy?" Dad shows no sign of hearing Blair. She licks her lips. "Could you pass the sugar?"

It sits by Dad's elbow. He nudges it in Blair's direction with no response.

"Thanks," Blair says after it's clear he isn't interested in conversation.

"Always a pleasure in the morning, aren't you, old man?" I sneer.

"Energy wasted is energy not spent on important discoveries."

Blair's eyes bulge. The hot burn of embarrassment crawls up my spine.

You haven't seen anything yet, angel. This isn't the worst this cold-hearted fucker has ever said to me.

Rubbing my jaw, I scoff, stewing for the fight I'm itching to pick with him. "Yeah. It's not efficient to talk to your son's girlfriend or interact with your family. Forget about affection, total time waster."

Blair's head snaps to me. I raise my eyebrows as I sip from my coffee. *Yeah, that's right*, my expression says. *You're my girl.*

Dad isn't ruffled by my jabs.

Mom walks in, dressed for work. Before they began traveling so much, they made a name for themselves in the medical field here in Ridgeview at a specialist clinic they started to treat various rare conditions. Through their clinic, my parents began to research experimental advancements in medicine and treatment that put them in high demand to speak and work around the country.

"Are we driving together or separate?" Mom grabs a granola bar from the pantry.

My teeth ache from how hard I clench my jaw.

"Separate." Dad sips his coffee. "Make sure the tech understands the parameters of the clinical trial. I don't want to explain it to him again."

Mom hums and turns to me. "Good luck on your tests this week. Your father and I might be here until Friday, but most likely will be flying out to Seattle before then. We're only in town to oversee the start of this trial before our next obligation."

Obligation. What bullshit. I feel like I'm one of their fucking obligations and I'm their son.

"Whatever," I mutter, turning away.

"One other thing, Devlin." Mom taps on her phone and shows me her screen. It's a monthly statement. "There's been an abnormal spike in your spending account."

Ice crystalizes in my stomach. "Why does it matter if you

give me the expense account in the first place? It's not like I've put that big of a dent in it."

Mom purses her lips. "We just want to make sure you're being responsible with your spending."

This is ridiculous. I have thousands left in the account. They fill it up every month, giving me more than I can spend in that amount of time, even when I'm being frivolous.

Blair has turned to a statue across from me, hunching her shoulders to make herself smaller. It pisses me off that she feels she has to make herself unnoticeable.

"I'm being responsible."

"That's all I wanted to know." Mom tucks her phone away. "Have a good day."

"Should we go, too? We'll be late." Blair slips beside me, grasping my limp wrist. Her touch is a balm, calming the rush of poisonous rage.

"Yeah." I dump the rest of my coffee in the sink and follow Blair to the garage. "I'm sorry. They're…"

There aren't words for what my parents are.

"It's fine." Blair tosses a concerned glance over her shoulder. "Want me to ride with you?"

"Yeah." It comes out gruff as I rake my fringe back.

I need her by my side now more than ever. I'm growing greedier with her time.

THIRTY-FOUR
BLAIR

The lines have blurred. In fact, the tasks have stopped completely. The deal is pretty much over without either of us saying it.

And yet, the new hospital bill I received is paid in full. There's extra money in my wallet.

Somewhere along the way, I blinked and didn't notice that Devlin and I fell into some undefined relationship.

It's undeniable. We're together often, all over each other once his parents leave the house empty. Our life at his house is domestic as fuck, leaving me squirmy and confused because I'm starting to catch feelings for something I can't have forever.

This has always had an end date on it. I've been living on borrowed time. Soon enough the issues I've been running from are going to catch up.

No matter how fast you run, your demons and problems always come for their pound of flesh.

"Hey, Blair! Wait up!" Sean calls from down the hall as I leave the library with an armful of books. He catches up to me and slings an arm over my shoulder as we walk. "What do ya got there?"

"The library gets rid of books once a month."

"Oh, so you were shopping for new stuff. Cool."

The way he says *shopping* hits me hard. It's not like once things shifted with Devlin and I, the rest of my school experience changed completely, but most of the relentless bullying stopped. Still, these privileged assholes can't help the way they talk. Disdain for my way of life bleeds into their tone when they're just making conversation. I didn't think these people were suddenly my friends, but Devlin's closest circle have been nicer since the beach party.

"Yeah, cool," I repeat in a clipped tone. "Can I help you with something?"

"Oh, yeah!" Sean snaps his fingers and yanks me closer to whisper in my ear. "I've been wondering about your rates. When Dev's finished, I was hoping to secure your services."

Every muscle in my body goes rigid. "Sorry, what?"

Sean chuckles and the sound makes me want to sink my fist into his gut. "Don't play coy. You don't really have the round features to pull it off. Girls like Thea have that shit on lock with the cute button nose and Bambi eyes, y'know? Shame about her fugly as shit granny sweaters, though."

A disgusted scoff rips from my throat before I can rein in my reaction. What a fucking pig.

"No, Sean, I don't know what you mean. Elaborate. Now."

Sean's head jerks. "Oof, girl. Is that attitude extra? I think I want to add some of that on every now and then. I like a little bit of fight. That's hot."

Slapping his arm off my shoulders, I plant myself in front of him. Passing students stare at the scene, but I don't care. I'm three seconds from kicking this dick-for-brains in the balls.

"What are you talking about?" I hiss.

Sean gives me a lopsided smile and leans close. "Dude, you're like, an escort. That's what you're doing with Devlin, right?"

My heart stops working as a pulse of adrenaline skitters across my nerve endings. Everything is icy and frozen inside.

"What?" I choke on my question. *Oh my god.* Willing myself to breathe so I don't pass out, I dig my grip into the books, grasping desperately at the way the spines dig into my skin to hang onto my temper. "Why do you think that?"

Sean shrugs. "It's been a rumor going around for a couple of weeks. Trent told me. So," he drawls. "Your rates? How much will it set me back for the 24/7 thing?"

My fist flies before I can control the anger coursing through me. I may not be physically strong, but I know how to throw a punch. Sean is caught off guard, doubling over with a winded groan when my fist lands in his gut.

"I'm not a fucking hooker, you dumb sack of shit!"

The people watching give up on pretending to do it on the down low, openly gawking. Some of them have phones out, because if there's drama it's getting filmed these days. Fucking posterity.

My chest heaves as I stalk away from Sean, seething.

Did Devlin know about this? He has to. Trent and Sean are his closest teammates other than Connor Bishop. How long has he let me believe that things between us were good?

He called me his girlfriend in front of his parents, for fuck's sake.

Tears well in my eyes. I swipe at them with a frustrated sound. I will not cry over this.

The bullshit at this school can't touch me.

It doesn't end there, though. Now that I'm aware of it and the video evidence of my showdown with Sean has spread around the school, I keep catching snide remarks about being Devlin's live-in whore throughout the rest of the day.

"Here comes Pretty Woman," a boy in my study hall announces, grinning at the wave of titters.

Nina's in my study hall. She sits in front of me instead of taking her usual seat with Bailey. I spend half the period shooting her bleached blowout a fierce glare, unable to get any homework done.

When Nina turns around to make the move she clearly has been wanting to, I'm ready for it. I set my notebook aside and cross my arms. She gives me a tight, prissy smirk.

"You can suck up to Dev all you want." Nina curls her manicured fingers around the back of her seat. A cruel, triumphant look flashes in her eyes. "Even ride his dick as much as I hear you have, but here's the thing, Raggedy Anne. It won't last forever. Guys like Devlin don't settle down with trash they picked up on the street."

My nails dig into my blazer. "Why don't you worry about yourself, Nina."

She shrugs. "I'm trying to help you out, girl. It's not my fault. That's just the tea."

"Thanks." *Fuck you.*

Even prepared for the attack, her words sting because they're true. It casts everything I've been doing in sharp relief. I've been playing house with Devlin, but it started with a lie.

Devlin turned me into everything I never wanted to be, forcing me across the last line standing that held my dignity intact.

Revenge doesn't end with happily ever after. My mistake was forgetting that.

THIRTY-FIVE
BLAIR

It takes almost all night, but I can't hold it in anymore. I have to know, right now, if this is real or not. If the rumor is truer than the feelings taking root in my being.

The feelings I thought might be love.

I was an idiot.

Gnawing on my thumbnail, I slip from my seat on the stool at the kitchen island. Devlin's back is to me as he organizes ingredients for a smoothie. We're supposed to go on a run, but I need to get this off my chest before the doubt eats me alive.

"So, Sean said something funny today."

Devlin rolls his eyes as he passes me to grab bananas. "Doubtful."

"He asked about my rates."

Devlin pauses across the island, narrowing his eyes as he plants his palms on the cool granite. "What?"

I chew on my nail and wrap an arm around my squirming stomach. "My rates. He's under the impression I'm available to purchase. As a prostitute. Well, *escort* was the word he used, actually, but semantics aside—"

Devlin snorts, the harsh sound caustic and dangerous. "If he comes near what's mine, he'll regret it. I'll end him."

The possessiveness in Devlin's tone twines around me, luring my hope out. It's been more difficult to keep it at bay. My survival skills are getting rusty.

"It's not just him. Nina brought it up, too. The rumor is all over the school."

He cuts his hand through the air with a sharp gesture. "You're mine, and that's the end of it in my eyes."

I jerk my head back. "Bullshit."

"What's bullshit is that you give a damn about this. Worse stuff has been said about you. How is this different from any other rumor? Besides, it's true that you're mine, so like I said, that's the end of it."

My shoulders tighten. I smack my palms on the counter, matching his stance. "I'm yours and that's the end of it? You can't control me, Devlin. No matter how hard you fight to pretend you can." I squint across the island at him, challenging his crappy logic. "And that bothers you, doesn't it?"

Devlin glares at me. "Willing to place money on that claim?"

I take an instinctive step back.

The expression on his face sends a frisson of unease through me. I've been able to read him easier than ever, but now it's like his walls have come back down. As if he's pushing me away, back to controlling me instead of fighting *with* me as an equal.

"What are you going to do?"

He stalks around the island, trapping me against the pantry door before I make a move. His hand holds my throat, thumb pressed to my pulse.

"Prove you belong to me. You're *mine*. That's all that matters."

I open my mouth to contest, but his tongue plunges inside as he kisses me with an angry edge. I grab his bicep and t-shirt, nails scrabbling as he controls the kiss. A small sound escapes me. His hand flexes on my throat. As he pulls back, he drags my lower lip between his teeth.

"Ah!"

Devlin growls and hauls me over his shoulder, leaving the kitchen.

"Hey! Where are you taking me?" A stinging smack on my ass makes me yelp.

I get my answer when Devlin dumps me down onto the plush rug in the lounge, next to the low, modern gray sectional that takes up most of the room. He's on me in a flash, caging me with his body. There's a hardness in his eyes.

"What are you doing?"

"No more questions."

"Fuck that noise." Twisting away, I drag myself across the floor.

Devlin wraps one hand around my thigh and hooks his fingers in the waistband of my jeans, yanking me back with a dark, sinister laugh.

"Stay," he orders while he attacks my neck, scraping his teeth over my skin.

"Ah! Damn you!"

I scrabble for purchase on the rug while I fight him. We both grunt, wrestling for the upper hand. As we roll across the floor, he claims my lips in another punishing kiss that makes my heart beat hard and heat pulse between my legs as they wrap around him like I'm coming home. He grinds his stiff cock against me, both of us consumed by the carnal excitement of struggling for power.

I don't know if we're fighting or fucking anymore, but it's turned into vicious foreplay.

And I fucking love it.

Fire burns inside, hotter than any I've experienced before.

It makes me feel alive, the pleasure and pain creating an intense mix.

The realization hits me hard—he's not pushing us back to our previous power struggle. When we're like this, I have power over him, too. We share the control, trading it back and forth.

A wild grin curves my mouth.

Devlin sucks hickeys into my skin and bites a trail down my throat, stretching my loose shirt down to expose my breasts. I don't have a bra on, giving him access to clamp his lips and teeth over my nipples.

"Fuck!" I arch with wanton abandon as he bites at my breasts hard enough to leave marks.

By the time we're done, I'm going to be covered, my skin branded by Devlin as if he's burning his name into my body with each scrape of teeth and forceful suck.

I'll brand him right back with the angry red trails my nails leave on his skin.

"That's right," Devlin rumbles between sucking on one of my nipples before he moves to the other. He strips me, ripping the clothes from my body to continue his bombardment of brutal pleasure. With each new bruising bite, his voice is like gravel while he declares, "Here? Mine. Here, too. All of you —*every inch*—you're all mine, little thief. That was the deal we made."

The urge to fight flares up. I pop up on one elbow, torn

between dragging Devlin closer or pushing him away by my grip in his hair. "So you'll just let them all believe I'm your live-in whore?"

Devlin gets in my face after tearing his shirt off. He grabs my jaw in his strong grip. "You think I give a *fuck* about any of those puppets or what they think? The only thing I care about is you." He gives me a searing, soul-twisting kiss. I gasp against his lips, and his tongue pushes inside my mouth, sliding against mine. The kiss is softer than the commanding arrogance clouding his actions. "They don't matter."

I bite his lip, giving as good as he's given me. He pins me to the floor, wrapping his fingers around my throat. It tugs on the desire pooling in my gut, throbbing through my body. I bare my teeth, ready for more.

Devlin's eyes flash with the challenge, his lips curling up. "Fucking fight me, angel."

With a raw sound, I buck up, managing to flip Devlin over to straddle him. My hands form claws as I scrape across his bare chest. He spurs me on with taunts, his ferocious grin devilishly attractive. The rush of power fills me as I roll my hips to feel him between my thighs while Devlin holds me in place by his grip on my waist with a groan.

The wonder in his expression as I peer down at him with heavy-lidded eyes pours warmth through my body.

"Give me all of your fight. This right here is why you're mine."

Devlin tackles me onto my back again, pinning my wrists above my head in one hand. I struggle against him, but he bears down on me, nipping at my swollen lips. The rug burns against my bare skin as he spreads my legs apart and presses his hips into mine, the material of his jeans scraping against my pussy.

My eyes roll back in my head and a guttural sound tears

from my throat at the sensation, the roughness of his jeans separating his cock from me.

He flips me over, forcing a knee between my thighs as he keeps my hands pinned above my head. His erection presses against my ass mercilessly. I moan, delirious with adrenaline and lust.

"I want you bare. Nothing between us this time." Swallowing, I can't stop my hips from rolling against him. Amusement laces his tone as he smacks my ass. "Oh? You like the sound of that, angel? You want me to fuck you raw?"

It's hard to cut through the lust fogging my head. "I'm not on the pill."

Not only that, a frisson of fear spirals through me, locking every muscle. My parents made that mistake. They were so young.

His grip flexes on my wrists. "I don't care."

The reckless disregard could bite us in the ass.

"I'd take care of you no matter what, angel." His husky voice softens at the edges.

My chest squeezes tight. That's all I want. "Okay."

"Stay." The command is barked in a dangerous voice. He waits a beat, then peels back. I make a sound of protest as the cool air hits my sweaty skin, squirming against the rug to feel the tingling burn in my breasts where the bitten skin throbs with a dull, sensual ache. "Good fucking girl."

I gasp, trembling as a burst of heat overwhelms me. His voice is gruff and it dances along my nerve endings.

When Devlin covers my back with his body, he's naked. A wild moan leaves me as he glides the head of his cock between my slick folds. With a sharp tug, he repositions me on my hands and knees. His controlling grip finds my hair and he pulls, stretching the column of my neck back.

"Ah! D-Devlin!"

"You're so wet already. Fuck, your pussy is glistening." As his cock lines up, he pulls my hair harder so I'm completely at his mercy. "Is this what you're moaning for? You want this cock?"

An internal struggle wars within me. I'm caught between the heady surge of dizzying arousal from his roughness and fighting back for power. But I feel alive right now and so fucking turned on, drunk with desire for this wicked side Devlin is letting free.

Not just letting free, but losing control of.

This is Devlin beneath everything. Ruthless and vicious. It should scare me, but it doesn't.

"Please," I beg, wound tight with the need he ignited like an inferno. "Come on, I want it. I want you."

Devlin's lips graze my ear as he palms my hip with his free hand. "You hear yourself begging for me, Blair? That's how I know you're mine."

"Yes," I gasp. He releases my hair to hold my hips in both hands. "Do it, just—" Devlin's cock slips through the slick wetness coating my folds. "I need you inside me."

Devlin thrusts inside with a depraved sound.

We both release choked groans. He fills me completely, so hard and perfect.

Before I've caught my breath, Devlin's hips snap, driving his cock into me.

"Give me your screams, little demon."

"Oh god." I arch my back as his dick hits a spot that sends electric bursts of pleasure to my core. "Fuck, yes!"

Devlin hums in aroused satisfaction. In the huge windows, I glimpse what we look like in the reflection.

Holy shit.

Devlin's head tips back as he pumps his hips, fucking me roughly. His hair is tousled, curling with sweat across his forehead. The muscles of his stomach and the cut V in his hips flex with each thrust.

We look like a Bosch painting. Wild, and unchained. Hedonistic.

"Christ, Blair. So fucking good. Clench that tight little pussy on my cock."

I gasp as I squeeze around him, feeling it more intensely. My nails dig into the thick carpet as his length fills me.

Devlin bends over, kissing the star tattoo on my back, his hand wrapping around my neck again in an iron hold. I scream as his open-mouthed kisses end in him biting it hard. At the same time, he slams into me, making my breath catch in my throat as my core erupts in pleasure.

"Oh fu-fuck, I'm coming!" My cries turn incoherent. Devlin doesn't stop, but picks up the pace.

"Yes," he growls. "I feel you."

Before my orgasm fades, another is creeping up. I pant as I rock back to meet Devlin's harsh thrusts. With a snarl, he whips my body upright by his tight hold on my neck.

My stomach clenches. The new position makes his cock slide deeper. I stretch my head back to lean into him. Devlin squeezes my neck, almost cutting off my air. His other hand goes between my legs, rubbing my clit relentlessly.

"You're going to come again on my cock," Devlin whispers darkly in my ear. "You'll only come for me. I'm the only one that can give you this."

Devlin's fingers circle my throbbing clit, making me feel so good that it's overwhelming. My words are stolen away by the coiling heat winding tight enough to snap. His touch edges on brutal as he pounds deep and sharp inside me. A sob tears from me as the stimulation becomes too much.

"I can't."

"You *will*." Devlin's skin slaps against mine with each sharp thrust. I can hear the wet sound of our bodies connecting as my pussy clenches on his cock. "Fucking hell, yes, my siren." The awe-struck words twine around me. His thumb strokes my pulse as his fingers put more pressure on my clit. "Tell me you're mine."

I gasp for breath, hanging onto the arm cupping my neck for dear life as he bounces me on his cock.

"D-Dev—"

"Say it."

Everything is too much. The coil in my stomach breaks in an explosion of electric heat. It runs up my spine while my core quivers with wave after wave. My orgasm threatens to shake me apart at the seams as I scream.

"I'm yours! I'm yours, yours, yours, fuck!"

Devlin's teeth sink into my shoulder with a fierce sound as his hips pump. His arms wrap around me as he tenses. His cock throbs inside me and I feel the hot sensation of his come.

My heart pounds, rushing in my ears and thudding through my body as we shake together, wracked by aftershocks of our releases. Our breaths come in ragged pants, dragging air into our lungs.

For a long stretch, Devlin holds me. I'm wrung out, my whole body aching pleasantly with the twinge of use, from my rug-burned knees to my tender skin where Devlin left his marks. He traces the tender bruise forming over my star tattoo with a gentle touch, following his caress with a light kiss.

There's a scary amount of truth in my answer to Devlin's demand.

I want to be his and I want him to be mine.

"Are you okay?"

I hum, too exhausted to form words and ready to collapse to the rug. Devlin places soft kisses wherever he can reach.

"Why don't you go upstairs. Put on one of my shirts and climb in bed."

I tense. "Where will you be?"

"Out for a little bit." A hardness creeps back into his tone. "I have a quick...errand to take care of."

"Now?" I twist to see him, but he hugs me tighter.

"It's important." Devlin mouths at the crook of my neck. "Promise, I'll be back soon."

"Okay."

Every muscle protests as Devlin helps me to my feet. I'm going to faceplant into bed. Devlin cups my face, gliding his thumb over my cheek. The wonder from before lingers, lighting up the ominous shadows in his eyes. He kisses my forehead tenderly.

After Devlin heads for the garage, I go upstairs, not bothering with any of the clothes he flung around in our romp. Despite the exhaustion and satisfaction of the experience downstairs, a niggling restlessness prods at me while I clean up in the bathroom. We didn't exactly address the point I brought up to him. With a ragged sigh, I slap the used washcloth in the sink, pad into the bedroom, and open one of the panels to Devlin's closet. As I poke through his hoodies, I chew on my lip.

It was great in the moment, but was I repeating the past by not using protection? There are options now, more than my parents had. Still, I can't beat back the uncertainty welling in my chest.

As I dig through the stack of t-shirts I love to steal from, a rustling makes me pause when I pull out the one I want. "What the...?"

I tug on the shirt and a folded magazine page flutters to the floor from inside the shirt. My stomach sinks as I pick it up and open it.

Our contract.

"Shit," I whisper, throat tight. "Why do you still have this if—?"

The niggling worry roars to life, making my stomach roll. I thought Devlin and I were fighting together, but am I wrong? Are we back where we started? Did we ever *progress* in the first place?

A pained gasp pierces the oppressive silence in the room.

Maybe he forgot he had it.

But the shirt I put on is one Devlin wore last week. The creases on the page speak volumes to how often it's been opened and folded.

"Damn it." Rubbing my forehead, I pace at the foot of the bed. "Is he playing me?"

He has to be if he still has this damn contract.

It paints everything we did downstairs in a harsh light. I thought I saw awe in Devlin's eyes, but now?

What did I actually prove to him? To myself?

Devlin never denied the rumor. He just wanted to claim me. How the hell can he go around calling me his girlfriend to his parents while he has the contract hidden in his closet?

He only cares about me? What a joke.

A lie.

One I fucking fell for.

With a frustrated grunt, I grab it by both ends, intent on shredding it. I stop before I rip it.

As much as it hurts to find this, I can't do anything yet. I need more answers first, and Mom is still in the hospital.

My heart feels fragile, as bruised as my body.

In a numb daze, I stick the contract in the stack of shirts in Devlin's closet. I'm not ready to face what I've discovered until I'm better prepared for the fallout.

THIRTY-SIX
DEVLIN

My grip on the wheel is tight as I whip the Mustang around the bend. Bishop whistles, tapping out a beat on the frame of the open window, night air gusting through his hair.

A muffled groan sounds from the backseat, where we stashed Sean after I knocked him out. He thought we were going for a cruise to pick up chicks. Nope.

I chose the Mustang because it's Dad's, so I don't give a shit if the blood trickling from the corner of Sean's mouth smears on the leather.

Bishop didn't ask questions when I called him up for help with this errand. He had a bat in hand and a cutthroat gleam in his eyes when I picked him up.

I want to get this done quick so I can get back to Blair, waiting at home in our bed. It killed me to leave her alone after the incredible fuck, but I couldn't let this fly. A growl rumbles in my chest, the anger a constant simmer.

Sean and those other puppets fucking thought they could get away with spreading shit about my girl? I'll end each one of them. He'll pay the price and meet the brunt of my wrath.

"Up here on the left." Bishop nods as the abandoned quarry site comes into view. "Perfect spot."

A hiking trail picks up at the back of the weed-choked gravel lot, the rest of the site cleared and filled in. All that remains is a rusted store building. It's the perfect spot to teach Sean a lesson.

I pull into the old lot and park the Mustang. Bishop grabs his bat, and we climb out to haul Sean from the backseat.

"God, you're heavy," Bishop grumbles, readjusting the distribution of Sean's weight to flick his lolling head.

Sean mumbles something unintelligible.

We drag him to the back of the storage building and prop him against the rusted metal wall. When Sean doesn't stir right away, I kick his foot. Hard.

"Wake up."

Sean jolts at the sound of my command. He spots Bishop first, then me. The relaxed look fades when he realizes my expression is deadly. His hand flies to his head.

That's right, shit for brains. I'm the one that cold-cocked you.

"Mornin', sunshine!" Bishop bends to get on Sean's level, hands dangling over the bat slung across his shoulders. "Heard you like to feed that beautiful beast, the Silver Lake rumor mill. Should we feed it some more?" Bishop's grin turns manic. "I've been holding on to the story of the time you pissed yourself freshman year for a long ass time."

Sean flinches back, hands up. "W-what's up guys? What is this?"

Bishop tips his head to me. I growl, advancing on Sean. He yelps like a little bitch, scuttling through the weeds.

"Nowhere to run from me, fucker."

"I, uh," Sean blathers, licking his lips, "thought we were going on the prowl for pussy."

Bishop chuckles sadistically, smacking his bat against the corrugated metal siding of the building. "Bro, do you see any babes around?"

Sean's throat bobs. "Uh..."

"Think hard, Sean." The moonlight shifts with the passing clouds, painting his fear in flickers across his face. I master the burning anger, ambling in front of him. "What did you do this week? Who did you talk to?"

"Is this because I was hitting on Davis? Guys, she's trashy. That's fair game."

The whoop Bishop releases pierces the night air as he laughs in disbelief. Bishop jabs the tip of the bat beside Sean's head. He flinches, glaring at us.

"Oh boy, you're stupid," Bishop says. "That's hilarious."

Gritting my teeth, I grab Sean by the collar, half-lifting him from his seated position. Sean jerks his head back.

"You'll kill that rumor, or I'll kill you for what you said to her," I growl.

"What is up with you this year? You've changed, man." The end of Sean's words ratchet up in pitch when I slam him against the wall.

"Really?" There's a dangerous amusement threading my voice. "I've never felt more like myself."

I drive my fist in Sean's gut, taking immense satisfaction in the way he groans and curls forward. Bishop snatches him before he can fall, standing him back up for my next hit. I pound Sean with my fists.

"You don't come near her! She isn't up for grabs." I hold

Sean by the throat, squeezing until I control his air supply. His eye is swelled shut and blood oozes from the cut on his lip. "Blair is off fucking limits. Clear?"

Sean nods weakly. "S-sorry."

With a disgusted snarl, I drop him. Sean crumples to the gravel like a sack of potatoes. I flex my hand, examining the redness. Two of my knuckles split, stinging with each movement.

"Enjoy your walk home." I spit on the ground next to Sean's foot.

"Oh, and if you think about talking about this..." Bishop flashes me a look, then crouches beside Sean, murmuring in his ear.

I can't hear what he says, but the curve of Bishop's mouth is savage. Sean goes pale in the moonlight. It must be one of his juicier pieces of blackmail.

"Cool?" Bishop smirks and pats Sean's head when he nods. "Cool. Good choice."

Bishop pops to his feet and twirls the bat up to rest on his shoulder.

"Let's go."

I promised Blair I wouldn't be long. Now that I've rained hell on Sean, the anger has bled away. The tether in my chest tugs, calling me home to her.

THIRTY-SEVEN
DEVLIN

I wait outside her bedroom, dressed and ready to head over to my aunt and uncle's for Thanksgiving dinner.

My knuckles have healed, but when I last saw Sean before the long weekend break began, his black eye remained purple and puffy. Whenever he sees me, he scurries away like the little rodent he is.

Blair opens the door, a knockout in the new dress I bought her. She tried to refuse it when I left it in her room, claiming it was too much. It looks damn good on her, but it isn't that the dress is anything special.

It's Blair—she's what makes the dress shine, not the other way around.

Her brows lift when she finds me there, flicking her gaze over me. A flare of heat fills her whiskey-colored eyes.

My cock twitches. It's hard to keep a leash on how much I fucking want her. The need keeps growing, like I'll never have enough.

"Perfect," I praise, taking her in.

Blair's dark lashes flutter, made darker by her light makeup and mascara. She smooths her hands over the deep jade dress that hugs her body and falls to her knees. "It looks okay?"

"Yes. Ready to go?"

"Okay."

I rest my hand at the small of her back as we descend the steps, but at the bottom she strides ahead of me to reach the garage first. Smothering a sigh, I retrieve the key fob for the Porsche from the hook and climb into the car, where she waits for me.

On the short drive, I keep an eye on her in my periphery. Blair clicks her nails together.

Things have remained tense between us since the wild sex last week. An uncomfortable feeling slithers in my gut like a poison. Blair is pulling away. I can feel it. I've been trying to mentally prepare for it if she does, giving into my coping mechanism to protect myself.

Even after reading through three of Mom's books on the brain science behind these habits, I can't cut them off just by reading about them.

It's frustrating to be so weak. To have the one thing that's made me feel alive, unable to stop myself from closing off to keep the fear at bay. No matter how strong I think I am, I'm still the same little boy inside, defenseless against the raw pain of everyone leaving.

When I pull up to Aunt Lottie and Uncle Ed's house, Lucas' car is there.

"They must be here already." Blair points at the car.

"Gemma said they'd be in town for the weekend to visit both families. Maybe we can grab breakfast with them tomorrow."

We head up the deck and enter through the kitchen where the scent of a home cooked meal hits us as soon as the door opens.

"Smells great, Aunt Lottie."

"Devlin!" Uncle Ed hauls himself out of a chair in the living room, followed by their plump pug dog, Lancelot.

Blair lights up, bending down to greet him. "Hi, my favorite knight."

"Looking sharp." Uncle Ed shakes my hand and beams at Blair. His usual gray stubble is shaved clean, his cheeks slightly pink from drinking. "We've been trying to get Dev to bring you over here for weeks. We're happy to finally meet his girlfriend."

A bubble of warmth expands in my chest at hearing Blair described as my girlfriend.

Blair tucks her sleek hair behind her ears, rising to her feet to shake hands. "That's all on him." She elbows me. "I love your dog and would've been happy to come over. Thanks for having me."

Uncle Ed laughs and reaches out to ruffle my hair, messing up the way I styled it.

"Ed," I complain, leaning away.

"What, you think you're too big for me to do that just because you're taller than me now? I still do it to Lucas, too. Don't I, son?"

"And I do it right back. You just have less hair to mess with," Lucas jokes from the couch, where his arm is around Gemma.

Uncle Ed laughs, touching his sandy brown hair that's shot through with gray.

"Come on in, you two. Anything to drink?" Uncle Ed waves us into the warm kitchen. It's cozier than my house. It feels like a family actually lives here. "Anyway, Dev, you don't have to duck our invitations. You aunt and I have been missing you after you were here so often at the start of the school year. You know you and your friends are always welcome over here. How's Bishop?"

"He's fine."

Aunt Lottie comes in with a couple of bottles of wine. "I brought reinforcements."

Lucas and Gemma come over from the couch to help her in the kitchen as Uncle Ed hands us appetizers.

Once she's taken care of the wine, Aunt Lottie turns to me, clasping my shoulders. "All right, let me see you." She gives me a once over and pulls me into a hug. "I see you make an extra effort for Blair. How come you don't dress up nice for us when you come over here?"

Lucas snorts as he pours wine, passing the glass to Gemma. She smacks him, and Lottie shoots him a flat look.

Blair laughs quietly, but it's not as relaxed as usual.

I wrap my arm around her waist, hiding a frown at the tense line of her body. "Aunt Lottie, this is Blair."

She gives Blair a warm, approving smile. She takes both of her hands. "Blair. It's wonderful to meet you. We're glad Devlin's met someone so lovely."

"Thanks, it's great to meet you, too." Blair directs a look at me from the corner of her eye. "Your home is really nice."

Gemma comes over and hooks her arm with Blair's. "Let's go snack on cheese on the deck. There's a great sunset this time of year. I was kicking myself for not bringing my camera when they had me over last year."

Blair relaxes as she pulls away from my side. "Sounds perfect."

The girls disappear on the deck with a platter of cheese and the dog, faithfully circling at their feet in the hope of morsels dropping. Gemma feeds him a piece of cheddar, smiling fondly at the pug dog.

Lucas slaps me on the back, drawing my attention from the girls. "Let them be for a bit. They never get to hang out without us."

My aunt and uncle commandeer both of us a minute later to help with dinner, delegating us to different tasks.

"So," Lottie drags out once the mashed potatoes are done. "Tell us about her!"

"I, uh," I glanced at Lucas for help. He's got a wide, cocky smile on his face. "Well, we actually used to go to the same school. She was in my third grade art class."

I swallow thickly at the surprised look all three of them give me. I tug on my ear and push my hand through my hair.

"Wait, Blair?" Lucas clarifies.

"Yeah." An affectionate smile curves my mouth. "She gave me her star drawings. Neither of us remembered until we recently...became closer."

Lucas lifts his brows knowingly. He's aware of the tenacity of our hatred and witnessed the shift at the lake party.

"How sweet," Aunt Lottie sighs happily, wrapping her arm around me in a half-hug while she cooks. "It was meant to be, then!"

My heart thumps.

When we sit down for dinner, the tension still rolls off Blair in waves. She's never talkative unless she's at ease, but she's quieter than usual. I shoot her a glance as my family digs into the meal.

Lucas, Gemma, and Uncle Ed get lost in a conversation about college while I'm distracted by Blair. She's been agitated all night.

"What about you, Blair?" Aunt Lottie asks.

"What?"

"Do you have a university picked out yet? What do you want to study?"

Blair turns into a statue beside me. "Not yet. Applications are due soon, though. I haven't decided, but I'll probably end up in nursing or maybe accounting."

Uncle Ed nods. "Smart fields to study."

Blair's gaze falls to her plate, a wrinkle marring her forehead. We haven't talked about it, but when I picture Blair as a nurse or an accountant it feels wrong. Neither of those are her passion.

Not like the number of art and history books she has in her growing collection.

"Did you finish your application submission, Devlin?" Uncle Ed asks, wiping his mouth on a napkin.

"Yeah."

Blair's eyes flick in my direction, and an uncomfortable tightness grips my chest.

Aunt Lottie tilts her head, pursing her lips. When she does that, she looks so much like Mom. "Any school will be lucky to have you, no matter what path you decide to pursue."

A hollow laugh leaves me. Her hidden meaning is clear: *you can do whatever you want, don't listen to your parents.* They've never approved of the way my parents push me to have a career in medicine. When Lucas came to them last year about his college dream, they were supportive. If I try to tell Mom and Dad I don't want to study medicine, I get shut down.

"Yeah, as long as it's part of the plan." I put an emphasis on *plan* with a capital P.

Blair frowns, playing with the corner of the napkin in her lap, pinching the corner.

"Not everything goes according to plan," Gemma says sincerely. "Do whatever you want to do, Dev." Her gaze slides to Blair. "That goes for both of you."

"Thanks." I sigh. It's easy for Gemma to say. Her parents are another perfect example of a loving, well-adjusted family. She wouldn't understand the years of investment my parents have put into my college plans. "How's Alec doing at University of Colorado in Denver?"

Gemma launches into a story about her twin brother. By the time she's done, she yelps at the time on her phone. "Oh man, I'm sorry, guys. I promised my parents we'd split so we could stop by their house for dessert."

"Oh! Here, take some extra sweet potato casserole for your dad. He's been asking for the recipe."

Aunt Lottie and Gemma get up to sort out their share of leftovers while Lucas shakes his dad's hand.

"Um, I'm going to head out, too," Blair says.

"What?" I lean my arm across the back of her chair. "I drove here."

"Gemma offered to drop me off when they left." She bounces her gaze between my eyes and sighs. "I want to go see my mom. We've never been apart for a holiday before. It feels wrong not to see her."

The irrational, possessive jealousy rears up and then blinks out as fast as it came on. I drop my arm to her shoulder and pull her closer, kissing her cheek.

"Do you want me to take you?" It's stupid, but I'm reluctant to let her leave my sight for long.

I've become so greedy the more time I've spent with Blair. Have I kept her from her mom by monopolizing her time? I'm a bastard. Her mom is important to her, I shouldn't do anything to mess with that connection.

Macy's health has turned rocky with the cooler weather.

Blair puts her hand on my leg. "No, it's okay. I'll—" Her gaze flicks to my aunt and uncle. I sense she doesn't want to admit to them she lives with me as she falters. "I'll call you later."

"Blair, it was a pleasure. Please come back soon, okay?" Uncle Ed gets up to hug her. She sends me a wide-eyed look. I hold back a smile. Uncle Ed is affectionate. "You're welcome anytime. You and Devlin should come over next week."

Aunt Lottie echoes his sentiments from the counter.

A few minutes later, I'm sitting alone at the table with my aunt and uncle after Lucas, Gemma, and Blair leave.

Uncle Ed and Aunt Lottie share a speaking glance. She smiles and reaches across the table to squeeze my hand.

"We really like her."

"Yeah," I agree, throat dry and scratchy.

I haven't put a name to any of these feelings that spread through me, twisted with my insides like a living organism. *Like* doesn't come close to what I feel when I'm around her. There's no way to stop it from flourishing, no way to cut it out without killing my heart. I have to live with it, every bittersweet second as she pulls further away from me.

* * *

Sitting with them is easy and comfortable until it isn't. The shift happens in a fraction of a second.

We've made our way through two different pies, laughing at a story about Lucas getting lost on the Oak Ridge College campus the first week of school.

All at once it's too much to sit with Uncle Ed and Aunt Lottie. Even though they're family, closer than my own parents, I'm still not their son.

Mom and Dad haven't spent Thanksgiving or any other holiday with me in years, not since I was nine.

It's times like these that their absence burns the most.

"I should go." They give me matching looks tinged in sympathy. I don't want to see it. Rubbing at the phantom pain in my chest, I come up with an excuse. "I want to be there when Blair gets back. So I don't miss her call to know she made it home safely."

"Okay, sweetie," Aunt Lottie says. "But please promise you'll come by soon. I worry about you, all alone in that big house. It's not right. You know you can come over and stay here whenever you want."

She drops a kiss on my head before I stand.

"Yeah. Thanks Aunt Lottie."

I say goodnight to them and head home with the leftovers they loaded on me. It's empty when I get there, the weight of loneliness crushing down on my shoulders.

Releasing a strained breath, I have nothing to do but wait for Blair to return. After I place a piece of the pie she was eyeing earlier on the counter, I sink to the couch in the lounge, staring at the spot where I fucked her, completely unrestrained, allowing the monster inside free rein.

And she took it.

Begged me.

She didn't look at me with disgust when she faced my inner monster, she spread her legs wider and gave me her claws, too.

My heart gives an irritating, needy flutter in my chest. I grab at the front of my shirt.

It's strange how one person can make you feel so much. Blair makes me feel hate, desire, anger, lust, and something even more dangerous—love. The kind of love that's unknown, like a star collapsing on itself to form a black hole. You can't help but get dragged in by the gravitational pull. A love that doesn't need light because it blooms even in the darkest depths.

I don't know how to tell her. Not when she's been closing

herself off. I won't bare my need for her when hers doesn't match it.

She's slipping away. All I want to do is hold on tighter. But if I do that, I'll only make demands I shouldn't.

If she wants to go so bad, fine.

I lean my elbows on my thighs and put my face into my hands, massaging the dull ache in my temples.

When she leaves, she's got her mom to go home to. I'll have an empty, overpriced prison cell all to myself once more.

The pang of jealousy gives way to the longing I've smothered. It seeps between the fractures in my internal boxes, bubbling to the surface with enough force to make me gasp for air. My stomach knots and my chest hurts.

I dig my fingers into my scalp in an attempt to shove it back down. The longing refuses to be tamed back into its place, eating at me instead as I wait for Blair to come back to me.

The door opens and the light in the hall clicks on. My head snaps up.

"Are you sitting in the dark?" Blair appears from the hall, shrugging out of the charcoal peacoat she borrowed from me. "Emo stereotype, much?"

I scrape my fingers through my hair. "I guess."

Blair's brow pinches. Her makeup is smudged, the mascara dried underneath her eyes like it ran. Was she crying?

"How's your mom?" My voice is too hard.

The grip on my composure is slipping thanks to the fear that's lingered in the back of my head for days.

But the look in her eyes is wary and distant.

"She's...stable," Blair says, exhaustion evident in her petite frame. "They've got the fever under control, but the inflammation in her heart hasn't cleared up."

"Are her doctors not doing everything they can to—"

"They are. Apparently there's just not enough known

about her illness, so it's not clear to them what caused her heart condition. All they keep saying is that autoimmune myocarditis is rare." Blair's eyes flash. "I'm going up to bed. It's been a long day."

I don't want her to leave like everyone else does. No one stays long enough to love me past my issues, but for a while I believed she might.

"Next time I'm going with you."

THIRTY-EIGHT
BLAIR

The laugh that escapes me is sharp.

"No, you're not. I don't care if you're paying for the bills, you don't get to just tell me when and where I get to go, or come with me like you're my boyfriend."

Devlin's jaw clenches, a muscle jumping. "I am. You're—"

"Mine? Is that what you were going to say?" I scoff, throwing my arms out. "Devlin, you never even asked me! You just started saying I was your girlfriend to your family without discussing it! You didn't talk to me, didn't ask me—you don't just get to decide. That's not how this works."

He shoots to his feet, closing the distance between us in two strides, towering over me with a dangerous glint in his eye. I jut my chin, unafraid of him.

"You're treading a risky path." He grips my arms. "Don't make me repeat how things work with us."

It's all becoming too much.

"There's no *us*!" I struggle free of his firm grasp and turn on my heel.

Devlin follows as I jog up the steps. The hair on the back of my neck stands, my instincts go on alert, expecting him to grab me. I'm faster, keeping out of his reach.

"What do you mean there isn't an us?" Devlin's tone is so rough, it's hard to make out his question.

The arrogant bastard has made a triumphant return. He's lurked beneath this whole time, waiting to remind me of the one truth I've burned into my brain since Dad first left.

Men can't be trusted. No matter what they say, or how sweetly they care for you, they'll all do the same thing—hurt you. Survival has to come first.

I stop in the middle of his bedroom, blinking angrily. My feet carried me here automatically, as if I can't shake how safe I've felt in this room. I kick off the short chunky heels I wore to his family's house and take a breath to filter out some of the agitation that's built in my chest since finding the contract hidden in Devlin's closet.

"Did I miss the part where I sold you the girlfriend experience?" The accusation leaves me on a pained shout, scraping my throat raw.

A flash of surprise crosses Devlin's face before he schools his expression into a controlled calm. It's fake, manufactured to hide his true feelings. I can see the white-knuckled fists he shoves in his pockets, though.

"I haven't set a task or paid for you to humiliate yourself in weeks. We've clearly been operating under different impressions of our relationship."

He's so careful about the way he words it, skipping over the way he's been manipulating me, treating me like he cares when he still has the contract. The blistering fury overflows, spurred on by the long fucking night I've had sitting with Mom, her body drained like she's going to be taken from me at any second.

"Goddamn it, Devlin! You can't buy love, it's not real! This has all been a fucking game to you!"

"The money doesn't matter." Devlin's mouth pinches, working like he's trapping his unfiltered responses, considering what to say before he opens those lying lips. "The arrangement doesn't matter, or anything else."

I jab my finger at him. "Doesn't it? You're so desperate for company, you *paid* me to play house with you."

Devlin's jaw clenches. Misery fills his eyes for a second before it disappears. Words keep coming, spilling from me without control. I throw everything in his face.

"You're a monster," I hiss. "You hated a girl so much you had to take your torment even further by diminishing me and manipulating my desperation to suit your sick game? You made me believe you actually—" I cut myself off with a harsh gasp before I continue in a low voice. "What a way to live up to your reputation as the devil. No wonder your parents are never around, because they probably can't stand to be near their demon spawn."

The only reaction Devlin gives me is a faint tightness around his eyes and the precise tilt of his head.

My throat burns with regret. The second the words are out, I wish I could take them back. It's a low, cutting blow, even for me. After seeing the way his parents treat him, I shouldn't have said it. That anger is born of the hurt Dad instilled in me, my rage is for him above anyone else, for leaving and destroying Mom's happiness.

I open my mouth to apologize, taking a step toward him.

"I see." Those two words are clipped and austere, freezing me in place.

It echoes in the silence, starkly outlining how little I mean to him. Nothing more than his paid toy. A game to play and no more.

Everything we had was fake.

I was so stupid to believe this cynical asshole could love a broken, beat down girl from the wrong side of town. Naive to forget how little I can trust men—in the end, they're all alike.

Releasing a watery breath, I go to the closet panels along the wall, opening the one where I found our contract when I was stealing one of Devlin's shirts to wear. I take out the magazine page with our deal written on it and spin to face Devlin. I knew when I discovered he still had it, in his bedroom no less, that things hadn't changed.

Devlin's eyes widen a fraction. He must have thought I wouldn't find the contract. It was bound to happen—I'm always stealing his clothes.

"This is over."

The sound of the tearing page grates on my ears as I shred it in front of him. My chest heaves with my agitated breathing, hoarse sounds slipping past my lips as I try to hold my emotions back. I'm in survival mode, there's no time for tears. Not yet. I can't crack until I'm in a safe space, where I can let go and bleed myself dry of this bleak feeling swallowing me whole.

Devlin watches with a detached disinterest, eyes hooded. The torn scraps of the magazine page fall to the floor in a flutter.

Part of me wants to storm out, but I'm not leaving my books behind. I have more clothes I left at the trailer, the ones here can stay. I gather the paperbacks from the nightstand into my arms and go into my room. Devlin follows, hands buried in his pockets. He doesn't say anything to stop me as I grab my duffel bag and stack my books inside.

It stabs like needles into my nerve endings. He says *nothing*.

Doesn't that drive the truth home? If he cared, he'd say something to stop me from self-destructing.

The tears I'm holding back leak free, but I can't break down yet. I finish gathering the books from the bedrooms, pull on shoes, and pause at the top of the stairs with the heavy bag weighing me down.

There are more books I've left all over the house. The one unaccounted for that hurts worst of all is my favorite book, the one I read with Mom. I can't find Stardust anywhere and I'm out of time. Devlin is breathing down the back of my neck.

I need to get out of here, far away from him, before I give into the weak rattle in my chest begging me to stay.

Shoving it down, I start for the steps.

A hand on my arm stops me. I glance down at Devlin's iron grip squeezing my bicep too hard. There's a tremor in his hand.

"You can't force me to stay here against my will like I'm your captive." My voice is cold. It's the only way I know to stay strong so I can leave. "Let me go."

Devlin releases a derisive scoff, dropping my arm. It throbs, the echo of his fingers lingering. My pale skin will probably carry his bruises.

"This arrangement is over then."

I hesitate at the top of the stairs, looking back. He could call the cops. It was the threat that kept me under his thumb at first, before I thought it changed.

It's a consequence I'll have to face later.

Devlin's stare is piercing, giving away nothing. Even when I hated him, I could read between the lines of his carefully constructed mask.

Gripping the strap of my patched up duffel bag, I make my escape. Every step makes my heart snap, the shattered pieces falling away. I don't reach my car before the tears bash through the thin wall keeping them at bay.

THIRTY-NINE
DEVLIN

Everyone leaves. That's my universal truth. I was an idiot to forget it or think this time would be different.

My body moved without my permission, holding her arm in a last-ditch effort, the instinct to stop her an innate thing I couldn't control.

No matter how much I prepared myself for it, Blair leaving hurts worse than anyone who's abandoned me before.

And I've never deserved it more.

FORTY
BLAIR

Mom was discharged from the hospital two days after I returned to the trailer. It's been a week, but we're getting by with her at home. The real problem is how we'll afford the medication the doctors prescribed for her autoimmune disease. It will be tough on us.

At least rent is paid on the trailer through the end of the year. I found out when I moved back. Devlin's parting gift, I guess.

It gives us a little over a month to figure something out.

More than anything in the last week, I hate the sickening ache in my chest, the one that stuck to my ribs like a burr after the fight with Devlin. It didn't sink in until I was standing outside the blue trailer how things had come to a screeching halt.

Regret slithers in my gut every day for the horrible things I said to him. He hid his reaction, but I must have cut him to use his awful parents against him. I'm no less of a monster than the one I accused him of being.

Seeing Devlin at school is torture on the days he decides to show up. He hasn't gone back to tormenting me, at least. The cops haven't shown up to cart me away, either. I'm beginning to let my hackles drop, no longer fearing my arrest at any second.

Through English and lunch I feel Devlin's unwavering gaze boring into me. Part of me wishes—*hopes*—he'll storm across the cafeteria and fight for me, rather than just letting me go.

Am I really so easy to toss away?

I must be, because my own father did it.

But Devlin and I haven't returned to hating each other. Instead, we're stuck in a weird, gut-wrenching limbo that hurts so much I can hardly breathe.

I have to, though. The thing I'm good at is being a survivor, and I need to be one now more than ever. For my future...for Mom.

When I make instant ramen for dinner, my stomach turns. It never bothered me before when it was the staple thing I ate for dinner on nights Mom worked late at the diner. Now, the salty chicken-scented broth tingles my nostrils and sends a wave of nausea through me.

I grip the sides of the cheap pink formica counter, breathing steadily to quell my roiling stomach.

The chicken flavor instant ramen is my favorite.

So why?

Maybe my dose of the high life has teased my taste buds too much. Bitter anguish wells up. So what if Devlin had good food to eat?

I chide the weakness, hardening myself back into the

person I've honed myself into ever since Dad ditched us. Scrunching up my face, I take a big bite of steaming noodles, waving my hand in front of my mouth when it's too hot.

"Ow, ow," I whimper.

"What are you doing, sweetheart?" Mom comes out of the hall.

"Nothing," I tell her in a garbled voice. Grimacing, I swallow the mouthful. "You should be in bed, resting. The doctor stressed how important it is to keep yourself relaxed so you don't have a flare up."

The terrifying beep of her heart rate monitor in the hospital haunts the back of my mind with a dissonant echo when the inflammation around her heart threw warning alarms to alert the nurse on call when I visited last week on Thanksgiving.

She touches my hair. "It's okay. I feel fine."

I take my ramen to the couch and prop my feet on the coffee table. "In that case, want to read with me?"

"Of course." Mom sits next to me, tucking her feet beneath her. She gives me an affectionate smile that soothes some of the pain hollowing my chest.

* * *

It's only two days later when Mom gives me another scare. Blood drains from my face as I enter the trailer and find her slumped on the couch, holding her head.

"Mom? Mom! What is it—what's wrong?" I rush to her side, taking one of her hands.

She winces. "Headache. It still won't go away."

Shit. She's had this headache for over a day, after she went out to find a job while I was at school. Mom gestures to the open pill bottles on the table, three different kinds to help headaches.

"Come on." I help her up and sit her at the kitchen table, crouching beside her chair. "We're going tonight."

"Blair—"

"No! We thought we could get by, but you don't qualify for the assistance program, not since I turned eighteen and you lost your extra boost from having a dependent. Fuck Dad's debt right now, we can't let that keep us from the help you need, no matter what it costs." I take a ragged breath. My voice turns small and hoarse. "I can't lose you."

"Oh, Blair. I'm not going anywhere." Mom brushes my hair aside. "I'm right here with you. If it makes you feel better, we can go to the clinic."

We've talked about this a little. I have money saved up, everything I ever received from Devlin. It's going toward a clinic in town that has several specialists. I've been in touch with them and they recommended her for their center when I explained I was trying to care for her at home, but it wasn't going well.

"Okay, so I'll just pack you a bag, grab the copy of your records from the hospital..." I tick off what we'll need, the mental tally continuing in my head.

Mom stops me from walking off, fingers curling around my wrist.

"What is it?"

A weary sadness is clear in her eyes and the age lines in her face. She strokes the inside of my wrist. "Nothing. I was just wondering when my baby girl got so strong. Most days I feel like you're the mom and I'm—"

I cup her face and kiss her forehead before hugging her. "I love you, Mom. I'll take care of you, and everything else."

"I love you, too, Blair. I'm proud of the woman you've grown into. So, so proud." Mom's voice cracks and I squeeze her tighter, a telltale sting in my nose and eyes warning of my own impending tears.

As I pack her a bag, I don't feel strong. I don't know how Mom can be proud of me. I'm weak, because the only thought running alongside my mental task list is how much I want Devlin to come help me so I don't have to face this alone. A broken exhale tears from my lungs. I lean against the wall in Mom's bedroom for a second, feeling the depth of my fears and mistakes.

Once I've given myself thirty seconds to feel fragile and vulnerable, I swallow and return to Mom's side.

The drive isn't long. The cheery holiday decor going up around Ridgeview for December is at odds with the knots in my stomach. Our destination is in the middle of town.

At the front desk, the receptionist is sweet. She takes Mom into a different area while I fill in forms and fork over my cash. The thick wad makes my hands shake.

"Ah, I'm sorry, Miss Davis," the receptionist interrupts me as I'm signing the emergency contact form. "You're short. This won't cover the clinic's program we talked about."

Dread spears into my gut and sinks it down. I rub my forehead. "Uh, okay. How much more...?"

"Without insurance this will cover two nights."

I keep my eyes from bulging by sheer force. Jesus fuck, that's a lot of money I handed over.

"Okay." My voice wavers. "I'll, um. I'll be back with the rest in a couple of days."

Panic surges in my chest. I need money and I need it *now*.

FORTY-ONE
BLAIR

There's no choice. If I don't do something to get money immediately, Mom's health is in serious danger.

The drive back to the trailer passes in a blur as my thoughts race.

My options are knocking over a couple of convenience stores near the interstate, hoping they have enough in the register, or the one line I've never been willing to cross. At least...not for anyone but Devlin. My broken heart pangs with a twinge thinking about him.

I can't believe I'm back to the same spot I was in months ago. Except stealing Devlin's car won't fly this time.

When I get home, I sit there, digging my nails into the steering wheel.

Time's ticking, little thief.

I hate my inner voice. Why does it always sound like Devlin?

With a bitten off sound, I storm inside. I run my fingers through my hair a few times, tucking everything into a tightly protected box. When I feel numb, I do what I have to.

It takes twenty minutes. I stop in front of the mirror I've been avoiding since I got dressed, rubbing my fingertips together. I'm afraid to look, but I do it anyway, forcing myself to face what I'm doing head on. It's the only way to put my mental armor in place.

The makeup I applied is thicker than usual, my eyes rimmed in black winged liner to make them appear bigger. An unamused smile stretches my plump red lips. Devlin would say I finally fit the cat burglar vibe with the winged style.

My hair falls around my shoulders, partially covering the sheer mesh top with tiny dots. The black lace bra is visible beneath it. I picked out a short leather skirt and the only pair of tights I own—they're sheer gray with a few holes, but they'll keep me warmer from the chill in the air. None of my coats give off enough sex appeal, so I opt for a thick long cardigan.

As I stare at the new phoenix I've morphed into, I tuck away the idealistic little girl inside who cries for crossing this line.

Bracing my hands on either side of the mirror leaning against the wall, I give myself a pep talk. "Buck the hell up. Life's not going your way. What the fuck else is new?"

I take the bus into town, too nervous I'll give into temptation to hop back in my car if I have an easy exit. The bus driver gives me a sidelong glance full of pity when she takes in the ripped tights and the sheer top peeking out of the collar of the cardigan I grasp closed. A man that gets on at the next stop leers at me, taking his time dragging his disgustingly open gaze up my legs.

By the time I get off the bus, my heart thuds. All around me, Ridgeview is bursting with holiday cheer. I pass a shop window on the main street with painted holly leaves and a scene of snow on the mountains decorating the display. Early birds and planners mill up and down the block, weighed down by shopping bags and packages purchased in time for the holidays. It doesn't click in my head that people can be so happy and festive when my entire world is crumbling.

Each step on the pavement clacks, echoing from the heels I snagged from Mom's closet. It's the soundtrack to my panicked plan.

I shiver as the breeze blows. It's cold out. The tights and cardigan don't do as much as I'd hoped to protect me from the wind.

"Damn it," I mutter, jogging a little toward my destination to warm my body.

The problem with jogging is it brings me to where I'm going too quickly.

Ash and acid creep up my throat as I approach the dark corner on the outskirts of the main strip in the middle of Ridgeview. It's known for sex workers, near enough to draw customers and secluded by the darkness enveloping the narrow, forbidden street.

I hesitate for a long moment a few feet before I reach the corner. There's a bustling cafe to my left. It would be so easy to slip inside the warm shop and forget about this harebrained idea.

This is insane. I'm eighteen and a scholarship student. I tug the cardigan tighter, gritting my teeth.

I'm a scared girl with no other options.

Steeling myself for how excruciating this will be, I make my feet move, walking to the dark corner. Men like the one on the bus will come here. With any luck, after a night of this I can figure out how girls end up as Sugar Babies or an escort. This town is full of rich upper class residents. They have to pay better.

It's hard to swallow past the lump in my throat as I pass two women near the entrance to the street. My skin crawls as I hear a faint moan further down, in the dark shadows. My limbs are jittery and stiff as I clomp along in my mom's heels.

Other workers look at me with understanding, sympathy, *solidarity* in their gazes.

A sharp breath catches in my throat as I find an open spot. Surreptitiously, I peek at one of the women nearby for an idea of what to do, how to stand so I don't scream newbie.

With monumental effort, I unclamp my clawed hands from my cardigan, allowing it to fall open and droop off one of my shoulders. The icy chill whips up my legs, moving over my belly. I smother a shiver and cant my hip to the side when a car turns down the street in a sedate roll. The other workers on the block prowl, some even calling out to the car.

Over here, honey.

Want a good time?

Right here, baby, I'll give you what you need.

My stomach revolts. It's all I can do to keep my sexy pout in place. Well, I hope it's a sexy pout and not a hint at the riot going on inside me.

The car stops and a girl that doesn't seem much older than me leans into the car with a smug smirk as she talks to the pudgy middle-aged man behind the wheel.

I twist my fingers in and out of the edge of the cardigan, wringing it into a stretched out shape. God, I wish I hadn't fought with Devlin right now. The broken heart I've been nursing without any sign of recovery gives a sad thump in agreement, as if it's saying *ya think, dummy?*

It never felt like I was selling my body to Devlin.

The money he exchanged to touch me was…different. Like it was his excuse to get close to me. Even if all of it was a lie, my feelings were real. They still are.

Enduring Devlin's storm was easier than the hell I'm sinking into tonight.

A familiar sounding engine tears my gaze toward the main street. My pulse ratchets fiercely as I keep my eyes peeled for the red Porsche.

Is he—?

The rev of the engine turns faint, driving away. My heart sinks.

Two more cars drive slow down the shadowed street, pulling sex workers out of the woodwork as they sell their wares —angling their bodies, puckering their lips, and flashing a teasing peek of bare thigh to the Johns.

I'm working up the courage to talk to the girls near me when a car rolls to a stop not far from my spot. The car is nice, a gunmetal gray with bright halogen headlights. When the window rolls down, the John waves me over with two fingers. Horribly, my mind flashes with a memory of my dad doing that same move.

"Come over here," the John calls in a gruff, authoritative baritone.

My pulse thunders in my ears and my palms turn clammy. I force air into my lungs, ignoring that my whole body feels cold. Unlocking my trembling knees, I take an unsteady step. Terror mixed with determination wars inside me, but my survival mode kicks on to shut up the side of myself I'm betraying.

I can't see inside the car past the tinted windows, but he's resting an arm on the open window. The crisp dress shirt looks expensive.

Please, please, please have a lot of money and no kinky requests.

Maybe the magic of the stars I used to wish on is finally kicking in and I've been sent a Sugar Daddy who will only want me to sit around doing my homework in my underwear. Looking, but never touching. *Yeah right.*

I wonder if this is what organ failure feels like as I trip on a crack in the curb. I wobble on the heels as I take stiff steps to close the short distance between me and the car.

The John isn't awful looking, so there's that. He has thick dark eyebrows, a square jaw, and a natural frown. He peers at me with clear blue eyes and I jolt into action, leaning against the open window.

"Uh, hi. *Hi*," I repeat, correcting my strained tone into something approaching sultry.

The John's eyes drop to where my hands clutch his open window in a death grip. His brow twitches and I jump back.

"Sorry. What, um," I'm totally fucking this up, but the nerves wracking my system are making it hard to think on my feet, "What do you like?"

The John stares at me for another beat, the silence stretching.

Fuck! Get it together!

Sucking in a subtle breath so I don't puke, I flutter my lashes and peek through them, biting the corner of my lip. Hopefully no red lipstick ends up on my teeth. I trace down the column of my neck, across my minimal cleavage—thank you, single push up bra from the back of my closet—down the sheer material showing off my stomach, and tuck my fingers in the top of my leather skirt.

"Want a good time?"

A grumbling sigh sounds from the John. He gives me another once over. "What do you offer?"

Shit. I didn't work up the courage to get a list of services from the other sex workers in the middle of my freak out.

"Ah, anything you want." The breathy voice I use makes me roll my eyes internally. I twirl a lock of hair around my finger. "See something you like?"

He taps his fingers on his thigh. "I haven't seen you around here before."

Translation: my fake it til I make it bravado isn't cutting it. I've got first timer written all over me.

I give him a girlish giggle, flapping my hand. "I'm here all the time. But if it's your first time, I'll be good for you."

Pouring acid on my tongue would hurt less than uttering those words.

The John hums skeptically. "You look pretty young. How old are you?"

I can't stop my eyes from widening. My nails dig into my palms. "Twenty-one," I lie, even though I'm not underage. "Want to go for a drink first to loosen up? Then we can go somewhere private. Um, like a hotel."

"Right." The John doesn't buy that for a second. He opens his door and steps out. He's tall, cutting an imposing figure in a dress shirt, tie, and charcoal slacks. Propping a hand on the roof, he leans into my space. I shrink back instinctually. Something shifts in his gaze and he nods. "That's what I thought."

"About my age?"

"Miss, you're under arrest for solicitation and prostitution."

My stomach drops. *What?!* I blink, faking a confident laugh. "I bet you play that with all the girls. Listen, if you want to use restraints, that's extra." I'm on a roll now, creating a whole story. I mime rubbing my wrists. "The last time a guy used handcuffs on me, it chaffed like a bitch."

He grants me an unimpressed look. "I'm not kidding. I don't really want to handcuff you, but I will if you resist arrest. Get in the car."

Another laugh leaves me, this one far less confident, tinged with dread. "If you're a cop, where's your badge?"

"Off duty." He checks his watch, sighing like I've caused him a huge inconvenience. "And late for a steak dinner I've been looking forward to."

"I want to see your badge."

With a grumbled mutter, he fishes out his wallet and opens it, flashing me the badge. Darting a suspicious glance at him, I snatch it, bringing it close to inspect if it's fake. It says *Ridgeview Police Dept.* across the top and *Chief* at the bottom, sending my stomach into panicked roiling.

"It's real." He takes it back, slipping the wallet in his pocket.

The fucking chief of police. *Oh god, I'm screwed.*

"I'm not going with you." An uncomfortable tightness sits on my lungs. I stumble back a step, losing my balance when my heel catches a loose rock in the road. "I need, ah—!"

He catches me before I fall with big, sturdy hands. Before I can get away, he gently pins my arms behind my back and guides me into the car.

"Wait, no, please," I ramble as he deposits me on the leather seat.

The officer blocks me in, leaning against the roof with a sigh. "Look, we're going to make it quick and easy, okay? You're a little older than my daughter, and I hate having to arrest the younger ones. I won't cuff you, but in exchange you're going to cooperate. Deal?"

A boulder-sized lump gets stuck in my throat when I try to swallow down the panic. "Will I go to jail?"

The cop doesn't answer. He frowns and shuts the car door, getting in the front seat.

As we drive toward the station, I chew on my nails. I failed. Hot tears slide down my cheeks.

I'm finally out of tricks. This time there's no smooth getaway.

FORTY-TWO
BLAIR

The light in the Ridgeview police station is too bright, making it impossible to hide from my failed plan. I caught a quick glimpse of myself in a mirror when the police chief brought me in. My stomach plummeted at the way I looked—exposed, destitute, desperate.

This is what I get for selling my soul.

A night in a holding cell by myself, too cold, tired, and out of options.

One of my cuticles bleeds from chewing on the nail. I keep picking at it. The sting reminds me I'm here and alive while time seems to tick by slowly and at a rapid rate, all at once. I have no way to tell what time it is. Like a casino, there's no window and no clock.

Let the good times roll...

Except all it does is leave me with my bleak thoughts.

Devlin would call it psychological by design, a tactic to let the criminals stew in the cage until they were ready to crack under pressure.

Scoffing, I curl up on the hard bench, tucking my bony knees to my chest. I lean my forehead against them, thumping my head with my eyes screwed tight. It doesn't change my surroundings when I open my eyes.

The concrete wall and iron bars with chipped white paint close in from all sides, distilling a sense of no escape. There isn't a plastic spoon in sight.

A hollow laugh puffs out of me, shaking my shoulders. I rub my arms, wishing the guard had let me keep my sweater. This sheer top does nothing to keep me warm.

Squeezing myself, I worry about Mom. What will I do? The clinic needs the money by tomorrow to keep her spot. Damn it, I shouldn't have gone to the streets. Devlin's cage was far cushier.

If only I wasn't so full of stubborn pride, pissed off about the contract.

The only noise in the echoing room comes from me. If I strain my ears, I can't catch any sounds drifting through the heavy door separating the holding cell area from the maze of the station beyond the hall. I imagine this is exactly what purgatory feels like. Harsh fluorescent lighting, hard seats, and a vacuum seal on the room that leaves you alone with your thoughts and your begging cries once the desperation takes root.

A wobbly sob gets caught in my throat, hiccuping to the surface out of nowhere. A deep sense of despair fills me as I wish for some way out of this.

Come on, stars. For once, please, just...do your thing.

I tuck my tender, nail-bitten fingers underneath my bent

knees, willing the wave of emotion to subside. Something Dad used to say pops into my head. *Crying is for quitters.* My lip curls in a fierce snarl.

I'm no fucking quitter. He's the deadbeat quitter.

There's no time for tears. If I don't get out of here soon, Mom will be in trouble. I can cry when I've clawed my way out of this mess.

What will you do?

That familiar, snarky voice needs to get the hell out of my head. With his voice comes thoughts of other things, like the shape of his full lips when he's pleased, the way he curls around me in bed, and the way his kisses steal my breath.

"Ugh, you freaking sap," I mutter, tipping my head to the bland ceiling.

All my wretched thoughts keep snagging on Devlin. I'm sitting in a jail cell, facing the one thing I've been running from all this time, and I still can't stop thinking about him. Am I pathetic, or what? It's ridiculous how easily someone can take root in your head and your heart.

I wish I'd never found the contract in his closet. My throat stings with my next thought—I wish I'd discussed it with him with a level head instead of assuming what it meant. I never gave him the chance to explain.

The only way forward is to swallow my pride, enduring the cactus tines prickling along my throat the entire way.

Devlin is the only person I know capable of getting me out of this holding cell.

I need his help. If I have to, I'll beg him for it. I can hate him later. Right now I need him.

I lick my lips. More than that, Devlin is the only person I'm more desperate to see tonight other than Mom, because when his arms wrap around me, I'm home.

There are millions of people in the world, and one person

can make you feel a full spectrum of emotions. Devlin makes me feel vengeance, resentment, desire, protection, and something even more deadly—love. The kind of love that's inevitable. You can't help but allow it to consume you. It's a love that doesn't need rules, because it's fate written in the stars.

"Oh my god," I whisper, staring past the bars of the cell without seeing them. "I love him."

Devlin challenged me, making me feel something other than the crushing weight of my life. I was happy with him, and now that it's gone, there's a gaping hole missing in my life.

I love him.

The bang of the door down the hall makes me jump, startled out of my ill-timed revelation. For a minute, my gut churns with worry that I'm about to get a cellmate. I wait, braced for a tweaked out drug addict or an angry drunk, but no one comes.

Putting my face in my hands, I sigh raggedly. My heart unfurls, giving off faint twinges of the hurt it suffered. I'm equally responsible for the pain I've forced myself through by running away instead of facing what my heart has known for a while.

The question is, if I call, will he come? He might not bully me in school, but I've sensed something intense in the way his gaze tracks me.

Well, if he hates me, tough shit. I need him, even if I'm still mad. Trusting Devlin is a risk worth taking.

What? I can admit I love him, want to trust him, and still be pissed at him. A wry smile tugs at my lips as I scrape my fingers through my hair.

"What a hot mess." Hopping to my feet, I grasp the cold bars trapping me and peer at the door. I stick my arm through the gaps and wave, hoping the camera feed above the door will alert the unobservant guards I need them. "Hey! Anyone there? Hellooo!"

It takes ten minutes, but finally the door clangs open. I drop my burning arm, grateful to rest it. A portly officer in uniform strolls down the row of holding cells with a sandwich clutched in his stubby fingers.

Leaning against the bars, I lift my brows. "Can I get my phone call?"

The officer chews for a long minute, eyeing me up and down. "That's only in the movies. I don't have to let you use the phone."

My jaw drops in surprise. "Uh...please?"

The urge to cover myself is strong, my lace bra snagging this guy's attention. I straighten my spine instead, willing him to do me a solid.

"Yeah, okay. Come on." Jangling the keys, he unlocks the cell with a metallic clang that sounds like freedom.

Somehow, when I step over the threshold to the other side of the bars, I feel lighter.

The officer on duty leads me down the hall with a greasy grasp on my elbow. "Do you have the number memorized?"

My heart stutters, but then it's okay. By some miracle, I do have Devlin's number memorized from the early days of our deal, before I programmed him into my phone.

"Yep."

The maze from the row of holding cells filters into a bullpen of desks in the center of a big room with two offices at the back.

"Okay, kid. Here you go." He waves a desk phone at me and props it on a filing cabinet. "Call your Mom."

"Thanks." A tremor of anxious anticipation travels through my fingers as I dial. Each ring has me sinking my teeth deeper into my lip. "Pick up...pick up..."

"*Who is this?*"

I nearly cry out in relief at his deep, curt voice. "Devlin."

The line is quiet for a beat. "*Blair?*"

"Yeah." My clammy palms slip on the phone, pulse fluttering. I crush the receiver to my ear. "Um, hi."

"*Are you okay? Where are you? Tell me now, I'm coming to get you. Christ, I've been trying to find you.*"

Emotion clogs my throat. "You have?"

Was it his Porsche I heard earlier in the night after all? We're like magnets, at odds with each other when we're flipped the wrong way, then undeniably drawn together when we're righted.

"*Yes. Tell me where you are.*"

"I'm downtown. At, uh, the police station. Can you bail me out?"

Devlin curses. "*I'm coming for you, little thief.*"

Air rushes from my lungs at his words. My world realigns, snapping everything into its rightful place. "Thank you."

FORTY-THREE
DEVLIN

The stars aren't helping tonight. They haven't in days. I'm beginning to think the one ritual I have finally lost the spark keeping me going. I sit on the roof to escape the empty, cavernous house, but it's not stopping the slow bleed out of my heart. The damn thing hasn't stopped oozing life since Blair walked out.

At first I was angry, because she left, and because I didn't stop her.

Despair crept in like shadows as soon as she packed up her books and walked out with that shitty duffel bag weighing her down. The rest of her stuff is here, stopping me like tiny grenades whenever I find something of hers.

The first few days, all I could think was how Blair was just like the others, ready to run away once she got to know the real me because I'm too hard to love underneath my mask.

A plume of smoke rushes past my lips on my exhale. I flick the end of the cigarette with my thumb, not in the mood to smoke it. The nicotine isn't numbing the constant dull thrum of pain.

I keep thinking I'll walk through the lounge or the bedroom and find her miraculously back, reading one of her books. Sleeping has become impossible. I'm lucky if I catch a few hours a night, if I can rest at all.

Somehow, it's easy to grow used to sharing a bed, so when you're faced with empty, cold sheets, the absence is palpable.

It's taken everything in me not to stalk up to her in school and kiss her. Today she kept peering over when she thought I wasn't looking. The agitation stiffening her shoulders called to me, begging me to go take her worries away.

I'm so sick of this. Sick of holding back, of living the way I am, closed off from everyone. It doesn't quell the disappointment or soften the blow.

For too long, I've used this excuse, pretending it made me better than my demons. But it does jack shit to protect me. In the end, I'm still alone and forgotten.

My lips pull to the side in a grimace as I put out the cigarette.

I fucked up by thinking I could just have Blair so easily without addressing how we started in the first place.

The boxes hiding everything I've locked up are breaking down, the visceral pain seeping out.

My fingers itch to comb through silky, soft, vanilla-scented hair. Her scent faded from my sheets and I've taken to walking around with a small bottle of her shampoo in my pocket. I take it out when things become too much, inhaling it while I picture her deep brown eyes, her lips, the way she fit so fucking perfectly in my arms.

"Goddamn it," I mutter.

This raw, aching feeling plaguing me like a disease sucks and I'm *done*.

Fuck this distrust my parents bred into me. I'm finished with it. I won't let it rule me anymore. Not when it could make me lose the one good thing in my life.

I know who will make it stop and it's about damn time I go get her. Wallowing won't bring her back. I need to go see her.

Rising to my feet, I send a wild yell to the sky. My throat is dry, scratchy with disuse. I pant, rubbing at the tender bags of exhaustion beneath my puffy eyes.

My breath is short as I climb through the window. Every nerve in my body spurs me on.

The abstract things I wish for when I look at the stars? I find it when I'm with her.

For the first time in years, I've realized I need to chase someone rather than accept being forgotten. I want to fight for my love with Blair because her heart is where I want to make my home. Even if she won't accept my love, I just need to tell her how I feel. If I don't, the decay eating at my heart is going to kill me.

* * *

Blair's trailer was empty when I got there. Worry niggled at me when I saw her car parked out front. I drove around town all night, searching. She wasn't at the hospital, the library, or any of the places I sped past.

Bishop checked in to let me know he hadn't found her after I recruited him to help.

I thought I saw her as I cruised down the main street in

town, but it was crowded with holiday shoppers and the girl disappeared.

When my phone rang with a number I didn't recognize, I was skeptical, but thank god I picked up and heard her voice on the line.

I break about four different traffic laws to get to the station. It's part of the collection of older buildings in town, the architecture from the Gold Rush era that swept the region.

As I wait for Blair to be brought out, I head for the police chief's office.

"He's out for the night." A night duty officer with mustard smeared on his collar tips his head at the dim office with glass walls at the back of the room.

"Fine, I'll call him, then." I nearly smirk at the bug-eyed expression the officer gives me. I press the phone to my ear. "He's a close friend of my uncle's."

Uncle Ed brought Lucas and I to the station plenty of times when we were kids. The police chief was a lieutenant then.

Chief Landry picks up on the second ring as I make my way back to the front of the station to wait for Blair. *"Yeah? You're interrupting my dinner, so make it quick."*

"It's Devlin Murphy. Edward Saint's nephew."

"Devlin!" His voice turns jovial. *"How are you, son? I hear the Coyotes varsity soccer team did well this season."*

"Yeah. Listen, my girlfr—someone important to me was picked up tonight. I'm at the station to bail her out, but I want to know what I can do to ensure the charge doesn't go on her permanent record." I lower my voice, glancing around to check that no one hears. "Whatever I have to do."

I've never been more thankful for Bishop's cutthroat interest in blackmail as I am in this moment. He dug up an interesting rumor surrounding the police chief's promotion from his previous rank. Ridgeview's top dog will do favors for the right price.

It doesn't matter that Blair hurt me by leaving. I'll fight for her and give her anything she desires. I'll do everything in my power to make sure she doesn't want to leave again.

"*Oh, the girl I picked up on Red Hill Road?*" His tone turns knowing.

My heart skips a beat and I suck in a sharp breath. Red Hill? It's where hookers pick up their customers. Fuck. *Blair, what were you thinking taking a risk like that?* Depraved old men prowl that dark street and girls are known to disappear. Some sleaze could've got his hands on her and—

I cut off my circling thoughts. "Yes. Her."

"*She seems like a good kid. I didn't make it an official arrest. I was going to let her go in the morning.*"

Relief floods my system. "Well, consider the bail I posted a generous donation to keep it like that."

Chief Landry chuckles. "*You're just like your dad. Tell your uncle I said I'll see him at poker night.*"

The line goes dead. Frowning, I shove the phone back in my pocket. Being compared to my dad isn't a glowing compliment.

Blair appears through a clear partition, accepting a bag of her things before she's allowed through the door. It takes all of my control not to gape at her skimpy outfit—the sheer top with little dots giving the perfect teasing view of her lacy black bra. We stare at each other for a beat. My fingers twitch with the urge to yank her against my chest and never let her go.

"Let's get out of here." Blair glances at the cops with a tiny frown and starts for the door.

Outside, the crisp winter air gusts through the valley. Blair shivers, her arms breaking out in goosebumps. She shrugs into her cardigan, wrapping it around herself and covering the tempting view of her body.

I unlock Red, parked in front of the station, and open the passenger door. Glancing up, I find Blair clomping down the sidewalk toward the bus station.

"Blair. Where are you going?"

She pauses, half-turning. An expression of longing lingers on her face when she finds me holding her door open, waiting for her. She worries her lip and gestures behind her.

"I took the bus into town."

"I know, I saw your car when I went to your place."

"You did?"

I close the distance between us and buff her upper arms when she shudders from the cold. "I told you, angel. I've been looking for you all night. There's so much I need to tell you."

Everything in me screams to take away the sadness in Blair's expression. She leans into my touch, making a small sound. A hint of vanilla tingles in my nose.

"Let me give you a ride."

Blair drags her teeth over her lip. "Okay."

Wrapping my arm around her shoulders, I walk her back to the car. When I get in, I blast the heat and click on the seat warmers. Blair blows breath on her hands and shoots me a grateful look.

"Thanks, it's cold as shit in the holding cell."

A short laugh barks out of me. "Little criminal."

"The real deal now."

"You were always the real deal." I lift my brow as I rev the engine. "This time you got caught."

Conflict twists Blair's features. "They didn't say anything about coming back for a court date."

"They won't."

Her head snaps to me. "What do you mean?"

"I know the chief. He's good friends with Uncle Ed. I called him before you came out. It wasn't official, so it's not going on your record. He said he wasn't going to hold you."

Relief melts her features as she falls back against the leather seat. "Thank god."

Now that I have her with me, safe in the car, the wave of protectiveness surges. I allow a few minutes to pass before I can't hold it in any longer. "Why'd you do it?"

Blair fiddles with her bitten nails. "Get arrested?"

"Come on, Blair. Don't play with me. What you did was dangerous."

She scoffs. "Walking on the street at night? Every woman lives that reality."

I grip the wheel tighter. "Yes, but you went out looking for trouble by walking down Red Hill Road. You're lucky it was Chief Landry and not some sick fuck who kidnaps hookers—"

"*Sex workers*," Blair interrupts to correct.

God, I've missed her fight. "Fine. My point stands."

"Fine." Blair sighs. "I don't want to fight about it."

"I don't want to either." Keeping my hands to myself is a challenge when all I want to do is put my hand on her thigh, to touch her and *feel* that she's okay. "Sorry. Just...tell me why you did it?"

"I had to." She shifts in her seat to peer at my profile while I drive. "My mom's health isn't great. It's worse than when I moved in with you."

"I thought she was discharged?"

"She was, but the medications they prescribed are hard to afford without insurance." Blair tucks her hair behind an ear. "I took what I had saved and took her to this clinic I've been talking to. She's there now, but the money you gave me isn't enough. The clinic is...expensive."

A band locks around my chest. "Clinic? New Horizons?"

"Yeah, that's the one."

Well, shit. Blair took Macy to the best medical clinic in the country—the one my parents are famous for starting.

"Don't worry. About any of it, okay?"

"Devlin, I can't. We still have the debt from my dad, and insurance companies won't accept my mom's condition as insurable."

"That clinic is my parents'. I'll take care of it. Please, let me help."

A shaky breath hisses through her teeth. "But...I don't want to be a charity case."

"Please, Blair." This is the right thing to do. "Look, you can pay me back. How's that? Deal?"

She appears prepared to keep protesting like the stubborn little spitfire I love.

"I just want to take care of you."

"Okay," Blair murmurs. "Thank you. For coming to get me, and for your help."

Licking my lips, I admit one of the things I need to tell her. "I'd chase you anywhere, Blair. I don't exist without you."

Her breath hitches and her eyes widen. There's something different shining in them. "Devlin..."

I squash the urge to hide the moment of vulnerability behind a shroud. Instead, I let her see the raw parts of me when I give her an open look.

Blair works herself up, her pink tongue darting out to wet her lips. "I'm sorry. God, I'm sorry for what I said about your parents." With a hesitant motion, she reaches across and presses her fingers to my shoulder. "I didn't mean it."

"I know." My voice comes out hoarse. "I'm sorry, too. I never meant to make you feel like that. I was an asshole." I hold my hand out, offering it to her to take. She glances down. "If you want. You don't have to do anything you don't want to. But I'm crazy about you and I want us to be together."

Blair grasps my hand tightly. Her touch is like a balm to my raw soul. It's the first I've felt grounded in days. A rough sound leaves me and Blair makes an answering soft sound as she clutches my hand.

In a gruff voice, I ask, "Where to?"

"Hmm?"

With my other hand resting on top of the wheel, I gesture a few lights ahead. One direction takes us up the mountain and the other winds through the valley toward the trailer park.

"Home." The piercing look she sends my way tugs at my heartstrings.

"Don't say that if you don't mean it, Blair."

She squeezes my hand. "I mean it. I don't want to be alone tonight. Home is when I'm with you."

A soft smile curves my lips. My fractured stone heart fuses back together one jagged edge at a time. "Okay. Home it is."

FORTY-FOUR
DEVLIN

It's surreal when we get back to the house. My hand hovers at the small of Blair's back as we enter through the garage. It's something we've done a hundred times when she lived with me, leaving a bittersweet twinge in my bones.

Blair showers and comes into my bedroom, where I wait for her. She's wearing one of my henley shirts. The gray shirt is loose on her, the top button open, the sleeves bunched up, and the neckline hanging precariously from one shoulder. It hits her mid-thigh and the top of her bra peeks out.

It takes an absurd amount of willpower to keep my hands to myself when all I ache to do is wrap Blair up and tuck her back in my heart, where she belongs.

Dragging in a breath, I erase the distance between us. "Feel better?"

"So much." Her mouth pulls into a lopsided smile. "Now that I'm out of the slammer, I'm like a new woman. I'm thinking about writing a memoir on the lessons prison taught me."

I chuckle, cupping her shoulders to bring her closer. It feels right to have her back in my room. I need to keep her this time. I'll do everything to be worthy enough to deserve her.

A loud growl sounds. Blair scrunches her nose, bunching the freckles scattered across the bridge. She covers her stomach with one hand. "How do you feel about ordering something? I didn't eat dinner."

An amused sound huffs out of me. "I'll go order and pick it up." I drop a soft kiss on her temple. "I'll be back soon. I have a couple of things to take care of."

Before I make it far, Blair tugs on my shirt with a vulnerable sound. "Wait."

There's a need in her eyes. It answers the matching one in my chest. Without words, we come together, both of us pulling until our lips connect in a tender kiss.

The world rights itself. Kissing Blair fills the empty cavern in my chest. Both of us release desperate sounds as we clutch each other. I want nothing more than to deepen the kiss, lay her down in my bed, and make her feel good. First, there's something I have to do.

"Wait for me. I'll be back soon."

* * *

On my way back from the clinic, I dial Dad's number. He better pick up. I haven't called or texted him since Thanksgiving, uninterested in trying to pretend we have a father-son relationship worth recovering.

At the clinic, the receptionist stared at me with wide eyes

as she copied my information to Macy's file from my license. "Murphy as in..." Her features stretched with her silent question.

"Yes." I signed the form for electronic payment authorization to pay the outstanding balance to keep Macy at New Horizons.

Dad actually answers the phone with a clipped, *"Hello?"*

"Dad. It's Devlin." He grumbles on the line. *Prick.* "A new patient checked in at your clinic tonight. Autoimmune disease."

"Oh?" I hate the interest that perks in his voice. Medicine trumps human fucking decency. *"How do you know this?"*

"She's my girlfriend's mom."

"Your girlfriend?"

"Yeah, Dad," I grit as I pull through the gate and park in the circular drive. "I tried to introduce you before, remember? That's one of the things you'd know about me if you cared to talk to your son about more than your career expectations for me. You know, like a real father."

"I am your real father."

"Are you?" Pent up rage I've smothered for years billows in my chest. I slam my hand on the wheel. "Bullshit, old man. Uncle Ed and Aunt Lottie have been better parents to me than you and Mom."

The truth of it burns my lungs. I've had parents my whole life, they just weren't my biological parents.

"Now listen here, Devlin!"

"No, Dad!" I stab a finger against the leather of the wheel. "For once, *you* listen! You're so obsessed with your career that you can't even see you missed out on my entire life. I've asked you for nothing, even though you both abandoned me."

"You're wrong. Your mother and I have given you the opportunity to continue our work and—"

A hollow laugh tears from me. "Are you kidding? Do you hear what you're saying?" I pull my fingers through my hair. "You left me to the nannies and Mom's sister. The only time you pay attention to me is to course correct if I veer from the med school expectations you cram down my throat. Why did you even have a kid if you wanted to work so badly?"

My raw yell echoes in the car.

Dad is quiet on the line for a minute. *"Your mother, she..."*

"Don't bother. It's not like I couldn't fucking guess." Blowing out a ragged breath, I sever any remaining vestiges of hope my parents care about me. It's freeing in a way, to let go of the broken threads I've been clinging to. I don't need them. I have a family—Blair, my aunt and uncle, Lucas, Gemma, and Bishop. I don't need anyone else. "You wanted me to be a man so bad, to grow up and be independent, well this is me doing that."

"Yelling at me like a child?" The distaste in Dad's voice is laughable.

Christ, who let him procreate? The detached, clinical way he approached fatherhood is wrong. Every one of my psychology books on the subject rings true on the importance during key developmental stages.

"No." My voice is cold and commanding. "Macy Davis. She's the patient. I want you to take the case or recommend a specialist."

"What gives you the right to give me orders or make medical decisions on behalf of someone else?"

I grind my teeth. "The entirety of my existence. I deserve retribution, but instead this is all I'm asking for. Take this woman's case and help her."

"Why do you care about this?"

A dull pain throbs behind my eye. "Because her daughter is my girlfriend and her mom is her whole fucking world—something you'd never understand! This is the girl I love. She's my family. My universe. I'll do everything to protect and care for her. If you don't do it, I'll come for you, old man. Do we have a deal?"

Dad is quiet for a long stretch. I contemplate threatening something more drastic to make him comply.

"*Very well.*"

I blink out of my day dream about digging up blackmail to bury his career with. "Good."

"*What are your plans regarding your future?*"

I bring the phone in front of my face to growl my point. "Anything I fucking want, because it's my life, not yours."

I hang up before he can curdle my blood. It felt good to finally stand up to him. I don't need either of them. I haven't for a while. Between my investments and financial manager, I have no use for their monthly expense account anymore.

What I wanted from them was never money. It was just the last lingering wishes of a lonely little boy missing the love of his parents, hoping they'd notice or care. I have the only family that matters to me and it no longer includes them.

With that issue seen to, I can finally go to Blair.

FORTY-FIVE
BLAIR

While Devlin is out, the sense of comfort hits me hard as I stand in the middle of his—*our*—bedroom. I go to his side of the bed, running my fingers over his pillow. The stack of psychology texts are present, and another book, one that makes my heart stutter.

Stardust sits next to Devlin's books, rescued from wherever I had left it before storming from the house when we fought.

It makes me want to apologize to him with more than words, to make up for fighting with him, and thank him for coming to save me when I needed him.

I used to think Devlin was nothing more than an evil, emotionless, manipulative asshole.

But he's not that. He's selective about the people he allows to see the real him, keeping those who don't matter at a distance with cruel words.

Devlin is someone aching for the magic of stars because a little girl gave him hope when he needed it. Underneath the jagged pain he's wrapped himself in, Devlin is a man that loves fiercely with his whole heart.

I love him, all of him.

From his sharp edges to his hidden charms.

His heart is my home. I never want to leave it again.

The supplies I bought weeks ago for a special room makeover pop into my head. "Yes!"

Hurrying into my old room, I dig through the closet, where I'd shoved the string lights and plastic stars away. They're tucked in the back, behind a stack of extra blankets. A tender warmth fills my chest as I get started.

I gave Devlin my stars once. It's time I gave them to him again.

In the bedroom, I hang the strand of tiny star-shaped lights over the bed. It casts a golden glow on the pillows. I stick the plastic glow in the dark stars to the wall, focusing them over the headboard and spreading the galaxy of my own making along the wall. They're different shapes, some large and some small.

I'm stretching to my limit, standing on the bed to reach the ceiling to put the finishing touches on my surprise.

A quiet laugh sounds behind me, followed by a sardonic voice. "Back home for five minutes and you're redecorating already?"

I jump, spinning around to find Devlin leaning against the doorway, watching.

"How long have you been there?"

"A few minutes. I was enjoying the view." His gaze skates down my body. "What's all this?"

I gesture to the stars. "Do you like it? I planned this a while ago, actually. These glow in the dark."

Devlin hums, taking in the new decor. "Yeah. You brought the stars inside."

"I did." A flutter tickles my stomach from the inside. "I wanted you to always have the stars overhead so you can whisper your wishes to them."

The corners of Devlin's eyes crinkle and his dimples appear with his surprised smile. "You…"

He crosses the room and grasps my waist. With a gentle tug, he guides me to my knees so we're closer in height. Our foreheads touch.

"I love you," I whisper.

Devlin wraps his arms around me and captures my mouth in a sweet, deep kiss that steals my breath. We kiss long and slow, with no purpose other than feeling. When we part, Devlin meets my eyes.

"I need to tell you."

He said he'd been out looking for me tonight because he had things to say.

"Tell me."

Devlin traces the freckles spread across my nose. His brow wrinkles and I reach up to smooth it.

"It hurt when you left." I open my mouth, but he shakes his head. "It hurts anytime someone leaves. I think it first started when my parents pretty much gave me up in favor of their work. People kept leaving, so I built up a shield. I stopped letting people in, stopped caring about them, so when they inevitably left, it wouldn't bother me. But deep down, it did. It doesn't stay buried forever."

A small sound escapes me. Devlin's mouth twitches into a quick grimace. He sits down on the bed and pulls me into his lap, holding me close as he continues.

"I've been this way for so long, when you dug your way into my heart, it scared me. I was too greedy. I just—I wanted too much because I stopped myself from feeling those things. I was drunk on you."

I lay my head on his shoulder, kissing his neck. Devlin rumbles, sliding his fingers beneath the hem of the henley shirt to trace my hip.

"I'm sorry for the things I did to hurt you." He licks his lips. "All I want to do is be worthy of your heart."

Devlin rustles in the pockets of his jeans, pulling out a folded paper. He hands it to me. My eyes go wide as I skim the words. It's long-term admittance paperwork for my mom at the clinic, paid in full and outlining a specialized program for patients with illnesses like Mom's.

I sit up. "You—Devlin, you did this?"

"I told you, it's my parents' clinic. I called my dad. They'll take good care of her. She'll have the best treatment."

My heart thuds as a wave of emotion wells from deep within me. I throw my arms around his neck. "Thank you."

Devlin rests his forehead against my shoulder. "You're my shooting star. My wishes come true when I'm with you." He turns his face, grazing his mouth over my neck. "My heart belongs to you."

My lips part and I kiss him again, losing myself in the way we intertwine. He makes a quiet sound and I move to straddle him, feeling him harden between my legs as we move. My fingers slide into his hair and our kiss deepens. He explores languidly, dragging his palms over my bare thighs, over my backside, and up my spine underneath his shirt.

"Please," I murmur. "I want you. I need to feel you right now."

"Yes." Devlin doesn't break the kiss as his arms lock around me, tugging me further onto the mattress as he lays back.

His shoes thump to the floor as I pull on his clothes. He slides his hands up my sides, peeling his henley shirt from my body, and undoes my bra with a skilled move. As soon as it falls, he groans, bending to suck one of my nipples into his mouth. His tongue flicks, making me shake in his arms. My head falls back as he moves to the neglected side, pinching the first one.

The flick of his tongue makes me buck, grinding down on his stiff length. We're only in underwear, and I need there to be no barriers between us.

"Dev, please. I want to feel you inside."

He releases my nipple to kiss me. "Patience, angel. I'm going to take my time, fuck you long and slow until we've touched every inch of each other."

An amused breath leaves me as I grind on him. "I've only been gone, like, a week."

"Felt more like a lifetime," Devlin grumbles against the sensitive skin of my neck. His fingers dip into the back of my underwear, squeezing my ass. The tip of his middle finger teases between the cheeks.

"Uh, Dev?" My voice is throaty when he bucks beneath me, pressing his cock into my throbbing clit. At the same time, he rubs his finger over my puckered hole. I drop my head back, lips parted on a gasp. "When you say every inch...?"

With a gravelly laugh, Devlin flips us so I'm on my back. He straddles my hips and traps my wrists overhead as his teeth nip down the column of my throat. I arch up to meet him, my body thrumming from his touch.

"I mean every inch. It's going to be a long night."

"Yeah, I want that, too." I bite my lip as he moves lower, peeling my underwear down while he settles between my spread legs.

"Keep those hands where I left them." Devlin peeks up. It shouldn't look sexy as hell, but it does. The wicked curve of his mouth, the gleam in his eyes, and the hint of mischief in his deep tone as he whispers, hovering his mouth over my pussy, all have me trembling in pleasure before his mouth descends where I need him. "I'm going to make you feel so good."

At the first swipe of Devlin's tongue on my pulsing clit, I cry out, fisting my hands in the sheets. He growls, licking and sucking my pussy. He drives me to orgasm so fast, I go lightheaded.

"Mm, that's it, baby. Are you ready? It's going to be like that all night. I'm not stopping until I make you collapse from coming so much."

"Ah!" I moan as Devlin's fingers tease my entrance before sinking inside. He curls them, stroking me and fucking me on his fingers. "Yes!"

I whimper as Devlin lifts his mouth off my clit when I'm close to another orgasm, but then it's back, working me perfectly.

His slick thumb massages my ass, circling with gentle pressure. It feels so good as I relax back into the bed. His thumb slides past the tight muscles, working into my ass as he thrusts his fingers in my vagina. My body hums with pleasure from Devlin's tongue and fingers. Devlin pumps his fingers and thumb in a torturous, sedate pace as he licks my clit, the euphoric sensations building.

Devlin fills me, my pussy and my ass clenching on his fingers.

"Please, more! I'm close, I just need—" Devlin hums against my pussy, pressing his tongue harder while he thrusts his fingers into the sweet spot deep in my core that pushes me over the edge. My back bows as I cry out. "Ah, god, yes!"

"Only me, baby," Devlin murmurs while he works his fingers perfectly, knowing how to touch me to keep my orgasm going. "Only me."

"Only you," I repeat in a ragged whisper.

Devlin pulls his fingers free and shifts up the bed to kiss me. I moan into his mouth when his cock glides against my slick folds. It takes monumental effort to keep my hands pinned to the bed when all I want is to touch him. Devlin ends the kiss to lean over, retrieving a condom from the nightstand.

"Please." I flex my fingers, glancing up.

A fond smile steals across Devlin's face. "Touch me, baby."

I grin as I sit up, skating my palms over the hard muscles and smooth skin, paying special attention to the cluster of shooting stars inked beneath Devlin's heart. My short nails drag lightly down his chest. I savor the way his eyes hood and his head tips back slightly. I take the condom from Devlin and stroke his cock, meeting his intense gaze. Parting my lips, I take him into my mouth, sucking down the shaft and bobbing back up.

"Fuck," Devlin groans, his hand cupping the back of my head. He threads his fingers into my hair, massaging gently. "So good. You're perfect."

I pull off and open the condom, rolling it onto his cock. He tips my chin up and kisses me. I fall back to the sheets and Devlin follows, entering me in a smooth glide.

"Mm, so perfect," he whispers against my lips, bracing on his forearm and cupping my jaw.

As he moves, my body opens, welcoming the fullness and connection.

My attention snags on the twinkling stars on the strand of lights and the homemade galaxy we're making love under. It fills me with a bright joy, feeling like I'm right where I should be.

Devlin moves in the same slow pace, rolling his hips in a way that drives my pleasure more intensely. A well of emotion bubbles in my chest, twining with the heat coiling in my core.

With a soft, needy sound, I snake my arms around Devlin's neck, holding on tight as he brings me to the edge over and over.

"Come here." Devlin picks me up from the bed and sits back on his heels with my legs wrapped around him. He rocks into my pussy, hitting my sweet spot and filling me deeper. A rough sound leaves Devlin as he cradles me close, stroking the star tattoo between my shoulder blades. "You feel that?"

"Yeah," I gasp, arms wound tight around his shoulders.

The emotion rises, misting my eyes. I capture Devlin's lips, kissing him tenderly as we move as one, climbing higher and higher. As I reach oblivion, Devlin tenses with parted lips, rumbling as he comes. I hug him tighter, smiling against the side of his face as he strokes my back.

With an attentiveness Devlin only shows when we're alone, he shifts us to the bed without breaking our embrace. He strokes my hair back from my face and places a soft kiss on my lips. So much devotion fills his eyes when he looks at me without any masks.

"Rest for a minute. Then we're starting again."

I chuckle, curling into his side. "Again?"

"Always."

Our fingers trace lazily as we catch our breath. Gradually, our touch grows more insistent, more purposeful, until we're chasing release again.

And again.

Devlin doesn't stop touching me, even when we finish, too exhausted to go another round. He tugs my thigh over his legs and brushes his lips on the crown of my head as I rest my cheek on his chest, mapping my own path on his skin. His heartbeat drums beneath my ear.

A smile curves my mouth as his hand finds mine, tangling our fingers.

We've always matched. Our bruised hearts are intertwined

and mending, tender and in need of the kind of love we give each other. We fit together, two broken shards showing off our damage by fusing together like my favorite Japanese art tradition, a delicate gold glue binding our hearts as one.

Fused together, we make a more beautiful work of art with proof of everything we've been through.

FORTY-SIX
DEVLIN

On the night of winter formal two weeks later, Blair is a knockout in a sleek fitted dress that steals my breath as smoothly as she's stolen everything else—my pain, my walls, my heart.

Beneath the silver and white decorations that transform the gymnasium into a winter wonderland, the dark gray material of Blair's dress sparkles when it catches the light, like tiny diamonds are woven into the fabric. She places her hand in mine as I offer it to her.

"Want to dance?" I ask.

A slow song filters through the speakers and other couples fill the dance floor. Mr. Coleman hovers at the edge of the room, smiling through his chaperone duties. Surprisingly,

Bishop dances with Thea Kennedy, who looks amazing in a sweet pink, flowing dress.

"Prepare yourself for some truly uncoordinated awkwardness." Blair waves her free hand with a flourish as I take her to an open spot. Color fills her freckled cheeks as I tuck her close, leading us in a smooth sway. She rests one hand on my bicep and the other curls around the back of my neck. "Well, actually. You seem to know what you're doing."

"You're light on your feet and among all of your other troublemaking skills, you're telling me you can't dance?"

"Not a lot of opportunities to bust a move while liberating wallets. Want me to moonwalk away next time?"

Blair smirks and I give into the urge to kiss her. I can taste her smile and her joy as we spin in the middle of the dance floor.

We dance for a few more songs. Blair grows more comfortable, letting loose with me.

When a break in the music comes, she fans her face. "Sustenance?"

"Come on, let's grab a drink."

I rest my palm at the base of her spine and lead her to the drink station set up in front of a fringe curtain of silver mylar. The table has an explosion of snowflake confetti. Blair picks some up and tosses it high enough to land in my hair, nodding with satisfaction flaring in her eyes when some sticks in my hair. I get her back, picking up a snowflake and pressing it to her cleavage.

Leaning in, I murmur, "I'll be back for that later. With my teeth."

She bites her lip around a grin and presses onto her toes to kiss me, grabbing my lapels. I squeeze her waist.

"How much later? Maybe I'm not too good for a little action in a deserted classroom after all."

A devious chuckle drops from my lips. Before I can retort with something alluring, Trent and Sean amble up to the drinks table with cocky swaggers. Sean darts a wary look my way. Trent nods to me, his attention quickly turning to Blair. These idiots eye her with a leering appreciation I don't like. Possessiveness rears up in my chest and I slip my fingers beneath the low cut of her dress to stroke her back.

Sean doesn't miss the move, his brows jumping up.

"Looking hot as fuck, Davis," Trent says.

"You really clean up," Sean adds. "For...you know."

I nearly growl, ready to teach him another lesson, but Blair presses her hand to my chest. We exchange a look. She silently gives me an *I've got this* expression.

Knowing she can hold her own, I let her take the lead, ready to enjoy the show of these two morons getting eviscerated by my feisty girl.

"Really? Thanks, guys." She inspects both of their suits. "Can't say the same for you, though. I can see the condom stash sticking out of your pocket, Sean." Blair *tsks*, shaking her head with mock sympathy. "A bit ambitious, and I don't think Bailey's DTF anymore after you started that rumor. You know, the one where you wanted a live-in sex slave to fulfill your needs."

Sean blinks stupidly. "Wh—You little—"

"Stop." The command in my tone pulls him up short before he can reach out to grab Blair. Sean flinches and Trent seems surprised by my expression. "You don't touch her. Or look at her like that."

Blair leans into me. We fight our battles together, balanced and unified as one.

"Shit—hold on to that thought." Blair peels away, hurrying to the other side of the room, where Bishop is in Thea's face, pinning her against the wall.

Trent scoffs. "What a bitch. Dude, when are you ditching that gold digging clinger?"

White-hot anger unfurls in my chest. I reach out and snatch Trent by the collar, jamming my thumb into the hollow of his throat. Trent's face melts into shock as he clutches my arm in an attempt to throw me off.

"Never. If you keep talking shit about my girlfriend, you're going to regret it." My gaze snaps to Sean. "Both of you. I hate repeating a lesson. Do I make myself clear?"

Trent and Sean nod. I press my thumb harder, enjoying the panicked way Trent's beady eyes flick around the room. A beat later, I release him with a shove.

"Get the fuck out of my face."

They leave, stumbling over themselves. I scan the room and find Blair jabbing her finger into Bishop's chest.

I can't see her face, but he is stunned, probably surprised she doesn't fear his reputation. Whatever she says pisses him off. Bishop stalks off from Thea and Blair with a thunderous expression. His shoulder slams into Mr. Coleman's on his way to the double doors draped in shimmering curtains. A worried frown tugs the corners of my mouth down.

Blair rubs Thea's back and leads her to the refreshment table to dab her tears away with a napkin.

I send a quick text to check on Bishop.

Devlin: You good?

Dots appear and disappear for a minute, then my phone vibrates with his response.

Bishop: Yeah. Whatever. Heading home.
Bishop: Make sure Thea gets home safe.

My eyes narrow. He should do that himself if he brought her here.

Bishop: Don't leave her there alone.

Devlin: Is that not exactly what you just did???

Bishop: [middle finger emoji] [middle finger emoji]
Bishop: Seriously, I don't trust anyone else. Give her a ride home.

I glance up. Blair has Thea smiling reluctantly as she chats. It does something to my heart to see her opening herself up to more people.

Devlin: Yeah fine. We'll take her.

Bishop: Thank you. Owe you one.

Pocketing my phone, I go to Blair's side, playing with her hair. She sends me a fond smile while Thea peeks at me shyly.

"Look, I was just showing Thea this dog account Gemma and I love on Instagram." Blair flashes me her phone.

"Is that the pug dog you're obsessed with?"

Blair sighs wistfully. "Sweetest, lumpiest prince. Here, Thea, watch this one."

Thea takes Blair's phone and soon enough the sadness lingering in her shoulders disappears as she laughs at the video.

I nudge Blair. "Ready to get out of here?"

"Yeah." Blair scrunches her nose. It's adorable and I have to struggle not to drag her in for a kiss. "I've had about enough of the whole winter formal scene."

"Come on, we'll give you a ride home," I say to Thea.

She glances at Mr. Coleman as he walks by. "Oh, I was going to ask…"

Blair shakes her head. "We've got a way sweeter ride. Are you hungry? We should stop for a pizza."

"Dressed up?" Thea peers down at her gauzy pink dress.

"Hell yeah!" Blair nods to me. "Last time we did it, we made up crazy stories about why we were decked out. It's fun."

Thea purses her lips expressively. "Well, okay. Thanks."

"Anything for a friend of Bishop's," I say.

Thea's expression falls and Blair elbows me.

"All I mean is he asked to make sure you had a good time and made it home safely." I rub my jaw. "Since he left early."

Thea studies me for a beat. I blink, taken aback by the perceptive shift in her eyes. Maybe she's not the quiet, mousy nerd we've all taken her for.

"All right." Thea gives me another challenging flick of her eyes. "I like pineapple on my pizza."

Blair lets out a laugh. "You and I are going to get along just fine."

I follow the girls out of the winter wonderland with a soft smile, hands tucked in my pockets.

***

The night air is cool, but we're wrapped in a cocoon of blankets on the roof. Blair nestles between my legs, her back to my chest as we gaze at the stars.

I don't feel like I'm escaping from an empty house, because the girl in my arms is the only home I need. It no longer seems like a cavernous, isolated prison because Blair is with me.

A profound sense of peace surrounds us. For so long this was a private ritual I did in secret, but now I can't imagine doing this without Blair, not when she was the one to give me this piece of hope in the first place.

I'm happy. The anger I grappled with for so many months has finally subsided. It doesn't have to rule me.

We're not watching the night sky because we need to make wishes, but because we want to show the stars we made our wishes come true anyway by finding love in each other.

Blair hums, turning her head when I kiss her cheek. "For a school dance, tonight was pretty fun."

"Teenage staple experience, check."

Blair snorts, shifting to get more comfortable. "Do we have to do the whole prom thing, too?"

"Only if you want."

"We should. You can go out with a bang. We'll really sell the dark devil of Silver Lake High." Blair shoots me a wry smirk over her shoulder. "Plus, you'd look super hot in a red velvet suit."

My chest vibrates against her back with my deep laugh. "Will you wear a dress like you did tonight?" I drag my teeth over my lip, picturing the sexy, sleek material hugging her body. "You'd look great in red, too. Maybe something with a slit." I move her hair aside and murmur more of the fantasy against her throat. "For easy access when I sneak you away to fill your pussy with my cock."

Blair tips her head to give me better access. I can hear the grin in her voice when she says, "I was thinking more like tight red leather pants and little demon horns."

The image she puts in my head makes my dick jump.

"Oh god. Fuck, I love you."

Blair reaches back, lacing her fingers behind my head to pull me down for a kiss. When we part, a smirk tugs at my lips. I press them to her ear, dropping my voice low.

"Want to play cops and robbers? I still have those handcuffs somewhere in the bedroom."

"Should I go to the garage? I can steal the car for old times' sake," Blair jokes. "Or pick your pocket."

I capture her hands and nip at her fingers. "You know what happens when you try to get in my pants, sticky fingers."

"That's what I'm counting on." Blair peeks over her shoulder, a playful mischief flickering in her pretty whiskey-colored eyes.

My heart thuds with devotion as heat spreads over my body.

"You've got a five minute head start." I kiss my promise against her cheek.

"Come get me." Blair gets up, luring me with a flirty look. She crooks her finger as she backs toward the window. "Catch me if you can."

"I'll always chase you. Five minutes," I remind her. "Then I'm coming to capture you again, little thief."

EPILOGUE

BLAIR
2 Years Later

Ridgeview is blanketed in fluffy heaps of snow, frosting the boughs of pine trees as I drive up to Mom's new house. It's a cute little cottage in the mountains. Mom was able to buy it earlier this year, before my fall semester at Oak Ridge College started.

Thanks to Devlin's financial advisor working pro bono with Mom and I in the second half of senior year, we created a plan to tackle the debt. Devlin offered to help, but it was something we both had to do for ourselves. We're finally free of the burden Dad left us. It's been liberating to have that weight lifted from our shoulders.

Mom is happy and healthy. At the end of summer before I went back to school with Gemma and Lucas, she found work as the manager of the new bakery in downtown Ridgeview. Her time at the clinic did her a world of good. Devlin's parents might have a complicated relationship with him, but their medical expertise gave Mom her life back. I'm grateful to have her living her best life.

The stone chimney emits a curl of woodsmoke. Mom must have a fire going. I smile as I hop out of my car, inhaling the fresh mountain air and the scent of firewood. My boots crunch on the snow as I head for the front door.

I'm home for winter break and I plan to spend the first few days with Mom until Devlin's break starts. We go to different colleges, but his is close to Oak Ridge. He'll drive down to Ridgeview from the townhouse we live in between both campuses at the end of the week after his developmental psychology final finishes.

I love my life in a way I never knew was possible. More than that, I love sharing it with Devlin. The things we face, we grow through together. I always think of the glittering gold that fuses over our old, healed cracks, not forgetting them, but making them shine.

We've barely been separated since graduation. It made sense to live together in our spacious townhouse when we already lived together at Devlin's house in Ridgeview. He picked it out specifically because it had plenty of room for my growing book collection. I tease him about it, since his library of books for his psychology degree rivals mine.

"Hey, Mom!" I call as I kick snow from my boots.

Her cottage is warm and inviting, the fire crackling in the stone fireplace filling the comfortable home with a drowsy sort of heat. I unwind my scarf and hang my coat up.

"In the kitchen! I'm making muffins."

"Smells great."

"How was the drive down?" Mom pokes her head out from the arched door to the kitchen. There's a smudge of flour on her cheek and my heart expands with a bloom of happiness. She beams. "Good to see you, baby girl."

I cross the room and envelop her in a hug. Our old tradition hasn't died. I'll always hug her when either of us walk in the door. She smells like sugary batter and cinnamon. Her arms close around me, squeezing me tight.

"Missed you! The video chats aren't the same as the real deal."

I laugh. "I know. I'm here now, though. The drive was good."

"I hope Devlin's drive isn't bad. They're calling for another storm."

"Oh, trust me, he's hoping for it. He's got a new addition." It's a BMW X1, perfect for driving in all terrains. Lucas has been by our townhouse to drool over it several times since Devlin bought it. I shake my head, affection lacing my tone. "He's been dying for a good snowfall to see what it can do."

Mom chuckles. "That boy and his cars."

"I know, tell me about it." I go about making tea on autopilot. "You should see what I rode here in. I was going to take my car, but he wasn't having it and made me drive the Land Rover instead."

The Corolla is no more. It died a pitiful, sputtering death days before our senior graduation, but Devlin had something waiting for me. He called the shiny red Audi Q7 a *congratulations for getting a scholarship to Oak Ridge College* present. I teased him that he wanted me to have my own red ride so I'd stop stealing his. Devlin's mouth had curled up at the corners and he reminded me how great he thinks I look in red.

Mom checks on the muffins baking in the oven and accepts the mug of tea I hand her when it's ready. "I like that he's so protective of you. It gives him the Mom certified stamp of approval."

I bite my lip around a fond smile. Secretly I like it, too. But it keeps him on his toes if I sass him with my independence.

We take our tea to the table.

"Well, go on," Mom encourages, relaxing in her chair. "I can see you're buzzing with it. How was your art history final?"

My grin breaks free, along with an elated sound. "Well, I don't know the official scores yet. But my professor said he was very impressed. He's recommending me for the internship at the museum over the summer!"

"That's wonderful!" Mom's eyes mist. "I'm so proud of you, Blair."

A happy spark of pride fills my chest. I love my studies as an art history major. These days my dreams reach higher than the stars I used to wish on.

As the oven timer rings, Mom pops up to take the muffins out. She bustles around the kitchen as the heavenly scent of cinnamon and brown sugar fills the room.

"Those smell amazing." The front door opens and my eyebrows hike up. "What, do you have a boyfriend you didn't tell me about? Or are you being robbed right now?"

"That's your area of expertise." A deep, familiar voice curls around my senses and a kiss drops on my head, enveloping me in the rich scent of leather and spice.

I twist in my seat. "Dev? What are you doing here? I thought you weren't coming down until the end of the week?"

Devlin grants me a charming smile tinged with mischief. He's pleased he surprised me. I saw him this morning before the meeting with my art history professor, but he has a way of igniting a constant ember of heat in my stomach with his dark tousled hair, his intelligent eyes, and his laugh. My fingers find his and he brings my knuckles to his mouth, kissing them with a tiny smirk.

"Surprise."

"Hi, Devlin." Mom greets. She doesn't seem as shocked as I am to see him. "How was your drive?"

"Great. Want to see the new love of my life? It comes in line after your daughter, of course."

Mom smirks and points at him. "Smart answer. Let me get a coat."

Devlin pulls me to my feet for an actual kiss. He grazes his nose along my cheek.

"If you were driving down the same time as me, we could've driven together."

Devlin hums. "Yes, but then I wouldn't have a chance to drive the X1."

I squint, my instincts tingling. "You're up to something. You've got your scheming face on."

"Is that so?" Devlin's arms lock around my waist and he hoods his eyes. "Pretty sure these are just genetics, angel."

Mom returns to the kitchen, bundled in a puffy parka. Devlin gestures us to the door. On the way, I grab my scarf and wind it around my neck to block out the crisp chill.

"Wow," Mom drawls as we step out. "It's so nice."

Devlin puffs up a little at the admiration, standing at my back with his arms around me. Mom walks around the vehicle as we amble over. He absently rubs my arms to protect me from the cold, his wool peacoat keeping me toasty.

"Very impressive, Devlin." Mom passes us, patting Devlin's shoulder. "I'm going to see if the muffins have cooled."

I turn to follow her, but Devlin catches my hand.

"Hang on. I have something in the car for you." He stares at me for a beat, a brief flash of nerves shining in his eyes before he opens the car door and retrieves a small package. "Here, I got you this."

"What is it?" I shoot him a smile as I unwrap it. "This feels book-shaped."

Devlin's mouth curves, but he remains quiet while I push

off the wrapping. My breath catches as I skate my fingers delicately over the cover.

"Devlin..."

He takes a small step closer, cupping my elbows. It's a copy of Stardust, the hardcover edition. The faint smell of an old book, musty with a hint of sweetness, reaches my nose. I trace the letters of the title.

"Open it," Devlin says softly.

I meet his gaze. He watches me with such intent focus that it steals my breath.

Tearing off the rest of the paper, a blue velvet ribbon bookmark attached to the book unfurls. A glint of metal dances from the end, where the ribbon is knotted. My eyes widen as Devlin cups my hands and kneels in the snow.

"Dev," I whisper hoarsely.

He unknots the ribbon and presents me with a beautiful platinum ring with a moon and star fitted together around a black opal that looks like a galaxy is locked inside. It's the prettiest piece of jewelry I've ever seen. Overwhelmed tears prick my eyes because this ring is...it's us. It's everything about Devlin and I.

"Blair." Devlin looks from the ring to me with love shining in his eyes. "You're my home, my magic star. I want to keep that, if you'll have me. Forever, preferably."

A shocked, breathy laugh leaves me. Devlin licks his lips, taking my hand. He places the ring at the tip of my finger. An excited squeal distracts me for a moment. It's Mom, filming with her phone. She has a hand pressed to her cheek, smiling joyously.

"Did you know about this?" I call to her.

Mom nods, squealing again. Devlin strokes my knuckles with his thumb, drawing my attention.

I swipe beneath my eyes to catch the leaking tears. "Is this really happening?"

The corners of Devlin's eyes crinkle. "When you're ready for it, will you marry me?"

Words have escaped me. All I can do is nod, watching as if I'm outside of my body as he slips the stunning ring on my finger. A watery gasp gets stuck in my throat as I launch myself at Devlin, snaking my arms around his neck.

A relieved laugh rumbles in his chest as he clutches me close. "Love you, angel. Going to love you forever."

Happiness like I've never known fills me to the brim as I hug him. Mom cheers from the front step as Devlin picks me up by the back of my thighs. My legs lock around his waist as he supports me. I grin, cupping his cheeks with cold hands and he gives me a matching expression. I kiss his smile, unable to contain my own.

"Are you sure?"

"Fuck yes." Devlin smirks, carrying me to the house. "I've known I wanted to marry you since winter formal senior year."

"Wow," I drag out. "Long game, huh?"

Devlin's voice drops as he brings his lips to my ear so Mom doesn't overhear. "You know how much I love playing games with you."

My delighted laugh echoes into the trees as we cross the threshold into the warm cottage.

EPILOGUE

DEVLIN
3 Years Later

After the last appointment for the day leaves, I lean back in my office chair, surveying what I've built for myself. The rooms are designed similarly to the rustic cabin-style house Blair and I have in the mountains, with wood accents and a focus on comfort. Art from the gallery Blair manages downtown lines the walls. My aim is to make this place feel as little like a counselor's office as possible.

The newly established therapy practice focusing on child and adolescent psychology stirs pride in my chest. My patient list is steadily growing, but it's not because of my parents' reputation. It's because of the dedication to make sure my patients are heard, determined that no child in this town will face the same lack of outlet I had growing up.

My phone lights up on the desk with a message from Bishop to our group text with Lucas. I snort at the picture he sent, helping his wife with one of her wild new ideas for her business.

Bishop: This Valentine's you too can have your very own chocolate dick mold. [eggplant emoji] Spread the word to your wives. Family gets first dibs on orders.

Lucas: Jesus. That is way more of you than I ever wanted to see again. I'll forward you my therapy bill. Dev, you got any openings?

Devlin: Fuck off, both of you.

Bishop: [smirking devil emoji] What, Saint, didn't you take any nude figure drawing classes at your fancy art school?

Lucas: [middle finger emoji]

Devlin: [GIF of Homer Simpson retreating into a bush]

It's strange to think of the anguish I once faced thinking my two best friends would someday leave me behind. Instead, we've grown closer than ever. Blood related or not, we're all family.

I don't have to wish for one anymore. The one I needed was there all along.

I spin the platinum wedding band on my ring finger, picturing the stars Blair had engraved on the inside when we got married last year.

As if I've conjured her, she texts me. The corner of my mouth lifts.

Blair: How do you feel about beef stew for dinner? I have the biggest hankering. Or maybe something with a little kick to it.

Devlin: What my wife wants, my wife gets.

Blair: [GIF of a beautiful woman in a crown]

Blair: Going hard for this year's best husband award?

A smirk crosses my face and heat tugs at my groin as I type my response.

Devlin: Not until I have you screaming my name tonight. You get beef for dinner and I get you to feast on.

It doesn't matter that we've been together for five years, I still can't control the need I have for her.

Blair: [smirk emoji] Going for gold, then?

Devlin: Always when it comes to you, angel.

Blair: Better hurry home, then.

She sends a surreptitious selfie of her plump red lips wrapped around her finger, sucking it to the knuckle.
"Fuck," I mutter hoarsely, adjusting my cock in my slacks.
I love my fiery little demon. Grabbing my key fob and coat, I let Blair know I'll be home soon after I stop to pick up stuff for dinner.
When I get in, Blair's not back from the gallery yet. I hang my coat in the cozy living room, filled with floor-to-ceiling

bookshelves for our book collection. On the shelf closest to our wedding photos, the hardcover edition of Stardust from my proposal is displayed front and center.

Once I have the groceries put away in the kitchen, I hear the front door open. Blair murmurs in a calming tone. My brow furrows as I sneak closer to see what she's doing.

Blair has her scarf bundled in one arm, bustling around the room to build a fort of sorts out of the pillows on the plush sofa. Once she's satisfied, she nestles her bundled scarf.

Intrigued, I move closer. Propping my shoulder against the doorway, I survey the attentive way she tucks in the edges of the scarf.

It's nurturing in a way, how she tends to the bundle. We've both talked about how we want a big family. My gaze sweeps over her frame. I'm ready to start one now, eager to see her belly swelled with our baby.

We've only come close once so far. Shortly after we were married, we took an at home test when we thought we might be pregnant, but it turned out to be a false positive. I haven't wanted to push her, not until she's ready to try again, too.

"What are you doing?"

Blair emits a startled sound and pops up. She spots me and huffs. "Jesus, give a girl a heart attack much?"

Humor injects my voice as I cross the room. "You shouldn't have taught me the trick to being stealthy then. If I can't use it to sneak up on you, what good does it do me?"

The lesson plays in my head, followed by the ways I've employed the new skill over the years. Usually it ends with both of us naked and sated. Blair tips her chin up with a wry smirk.

My hand rests on her ass when I reach her. Giving it a squeeze, I peer into the scarf mound. A ball of black fur greets me.

"I found her behind the gallery. She was all alone, crying up a storm." Blair reaches out to stroke the kitten's fur. "I couldn't leave her there."

The little kitten pops her head up, peering at me with big yellow-green eyes. She's a tiny, pathetic thing. I can see why Blair was immediately drawn to the kitten.

I take a seat next to the pillow fort Blair constructed, leaning an arm across the back of the couch as I watch the kitten. "So my stray brought home a stray?"

Blair snorts and plops onto my lap, pinching my arm. I tug her closer, and she snuggles against my chest as we study the tiny kitten.

"Isn't she cute? She reminded me of you."

I run a finger down the kitten's back. My lips twitch up at the way the kitten leans into my touch like it's starved for affection, needy for a connection. The kitten releases an indignant mewl, demanding more attention. I resume petting it, astonished by the loud purring.

"I think she looks more like you," I counter in a teasing tone, patting Blair's thigh. "So a cat, huh?"

"Yup." Blair bites the corner of her lip, reaching for my hand. Our fingers intertwine, the same as they have a thousand times. "And that's not all."

"More surprises?"

"Well, I made an appointment to confirm, but I'm pretty sure." Blair tugs my hand over her stomach, covering it with her palm. Her eyes are soft as her mouth curves. "I think…"

Eyes wide, I cup her jaw. "You—Really?"

Blair nods, swooping down to kiss me. I cradle her close, tracing her stomach with care, searching for the feel of life we created together.

She releases a breathy laugh. "You won't feel anything yet."

"That won't stop me from imagining."

Elation builds in my chest as it hits me. Blair and I are having a baby.

A piercing meow interrupts our celebration. The kitten clumsily climbs from the makeshift swaddle and jumps between us, curling up once more.

The family I found is growing. A warm glow rises inside me. I think it might be happiness.

Blair rests her forehead against mine. I hook my hands around her waist and kiss her.

My thumb strokes over her freckled cheek when we part. "My shooting star. You're better than a wish."

* * *

Thank you so much for reading TEMPTING DEVIL! The Sinners and Saints series continues in Bishop and Thea's book, RUTHLESS BISHOP.

THANK YOU + WHAT'S NEXT?

Need more Sinners and Saints series right now? Have theories about which characters will feature next? Want exclusive previews of the next book? Join other readers in Veronica Eden's Reader Garden on Facebook!

Join: BIT.LY/VERONICAFBGROUP

Are you a newsletter subscriber? By subscribing, you can download a special bonus scene featuring Blair and Devlin from Tempting Devil, as well as a bonus epilogue from Wicked Saint.

Sign up to download it here: BIT.LY/TDFREEBONUS

ACKNOWLEDGMENTS

I want to thank you, readers, for reading this book! It means the world to me that you supported my work. I wouldn't be here without you! The response to this series and these characters has seriously blown me away. I love all of the comments and messages you send! I hope you enjoyed your read! I'm really excited to bring you more from this series!

Thanks to my husband for being you! He doesn't read these, but he's my biggest supporter. He keeps me fed and watered while I'm in the writer cave, and doesn't complain when I fling myself out of bed at odd hours with an idea to frantically scribble down.

Bre, I seriously couldn't have written this book without you. Our many chats were amazing. You never fail to make me laugh, cheer me on, and inspire me to write. Your love and understanding of my characters is amazing! Thank you for your friendship and support, and no, I will not apologize about my love of pineapple on pizza haha!

Thank you to Jade Bones for help whipping this problem child of a book into shape and helping me make it something I'm proud of! I always appreciate your help and love chatting writing with you!

Thank you to Ashlee of Ashes & Vellichor for the amazing book trailers for this series! I love the way you can look at something and get it, and I've been in awe of what you've come up with to bring these books to life!

To my beta readers, thank you from the bottom of my heart! I appreciate that y'all read my raw words and offer your time, attention to detail, and consideration of the characters and storyline in my books! You're a dream team and I'm so glad I met each of you! Your time and hard work are much appreciated!

To my street team and reader group, y'all are the best babes around! Thank you for your help in sharing my books and for your support of my work!

To the bloggers and bookstagrammers, thank you for being the most wonderful and welcoming community! You guys are incredible and blow me away with your passion for romance!

As always, I want to send a big shout out of love to my writing hags, the best bunch around! I always cherish your support and encouragement of my writing, no matter where my heart eyes and the muse take me. Every book I publish is thanks to you guys.

Ruthless Bishop
Sinners and Saints Book 3
Available Now

* * *

THEA

ONE WRONG MOVE AND IT'S OVER.

I was invisible until I wasn't.

One mistyped number became the catalyst to my hell on earth when I accidentally sent a risqué photo to the blackmail king of Silver Lake High. Now Connor Bishop holds it as a bargaining chip over my head. I've become his doll, at his mercy in a corrupt castle.

Better do as he says or else, or else, or else...

His thumb is on the send button every time I try to buck his command. Can I survive a private photo going viral instead of living this life of torment?

It's not right. Maybe it's time his castle burns down.

CONNOR

SECRETS AND FAVORS BUILT MY THRONE.

Meek. Shy. Wholesome.

Thea Kennedy was picture-perfect innocence until she wasn't. The unexpected photo is the juiciest secret to land in my lap in a while. Who knew she was hiding luscious curves under frumpy sweaters?

With one racy selfie, Thea stepped into my world. I'll trap the little mouse and won't let her escape the depraved kingdom I built. No one tests my power because I control the board through merciless blackmail.

But there are darker monsters than me lurking in the shadows. They want to take a bite out of my little mouse. I don't like sharing what's mine.

One-Click: bit.ly/BishopSAS
Add to Goodreads TBR: bit.ly/GRruthlessbishop
Sign Up for Updates: bit.ly/veronicaedenmail

PREVIEW RUTHLESS BISHOP

THEA

Sexy selfie attempt number twenty and I still don't have a winner I totally love on my phone's camera roll.

"Just do it," I mutter, arguing with myself. "Spontaneity is a good thing. He'll like it. Be cool."

I've been going in circles for five minutes, getting nowhere as I pace my bedroom.

My school uniform hangs on the closet door from a funky sun-shaped brass hook, the plaid skirt in the school colors—evergreen and white—and the black blazer with the gold embroidered crest mocking me. At school I'm known by cruel names because I prefer wearing my uniform a couple of sizes too big to hide my body, unlike the girls who wear their skirts short enough their asses almost hang out and their blazers fitted to their petite waistlines. The other students are labelled cool because they break the uniform code with designer fashion, but I'm not because my rebellion isn't worthy in their eyes.

At least most of the time I'm invisible to them.

Narrowing my eyes at the uniform, I turn my back, where the riot of color on the other side of the room makes me smile.

The wall is a pastel rainbow of baking-themed art with funny sayings like *bake the world happy* and *happiness is homemade*.

"Okay, focus. Send the photo," I coach.

My stomach protests with a wave of butterflies. All of my positive thinking flees.

I can't believe I'm losing an argument against myself. I blow out harshly, deflating my ballooned cheeks along with my nerve. A wayward auburn curl ends up in my eyes. With an impatient flick, I brush it aside.

It's taken me weeks to work up the courage for this step with Wyatt, the cute lifeguard at the summer retreat my parents sent me to. We had a sort of fling. Well, okay. Not really.

It was fling-like. *Fling adjacent.* We were on our way to flirting.

At least, that's what my friend Maisy assured me between yoga class and gourmet s'mores by the campfire.

The air hisses from my lungs in a soft, flat laugh that caves my chest.

You? Dream on. He was only being polite. As a staff member, he was probably contracted to be whatever the guests needed. Even appearing interested romantically.

I shake my head to dispel the depressing inner voice. Wyatt wasn't only being a nice guy, and I am a damn goddess he would love to be with.

Forget the short-girl-with-an-ass figure it's difficult to find jeans for, the stretch marks on my hips and boobs from puberty growth spurts, and the memories of shopping for bras when my friends were still playing with toys.

"A goddess," I repeat, letting the affirmation give me the mental hug I need to restore my confidence.

My tongue pokes out of the corner of my mouth as I hesitate to click on the message icon in his contact, where I saved his name with waves. As if I'd forget about how he looked in his red lifeguard trunks with a deep golden tan. Maybe I should go for a Facebook message or an Instagram DM first to double check I have his number saved correctly.

I shake my head. "Be bold."

This is my chance to keep our tiny spark alive before it snuffs out. I have to act fast. I arrived back in Ridgeview the week before school at Silver Lake High started, and Wyatt went home to Colorado Springs. The drive down is under two hours if this works out—but I'm getting ahead of myself.

First I have to buck the hell up and send the photo.

I've decided. Senior year is my year. I'm eighteen and it's time I stopped hiding myself from the world.

Mom can spout her crap until she's red in the face, but I'm not listening anymore.

A whine sounds at the locked door, followed by a muffled scratch.

"Not tonight, buddy. Go to your bed," I tell my rottweiler. He's an oversized lapdog that usually shadows me all over the house. He whines once more. "Bed, Constantine."

The dog makes a put out sound as his nails click down the hall.

My grip tightens on my cell phone. The picture I took is all right. Not my best, but like the hundreds of photos in a secret folder, it's the version of the girl I want to be.

Confident, sexy, and owning my curvy body.

Ah, the pipe dream.

I pluck at the sunflower yellow chunky knit cardigan I tugged on over the lace-edged romper that barely contains my breasts. It's designed to drape nicely on elegant bodies with long limbs and chests much flatter than mine. Instead, the romper fits to my big hips and rides up my thighs. Thank god for still photos where I can fake like I'm not trying to pick the material my ass is eating every two seconds.

Mom doesn't know I own the romper, or some of the other clothes hidden in the closet. I have to rotate my hiding spots because she is a notorious snooper.

Photo-me looks up from the phone screen with bedroom eyes, my lashes fluttered low over my blue-green eyes. My dark red curls are tossed over strategically to give my hair that bombshell volume, spilling down my neck and over one shoulder as I lean forward to show off my cleavage. My plump lips are puckered into duck lips. I can't help it, duck lips are my go to when I put myself on the spot in the hopes I'll capture something natural and effortless. It's me, and yet...not.

My gaze slides to the mirror and my shoulders droop as soon as I eye my reflection critically.

Mirrors and phone cameras must have a deal with the devil.

Somehow the reflection and the pictures never match up. Maybe the girl I am in my secret folder of photos exists only in digital format.

Squinting, I lean closer. Is that—? *Yup.* That's flour in my hair. I sink my fingers into my curls with an aggravated sigh and shake them out as I check the photo. Fan-flipping-tastic.

I thought I cleaned myself up after baking the rustic cranberry tarts I've been trying to perfect when I got home from school, but I must have missed some. What else is new? I'm almost always covered in some ingredient with my love of baking.

Okay, attempt number twenty-one.

This time I crop part of my face out of the frame and go for a coy smirk. Once I snap the photo, I drop out of the pose and perch on the arm of the floral print cushioned chair by the window, nudging one of my infinite recipe notebooks onto the seat.

"Not bad." I tilt my head and scrunch my lips to the side. The next dilemma occurs to me and my eyes widen. "Crap."

I'm already being bold with the photo, but should I say anything or just send the picture? What do people normally say when they send selfies revealing their thirst levels to their crush? Oh god, I'm going to screw this up. I'm so bad at this!

The glow of headlights shining through the window distracts me from my momentary panic as a dark silver SUV pulls into the house next door. The Bishop's place. I'm the lucky duck who not only has the school principal for a neighbor but also his vicious son, Connor Bishop. Most of the time he ignores my existence, but on days he doesn't, he's the champion of the crusade against me and my favorite sweaters.

"Oh freaking great," I mumble, ducking down in the chair so he doesn't look up to my window and think I'm creeping on him.

I'm not risking Connor seeing me in this romper, either. No free shows for that asshole.

The headlights cut off as he parks outside of the garage. Their house looks like it belongs in the Hollywood Hills with its sprawling paved terraces, huge arched windows, and terra-cotta tiled roof. It stands out against the other houses, like mine, that resemble mountain lodges and chalets with stone columns and dark accents. Almost everything in our town matches the same mountain vibe. Our neighborhood is comfortably upscale as far as Ridgeview goes, but Connor's is the biggest on the street.

Curling my fingers over the back of the chair, I peek past the sheer lavender curtains and watch him slam the door of the Lexus GX with a bag of soccer balls hooked over his shoulder.

It makes his bicep flex, stretching his green varsity soccer shirt taut.

Why do mean boys always have to look like that? He's an angel-faced demon in disguise with his striking gray eyes, floppy light brown hair, and a dangerous, dazzling smile he uses to melt the panties off of his adoring fangirls. Not that I know what his charm-up-to-eleven smile looks like up close. I only get the cruel smirks directed my way when I have the misfortune of catching his attention.

Collapsing back into the chair, I bite my lip and push Connor Bishop from my mind. I'm a girl on a mission to flirt. He isn't messing this up for me.

As I tap my nails against my phone and tug my lips side to side in thought, different options scroll through my mind. *Hey cutie?* I shake my head. *No, that's too much. Hope you're having a good day?* I groan, scrubbing a hand over my face.

"Why are words so hard?"

The stuffed sea lion on the bed doesn't answer. I'm terrible at this stuff. A 4.0 GPA and all my baking skills, yet I can't flirt for shit. It's like I'm defective, missing a social skill or two because I listened to all the things Mom has always warned me about boys, and ran in the other direction when one spoke to me.

Except for one. But that didn't end well.

I cock my head to the side as a thought occurs to me while I'm wallowing in self pity. What would Connor say in this situation if he was going to sweet talk a girl he wanted?

My gaze flicks to the window where his bedroom light is on. I only know it's his room because he refuses to change with the curtains closed, the self-obsessed exhibitionist. I may have caught sight of his bare chest—*briefly*—a time or two over the years. He has abs, and that's just completely unfair.

Dropping my voice into a lower register and pretending to

be all macho, I shoot my stuffed sea lion a sly look and say, "Baby, you light up the sky with your pretty smile."

A beat of silence passes before I make a sound like a dying animal in my humiliation. I sink further into the seat, wishing for the ground to open up and swallow me. Thank god no one actually witnessed that train wreck.

"I'm hopeless!"

With a sigh I scoot up and type out *missing your smile*. I chew on my lip. It's not bad. Maybe an emoji? But then again, emojis change meaning by the day.

"Ugh. No."

I jab the delete button, erasing the message letter by letter. Frustration mixes with a heavy bubble in my chest. It swells until it chokes me. Before I finish deleting the text, I let my phone slip from my grip to plop in my lap, rubbing at my stinging eyes. The mascara I applied is probably smearing, but I don't care. I can't get this right, so why does it matter anymore?

An innocuous computerized *whoop* sound makes me freeze. Oh no. Oh no, no, no. *Shit*.

Mortification crashes through me as I scramble to flip my phone. The evidence of my clumsy mistake glares back at me, punching through my stomach and making it plummet faster than concrete shoes dragging someone to the bottom of the ocean.

Thea: Missing you [Photo attachment]

The message sent. There's no way to unsend texts, because the technology gods like to laugh at us unfortunate souls who send embarrassing shit and regret it the minute it transmits. Maybe I'll get lucky and he won't see it.

How will I know, though? Wyatt never struck me as the

type to leave his read receipts on. He could look at the text and I would never know.

"Fuck," I drag out in a harsh whisper.

What if Wyatt does open it and hates it? I already see three things wrong with my photo. I wish more than anything I could yank it back. Erase it from existence. Keep it tucked away in my secret folder.

I try to suck in a slow meditative breath through my nose like Maisy always instructs, but it catches in my throat while my pulse thunders in my ears.

A million thoughts scramble through my head. Pictures, too. *Thanks overactive imagination.* I see Wyatt with his long-time girlfriend when he reads my text. In my head, they laugh and I feel like the world's biggest idiot.

Squeezing my phone with sweaty palms, I search the internet, scanning articles and results with a jittery focus.

Does the throbbing-prickly sensation in my palms mean I'm experiencing an adrenaline surge?

How do I unsend a text message?

Can I delete a photo from someone else's phone before they see it?

In the middle of my fruitless searching, a notification banner pops up at the top of my screen for a few seconds before disappearing. Wave emojis bracket his name.

My heart stops.

He texted back.

ABOUT THE AUTHOR
STAY UP ALL NIGHT FALLING IN LOVE

Veronica Eden is a USA Today and International bestselling author of romances with spitfire heroines, irresistible heroes, and edgy twists.

She loves exploring complicated feelings, magical worlds, epic adventures, and the bond of characters that embrace *us against the world*. She has always been drawn to gruff bad boys, clever villains, and the twisty-turns of morally gray decisions. She is a sucker for a deliciously devilish antihero, and sometimes rolls on the dark side to let the villain get the girl. When not writing, she can be found soaking up sunshine at the beach, snuggling in a pile with her untamed pack of animals (her husband, dog and cats), and surrounding herself with as many plants as she can get her hands on.

* * *

CONTACT + FOLLOW
Email: veronicaedenauthor@gmail.com
Website: http://veronicaedenauthor.com
FB Reader Group: bit.ly/veronicafbgroup
Amazon: amazon.com/author/veronicaeden

facebook.com/veronicaedenauthor

instagram.com/veronicaedenauthor

twitter.com/vedenauthor

pinterest.com/veronicaedenauthor

bookbub.com/profile/veronica-eden

goodreads.com/veronicaedenauthor

ALSO BY VERONICA EDEN

Sign up for the mailing list to get first access and ARC opportunities! **Follow Veronica on BookBub** for new release alerts!

DARK ROMANCE

Sinners and Saints Series

Wicked Saint

Tempting Devil

Ruthless Bishop

Savage Wilder

Sinners and Saints: The Complete Series

Crowned Crows Series

Crowned Crows of Thorne Point

Loyalty in the Shadows

A Fractured Reign

The Kings of Ruin

Standalone

Unmasked Heart

Devil on the Lake

REVERSE HAREM ROMANCE

Standalone

Hell Gate

More Than Bargained

CONTEMPORARY ROMANCE

Standalone

Jingle Wars

The Devil You Know

Haze

Printed in Great Britain
by Amazon